# Supercute Second Future

## Martin Millar

Refutured Media

## Supercute Second Future

Mox and Mitsu, owners of Supercute, have millions of dedicated fans all over the world. Supercute has grown into one of the world's largest and most powerful conglomerates. They now own their own weapons company and their London headquarters is protected by an advanced array of drones and missiles. Despite this, they're in danger again. An international force of hostile consortiums, armed mercenaries and artificial intelligences is conspiring to bring them down. Mox and Mitsu would much rather concentrate on their cute clothes and toys but once more they're obliged to fight to survive in their ruined, flooded, irradiated future.

*'You're spending the whole day at a photo shoot? With everything else that's happening at the moment?'*

*'Life must go on,' declared Mox. 'When there were rumours of a rogue submarine about to nuke London, did we panic? No. We kept right on with the Plumpy Panda promotion and now Plumpy Panda is one of the world's best selling soft toys. We've always shown courage in the face of adversity.'*

Cover by Simon Fraser

Thanks for help: Gordon Millar, Nicolle Leitch, Marie Heibel, Simon Fraser, Derek Judge.

Also available by Martin Millar: Supercute Futures

# Supercute Second Future

'We killed Moe Benny because he attacked us. We considered killing AIFU because he let us down badly, though we decided just to send him away instead. We did arrange for the assassination of Ms Mason, CEO of RX Enviro. And Captain Edwards, who worked for us.'

Mitsu paused. She glanced at Mox, then stared at the miniature rock garden at their feet. Their therapist waited patiently for her to continue. 'We didn't expect to be killing anyone when we started Supercute.'

'You were attacked. Many people would say you had a right to defend yourselves.'

'I know. But there were others. Some of them a long time ago. *Business disputes*, you might say.'

'Has this been troubling you?'

There was another pause before Mox replied. 'Troubling us? Not exactly. It doesn't make us feel great.'

Mitsu brushed a strand of pink hair from her face. 'Supercute is now one of the largest and richest organisations in the world. You can't achieve that without some deaths along the way. Not with the way the world is these days.'

They fell silent. Their artificial intelligence therapist waited for either of them to continue. He never hurried them.

'After we killed Moe Bennie we took his jacket and nailed it to the wall in one of our private apartments.'

The therapist had heard many strange things from Mox and Mitsu. This made him raise his eyebrows.

'*Spolia opima*,' explained Mitsu. '*Rich spoils*, in ancient Rome. When a Roman commander defeated an enemy commander in face-to-face combat, he took his armour. It was a big honour. Like a Triumph, but better. We thought we'd revive the custom. We stuck Moe Bennie's jacket on a wall and wrote *spolia opima* underneath. It's an ugly scrawl, we didn't make it look neat.'

Their therapist nodded. He was never critical which was one reason they liked him.

Mox sighed. 'Sometimes we're not very nice, really.'

—

Mitsu rushed over the stage and grabbed Mox's arm.

'Mox, we're in trouble!'

'What's wrong?'

'The kittens are angry again!'

'Oh no! Not another super-kitty rampage!'

Suddenly the Supercute stage was full of stampeding kittens. There was nothing to do but flee. Mox, Mitsu, Presenter Bear, Plumpy Panda and the host of brightly dressed teenagers around them rushed for the cover of the *Stonehenge Cuddly Super Set* at the side of the stage. All around the world, the Supercute audience, connected to Supercute Space, ran with them, fleeing from the angry kittens. Mox's *Supercute Big Colour Super V-Hair* streamed over her face as she crouched behind the one-metre-tall henge. 'These naughty kittens!'

'They never behave themselves!' cried Mitsu.

There were shrieks of laughter as the cute kittens began to scamper around the Stonehenge Cuddly Super Set, threatening to overbalance some of the henges. Above them in the control station Morioka Sachi added a little more laughter to that coming from the stage. She didn't have to strengthen it much; there was already a lot of mirth. A lot of amusement around the world too. Supercute was the world's most watched show and the *Super-Kitty Rampage* was a regular and popular feature. Many were realistic renditions of actual kittens but some were pink or blue or yellow, with slightly larger eyes, part of the super-kitty pack that was always on hand to threaten chaos. As they began to invade the inner circle of Stonehenge, Mitsu rose to her feet and sternly addressed a young white and tabby cat, larger than her companions.

'Small Cute Presenter! What's the meaning of this outrage? You're destroying Cuddly Stonehenge!'

'We want to be fed!' cried Small Cute Presenter, leader of the band and a well-known character on the show.

'We don't have any food,' replied Mox. 'The shipment didn't arrive!'

This resonated with their audience. Many of their fans were familiar with food shortages. There were plenty of places around the world where it was easier to put on your visor and connect to Supercute that it was to find a regular meal.

'The super-kitties demand to be fed!' The kittens meowed furiously. More henges were toppled over.

2

'Help!' shouted Mox. 'There's a super-kitty nibbling my ankle! Bad kitten!'

Just as the chaos threatened to overwhelm them, a large pink and white valocopter appeared above their heads. The advanced craft hovered noiselessly. A hatch opened and Captain Yến appeared. At the sight of her, applause erupted from all sides. Phan Thị Yến was a highly regarded person in the world of Supercute. The Vietnamese pilot was well-known outside of Supercute too. As leader of the Supercute Rescue Mission, she'd participated in numerous relief operations in every continent. Captain Yến, dressed in her pink Supercute camouflage flying suit, was a dashing figure, a real life heroine among the cute clothes and kittens. Tall, athletic, good-humoured even in difficult circumstances, she was the visible face of Supercute's relief work. This work was expensive, expansive, and had saved many lives, bringing fresh water, food and shelter to millions of disaster victims. On the walls of Supercute's huge London headquarters were awards, certificates and commendations from the United Nations, UNESCO, the World Health Organisation and many other official bodies thanking them for their assistance.

'I've brought food for the kittens,' cried Captain Yến, smiling. 'Tuna steaks for everyone!'

The kittens leapt around excitedly as Captain Yến began to unload her cargo. The AI controlling the kittens boosted the volume so that Supercute's audience were overwhelmed with the happy sound of kittens purring with pleasure. Had they been real the kittens would have had good reason to purr. Tuna was rare and extremely expensive. Only the richest people could afford tuna fish for themselves. It was highly unlikely that anyone was actually feeding it to cats. However, that was the real world. Here in Supercute, life was much happier.

—

Mox and Mitsu walked from the elevator towards the meeting rooms on level two of their headquarters. Both were exactly the same height. A long time ago Mox had been a centimetre taller but as part of their many biotech advancements they'd evened it out, by choice.

'It's still surprising how many boards there are in Supercute and how many we're on.' Mitsu sounded mildly irritated. 'We try and keep it simple but they still accumulate.'

Mox and Mitsu were joint owners of the vast Supercute Empire, a conglomerate that included Supercute Entertainment, Supercute Communications, MitsuMox Global Merchandise, Supercute Greenfield, Supercute ZanZan Defence, Mokusei Space Transit, Supercute Mokusei Financial Holdings and others. There was no place on earth in which they did not have a presence. Supercute Greenfield, the desalination business on which much of their wealth was based, was ubiquitous around the world's coastlines. For years their advanced technology and superior business acumen had enabled them to bring fresh water to a large proportion of the world's population making them an unmatched giant in the field of environmental relief and repair. Their show, with its focus on cute toys and clothes, had first brought them to public attention, but it was their desalination work that made them a business giant. Much of the ruined earth was crying out for fresh water; Supercute could provide it more quickly and cheaply than anyone else.

The administration of their huge empire was a formidable task. This was made easier by their policy of delegation in which Mox and Mitsu trusted the boards of each part of the conglomerate to run their businesses efficiently, and also by SAID. Supercute Artificial Intelligence Development had grown out of the company's translation expertise, which in turn had grown out of Mox and Mitsu's considerable language skills. They now controlled an array of advanced artificial intelligences. These days it was not unusual for the largest companies to have very diverse interests. These conglomerates were huge in comparison to their historical counterparts. C19 covered virtually every aspect of human existence and since the acquisition of ZanZan Defence, Supercute were now one of C19's strongest members.

Such a huge empire did require many layers of management. The Supercute Board was the most senior executive layer but each subsidiary had its own board. Here in Supercute Headquarters they were responsible for producing the Supercute show, the flagship of the whole empire. Just as important was Supercute Space Warriors, the gaming galaxy that had grown into an extremely popular franchise, more popular even than some of the specialist gaming companies that had previously dominated the market.

4

Mox and Mitsu had two meetings scheduled. The first was with the Board of Supercute Entertainment. 'That shouldn't take long,' said Mox. 'We need to buy Spacewalk no matter what it costs. Most of the board agrees and if some don't then they'll just have to fall into line.' Mox and Mitsu owned the company as majority shareholders. There were investors who had to be catered for and business realities that couldn't be ignored but ultimately they were in charge.

'I hope it's quick because the meeting with the production committee's going to take longer. We've got new ideas and Sachi always takes some persuading.'

'Then there's Castle.'

'We don't have to meet him.'

'We do really.' Despite all their official boards and committees, Mox and Mitsu tended to rely on their most trusted advisors. One of those was Ben Castle. He'd only recently been brought back into the fold as Head of Security, but they trusted him. Not long ago he'd stood beside them in a dank, underground, radioactive tunnel, risking his life in a desperate battle with hostile drones. After such violent combat they knew they could rely on him, providing his drinking was under control, which it seemed to be.

The board of directors meeting went smoothly. The production meeting took longer, as anticipated. Mox and Mitsu had new set designs, new outfits to suggest and several new characters they wanted integrating into the show. There was some resistance. Their senior producer, Morioka Sachi, was unconvinced. 'Do we really need a new cute Brazilian girl on stage? We've got plenty of cute girls already.'

'We have a lot more opportunities in South America. 5-Research think Cute Brazilian Girl will help with that.'

'5-Research always sees room for expansion,' said Sachi, sourly. 'Their ideas generally involve adding characters to the show whether we need them or not.'

'Igraine?' Mox turned to their Artificial Intelligence Forecast Unit. 'Do you agree with 5-Research?'

Igraine, a pale, dark-haired and extremely lifelike android, nodded her head. Since arriving at Supercute, her movements and facial expressions had greatly improved. Were it not for the small traces of metal on her face she'd have appeared entirely human. Igraine was an extremely powerful unit with many capabilities.

5

She could forecast future trends more accurately than most of the AIs used by large investment companies. She was connected to every AI used by Supercute and was able to give an accurate summary of current events in any part of their empire. Since joining Supercute she'd brightened her appearance. Her trousers and sweatshirt were still the basic black of the standard AIFU but over them she now wore a Supercute yukata with a pink and white pattern based on one designed and bequeathed to Mitsu by her mother.

Mitsu's mother had died a long time ago, killed by one of the tsunamis that swept over Tokyo after the impacts. Mox's mother had died some time before that, while giving birth to her. Neither Mox nor Mitsu's parents had lived long enough to see their daughters reach adulthood. It was a taboo subject at Supercute. No one ever mentioned it.

—

Amowie in Nigeria, Birgit in Iceland and Meihui in China met in Supatok as they did every day. They were excited by Amowie's news. 'They're really taking you?'

'Yes! Mox and Mitsu are going to the Paris show themselves but they'll be opening a space for visiting other fashion shows and they said I can come with them!'

At one time it would have been an unbelievable development. Actually joining Mox and Mitsu in some of their own personal space to visit fashion shows in Paris was a remarkable honour, not one normally extended to fourteen-year-old fans, no matter how devoted. Amowie was more than a normal fan. She'd been made a Supercute SuperSuperFan last year after helping Mox and Mitsu in their struggle against Moe Bennie. She'd rendered them great assistance, even if she was reticent about some of the details. Afterwards, Supercute had rewarded her handsomely. Amowie could now be found walking around her village in Igboland dressed in a complete set of Supercute camouflage in four shades of pink, wearing the highest grade visor which could connect her to Supercute from anywhere. She had a special edition of every Supercute Space Warriors game and a *Stonehenge Cuddly Mini Set* assembled in her bedroom. Not only that, Mox and Mitsu had asked her for her opinion on new developments in Supercute Space Warriors. Her friends were pleased for her. Amowie deserved it.

She'd put herself in danger for Mox and Mitsu. Besides, her connection was proving beneficial to them too. Mox and Mitsu had asked Amowie to talk to her friends about gaming, meaning they all had some input into the new Space Warriors expansion pack which was a very exciting thing to happen.

'I want Roota to move on from Jax.' Meihui's Mandarin was instantly and accurately translated into Icelandic and Igbo by the Supatok space they shared. Mox and Mitsu had risen to prominence partly through their ability to communicate with the whole world. In the days before instant translation their phenomenal language skills had allowed them to talk to more people in more countries than anyone had managed before. Later they poured resources into their translation services, outshining their competitors. Anyone meeting their friends in Supatok had no need of their own translation device; the space now did it for them.

'Really? Jax and Roota?' Birgit was doubtful. 'Shouldn't they keep trying?'

It was a contentious subject in Supercute fandom. The romance between Roota Space Warrior and Jax the Astronomer Poet never worked out well in Supercute Space Warriors. No matter how players approached it in the game, no matter what choices they made, the relationship would always falter. Players had tried everything to bring them together. Every option had been examined. New ones had been developed. The procedural nature of the games allowed for new combinations of events to occur. It seemed there should be some way to bring Jax and Roota together; they obviously had strong feelings for each other. Somehow it never worked out. At best, circumstances would oblige them to part in sadness. At worst, one or both of them would die.

'You can't even get them to kiss,' said Birgit. 'Last time I played solo I thought they were going to do it right there in the gun turret but then the Krogdar Mercenaries attacked and they both got killed. I was really frustrated. I hate these Krogdar.'

'Last time I tried, Roota found a message from Jax's old lover. She thought they'd been meeting behind her back so she flew off in a huff. Crossed a whole galaxy. Then Jax was so sad he flew his own ship into the sun!' Meihui winced. 'It really is a painful love affair. I think they should just give up.'

'But it's so romantic!' protested Birgit. 'Sometimes it even says they met when they were at school.'

7

'She was at that rich girl's school and he was poor and too shy to talk to her and fell in love with her right away!'

They asked Amowie if Mox and Mitsu had mentioned Jax and Roota. Amowie brushed her hair back from her eyes. In real life her hair was short, cut simply like other girls her age in her school. Here in Supatok space it was long, voluminous and multi-coloured. Almost everyone's was, thanks to the ubiquitous *Supercute Big Colour Super V-Hair* program. This was continually updated by Mox and Mitsu themselves, giving their followers an endless supply of the most colourful hairstyles imaginable.

'I don't think they mentioned them,' said Amowie. 'They were talking about some sort of expansion for Supercute Fairy Realm. They know we sneaked in there, which is still a bit embarrassing. Now they're wondering if they should let more teenagers in instead of making the age limit eleven. But they don't want to spoil it for children by having adults there. So we talked about that.'

'I miss the Fairy Realm.' Birgit looked wistful. 'I was a beautiful fairy.'

'It was so great flying around the space forest, playing with the blumpies.' Meihui shook her head. It had been a sad moment in all their lives when, on their twelfth birthdays, they had been forbidden entry into Supercute Fairy Realm. 'Tell them to increase the age limit!'

'And they were talking about Spacewalk,' continued Amowie.

'What's that?'

One of Amowie's Blue Brontos floated over to her and she put her arms round it. The one metre tall blue fluffy dinosaur was a great favourite. 'I'm not sure. Some sort of connection thing, but they didn't say much about it.'

'Raquel would know. Where is she?'

'Probably in trouble.'

They all laughed, making their eems turn pink and rise in the air. The tiny floating spheres reflected the moods of their owners. Supercute eems were much better than anyone else's and they gave you hundreds of them free when you watched their show.

'Raquel's always in trouble.' Their friend in Paraguay had very advanced programming skills. Unfortunately, though also amusingly, this tended to get her into trouble. Raquel had no qualms about altering school records as necessary, infiltrating places she wasn't meant to be, and generally making fools of some of the most advanced security systems ever devised. Mostly she got away with it but on occasion she didn't. It wasn't unusual for her to be grounded by her exasperated parents.

'I'll call her,' said Amowie. 'Supatok, find Raquel.'

—

Mitsu wasn't satisfied. 'I don't like the designs for this new Brazilian character. She's too average. 5-Research suggested she should be Brazilian because that's the largest population in South America. He skin tone is Supercute Brown 14 because they measured the entire population's skin tone and took the midpoint. Supercute doesn't work like that. We never have.'

Mox agreed. 'We didn't grow big by being average. We created our own audience. Nothing began as a marketing exercise. Everything came from our own preferences, even if they were weird by other people's standards.'

Juha Soini from 5-Research was used to their ways and not surprised by their objections. 'What would you suggest?'

Mox thought for a moment. 'Make her come from Suriname. That's the smallest sovereign state in South America.'

'There's not much left of Suriname these days. 9HC pretty much wiped them out.' 9HC, the nine-year hurricane cycle, had devastated the east coast of the Americas from Maine to Buenos Aires. Coastal areas had been battered, flooded and sunk. The death tolls had been huge and none of the land was now inhabitable.

'All the better. She'll be a sympathetic character. Her family is bravely struggling on.'

'Try making her darker than average,' suggested Mitsu. 'Lighter too. And try some shades of blue and purple. We'll pick which looks best.'

Juha Soini agreed to take the new character back for re-evaluation. Discussion moved on to the *Supercute 4Koma Maker* they were remodelling. Finally there were decisions to be made as to which presenters at Fab 306 would be wearing the new *SuperGlam SuperNails* with purple and silver stripes. The meeting ended, having gone quite smoothly. Mox and Mitsu had a very clear vision for the Supercute Show.

Their later, informal meeting with some of their advisors did not go as smoothly. The projected trip to France led to heated debate.

Ben Castle didn't like the idea of them travelling. Castle was a forceful character who wouldn't hold back from criticising Mox and Mitsu if he thought it was warranted. They weren't intimidated by this though it was an unusual experience. Mostly their organisation protected them from hostile opinions.

'Why travel to France to meet Pharma Xeng Port? It's an unnecessary risk. Just talk to them from here.' Castle had a lot of dark, wavy hair, not particularly well cared for, that would fall over his forehead on occasion. He was rarely clean shaven. Whether this was for reasons of style or because he couldn't be bothered to do anything about it was debatable.

'Face-to-face still has its uses,' replied Mox. 'We've clinched deals that way when virtual meetings haven't worked. Besides, PXP are nervous about anyone knowing they're doing a deal with us over Spacewalk. They haven't even admitted they acquired it. They put it about that Spacewalk died in development and was discontinued.'

'Why are they so worried?'

'AimYa, mainly. PXP are scared of offending them. They wouldn't even have offered Spacewalk to us except they knew we'd pay an extortionate amount, as well as doing them a favour no one else can do.'

'It's all been awkward,' continued Mitsu. 'They don't even like mentioning it in encrypted private communications in case anyone's listening.'

'So how are you meant to do the deal?'

'Meet them in some place we both happen to be — like a fashion show — whisper in their ear how much we're paying them, and they slip the coding to us in a little box. Something like that.'

Castle was sceptical. 'This all sounds very dubious.'

'It can't be helped. Pharma Xeng Port just don't want AimYa finding out.'

Castle shook his head. 'I don't like the idea of you travelling. It wasn't that long ago that RX Enviro nearly destroyed you.'

That was true. The shocking attack had almost cost Mox and Mitsu their lives. Castle, reappointed as their Security Chief, had now become extremely cautious. Mitsu didn't share his concerns. 'C19 won't allow any trouble in Paris. They weren't happy we were attacked and they've made it clear to all their members that they won't tolerate any more incidents.'

'Just because no one wants to offend C19 doesn't mean they won't try something if they think they can get away with it. Chang Norinco and Goodrich ATK might pretend they had nothing to do with the attack on you but we know they were turning a blind eye at the very least. Wouldn't surprise me if they were more involved. Till things settle down you shouldn't be travelling. If you really have to, you shouldn't be travelling without me.'

The meeting rooms on level two were soberly furnished, sharply contrasting with Mox and Mitsu's current extravagant outfits. They'd been experimenting with pale blue tartans and their full range of pinks, from Supercute Pink 1 to Supercute Pink 44. Not only were they dressed in this combination, they'd managed to extend the tartan and pink mixture into their hair. Even Supercute employees who thought they'd seen everything in the way of bright hair and clothing were quite startled by this development.

'You're Head of Security, we need you here. Look what happened last time we let things slip.'

Supercute's enemy Moe Benny had actually taken control of their headquarters, the huge pink and white building that stood out among the ruins and desolation of North London. Mox and Mitsu would never let that happen again. 'We'll have Ms Lesuuda with us. She's a good operative.'

Castle acknowledged the truth of this. Ms Lesuuda, head of external operations, *was* a good operative. He still wasn't satisfied. 'She doesn't have my experience. I should be going with you.'

'No. We need you to keep this place safe. We trust you to do that.'

'We'll be fine,' said Mox. 'Paris is only an hour away and Igraine doesn't foresee any trouble.'

Again, Castle was unconvinced. 'Igraine's a powerful AIFU but she's inexperienced. She doesn't know how duplicitous these organisations can be. Put her up against the AIFUs of a weapons giant and they'll trick her.'

Mitsu shook her head. Her hair tumbled around her shoulders. Mysteriously, the chequered lines in the tartan pattern remained in alignment. 'We'll be fine. Two days away from you won't be fatal.'

'Think of the benefits.' Mox smiled. 'You can snuggle up with Dr Ishikawa without turning off the cameras.'

Castle refused to engage with this though he was quite open about his relationship with Dr Ishikawa, Supercute's chief medical researcher. Ishikawa herself was considerably more reticent.

'Except Dr Ishikawa's coming to Paris with us,' said Mitsu.

'Right, I forgot. Well, think how happy she'll be to see Castle when she gets back.'

Ben Castle looked sourly at them. 'What the hell have you done to your hair?'

'It's our new combination — eight shades of pink mingled with Dress Blue Menzies tartan.'

'How is it when you hair moves it still keeps the tartan stripes aligned properly?'

'Nano bots. We've been programming them for months. They can all communicate with each other.'

'In your hair?'

'Yes. They're linked to our central AI. Keeps it all working in sync.'

'That's a lot of technology for a hairstyle.'

'True, but it does look fantastic. Isn't the modern world great? Apart from the famines and drought and radiation and warfare and climate disaster.'

Mitsu laughed. 'You forgot the flooding and chemical contamination.'

'I'm so looking forward to the Paris fashion show,' enthused Mox. 'People are going to love our hair.'

'You said this was for business. Is the real reason you're traveling to Paris just so you can sit in the front row at a fashion show?'

'Certainly not,' said Mitsu. 'It's business. It just so happens we really want to go to the fashion show too. *Paris Winter*, sponsored by PXP. One of the biggest dates in the calendar.'

'Theme of *Melancholic Beauty*,' added Mox. 'We have to be seen in public occasionally. It's important for the brand.'

Castle looked like he had more to say on the subject but Mox and Mitsu brought the conversation to an end. 'We have to go now, we've got outfits to plan.' With that they departed, not wishing to be harangued any further. They trusted Ben Castle and even rather liked him, but he did have an unfortunate habit of lecturing them about things they'd rather not be lectured about. This was permissible from their Head of Security, but not something they enjoyed.

—

Nothing about the European Review Group would ever be written down. Nor did they ever meet in person. Despite this, Kadri-Liis did sometimes imagine that the ERG were in formal session, with a written agenda.

*Meeting of the European Review Group*
Chair - Kadri-Liis Mason-Eensaar
 *Those present*
Eupraxia
Penny Cutie (AimYa)
Xiàngrìkuí (Chang Norinco)
Nguessan (Ivo CC)
 *Agenda*
The Destruction of Supercute

—

When Raquel finally appeared in Supatok her friends were astonished to see she was wearing a Kyutu-Kyutu SupaTech jacket.

'Raquel! When did you get that?'

Here in Supatok, the jacket was virtual, translated into the space, but that could only happen if you owned one in real life. That meant the fourteen-year-old Raquel was at this moment lying on her bed in Paraguay wearing a jacket so prohibitively expensive that few Supercute fans had ever seen a real one up close.

'Bought it yesterday,' announced Raquel.

'Did you rob a bank?'

'Of course I haven't robbed a bank! Think of the trouble I'd get into at school. Supercute are paying me for the security checks. Full rate for my services.'

The other three leaned forward eagerly. Supercute's security systems were unrivalled in their complexity and completely resistant to infiltration. Or so Supercute had thought until Raquel successfully breached the advanced biometric protection that prevented anyone over eleven from entering the Supercute Fairy Realm because she and her friends wanted to see the new fairy wings. Mox and Mitsu had been both horrified and impressed to

13

learn of this. With security all over their organisation now being strengthened, they'd hired Raquel to find out if there were any other parts she could still infiltrate.

'Did you find any flaws?' A cute Plumpy Panda made its way through Amowie's voluminous Super V-Hair to nestle in her lap.

Raquel grinned. Her eems looked happy. 'A few. Nothing too serious, but I found an old server that still gave access to Mox and Mitsu's private messaging to Supercute Greenfield. I'll probably find more. You'd be surprised how often these things happen, even when they've got experts looking after everything.'

'I still can't believe you've got a Kyutu-Kyutu jacket.'

Mox and Mitsu's business expansion had originally been driven by sales of their cute clothes. These had never been expensive. They were careful not to price their fans out of the market. However the collapse in living standards around the world hadn't eradicated the rich. Supercute became aware that there were people who were still determined to spend a lot of money. To cater for this they'd established several new subsidiary brands. Everything on the Kyutu-Kyutu label was expensive, including Raquel's jacket, made from leather grown artificially by the German textiles giant Amohr, pink with grey trimmings. Amowie was as interested in the Kyutu-Kyutu jacket as the others but she had something else on her mind. 'Raquel, what's *Spacewalk*?'

'Spacewalk? Why?'

'I heard Mox and Mitsu mention it.'

'Spacewalk was a connection program. It was meant to let you go from one company's space to another. Virtual game spaces, or education spaces, anywhere really. For instance we can't go directly from *Supercute Space Warriors* to *The Star at the End of the Universe* without leaving one and then entering the other, because they're owned by different companies and they don't want you to have direct access. You have to pay for them both and use their own networks. Some companies have reciprocal agreements but AimYa never allows that because they're the biggest and don't want to share with anyone. Spacewalk was meant to get around that. It was a big prospect at one time but I don't know what happened to it.' Raquel brought up her screen. 'It says here it was discontinued after Varsoon went bankrupt. Pharma Xeng Port got all their assets but they must have abandoned the project. I remember AimYa were making a fuss about it, that's probably why PXP dropped it.'

'AimYa is stupid and boring.' Amowie was dismissive. Though there was no single company that dominated the world's alternate realities, AimYa was the largest and most used. Consequently, it held little of interest to Supercute fans who didn't want to go anywhere they might encounter their parents.

'It is boring,' agreed Raquel. 'But plenty of people can only afford to subscribe to one service.'

'How do you know all this?'

Raquel shrugged. 'I read a lot in class. I'm so far ahead of the teachers it's not worth paying attention to them.'

—

Mox and Mitsu were surprised when Igraine informed them that Penny Cutie wanted to talk to them.

'Cutie?' Mox's lip curled. 'We detest her. She knows that. We told her last time she called.'

'Maybe we didn't make it clear enough?'

'I think our language was quite forthright.'

Penny Cutie worked for AimYa as a host on one of their youth shows. She'd copied her style from Supercute. She'd admitted as much, even going so far as to praise Supercute in public, something that had not gone down well with Mox and Mitsu.

'I don't know what I dislike most about her,' muttered Mitsu. 'The way she copies us or the way she gets it wrong and looks terrible anyway.'

'Calling herself Cutie is fairly annoying as well. Couldn't she come up with anything better?'

'OK, Igraine. We'll take the call. Make sure you monitor it in case she's up to anything. Keep a double encryption shield in place. I wouldn't put it past AimYa to try and slip some virus into our communications.'

'There's no chance of that succeeding.'

'I know, but they're foolish enough to try.'

Igraine connected them and a life size hologram of Penny Cutie appeared in their office. 'Mox Bennet! Inamura Mitsu! It's always so nice to see you.' Penny Cutie was wearing a pink and lilac blouse which, Mox noted sourly, bore a strong resemblance to one from their own *Beautiful Lovely Sky* range. Her hair, while not so voluminous as Mox and Mitsu's, was nevertheless multi-coloured, mainly yellow and pink, and arranged around her face in an artfully disorganised style that made her look like an eager young teenager.

Mox scowled at their visitor. 'What do you want?'

Cutie had a dazzling smile and her eyes had been slightly enlarged to emphasise the effect. Mitsu and Mox acknowledged it was good work; bio-enhancement almost equal to their own. Eye enlargement could be difficult to get right. The end result had to appear natural; even a fraction too much made a person look strangely non-human. Penny Cutie looked very human, a beautiful nineteen-year-old straight out of a wholesome anime adventure.

'I just came to say hello. We're such fans of yours over at AimYa.'

'I don't think your board of directors are fans of ours, Penny Cutie.'

'Please, call me Cutie! All my friends do. Did you watch my show last night?'

'No.'

'You should have! I was super nice about your new Big Purple Glitter Boots. I'm wearing them now.' Cutie looked down at her feet. The Supercute boots were solidly constructed, only ankle height but with a five centimetre platform and three leather straps over the laces. Supercute sold a wide range of glitter boots, some quite delicate and some, like those Cutie was wearing, very solid. 'I expect I made you a lot of new sales.'

'Thanks for the endorsement, Cutie.' Mox remained guarded, not sure why Cutie was here.

'Are you going to the Paris Winter fashion show, *Melancholic Beauty?*'

'We haven't decided.' Mitsu was equally guarded, having no wish to give away any hint of their movements.

'You should go! We could meet up. I've been planning my melancholic beauty outfit for such a long time.'

'We'll think about it. We'll probably be too busy.'

'We're such big fans of yours at AimYa! Do let me know if you make it to Paris. We can all meet.'

And with that, Penny Cutie was gone, leaving Mox and Mitsu puzzled and dissatisfied. Mox was scowling, as she had been since Cutie appeared. 'What was that about?'

'I doubt it was a friendly visit. Was it meant to be some sort of warning? Do they know about Spacewalk? Was she letting us know that AimYa knows we're meeting PXP in Paris?'

Mitsu connected to Igraine. 'Igraine, did you pick up anything strange?'

'Nothing untoward. No attempt at breaching our systems.'

'What about voice analysis? Was she threatening us?'

Their AIFU's eyes flickered as she analysed her recording of the conversation. 'Her voice was artificially modulated to filter out any emotional clues. Her holo was using a standard mask to avoid any sort of identifiable body language. I'm afraid there's no way of discerning any hidden meaning in her words.'

'Do AimYa know we're trying to buy Spacewalk?'

'Very unlikely. As far as the outside world knows the project is dead. Every mention of it in this building has been well shielded.'

'Pharma Xeng Port might not have been as careful,' said Mitsu. 'Word could have leaked out from their end.'

Igraine's eyes flickered again. She was designed for intellect rather than strength and was no taller than Mox or Mitsu and almost as slender. 'There's an interesting lack of background on Penny Cutie. Her official background of being a nineteen-year-old from Southampton is undoubtedly false but there's no path back to her actual origin. It's been well covered up.'

'I hope she wasn't really here to invite us to a fashion show.' Mox sounded withering, and decidedly English upper-class, as she did when she disapproved of anything. 'The mind rebels at the thought of spending time with that fraudulent little imitator. Her blouse was simply copied from our *Beautiful Lovely Sky* range.'

'She didn't suit these boots either,' added Mitsu.

'Are preparations ready for our journey to Paris?'

'Yes.' Igraine nodded. 'Mr Castle has been raising objections with me all day. Did Mr Mech mention the unusual graffiti?'

'Khary Mech? Graffiti? What's this?'

'I thought he may have mentioned it. I advised him to.'

Khary Mech was Supercute's Senior Game Director. His offices were on the west of their headquarters where he directed and co-ordinated the work of all the various studios around the world involved in the production of Supercute Space Warriors and other Supercute titles.

'Connect us to him.'

17

Khary Mech appeared on a floating screen. He looked young for the seniority of his position but he'd been involved in gaming worlds all his life and had an outstanding reputation. Supercute had poached him from a rival some years ago. 'Khary, what's this about strange graffiti?'

Khary Mech scowled. Noticing Igraine on another screen next to Mox and Mitsu, his scowl intensified. 'It's nothing. I don't know why Igraine is so concerned.'

'What was it?'

Khary Mech brought up a picture. They recognised it immediately as Helixio, a city on the southern continent of Planet Vespasian. Helixio was blanketed in thick green smog as it always was. Various important events in Supercute Space Warriors took players to the city though it was never a pleasant place to visit. The Senior Games Director zoomed in through the smog, into the heart of the city then out towards the industrial zone to the West. There, through the gates of a chemical processing plant, he showed them a small, dark space behind a warehouse, where someone had scrawled on the wall.

*When the revolutionary proletariat manifests itself, it will not be as a new audience for a new spectacle, but as people actively participating in every aspect of their lives.*

Mitsu laughed. 'Well, that makes a change. Usually people just draw penises.'

Khary Mech nodded. 'It's unusual graffiti but I don't know why Igraine is worried. It's just someone playing a joke.'

Mox turned to Igraine. 'Why does this bother you? It'll be automatically removed when the game resets tomorrow, same as always.'

Igraine frowned, awkwardly. Frowning was one of the expressions she was yet to master. 'It bothers me for several reasons. It's in a very obscure location. No one has any reason to visit that chemical factory. Why travel all the way there to deface a wall behind a warehouse where no one will see it? Further, I can't trace the quote. I assume that talk of the *revolutionary proletariat* relates to a Marxist position but the lines don't appear in any Marxist text I have a record of.'

'Maybe we have an original thinker?' suggested Mitsu, still amused. 'People all over the world play Space Warriors, we've had strange graffiti before. Can't you identify who did it?'

'No,' admitted Khary Mech. 'The camera records are unclear.'

Mox and Mitsu's amusement vanished. Everything that happened in the Space Warriors Galaxy should have been recorded. 'Do you mean someone's altered our records?'

'The smog is particularly thick around there. I can't tell if it's been altered or not.'

'Keep investigating,' ordered Mox. 'I don't mind student revolutionaries writing radical slogans but anyone blocking our in-game cameras would be serious.'

Khary Mech disappeared from the screen. Mox turned back to Igraine. 'Is this really a worry?'

Igraine was silent for a moment. Her eyes flickered. 'Something about it concerns me. However I can't extrapolate from a single example. I've asked Mr Mech to inform me of any others.'

'Right,' said Mitsu. 'Has he been to surgery again?'

'One moment while I access his financial records. Yes, he recently visited his preferred cosmetic practitioner.'

Mox smiled. 'He's getting pretty close to Margaret K these days. Another few tucks and he'll be there.'

For some months Khary Mech had been altering his appearance so that he more and more resembled Margaret K, a member of the Space Warriors crew. She was a weapons expert with super assassination powers, notably bright red hair and the largest collection of shoes on the space cruiser.

'She is a popular character,' said Mitsu. 'Great hair too. I can see the attraction.'

'Is this important?' Igraine appeared confused. 'Do you require regular reports on his surgery?'

Mox and Mitsu laughed. 'Of course not. We're just gossiping.'

'I see. I'm not very good at gossip.'

'Our headquarters is awash with gossip. You'll get used to it.'

—

Sorg Message Number 6hket04: *I'm so insignificant. No one notices me. No one cares if I'm alive or dead.*
6hket05: *My gran died. She was the only person that liked me.*

—

19

Sorg/Sadness was a well-known part of Supercute; a place for anonymously writing down your problems. Every day, the anguish of mainly young people around the world would be recorded. Miseries of all sorts could be found there, from a crush going wrong to bullying at school to chronic disease. Personal problems, fashion mistakes, family problems, loneliness, miscarriages, war, famine, disease: everything appeared on Sorg/Sadness. Anyone leaving a message there received a free fluffy virtual kitten, a beautiful little ball of fur that came into your own personal space to comfort you.

No one could abuse Sorg. It was heavily moderated by a dedicated AI and anyone leaving inappropriate messages or attempting to mock another's sadness would be swiftly identified and removed from the gameworld. Sorg had become an institution. As few places in the world could be said to be happy these days, it was used more and more. Millions of free virtual kittens had been handed out and would continue to be as part of Supercute's service to their fans.

—


Mox and Mitsu travelled to Paris taking suitable precautions though not anticipating trouble. Most events involving members of C19 were peaceful because C19 had the power to enact crippling sanctions against members who stepped out of line.

After landing at le Deuxième Nouvel Aéroport near Paris they were taken by armoured vehicle towards a small private hotel on the outskirts of the city. They travelled in a convoy, armed guards in front and behind, marshalled and directed by Ms Lesuuda. As always while on active duty, Ms Lesuuda wore her faded Ugandan combat jacket, a garment she'd first put on as a teenage army recruit and retained throughout her subsequent career as a mercenary and security operative. Mini-drones accompanied them above, their screens and sensors being monitored by agents already stationed at the hotel. Back in London, Castle was also monitoring their progress. He maintained an open link to Igraine who travelled in the same car. Mox and Mitsu wore their Supercute business suits from the *Girls Fun Work Party* range. These were unlike anyone else's business suits, being coloured in Supercute Peach 8, Supercute Blue 16 and Supercute Pink 19, but they always made them feel professional.

Moving rapidly along private roads they arrived at their hotel. They emerged from their vehicle into relentless heat. Under the constant burning sun the grass surrounding the building was parched and yellow; even the gardens maintained by the luxury hotel wilted under the constant high temperatures and increased ultraviolet radiation of the post-impact world. Mox and Mitsu were closely guarded by their bodyguards as they walked the very short distance from their car to the hotel. It wasn't enough to prevent a plasma bolt from hitting Mox's left elbow. Nor was the advanced shielding built into her clothing enough to prevent the plasma bolt from removing her forearm and hand. Before Mox's yell of pain had died away, Ms Lesuuda had picked her up and sprinted inside. Mitsu ran beside her, her gun now in her hand.

'Where did that come from?'

The agents in the control room couldn't say. They'd been monitoring the surrounding airspace but hadn't detected any hostile drones. Nor was there any sign of enemies nearby. Ms Lesuuda didn't panic. With Mox in her arms she ran straight past the startled employees at the front desk and up the stairs to the suites on the first floor. As she ran she was already communicating with Dr Ishikawa. 'Medical emergency. Ms Bennett's arm blown off at elbow. Arriving in fifteen seconds.'

Dr Ishikawa sprinted towards the large room set aside as a medical unit. Two doctors and two nurses ran at her side. Inside the medical room, small drones took to the air. Less than thirty seconds after the attack, Ms Lesuuda and Mitsu were laying Mox on an operating table and Dr Ishikawa was sterilising her hands as she made ready to direct the surgery. Mox was very pale. Her wound was painful. Normally she had some control over her pain receptors but the plasma bolt had sliced though the tiny relay that modulated the nerve signals to her brain, meaning she could not reduce the discomfort. Despite this, she remained silent. Mitsu gently took her other hand. 'You're safe now. We'll fix you in no time.'

Dr Ishikawa ushered Mitsu out of the way. As she began examining Mox's wounds on the screens that now floated around the operating table, Castle's voice could be heard on the communications channel, berating Ms Lesuuda. 'What the hell? How were you attacked?'

21

Ms Lesuuda didn't know. They'd found no trace of the attackers. She looked on with concern as Ishikawa's team worked rapidly to stop the bleeding, putting Mox into artificial sleep as they sealed up the wound and treated her with tranexamic-d, an artificial compound made for halting artificial blood loss from Mox's mostly artificial body.

—

Amowie, Birgit, Raquel and Meihui crept silently through the bushes that grew over the low hills surrounding Blaise Valley. The atmosphere on Planet Radiant 2 was thin and each wore a Supercute oxygen mask. All four had pistols at their hips. They were on a mission to steal advanced laser rifles from a supply dump owned by the Kernen Mercenary Army. Amowie came to a halt. Crouching low to remain out of sight of the spy towers further up the valley, she signalled to the others. They'd found the entrance to the secret tunnel that led down into the ammunition dump. If they could make their way inside without being spotted they could steal the laser rifles unobserved and leave the planet without having to fight. That would be a good outcome because the Kernen mercenaries were a strong group, well-armed and aggressive. If they brought up one of their Mk 6 hover tanks it would mean certain defeat. Birgit stepped into the tunnel, examining the way ahead with her level two scanner. Messages from the scanner were relayed to the screen inside all four girls' visors.

*No enemy activity ahead. No enemy traps located.*

'Keoma Bishōjo, advance,' whispered Amowie. The small squad had taken on the name *Keoma Bishōjo* when they'd started the game, Keoma being an Igbo word meaning good or attractive, and Bishōjo being a Japanese term for a beautiful young girl. *No harm in giving ourselves a boost*, as Amowie had said when they registered the name. They advanced, making their way down the worn grey stone steps that led into the cave. The lighting was dim but night-vision mode was incorporated into each of their Space Warriors visors. The four girls had been together in Supercute Space Warriors cooperation mode in many missions and acted as a well-disciplined unit. When they reached the end of the stairs, Meihui accessed the map they'd purchased in Lundra and aligned it with the ground ahead. Immediately, a dim blue light snaked its way from her screen towards the trapdoor that opened up on the cave below, revealing its location. Excited now, but maintaining their silence, the girls hurried towards the trapdoor. Raquel pulled it open. Birgit again consulted her scanner.

*No enemy activity ahead. No enemy traps located.* They dropped down into the cave, landing silently, cushioned by their combat suits which were black, for night-time missions, with pink trimmings. All around were huge supply crates marked *Weapons*.

'The laser rifles should be—' Amowie didn't manage to finish the sentence. An alarm went off and the lights came on. Four turrets descended from the roof and another four rose from the floor, opening fire immediately. The girls' shielding wasn't strong enough to protect them from the fusillade and they were cut down in an instant. Their mission was a failure and they were dead in the game. They were ejected from the Space Warriors Galaxy. Each of them ended up floating in Amowie's personal space, quite baffled by their sudden disastrous defeat.

'Where did these turrets come from? The scanner said there were no traps!'

Raquel scowled, quite fiercely. 'Our scanner is level two. Obviously their cloaking defences were level three.'

The four girls were disconsolate. It had been an ignominious defeat. Meihui sighed 'We're never any good at stealth missions.'

Birgit agreed with her. 'We're better when we can just go in shooting.'

Amowie's personal space was normally a pleasant place to be. There was a large pink bed laden with Supercute cushions and representations of her favourite toys. A miniature Supercute Space Shuttle rotated slowly overhead. Everything was colourful. Despite this the girls were gloomy after their defeat and their eems turned green and sank to the floor. Amowie embraced her Blue Bronto toy for comfort. 'We need a better scanner.'

'I wish we could just buy one.' Raquel sounded annoyed because in this, Supercute's policies were against them. No one could gain an advantage in any Space Warriors game by spending real money to advance. It was possible to buy new outfits for your characters or new interior designs for your spaceship, but it was not permitted to buy equipment that would give players an advantage. All upgrades had to be earned by completing missions and levelling up. Mox and Mitsu maintained this policy because they remembered being young and poor, and how annoying it had been if games forced players to spend money to advance. Everyone who bought Supercute Space Warriors knew they wouldn't have to pay more to complete it. Supercute's marketing division was not in total agreement with this policy, but it engendered fan loyalty and Mox and Mitsu would not be swayed.

Now that the girls' combat uniforms had disappeared, their Supercute clothes were visible. Raquel was dressed in an array of bright, ultra-thin Supercute blouses layered on top of each other with extravagant additions from the *Supercute Super Colour Super Plastic Beads Set, Deluxe Edition*, and Birgit had a new *Silvex and his Supercute Boyfriend* T-shirt in luminous Supercute Yellow 18. Meihui wore a Supercute medical mask with a glittering logo, *Fab 306*. Fab 306 was the main entertainment channel in Supercute Space Warriors and an important part of their empire.

Amowie's arm bleeped. A small transparent screen projected upwards from her wrist. 'What's this?' She read from the screen. *'Two adventurers in Space Warriors Nine have discovered a fragment of poetry written by Jax the Astronomer Poet.'*

'What?' Birgit looked incredulous. 'That's impossible. We're never shown any of his poetry. Everyone knows that.'

—

When the wound was carefully sealed, Dr Ishikawa inserted a thin defiplate into the appropriate slot in Mox's chest to ensure her heart rate remained steady. Next she supervised a swift, partial removal of the stress chemicals currently circulating in Mox's injured body. Here in the hotel they didn't have the nanotech facilities to manage this completely but it would be enough to prevent long-term damage. Two small tubes were connected to her thigh, measuring and maintaining blood pressure and hydration. Satisfied that her patient was now ready to travel, Dr Ishikawa stood back as Mox was strapped to a stretcher and taken to the roof where four valocopters were waiting. Two of those were their normal means of transport; the other two had been called in by Castle for additional armed protection on their way back across the channel.

They took off less than fifty minutes after the attack. In London, Doctor Prasad and her medical team were making ready to receive their patient. Supercute Headquarters was on high alert. Castle had every new drone in the air, every turret armed and ready, and the newly relocated support squadron surrounding the building. Movement in and out had been locked down and two more advanced, fully armed valocopters had been rapidly disgorged of the emergency supplies they were carrying and sent to meet and escort those arriving from France. The journey from Paris to London would take less than forty minutes. Dr Ishikawa sat on one side of Mox, monitoring her vital signs while Mitsu sat on the other, very anxiously.

The airborne procession crossed the English channel without incident. They sped towards London, meeting their additional escorts on the way. By the time they reached Supercute Headquarters in London night was falling. Dr Prasad was waiting on the roof along with Castle. Neither spoke. Castle was concentrating on two screens which floated in front of him, assessing any security risks in the area. Dr Prasad was studying a screen of her own that was now connected to those of Dr Ishikawa, reading her medical reports in advance so there would be no delay in treating Mox. Already their biotechnicians were preparing the new parts to replace Mox's arm and hand.

Two valocopters landed on the roof while the other four remained in the air. Mox was brought out on a stretcher and taken rapidly down to the heart of the building, accompanied by Dr Prasad and Dr Ishikawa. Mitsu went with them, as did Ben Castle. One hour and twenty minutes after the attack in Paris, Mox was safely back in London and Supercute's advanced medical team were assessing the damage before beginning treatment.

Mitsu sat close by in the operating theatre. Both she and Mox wore regulation, undecorated medical facemasks rather than the cute Supercute versions they'd usually favour when visiting their medical centre. Mitsu's hair, as voluminous in the real world as it was in Supercute space, was neatly tucked away beneath a hair net, something she'd only permit in the gravest of situations. She watched as the remaining parts of Mox's upper arm were removed. Dr Prasad had decided that a complete new arm would be preferable to repairing what was left of the original. The main bones were connected quickly, the humerus, radius and ulna fitting perfectly around the new elbow, but it took longer to properly align the forearm with the seven bones that made up Mox's new wrist. Tiny medical drones flew around as the work progressed, sometimes disappearing inside Mox's skeleton where laser-assisted measurements were taken to ensure that everything was in perfect alignment. Screens floated beside the operating table, showing the results of these tiny drones' work. Dr Prasad, with Dr Ishikawa at her side, checked their readings, sometimes making small adjustments to a drone's settings. Only when they were satisfied that each new bone was perfectly connected did they move on to the next. The new left hand had been constructed in advance. Dr Prasad's team had been working on it before Mox arrived back in London. Using Supercute's existing medical records, an exact replica was ready and waiting to be attached by the time her wrist was complete. The twenty-seven bones in the hand were similar in chemical composition to normal human bones, but greatly strengthened. The customised biotechnology available to Mox and Mitsu was equal or superior to anything available elsewhere. No specialised clinic for the world's wealthiest inhabitants could offer better. Mox and Mitsu's body enhancements rivalled even those available to the military. Each of them was now ninety-four percent artificial, only parts of their brains remaining from their original organic forms, and those parts had been refreshed many times.

The attachment of the artificial biological materials making up Mox's new muscles, nerves, ligaments, blood supply and skin all proceeded smoothly. Mitsu looked on, worried at first, but reassured by the medical skills on display. Both she and Mox had received treatment here many times. They were used to their doctors opening them up, renewing, regenerating and replacing parts of their frames. Mox remained asleep and would not be woken till the next day when her new limb would be fully tested. Mitsu followed on as Mox was wheeled into the recovery room. In contrast to the stark surgery room, the recovery room was discretely colourful, a soothing light blue shade with pink furnishings, with many of Mox's and Mitsu's favourite toys scattered around. Knowing that Mitsu would want to remain with Mox while she recovered, two beds had been placed next to each other, each covered by a *Blue Bronto and Dinosaur Friends* quilt.

Mox was placed in her bed. She slumbered peacefully as several small adhesive pads were placed on her frame, monitoring her vital signs. Readings were all satisfactory. Her arm had been repaired and all harmful hormones and chemicals cleansed from her body. The medical personnel withdrew, leaving them alone. Mitsu sat on her bed. She looked at Mox and smiled. 'Now you have a better left arm than me. Dr Prasad's going to make me get mine renewed too, so we match up.'

—

In the nearest conference room Castle was furiously berating Ms Lesuuda over the incident. Ms Lesuuda defended herself. 'All security procedures were carried out properly. All checks were made, exactly as if you'd been there.'

'If I'd been there this wouldn't have happened. I knew you didn't have the experience for this sort of job.'

Ms Lesuuda did not like being criticised. Voices were raised and the argument intensified. Curiously, it was not that long ago that both Castle and Lesuuda had been enemies of Supercute. Ms Lesuuda had been hired by Supercute's enemies to kill Mox and Mitsu. Ultimately she'd failed but, recognising her many talents, they'd hired her afterwards. As for Castle, he'd never actually tried to kill them but he had spent a long time telling anyone who'd listen how much he hated Supercute, berating Mox and Mitsu at every opportunity. They'd sacked him from his position and he'd blamed them for his subsequent problems. He too had changed his mind after the affair with Moe Bennie. Since being rehired as Head of Security he'd shown himself to be solicitous about their safety.

The argument continued. Neither showed signs of backing down though Castle was senior and therefore would prevail eventually. They were interrupted by Igraine. The AIFU strode silently into the room, regarded them with disapproval for a few seconds, then informed them sharply that they should be upstairs in security central where their analytical team was busy examining and expanding new information from the Supercute Satellite that might be able to detect where the attack had come from. Castle and Lesuuda left the room to examine the new findings. Igraine remained behind, expressionless. She'd already been in contact with Pharma Xeng Port to make excuses for their failure to meet them. She promised to be in touch soon to rearrange their meeting. Igraine was well adapted to predicting human behaviour and knew that Mox and Mitsu would not be put off from business by this attack.

—

Amowie had strong opinions about the report that a fragment of poetry by Jax the Astronomer Poet had been located. 'It's ridiculous. Someone must be lying. Everyone knows you never get to see any of his poetry. Who makes up this rubbish?'

'Jemima Dreem says some people saw Jax write these lines.'

'It's impossible! Jemima Dreem is talking nonsense.'

Jemima Dreem was a well-known figure in the world of Supercute. She presented a very popular fan show every week. Amowie and her friends watched this show religiously, strongly agreeing with her on some things and relentlessly criticising her on others.

'Everyone who's ever played Supercute Space Warriors meets Jax at some point and he's never written any poetry before.'

'But he is a poet.'

'We never see his poetry!' The conversation became animated. Meihui spoke Northeastern Mandarin, Amowie spoke Central Igbo, Raquel used both Paraguayan Spanish and Guarani, and Birgit spoke Icelandic. All four also used English to some degree, which often veered into Supex, a pidgin language composed of many different elements that was now becoming more common inside Supercute gameworlds as a lingua franca. This language, unintelligible to parents around the world, had grown in complexity and popularity in recent years. No matter which language was used, the girls' conversation flowed smoothly. The automatic translation in Supatok was so advanced as to cope easily with excited conversations between teenagers in seven languages. It had become so efficient that Supatok space was now used by many people otherwise uninterested in Supercute. That was interesting for Mox and Mitsu. The rise of Supex, effectively their own language, was interesting too. Despite Mox's rather severe defence of standard English in most circumstances, some in-game announcements and advertisements had started to appear in Supex, the feeling being that having their own private language invited greater loyalty from their already fanatical followers.

Meihui stared at the lines of poetry in question.

*Fourteen levels inside*
*Neutrinos: three flavours: electron, muon, tau*
*Each neutrino a quantum superposition of all three*
*flavours*

28

'What's it supposed to mean?'

'It's not like a poem at all.' Raquel was dismissive. 'More like something from a textbook.'

'It must mean something if Jax wrote it.'

'He can't have written it.'

—

Mitsu perched on the side of Mox's bed, partly for companionship and partly to prevent Mox from getting up. 'You need to rest while you recuperate.'

'It was only an arm. I'm fine. Look, I've got a new one.'

'Stop flexing it, it needs another twelve hours to fully integrate. And after that, biotech still has electronics to fit in.'

Mox scowled. Her strong aversion to hospitals had been the original reason behind Supercute opening their own medical centre but even here, in the safety of Supercute Headquarters, she didn't like undergoing treatment. 'Dr Prasad wants me in here for another whole day. Can you believe it? The woman's a fanatic.'

'She's one of the finest doctors in the country and we're lucky to have her.'

Mox was still scowling but she wasn't really upset. Mitsu's presence was enough to make her feel secure.

'Prasad's scheduling you for trauma therapy.'

Mox shook her head. 'We reached maximum trauma when we were four years old and watched our teacher being stabbed to death right next to us. We can't suffer any more trauma, there isn't room.'

Mitsu smiled, rather grimly. The effects of seeing Miss Evans being murdered had never fully left them. They were both aware of this. 'I brought you some things.' She produced a badge. Yellow, once shiny but now dulled with age. It read *Art-I-Ficial*.

'X-Ray Spex?'

'Yes. Made long before we were born. Appropriate, as we're mostly artificial these days. And I got the factory in Norwich to make a rush edition of our new *Super Space Unicorn*.' Mitsu handed over the cuddly toy. *Super Space Unicorn* was a popular character from Supercute Fairy Realm. Mox clasped the pink and white winged unicorn to her chest. She looked happier. 'Good toy.'

'Pre-orders are excellent.'

'Fairy Realm gets more popular every day. We're going to have to think more about letting older kids into some version of it.'

Mitsu nodded in agreement. There was an increasing demand from older teenagers, and indeed from adults, to travel there. They were considering ways of facilitating this, without spoiling the children-only experience of their younger fans.

'I made you this.' Mitsu handed over a screen. On it was a cartoon, made from the popular, improved Supercute 4Koma app. The cartoon had four panels, laid out in a single vertical strip, one below the other. The characters were cute, appealing and well drawn. The app would do that automatically for anyone, no matter how deficient their artistic skills might be.

Mox and Mitsu are wearing their Supercute Girls Fun Work Party outfits for a big meeting in Paris.

They go to their hotel but then Mox is shot!

Who could do such a terrible thing? The whole world loves Supercute! Supercute have the best clothes and the best toys.

Mitsu rushes Mox home where the Supercute doctors make her all better! Here she is in her cute bed. Mitsu has brought Mox more toys and nice hot chocolate and now everything is fine in Supercute World!

Mox laughed. They often used their app to make their own 4Koma comics. They'd liked the format for many years and still remembered the earliest examples they'd seen, like Lucky Star and K-On. They were silent for a moment.

'So who blew my arm off?'

Mitsu produced a paper and pencil, objects so ancient it was probable that no one else in Supercute Headquarters had ever used them. 'I thought we could make a list of suspects.'

'We've always enjoyed making lists.'

'And getting back at our enemies.'

—

30

'*To everyone in Supercute, hello from Kirei19, number one host on the number one in-game channel, Fab 306!*'

Fab 306 performed an important function in Supercute. It could be heard all over their gameworlds. It played music, gave out news, hosted its own shows and acted as a unifying central source of information for all players. As tended to happen with Supercute, elements that were successful in their shows and games often leaked out into the real world. In the same way that Shanina, captain of the Space Warriors, could now be found modelling clothes in actual fashion shows, Fab 306 had emerged into reality with its own fashion label, its own celebrities, its own culture and its own music.

Supercute dance music was especially notable. Arising from a mingling of many different cultures it had finally merged into an identifiable genre, SupaCore. SupaCore had spread to the clubs and dance halls of the Supercute galaxy and from there entered the outside world. It could now be heard in many regions, played by many DJs. Though not quite mainstream it was influential in a way that rival organisations had not been able to imitate. Even MazeCam, who dominated the music market, creating entire worlds dedicated to music production and marketing, had never been able to come up with anything quite as influential as SupaCore, which seemed to have emerged organically, without guidance, the result solely of the enthusiastic creativity of Supercute fans.

'We don't know what's going on with these reports of Jax's poems,' continued Kirei19. 'We think someone's playing a joke on us. Surely no one's ever seen any of Jax's poetry? The Astronomer Poet is very secretive about his writings!' Listened to in English, Kirei19 had a slight Japanese accent. In Japanese and other languages she had a slight English accent. 'But who knows, perhaps there's something unusual going on? Supercute Space Warriors has the best galaxy, you never know what might happen!'

The computing power and artificial intelligence involved in the running of Fab 306 were immense. Many of the servers and memory banks responsible for this were kept safely underground near Stabbursdalen National Park in Norway, where Supercute owned huge tracts of land, cool, uncontaminated and safe for storage.

31

'Don't forget the Fab 306 Super Dance Party this Saturday on Krisna Mag. We'll be dancing all night under the blue illuminated rings. I'll see you all there!'

The name itself, *Fab 306*, was something of a private joke between Mox and Mitsu. It was resonant of the 1960s, a period about which they were particularly well-informed. In the very earliest days of Supercute, when the show had been just the two of them in a bedroom filming themselves with an iPhone, they'd sometimes pretended to be presenters of their own imaginary show, Fab 306, where they'd give reports about their favourite toys and clothes. In their private rooms at Supercute Headquarters they still had some of the earliest T-shirts they'd made, lovingly screen printed with the Fab 306 logo they'd designed themselves.

—

Sorg 3hzaw18: *My so-called friends are going to the dance party on Krisna Mag and I'm not invited. I want to kill myself.*

—

Mox and Mitsu studied their list. The words were elegantly written. Both retained the extensive cursive and calligraphy skills they'd developed at their advanced nursery school.

'We have a lot of potential enemies but not that many who'd actually be prepared to attack us.'

'The two weapons giants are the most obvious candidates. Chang Norinco and Goodrich ATK still don't like it that we acquired ZanZan.'

These huge conglomerates had previously shown no real animosity towards ZanZan Defence, a smaller company. They were known to be unhappy that Supercute had made the acquisition. Considering Supercute's financial might and political influence, they had reason to fear that ZanZan might end up overtaking them. Supercute was now one of the larger members of C19. Procuring ZanZan had boosted both their turnover and their strategic importance. ZanZan Defence was ripe for investment, with plenty of potential for growth.

'C19 didn't raise any objections to us acquiring ZanZan. Chang and Goodrich have no legitimate reason to complain. Still…'

'When we met up in Rome they seemed to have accepted it. They were probably lying but are they annoyed enough to actually attack us?'

Mox considered this. 'Of the two, I'd say Chang Norinco were the most likely to take action.' She sat up in her bed. 'Goodrich are concentrating a lot on South America and they've had problems with some of their contracts. The Central American Recovery Agency is investigating them over illegal payments so they're probably keeping their noses clean at the moment. Unlike Chang Norinco.'

Since the destruction of Beijing, Chang Norinco had been based in Shanghai but in recent years they'd moved much of their business to their own artificial islands. 'No one's controlling them there. They're probably hiding a lot of things they'd shouldn't be from the New Chinese Republic.'

'Spying on Chang has never been easy. We'll see what 8-Research can tell us.' There were several research departments at Supercute. 5-Research carried out their standard marketing and commercial analysis. The rather more secretive 8-Research was involved in the espionage work necessary to combat external threats.

'What about AimYa?'

Mitsu pondered this. 'AimYa haven't been known to take violent action for years.'

'They did in the past. They wouldn't have become the number one alternative cyber life company if they hadn't wiped out half of Maegfix's board of directors and blackmailed the rest.'

'Not that that was ever proved.' Mitsu and Mox laughed. They were both aware of AimYa's illegal actions which had taken them to their present dominant position, even if the public were not.

'They've been trying to remain clean for a long time. The war with Maegfix brought them close to the edge. C19's council sanctioned them and warned them not to let it happen again.'

Mitsu had her suspicions. 'If they've found out Spacewalk still exists and we're trying to buy it, they might have decided it was worth the risk.'

'All our negotiations with Pharma Xeng Port have been secret. We've taken a lot of care.'

'We'll need to check them out anyway.' Mitsu looked down at their list. 'What other enemies do we have?'

'Nothing major, as far as we know. RX Enviro are out of the picture and we've maintained good relations with the rest of C19. There is Ivo CC, I suppose, but they're too small to bother us.'

Mitsu screwed up her face. 'I've always thought there might be some repercussions from the Cote d'Ivoire. Ivo CC is virtually synonymous with their government. They hated us for the move.'

Supercute were a very large purchaser of cocoa beans. Supercute cafes brightened up desolate high streets all around the world and their Supercute chocolate treats sold in huge numbers. A year ago they'd switched their supplier from the fields of Cote D'Ivoire to an artificial bio-production plant in Normandy. It saved them a lot of money: it had a bad effect on Ivo CC.

'We didn't have a choice. Normandy was much cheaper. Better beans too. Ivo CC's fields have never been completely free of plutonium, there were still traces.'

'Even if we think they're too small to trouble us we should still check them out. I'll add them to the list. Anyone else?'

'No one I can think of. Unless we're facing some malign unknown AI.'

Mox made a face. 'I've never really thought a malign unknown AI was all that unlikely, honestly.'

'Why would it dislike us? There are plenty of worse people around. Plenty of worse companies too.'

'Maybe it's an AI that hates cute clothes and toys.'

'Then we'd really be in trouble.'

—

Krisna Mag was a beautiful moon with beautiful rings. It hung low over the Fabulous City of Lundra, always visible in the night sky. Supercute's game designers had created it as a place where players could forget their troubles and relax in the warm sunshine. As the long twilight set in, the silver beaches would fill up with revellers for the frequent dance parties hosted by Fab 306. On one of these beaches an illuminated sign spun lazily in the air.

*Tonight - Fab 306 Super Dance Party - Your Host - Kirei19*

A few people lay on the beach, early arrivals, resting, gathering their energy for the night's events. Ignoring them, a tall figure walked up to the sign. He wore a dull blue jumpsuit with a

Supercute mask covering the lower part of his face and a dark hat shading his eyes. He examined the sign. After pondering for a few moments, he reached out and began to change the letters. How he did that was unclear to the onlookers but the floating, illuminated sign altered under his touch.

*Dance back into your ruined homes*

The masked figure took a step back, examining his work. Satisfied, he strolled off, disappearing behind the beachfront shops that were full of new Supercute summer merchandise.

—

The four dancers collided in a manner which would have caused bruises had it happened in real life. Here in Supatok dance practice space they were spared injury, if not embarrassment.

'Raquel, you were meant to step left, not right.'

'I did. You all got it wrong.'

Meihui, Amowie and Birgit stared at Raquel with some exasperation and some sympathy. She was not a talented dancer and didn't claim to be. Nonetheless, they needed her to improve. 'If we're going to get these laser rifles we need to win the dance contest.'

Raquel scowled. 'I never enter dance contests when I'm playing on my own. I look for another way.'

It was a feature of Supercute Space Warriors that there were always several ways to succeed at any of the missions and quests in the game. When you needed an item you might win it by all out assault. Or, as they'd recently attempted, you might obtain it by stealth. Sometimes you just needed enough in-game experience, which gave you credits to buy it. If these all failed, there was generally a cute route. By careful study of fan pages, Amowie had discovered that winning the dance contest on Krisna Mag brought a key that would unlock the Kernen mercenaries' cave and turn off their secret defences.

'It's our only way in. We can't attack it and we can't get in by stealth. We need this key and to get it we have to win the dance competition.' Meihui looked pointedly at Raquel. 'So we'd better practice.'

35

Raquel got to her feet, grumbling about the indignity of it all. As always, she was extravagantly dressed in Supercute finery. This was not so hard to do in Supercute space but Raquel dressed like that in real life too, walking around her Paraguayan city in the brightest and cutest clothes and enjoying all the attention.

'Let's try again,' Meihui was the best dancer in the group, closely followed by Amowie. Birgit was less talented but was prepared to practice and had so far managed to keep up. Raquel lagged far behind. 'We could try bargaining for better rifles with Emerald Yoon-Ah.'

'Emerald Yoon-Ah's the meanest weapons trader in Lundra,' said Amowie. 'She never bargains.'

'And she's scary,' added Birgit. 'I don't even like talking to her.'

Emerald Yoon-Ah was a weapons dealer in the Fabulous City of Lundra. She had good equipment for sale but her prices were high.

'Just concentrate on your moves.' Meihui took up her position. 'The Phnom Penh Skip isn't that hard.'

'I hate the Phnom Penh Skip,' muttered Raquel, though she stepped back in line to try again as Meihui counted them in.

'Five, six, seven, eight…'

—

Mitsu spoke to her therapist. 'Mox won't let it go. It's going to lead to bad things.'

'You said the injury wasn't serious?'

'Not serious for Mox, given our medical resources. But she still had her arm blown off. She's not going to ignore that. Even if it was good for business to let it pass, she wouldn't. Neither would I.'

Mitsu paused. Their therapy space was a soothing room with a small Zen garden on the floor, designed by Mitsu, inspired by one she'd known from her parent's home city of Kanazawa, capital of Ishikawa Prefecture. Like many of the cities, town and villages on the west coast of Japan, Kanazawa longer existed. On the walls were virtual copies of pictures by Narbian, one of their favourite contemporary painters. The young German's paintings of fruit and flowers were highly detailed and very traditional. So far she had found little favour with art critics.

'Mox always had a vengeful streak. I knew that from a young age. When she came to live with us she had a lot of resentments. She was quite angry with the world. Her mum died giving birth to

36

her and her dad committed suicide before she was one year old. By the time she was two she was already showing signs of being a super genius and her carers found that difficult to cope with. She was resentful about some of the treatment she'd received. A lot of that vanished after my parents started taking care of her. But her vengeful streak didn't completely disappear.'

'When we were nine, at Oxford, we had this tutor who didn't take to us. By that age we were far ahead of virtually everyone else at university. We were studying physics and computer science which involved a lot of advanced maths but we'd learned all the maths already before we got there. We were a long way in front of all the older students. We already had pink hair and colourful clothes and this tutor just didn't seem to like us. In the tutorial group she'd be quite unfriendly. It went wrong one day when Mox corrected her maths in front of everyone. Mox was right of course, but the tutor just went mad. Shouted at Mox, called her arrogant, accused her of being purposely disrespectful. Then she physically marched her to the door and threw her out the room. It really was an over-reaction on her part.'

Mitsu paused. 'Of course, you never know what's going on in someone's life. Maybe that tutor had problems. Family problems. Money problems. Mental problems. Who knows? But Mox didn't like being criticised in public, and worse, the tutor had actually laid her hands on her. Mox wouldn't let that go.'

'What did she do?'

'You should ask *what did we do?* Because I helped. We hacked into her phone and her computer at home and emptied her bank account. Erased her mortgage details, her work contracts, cancelled and erased her insurance records, tax records, all her personal information, years of texts and emails, pictures, everything. Just deleted her past. It really screwed up her life. She was away from work for months, sorting the mess out.'

'How did you feel about that?'

Mitsu's brow furrowed, very slightly. 'I felt fine about it then. Turned out I had a mean streak as well. Mox and I have grown to be very alike over the years but in a lot of ways we were very alike when we met. We're not good at letting things go. Vindictive. Generally we keep it under control. Sometimes it still appears.'

'You don't seem entirely comfortable with this.'

37

'If I was comfortable with everything I wouldn't have paid so many millions for this *Perfect Therapy Suite*.'

Mitsu touched a button on her wrist. The therapy room faded away and she was back in the medical centre at Supercute Headquarters. She stared out of the large window, made from treated glass that kept the hostile elements at bay. Outside she could see the well-tended grounds surrounding Supercute Headquarters and their huge bank of solar panels, but beyond the walls a large tract of barren land was visible, a parched, sunken mess which had once been part of the heavily populated London Borough of Barking and Dagenham. Much of London was still in ruins. In the distance were the tall skyscrapers of the financial district, blue-tinged from their shielding, but next to them were devastated areas which showed no signs of recovery. Beneath them the water table still leaked radiation: without fresh water pumped from Supercute Greenfield's desalination and purification plants on the South Coast, London would have been uninhabitable. Even the seat of government had moved further south, to the administrative centre of New Salisbury. Mox was sleeping peacefully in the recovery room next door. Slightly guilty about leaving her for even a few minutes Mitsu hurried back to her side.

—

Sorg 3mkrb22: *I'm a mess. Nothing ever goes right. I have dreams I don't like.*

—

Igraine met Raquel by appointment in Supercute's security space. The measures taken by Supercute to avoid any sort of hacking or spying were costly, comprehensive and the equal of any organisation in the world. 'Despite this, you keep finding flaws. It's...' Igraine paused. Emotions in her android brain were sometimes difficult to describe in human language. '...curious.'

'Don't feel bad,' Raquel grinned. 'I mean, you're a really advanced Artificial Intelligence Forecast Unit and you've got loads of AIs working with you and plenty of experts making sure everyone is secure, and I'm just a fourteen-year-old school student who keeps finding flaws...maybe you should feel bad, now I think about it.'

'Thank you for your latest input.'

Raquel had identified a weakness in the encrypted communication between Supercute Headquarters and one of their financial centres in Berne. It was an oversight which should never have been allowed to happen. Raquel was still grinning. She liked Igraine, the only person or android she'd ever met who could equal her own knowledge of cyber security. 'The main problem is people. You have everything protected correctly and then someone in an office just doesn't bother to do something properly and it leaves a little gap for someone like me to worm their way in. Don't worry. We'll close all the gaps eventually. I can't meet you tomorrow though, I have extra dance practice.'

'I didn't take you for a dance enthusiast.'

'I'm not. I've been trying to learn the Phnom Penh Skip but it's not going well. Keoma Bishōjo need to win a dance contest to get a key so we can steal laser rifles but I'm not much good at it.'

'Is there no other way?'

'We failed at all the other ways. Now Meihui and Amowie and Birgit are all dancing like crazy and I'm trying to keep up.' Raquel scowled. 'It's OK for Meihui. Every week she meets people in Cambodian Supatok to go raving and they all dance for twelve hours or something like that. Sometimes Amowie and Birgit go with her. But I'd rather be at home, just playing with my code, mostly. So my dancing is nothing like theirs.' Raquel looked sad. 'It's becoming embarrassing.'

Igraine was sorry to hear this but unsure what to say. She wondered if a compliment would cheer Raquel. 'You always wear the most beautiful Supercute clothes.'

That was true. Raquel's father in Paraguay was a general in the Fuerza de Defensa Combinada Sudamerica. She was wealthier than her friends and could afford any clothes she wanted. 'Thanks Igraine. Do you like my jacket?'

'I do. I don't think I've seen anyone your age wearing the Kyutu-Kyutu SupaTech.'

'I bought it myself,' enthused Raquel. 'With the money you're paying me.' Despite her youth, Raquel was being well paid for her consultancy work. Supercute remunerated all their employees well. From the most skilful artificial-world renderers at their studios to the serving staff in their Supercute cafés, from the heads of their financial institutions to the cleaners in the vast warehouses that sent their goods around the world, Supercute paid well. No

Supercute employee was on minimum wages in any country. This was the declared policy of Mox and Mitsu from which they had never deviated.

—

The Fabulous City of Lundra was one of Supercute's greatest assets. The futuristic metropolis was one of the wonders of alternative reality. It was such a glorious place to be. Huge high rise buildings linked by extravagant walkways, interspersed with the most beautiful parks where the air was clear and the flowers bloomed in the brightest colours. Whole neighbourhoods dedicated to Supercute fans who paraded in their clothes through streets lined with small shops and boutiques bursting with Supercute merchandise, small shops the likes of which could hardly be found these days in the bankrupt high streets of real cities around the world. Most often the city was pleasant, warm and sunny, but there were occasions where it would rain or even snow, all making life more interesting. Occasionally the huge swathes of Supercute-clad young people would have to run shrieking and laughing from a sudden rainstorm into the cover of the nearest shop or arcade where they'd talk excitedly about the latest goods on display and show off their new outfits to each other, and talk about which Space Warriors mission they were on, or which concert they might go to tonight, or which picnic in which park, or what they'd just seen or heard on Fab 306. Was Jemima Dreem's latest gossip reliable? Were Silvex and his Supercute Boyfriend really having problems? Did Ammo Baby, leader of the Ultra Waifs, really defeat a level 53 Gro-Tek fighter on Planet Excalibur 6, all by herself? Were the new *SuperGlam SuperNails* with purple and silver stripes really only going to be available to players who'd reached level ten? That didn't seem fair! There were the regular adventures of Captain Shanina and the Supercute Space Warriors to discuss. Shanina was facing a tough decision on who to appoint as their new tail gunner after Markus Space Warrior left to follow his ambition of being a doctor. As for the ongoing drama in BetaStarGirl, where Beta had just been betrayed by her fashion consultant, that was building up to be a shocking scandal. BetaStarGirl, an animated series shown only in the internal world of the Supercute Galaxy, could bring Lundra to a halt, with inhabitants simply stopping whatever they were doing to watch the latest events.

On the outskirts of Lundra were the weapon dealers, the shielding merchants, the space armour brokers who sold all the in-game merchandise you needed for the gameworld you were in, and the information sellers where you could pick up missions. There were recruitment offices for the Space Warriors themselves. When you'd progressed far enough in the game, you could join them for missions.

Even Mox and Mitsu could be encountered on the streets of Lundra. The real Mox and Mitsu, not imitations. Their bodies might be back in Supercute Headquarters but they'd put on their Supercute Visors and visit their virtual city, just like everyone else. They liked the city. Like many things involving Supercute, it had not been deliberately planned. They'd originally intended it as a town in their gameworld where players could buy and exchange merchandise. As it grew in popularity, they'd found it becoming more and more important. Ostensibly, the population of the city was 20 million. In reality it was much larger, as the computing power available to Supercute allowed players around the world to experience the city slightly differently, keeping the population manageable for each player's timeline. Apartments in Lundra were not available to beginners. Inhabitants had to have made some progress through the game before they could even visit. Amowie, Meihui, Birgit and Raquel had all made their way through solo versions of Space Warriors and had lived there, but now, playing as a team, they still had to earn the right. That was almost as big an incentive as becoming eligible to fly with the Space Warriors.

Already fabulous, the city had recently been improved by two events. Firstly, Igraine's arrival at Supercute. She had great powers of world building and used it as a means of relaxation. She loved the complexities of the gigantic city. Secondly, Supercute's new quantum supercomputer, Welcat, had recently been completed. Now they owned one of the world's most powerful supercomputers. The huge additional computing power would help in many areas of business and research. It was already enabling them to increase the complexity of the algorithms governing the City, giving an ever more realistic alternative life to its population.

'*The Fabulous City of Lundra is better than ever!*' as Kirei19 enthused on Fab 306, every day.

41

Mox and Mitsu were aware of their city's elevated status. They weren't quite aware of the extent of AimYa's jealousy. AimYa had been unable to construct anything as popular. It was annoying to their board of directors. Some wondered if it might be possible to take over Lundra. Failing that, perhaps they could destroy it.

—

In her office adjoining the main laboratory, sharing a pot of green tea with Castle, Dr Ishikawa was in a good mood. In recent weeks she'd found herself relaxing more in Castle's company. She'd stopped denying to herself that they were having a relationship, even if she wasn't keen on hearing anyone else mention it.

'I see you got rid of everything colourful.'

Dr Ishikawa scowled. 'What were they thinking, hanging a string of dancing fairies on the wall?'

'I think Mox and Mitsu were welcoming you back.'

'Hah. This is a place of science, not a child's playroom.'

Castle laughed, and reached out to place his hand on hers. 'You said you'd made some breakthrough?'

'The virus vector for causing genetic changes in two childhood cancers is showing very positive results in my *in vivo* studies. In six months I should have a successful treatment.'

'I'm happy for you.' Castle was sincere. He admired Dr Ishikawa's work. He knew that once she'd developed the treatment she'd give it away for free, spreading the knowledge around as her service to the world. There were a lot of brilliant minds inside the Supercute building — some organic, some artificial — but Dr Ishikawa was both brilliant and ethical. Though she was employed to look after Mox and Mitsu, much of her research was dedicated to assisting children around the world, many of whom had far less access to health care than past generations.

'I suppose I should thank Supercute,' continued the Doctor. 'Welcat is making a difference. Some things I can now test a thousand times faster than before.'

Castle grinned. 'Do you know what Welcat stands for?'

'No.'

'We Love Clothes and Toys.'

Dr Ishikawa grimaced. 'Now you're ruining my good mood.'

—

42

Mitsu sat next to Mox's bed, reading reports from some of their Heads of Departments. 'Mox, remember our first employment? When we were waitressing in Camden?'

'Of course. Terrible place. They kept making us do double shifts when people got sick.'

'And remember what we decided when we were working there?'

Mox narrowed her eyes and assumed an expression of exaggerated suspicion, something she'd do in private to amuse Mitsu. 'What's this leading up to?'

'We decided if we were ever employers we'd be nice to our staff.'

'And we always have been. Supercute are good employers.'

Mitsu smiled. 'Yes, we are. Except for the occasions you forget we're not living in Victorian times and start trying to fire people for not meeting your exacting standards.'

'Do I do that?'

'I just talked to Ms Ghent. I assured our Head of Staff you were only joking when you threatened to discharge her new assistant because he can neither read nor write in longhand.'

Mox looked at Mitsu in mock outrage. 'Are we employing children now? What sort of person can't read joined-up writing?'

'Americans. They gave it up a long time ago.'

'No wonder the country collapsed.'

'That was really more to do with both coastlines going under water and Yellowstone getting rid of the middle. The bits that are left are still struggling on. Anyway, you can't fire junior members of staff because they can't write in longhand.'

'If you say so.'

'Just like you couldn't demote our young science illustrator for not knowing there are twenty-two proteinogenic amino acids.'

'She thought there were twenty. It's a serious scientific error.'

'Not for the woman who colours in *Happy Little Science Pixie and his Adventures on Pluto*.'

Mox had the good grace to laugh at herself. 'I'm just trying to maintain standards.'

'You really have to stop getting upset over this sort of thing. When Ranbir used the word *sassy* I thought you were going to have a heart attack. And that's not easy, given our advanced artificial organs.'

'I deplore the word *sassy*. It implies that normal female confidence is somehow impertinent. I refuse to allow it anywhere in Supercute. There's nothing wrong with being careful with our language. It's not like I overdo it.'

'You still complain about the word *sneakers*.'

'What's happening here? I'm a sick woman in a hospital bed. Is this the time for complaints?'

Mitsu laughed, and stroked Mox's shoulder. 'You're much happier discussing declining standards of literacy than you are lying here doing nothing.'

Mox scowled, though again her scowl was exaggerated for effect, designed to make Mitsu laugh, which it did. '*Sneakers*. I hate the way that word took over. We should have resisted it.'

'It was too late. It had gone around the world before we entered the market. We did successfully repel *plushie*. Anyway, we sell an incredible amount of Supercute sneakers. Number one worldwide brand for under fourteens, highly placed in most other categories. We even got commended by World Health Organisation for our cheap range, *Cute Basics*.'

'I was proud of that. Every time the cameras went to the famine zones there were thousands of kids wearing Supercute pink sneakers. They were still starving but they had excellent footwear. These Cute Basics can keep out fire, water *and* radiation.' Mox looked up at Mitsu. 'You know, there was a time when you had your own super-traditional phase. We were walking around London in Kimonos for two years. Wooden sandals and everything.'

Mitsu's parents had died in Japan a long time ago, victims of one of the series of terrible tsunamis that swamped the country. Both Mox and Mitsu had grown up in their care in London. Their loss had been a terrible blow. Afterwards Mitsu had gone through an intense phase of Japanese traditionalism.

'I know. I still appreciate the way you supported me.' A discreet alert informed Mitsu that marketing had sent her material for approval. She brought it up on a screen.

*Sumair04 exclusiv oshberi khunni ₡ Kirei19 @ Fab 306*

Mox raised her eyebrows. 'Talking of language…'

Mitsu nodded. 'I never thought we'd be responsible for a new one.'

'It's an interesting phenomenon. We didn't encourage Supex. In fact, with our perfect translation services, you'd have thought it wouldn't need to happen, but it has.'

'All these young people from all around the world, meeting in our gamespace. It seems there's still some need to talk face to face, without a translator.'

'Igraine says it's starting to develop its own consistent grammar.'

'Are we happy using this made-up fan language in our own marketing?' wondered Mitsu.

'I don't think we have a choice. We can't let our own fans leave us behind.' Mox took Mitsu's arm. 'Anyway, I resolve to no longer be overly fastidious about words.' They watched as Mox's new Super Space Unicorn toy strolled over the bed before lying down comfortably next to her.

'I'm not really happy with the name Welcat,' said Mox.

'You just said—'

'It's a defective acronym for *We Love Clothes And Toys*. We've used two letters from the word 'we.' Really it should be *Wlcat*.'

'That's difficult to pronounce.'

'The whole thing is unsatisfactory.'

'I think this probably counts as being too fastidious about words. Though you're right, it is unsatisfactory.' Mitsu thought for a moment. 'We could fit another word in for the letter E. Some suitable adverb.'

They both considered this. 'Emotionally?' suggested Mitsu. 'We emotionally love clothes and toys?'

Mox wasn't satisfied. 'That seems redundant. Love already implies emotionally. What about enthusiastically?'

'Wouldn't that also be redundant? Can you love something unenthusiastically? How about eternally?'

'We can't really claim that. Not while there's the heat death of the universe to contend with.'

They came up with a few more suggestions but weren't enthused by any of them. Finally Mox connected to Igraine and explained their problem. 'Do you have any suggestions?'

Igraine checked through her memory banks of every known word. 'I have two suggestions. *Exuberantly* or *especially*. Both would be accurate.'

'We exuberantly love clothes and toys.'

'We especially love clothes and toys.'

After some consideration, Mox and Mitsu decided on *especially*. 'It scans well and it's quite a Supercute word,' said Mox. 'All right, Igraine, please enter it in the official files that our quantum supercomputer's name Welcat now stands for *We Especially Love Clothes And Toys*.'

'The long name doesn't appear in any official files. It's always simply referred to as Welcat. You only used the full name in conversation with each other here at headquarters.'

'Oh,' said Mox. 'Well, now I just feel silly.'

'There may be worse problems,' Igraine informed them. 'Welcat is scanning your gaming worlds much faster than we could before. Moments ago it notified me of two further instances of hostile graffiti, revolutionary in tone and content.'

Mitsu screwed up her face. 'We really have to sort this out.'

—


Kadri-Liis Mason-Eensaar and Penny Cutie met in Kadri-Liis's private space. She'd decorated this to resemble a stylish art deco drawing room from the 1920s, with smooth lines and geometric shapes in silver, crystal and jade. She was displeased by recent events. 'The attack on Ms Bennet and Ms Inamura was a mistake. All it's done is give Supercute a warning.'

Cutie didn't seem so upset. 'They saw it as a rare opportunity. It might have worked.'

'It failed. Supercute won't leave themselves so vulnerable again. They'll be looking for whoever carried it out.'

'It would be extremely difficult for anyone to find Ruosteenoja,' said Cutie. 'Even AimYa don't know who he is.'

Kadri-Liis raised her eyebrows. 'That doesn't mean Supercute can't find out.'

'If AimYa can't find someone then neither can Supercute.'

'Just because AimYa is so large, it doesn't mean you know everything. Supercute are one of the most dangerous organisations in the world. We should end these pointless physical attacks until we're capable of subverting them from the inside, as previously agreed.'

Cutie twisted a strand of pale blue hair round her fingers, a habit which Kadri-Liis found annoying. 'You assembled a group of people who hate Supercute but it's not like you can really order them around. Nguessan at Ivo CC isn't one for stealth. He hired Ruosteenoja to assassinate them. I can understand that.'

'Nguessan might regret it if Supercute ever find out he was behind it. I know that from experience.' Kadri-Liis's eyes glinted and for a moment her face took on an expression of fury. The death of her mother at the hands of Supercute still enraged her. To cover for this, Eupraxia, her AI, spoke from the screen he never left. 'Ms Cutie, what progress have you made with visor interference?'

'Not as much as I'd hoped. It would be difficult to inflict serious physical harm on Supercute's users. AimYa has researched inflicting neurological damage on connected people but it's usually only effective on people with chips in their heads. There's a chance we could attack Mox and Mitsu if we caught them unprepared. We might be able to interfere with the connection between the chip and the artificial parts of their brains.'

'Do we know they've had brain replacement?'

'They must have had, at least partially, to be functioning at such a high level for such a long time.'

Kadri-Liis wasn't convinced this was a weakness. 'Artificial brain replacement is done molecule by molecule. It's more replenishment than replacement. It's a very exact process and hasn't been shown to be susceptible to attack.'

'I know,' said Cutie. 'But there might be a vulnerability there. We're researching it. As for Supercute fans, they're not chipped and the commercial visors most of them wear have effective fail-safe devices. We're looking at the possibility of trapping visitors to Supercute Space so they can't leave. In some circumstances neural exits can be blocked.'

Eupraxia agreed this was worth investigating. 'Children unable to return to reality would be a devastating blow.'

Cutie twirled her hair around her finger again. The blue took on a darker shade. 'Xiàngrìkuí's been looking at ways to affect their gaming spaces. She says if she's going to find the Supercute test gate she needs to be able to take some control of their code.'

'What's she been doing?'

'Writing graffiti on walls.'

'Pardon?'

'In Space Warriors. She's experimenting with altering the behaviour of some of their non-playing characters to make them write graffiti.'

Kadri-Liis frowned. 'That sounds like a pointless distraction.'

Cutie shrugged. 'She does tend to be erratic. She's a brilliant AI though. Making any change in a Supercute world has never been done before. Maybe it will lead her to finding the test gate.'

'Eupraxia, you should talk to Xiàngrìkuí,' said Kadri-Liis. 'Find out more about what she's been doing. I want to know if she's receiving any useful information from her contact in Supercute.'

'I don't want to talk to her.'

'Why not?'

'I don't like her.'

Kadri-Liis smiled. She'd never known two artificial intelligences to take such a dislike to each other. It amused her, though it wasn't helpful. 'I'm sure you can get over that. We all need to communicate. Time is limited. We need to be ready before Supercute fully integrates Victoria Decoris.'

—

Mox was conscious as she had new electronics implanted into her arm. Mitsu sat next to her as the doctors, technicians and medical drones did their work. Mox had shown signs of irritation bordering on distress and Mitsu knew her tolerance for being in the medical unit had almost worn out. She talked to her to divert her attention.

'People are still saying Jax wrote poetry. It can't be true. He's an imaginary figure.'

'Of course. Strange how the story spread though.'

'Fab 306 picked it up from Jemima Dreem. It's not bad for publicity, I suppose. Jax and Roota are always popular even if the game never lets them get together.'

'Maybe we should think about that some time,' said Mitsu. '*Space Warriors Ten — the Big Wedding*. Have you thought about Sachi's suggestion?'

Their chief producer had suggested they film an episode from the ward, with Mox still in her recovery bed. Mox shuddered. 'I'm not staying here any longer than necessary. I had to listen to Dr Ishikawa lecture me today while she was calibrating the muscles in my palm.'

'What was she lecturing you about?'

'The usual. The general immorality of Supercute and the worthlessness of our existence.'

Mitsu laughed. 'Our chief medical researcher still shows no signs of liking us, even though we're protecting her.'

Dr Ishikawa's habit of stealing exclusive private research from the world's leading medical companies had almost caught up with her. These companies had been very close to tracking her down before she came under the protection of Supercute.

'They would actually have assassinated her. You'd think she'd show some gratitude.'

'Dr Ishikawa knows no gratitude. She complained when we asked her to return the equipment she stole from us.'

Dr Prasad stood waiting as tiny medical drones flitted about, checking the results of their work. The last of the drones closed up the skin on Mox's forearm, sealing off the advanced electronics. 'Everything is satisfactory, Ms Bennet. We've replaced everything you had before and made improvements to your internal communication with the Supercute satellite.' Dr Prasad turned to Mitsu. 'We should improve that for you as well.' Mitsu nodded, unperturbed by having her arm opened up for improvement.

'You need to rest that arm for another eighteen hours.'

Mox sat up in her bed, 'No chance. I'm getting up right now.'

Mitsu laid her hand gently on Mox's shoulder. 'I'll make sure she rests, Dr Prasad.'

After Dr Prasad left Mox still seemed determined to rise. 'I'm supposed to lie here for another seventeen hours. What am I meant to do for seventeen hours?'

Mitsu was prepared for this. 'We can design clothes for Victoria Decoris.'

Mox was partially mollified. The acquisition of their new game did give them a lot of scope for character and clothes design. They'd always enjoyed that.

—

Amowie, Birgit, Raquel and Meihui all agreed it was unexpected that Supercute had bought Victoria Decoris. They'd watched the edition of Jemima Dreem's show where Jemima had explained the purchase to fans. The company behind the game had overextended themselves, running into financial difficulties. Supercute had stepped in, paying for its further development and eventually adding it to their own franchise. Jemima Dreem showed pictures of some early clothes designs. The girls admired these designs though Raquel had her doubts about the enterprise.

'I don't see how they're going to fit this into their other game worlds. Supercute Space Warriors is strictly scientific. There's no magic involved. Doesn't steampunk always have some magic thing so the Victorians get super energy supplies or something like that?'

Raquel was correct about Space Warriors; it did exist in a scientific universe. Some elements did need to be glossed over without too much scientific analysis — faster than light travel being the principal example — but it mostly relied on probable scientific realities. Players could have extraordinary weapons and equally extraordinary abilities but everything was couched in logical, scientific terms. In contrast to this, the cities of Victoria Decoris were powered by a mysterious golden force that emerged from the world's volcanoes. That didn't sound scientific. Meihui was sceptical. Her home had been destroyed by the violent eruptions of the volcano in Wudalianchi province; there had been nothing magical about that. Her family was still housed in temporary accommodation and there was no prospect of things improving in the near future. 'Volcanoes don't bring anything good.' She shook her head sadly. 'I won't be able to afford a new game extension anyway.'

'Supercute will probably include it free in the *Extra Super Always Happy Bundle*,' said Raquel.

'My family can't afford that either.' Meihui sighed. 'We just connect with the *Super Always Happy Bundle*.'

'Us too,' said Amowie.

Supercute's subscription rates were low compared to others. The basic *Super Always Happy Bundle* was an inexpensive entry to their worlds. There were more expensive packages such as those used by Raquel and Birgit, but for Amowie in Igboland and Meihui in her disaster relief location in North East China, money was tighter. Their families couldn't afford any extras.

'Don't worry,' said Birgit, brightly. 'Amowie's a SuperSuperFan now. They'll give her a free game. And you can play with us, Meihui. There's always a plus-one player option when you get the *Extra Super Always Happy Bundle*.' Birgit was optimistic about Victoria Decoris. 'Supercute always have the best games. I want to wear those boots Jemima showed us.' As always, the clothes were a powerful attraction.

'I don't suppose the Fairy Realm is scientific,' Amowie pointed out. 'And we used to love that.'

'It's different though. That's for kids,' said Raquel.

Amowie sighed. 'I still miss the Fairy Realm.'

Raquel laughed. 'You still miss the fairy roundabout!'

Amowie rushed to defend herself. 'I do not! I never said that!'

There was more laughter. Raquel had only been joking but Amowie bristled at the accusation. The roundabout in Supercute's Fairy Realm was for two and three-year-olds only. It was many children's first introduction to Supercute space. Infants at home put on their visors and were transported to the roundabout, an extremely gentle and slow-moving device. There they sat on small, colourful, friendly unicorns and trundled sedately round a circuit of lush green foliage while small laughing fairies fluttered over their heads, to a background sound of lutes and running water. Infant visitors sat on these unicorns as if hypnotised, entranced at everything around them. Fairies and fluffy little chicks would perch on their laps as they made the circuit. It was well-known in many regions of the world that if you wanted to entertain your toddler for an extended period of time, sending them to the fairy roundabout was an effective way of doing so.

Amowie could not admit to missing this childish adventure, even if it was true. It had been a cause of regret when she was no longer permitted on the roundabout. She needn't have worried. Many older children missed it too. They all might have been surprised to learn that Mox and Mitsu had their own, real-world version. In one of the largest of their private rooms at Supercute Headquarters there was an exact copy, an actual physical rendition where you could climb on to a solid little unicorn and sit there among the fairies as it circuited the room which itself was decorated exactly like the virtual version. No one had ever witnessed them there, sitting contentedly, trundling happily around the long circuit, entranced like children by the fairies flitting around their heads, the green surroundings and the sound of running water.

The four young fans would have been extremely distressed to learn of the attack on Mox, and utterly horrified to learn that her arm had been blown off. News never reached the outside world. Supercute's powerful media empire suppressed the story completely. No word of the incident ever leaked out to the public.

—

Mox and Mitsu sat motionless in the lifeboat, huddled together for warmth. The small wooden craft was packed to capacity and floated low in the water. Beside them a young girl with damp blonde hair was weeping. An older woman sat beside her, ignoring her, too shocked by events to do anything but stare into space. Mox and Mitsu watched as the Britannic reared in the water before breaking up, the entire stern tearing off with a terrible wrenching sound as hundreds of tons of buckled metal came loose from the main body of the ship and plunged into the water. The rest of the broken hulk slipped smoothly under the surface. Now there were just the lifeboats dotted around the sea. It was eerie, calm, and cold.

'What now?' whispered Mox.

'I don't know.'

It was early morning on 19 August 1916. The Britannic, a passenger cruiser, had been repurposed as a hospital ship for the duration of the war. After striking a mine it took only fifty minutes to sink.

Mitsu looked around 'Maybe we should comfort the crying child?'

Mitsu reached out to touch the child's shoulder. 'Don't worry, we'll be rescued soon.'

The child kept on crying. 'I did my best,' whispered Mitsu.

Mox squirmed on the hard wooden bench. 'This lifejacket is really uncomfortable.' She reached over to the crying child. 'Would you like some emergency chocolate?'

The child's crying intensified. Tears poured down her face. Mox looked defeated. 'I'm cold and miserable. I don't think I'm getting anything out of this.'

'It's beautifully detailed. I don't know what we're meant to do.'

They looked around them at the shocked, shivering figures crammed into the lifeboat. In the anxious silence the sound of the child crying was quickly becoming intolerable.

'Are we meant to make an inspiring speech to cheer everyone up? Maybe something about the super-kitties?'

Mitsu made a face. 'It's 1916. There are no super-kitties.'

They shivered. Both felt unhappy. Rain began to fall. The nearest lifeboat drifted further away, leaving them isolated in the lonely sea. Neither had any inspiration as to what might be a good course of action.

'Let's go home.' Mitsu touched a spot on her wrist and the whole scene faded away. They were back in the recovery room, Mox in bed, Mitsu sitting beside her. The visors generated by the chips in their temples disappeared. 'Why do we play these art-house simulations? "*You're a survivor from the wreck of the Britannic, adrift in a lifeboat in the Mediterranean.*" It's hardly promising.'

'Do you think we did OK?'

There was no telling. Sadanumi's simulations never gave you a score. They never gave instructions. What you were meant to achieve was never made clear. Possibly there was nothing to achieve. They just put you into an uncomfortable situation, with a friend, and you made whatever you could of it.

'Did we learn anything?'

'We're not much good at comforting children.'

'Strange that, with us running the biggest children's show on the planet.'

Mitsu wasn't satisfied. 'Why do Sadanumi make these strange simulations? *Friendship in Discomfort?* What sort of title for a series is that? And again, why do we play them? I'm sure no one else does.' Sadanumi were a small company. Their simulations were high quality but not widely known. They seemed to have no desire to make anything that might have mass appeal.

'I'd like some gin. And sake.'

Mitsu shook her head. 'Alcohol is forbidden in the recovery room.'

'How can it be forbidden? We own everything in this building.'

'Somehow our doctors can still order us around.'

Mox made a face. Her hair had been tied back in a ponytail while she was undergoing treatment and it was irritating her. 'Release hair.' At her words her hair automatically rearranged itself around her shoulders.

'At least it stopped you complaining about wanting to get out of bed.'

'I still want to get out of bed.'

'You have another eight hours. Are we going to authorise troops to protect our desalination plant in Baaska-Tera?'

Mox grimaced. 'It's quite an escalation. We've supported military action before but we've never actually authorised our own troop placement.'

'We can do it now, with ZanZan. Ms Lesuuda has worked with the mercenaries we'd be using. It's expensive but less expensive than losing the plant.' It was a problem Supercute Greenfield had encountered before. In a crisis-struck, drought-ridden area, Captain Yến and her relief team would install an emergency desalination plant. Soon afterwards, Supercute would build one of their highly efficient permanent plants, capable of transforming one thousand million litres of seawater into fresh water every day. This would be done with the co-operation of the government or local authorities. Usually it turned out well. There were exceptions. Unrest and revolution might threaten the plant as was happening now in Baaska-Tera.

'The leader of the insurgents is planning to take it over without compensating us. He's not much of a negotiator.'

'We can't really blame him. The Baaska-Tera regional authority is corrupt from top to bottom. We should never have become involved there.'

'We had no choice. Either we became involved or everyone died.'

Inside Mox's recovery ward there was the sound of gentle rain, which she found soothing. 'So we can either give up the plant, defend it, or decommission it remotely. Do they realise we can decommission it?'

'We warned them but they don't believe us.'

Supercute retained ultimate control of every desalination plant they installed. Each could be remotely put out of service. 'I'm not sure what to do. I refuse to give up the plant but if we put it out of action people will die.'

'I'm not sure either.'

Mitsu had brought Mox a soft silk jacket which was now draped round her shoulders. 'Perhaps we should have stayed on the lifeboat longer. Maybe it was going to teach us something.'

'I doubt it. Let's talk to Lesuuda again about the possibilities of military action. If we don't like that, we'll just have to decommission the plant. We can't let ourselves be blackmailed.

54

Anyone around the world who tries to steal our desalination plants has got to know they'll end up with nothing.'

There was a gentle beep on Mitsu's screen. Igraine's face appeared. 'More unusual graffiti in Space Warriors. Look at this sign on Krisna Mag. It's been changed.'

*Dance into your ruined homes*

They stared at the altered sign. 'That's very depressing.'

'Really puts a downer on the dance contest.' Mitsu looked puzzled. 'Who changed it? And why?'

'We don't know who,' replied Igraine. 'As to why, I suggest it's an example of détournement.'

'What?'

'Détournement. A method of defacing any type of media. It's been defined as *turning the expressions of the capitalist system against itself*. Following this insight, I re-examined the previous graffiti located on Planet Vespasian — *When the revolutionary proletariat manifests itself* — and found it to be an imperfect translation of the French original, from a Situationist text.'

'Situationist?'

'French revolutionaries during the 1950s and 60s, much involved in the Paris riots in 1968. An interesting group, I've been reading about them.'

Mox and Mitsu were both looking blank. 'What does it mean?' ventured Mitsu. 'Has some political faction invaded Space Warriors?'

'I think that's unlikely. Much more likely is one lone prankster. I'd say it was only a minor problem were it not for the fact that the gamespace cameras haven't picked them up. That could suggest something more sinister.'

Another gentle buzzer sounded, contact from Marlene Stevens, one of their senior designers. 'We have the samples for our Neo Decora sweatshirts. Would you like to see them?'

'We're busy dealing with a revolution,' Mox told her.

'We probably should look at them before we're overthrown and led away to the guillotine,' said Mitsu.

'You're right. Bring them in, Marlene.'

—

Kadri-Liis had been depressed all day. It made her pessimistic. 'We're wasting energy. We have attacks that might not work and research that might go nowhere.' She gazed out the window at her gardens. 'I wish I could have declared open war.'

'Not possible. Supercute are far too powerful.'

Kadri-Liis Mason-Eensaar's office was modest and rather nondescript though it overlooked an extensive, well-tended garden through which ran a small stream of purified water, an extravagance rarely seen among the parched wastelands of southern Estonia. She herself was elegantly dressed in a long white and gold gown that seemed out of place among the office furniture. 'Supercute don't deserve their success. They got lucky with desalination. That's what really boosted their growth. They'd never have got anywhere with their show, selling their ridiculous clothes to infants.' Kadri-Liis shuddered. She had a particular aversion to Supercute's clothes.

Eupraxia, her AI, didn't reply, though he knew the allegation was not entirely true. It was Mox and Mitsu's exceptional language skills and talent for communication that had first caused their show to grow. After that, their genius for designing and marketing their own merchandise had started to bring them wealth. However, it was true that the desalination business had made Supercute a global giant and a member of the C19 cabal.

'How they developed that technology is still a mystery. I assume they stole it from someone.' Kadri-Liis sipped from a tumbler of brandy on the desk. Ever since her mother had been killed she'd been drinking more. 'What chances do you give us of success?'

'There are too many variables to calculate a meaningful figure.'

'Can't you make an estimate? AIFUs predict the future all the time.'

'I hold AIFUs in low regard. Predicting stock positions only puts them one step ahead of adding machines.'

Kadri-Liis Mason-Eensaar scowled. 'Eupraxia, you're the offspring of two of the most advanced artificial intelligences developed in the last decade. My mother was CEO at RX Enviro before Supercute killed her. She helped develop you. When I pulled you out of the wreckage of RX Enviro I was expecting better.'

Eupraxia laughed. For an artificial intelligence, he had a good sense of humour. 'I'd say I'd done well for you so far. I discovered

Supercute's attempts to buy Spacewalk. That's how you persuaded AimYa to cooperate. If that hadn't happened Chang Norinco and Ivory CC wouldn't have come on board. You've built your European Review Group quickly because of my help. You have a reasonable chance of bringing down Supercute. I can't give you an exact estimate.'

Kadri-Liis sipped her brandy, and looked sour. She liked Eupraxia but sometimes had the feeling he could be doing more. 'Do you like my dress?'

'Yes.'

'Yes? Is that all you have to say?'

'Very well, it's a fusion of geometry, metal and graphic florals exploring urban and natural spheres, interpreting contemporary femininity through its opposites.'

'Are you just quoting from the catalogue?'

'Yes. But again, I provided you with all of Ralph and Russo's records, even though the originals disappeared in a firestorm.' Eupraxia's voice changed. He sounded more sincere. 'It suits you well. You look beautiful.'

Kadri-Liis leaned forward and patted the screen. 'Thank you. It's nice of you to say so.' She finished her brandy. 'I need to destroy Supercute. They put a bullet through my mother's head.'

'We'll bring them down. They're not as well-protected as they believe.'

Outside it began to rain; grey, acidic rain, polluted by high levels of soot in the atmosphere. The garden outside reacted instantly, transparent walls shooting from the borders to form a protective pyramid over the plants, reminiscent of the pyramid that had once stood in front of the Louvre. Kadri-Liis Mason-Eensaar looked out at the rain impassively. Here there was some protection: Elsewhere in Estonia there was none. The country was still in ruins. She didn't expect it ever to recover.

—

Meihui, Amowie, Birgit and Raquel are practicing for the big dance competition!

See how good they are!

Apart from Raquel. She's a big idiot.

Now she's fallen over again.

All four girls laughed at Meihui's 4Koma, even Raquel. 'I've been practicing my dancing. We can do more now if you like.'

Meihui shook her head, causing her Super V-Hair to tumble around her shoulders. 'Can't tonight, I'm off to dance in Cambodian Supatok.'

'I wondered why you were wearing so little.'

The young Chinese girl shrugged. 'It's all in Supatok. It's not like I'm really meeting anyone.' Meihui was wearing a violet Supercute top that had been small to begin with and had been altered to make it smaller. On it were two badges. One, in English, read *Kill Me Baby*. The other said *Ég lifði eldfjallið af* which was Icelandic for *I survived the volcano,* and had been given to her by Birgit. 'You should come to the rave.'

Raquel declined the invitation. She didn't feel that she was up to dancing in public yet.

'No one will care. Loads of people dance just as bad as you.'

'Thanks. That makes me feel much better. I'll stay home for now. I have more work to do for Supercute.'

'Did you learn any new secrets?' asked Amowie.

'I'm just checking their security, I don't get to see secrets. Though Igraine did show me a new outfit they'd designed for Victoria Decoris.'

That was interesting news and the others clustered around eagerly to study a picture of a young woman in a Victorian-style dress with a full skirt. She had a brown leather hat, very sturdy boots, ammunition belts over her dress and a musket slung over her shoulder. They were all amused at the though of wearing such a long dress, very unlike any of their Supercute clothes, but they all liked the outfit.

—

Ben Castle was an experienced military man with a lot of useful biotech enhancements. Mox and Mitsu were pleased they'd appointed him as Head of Security though cautious as he appeared in the recovery room.

'New suit?'

'Ishi made me buy it.' Castle was the only person who'd ever use any sort of familiar name for Dr Ishikawa. 'I thought you'd be up by now, looking for revenge.'

'They're keeping me in bed against my will. Another four hours to go.'

'What difference will four hours make?'

'Don't encourage her,' said Mitsu. 'She needs time for her new electronics to settle in. With a better connection to our satellite.'

Castle didn't look impressed. 'Never mind the satellite. You don't need a satellite. What you need is to start listening to me when I tell you about security.'

Mox was dissatisfied with this. 'That was a very weak transition from one subject to another. It hardly made sense.'

'Also, we do need our satellite,' added Mitsu.

'You're almost dead because you went gallivanting off to France instead of staying here like I told you to. And if you had to go you should have taken me for safety, as I also told you.'

'Yes, fine, Castle. It may have been a mistake. No point going on about it.'

'It's the same sort of irresponsible behaviour that made me leave Supercute in the first place.'

'That's not quite what happened…'

'And I'm not allowing it again. From now on you need to take my advice.'

Mox tightened her grip on her Super Space Unicorn and turned to Mitsu. 'Did I miss something? Don't we own Supercute any more? Did someone make Castle our boss? Mr Castle, are you suffering from delusions? Is that why you haven't bothered shaving for a while?'

'You employ me to keep you safe. You have to follow my advice.'

'We'll bear it in mind. Is there anything else you'd like to complain about while I'm in my sick bed?'

'Yes. I still need another two high altitude drones over the building. The new 8-Mv4 models from ZanZan.'

'We already have more firepower protecting this building than most countries could muster.'

'We need more. Authorise the money.' Castle's desire for additions to the already formidable defences around Supercute Headquarters touched on a deeper problem. Here in London, Supercute were protected to an extent by the British state. It would be difficult for an enemy to launch a prolonged, full scale attack. That also made Supercute subject to certain restrictions placed on them by the government. Not too many restrictions, given that Supercute was such a vital contributor to the perennially struggling economy. The authorities didn't want to offend them and largely left them alone. Few governments around the world were keen to confront any of C19's largest members. Even so, they weren't free to do anything they wanted. For some time Mox and Mitsu had been considering the possibility of moving Supercute, perhaps to one of the islands they owned, essentially setting themselves up as their own country. That would present its own problems. The issue remained unresolved.

'We'll think about it,' said Mitsu. 'We already increased our drone protection and guard regiment, we should have enough.'

'Last week we paid thirty-two million for a shielding upgrade, on your advice,' added Mox. 'Boosts the shielding in our clothes by 1.4 percent. Which is not a lot for thirty-two million, when you consider it.'

'Espionage isn't cheap. It cost a lot to steal that. You'll be pleased at the extra 1.4 percent some time.'

'Maybe. But we can't keep pouring endless resources into your security concerns.'

'There would be more money for security if you stopped spending money on things you don't need. The Mondrian you bought last month. How much did that cost?'

'380 million. It's the best piece to come on the market for a long time.'

'You have enough art already. Too much, probably.'

'How can you have too much art?' demanded Mox.

'Just get me the drones.' Castle also raised his voice. 'And don't wander off to fashion shows without me there to protect you.'

Mox and Mitsu were now thoroughly irritated. 'We'll go wherever we want,' said Mox. 'You can protect us when we get there. That's why we employ you. I'm not staying a prisoner in

Supercute Headquarters.' Because she was annoyed at Castle, she added, 'We might go back to Paris. PXP are hosting another fashion show and they're sponsoring a performance of La Traviata at the opera afterwards.'

'You just had your arm blown off in Paris! You can't possibly think about going back there now.'

'We can take better precautions this time. We still need to talk to Pharma Xeng Port in person about Spacewalk.'

'Is this thing really worth all this trouble?'

'Yes. It'll allow everyone in Supercute space instant access to any other company's space without subscribing to their service. It will be huge for our business.'

'No wonder they're all trying to kill you.'

'It shouldn't be that controversial,' said Mitsu. 'Lots of companies have reciprocal arrangements with their alternate worlds anyway. AimYa just wants to keep us out because they're trying to dominate the market. If we do nothing then one day they'll try to replace us. You've seen Cutie and her show, that's a first step to siphoning off our fan base.'

Castle nodded, calming down a little. 'OK, I see why you need it. But you can't go to Paris at the moment. Talk to PXP from here.'

'And miss the opening night of La Traviata? There's an excellent cast. Nabanji Nganga is singing Violetta and she's commonly regarded as the finest soprano in the world.'

'So what?' Castle regarded them more quizzically than sternly. 'Why are you so keen to attend the opera?'

'It's really the only chance we get to wear long gloves.'

Castle shook his head, irritated but now fed up with arguing. 'I'll protect you if you go to Paris, but it's a stupid move. And you should buy me the drones.' With that, he walked out of the recovery room.

Mox and Mitsu sat in comfortable silence for a few minutes but it didn't last for long. Dr Ishikawa entered the room unannounced. Ishikawa, a Japanese woman who'd just turned forty, was wearing her white medical coat, as she usually did at work. Her black hair was short and neatly styled. 'What did Castle want?'

'To moan at us,' replied Mitsu.

'We're glad you made him buy a new suit. It's an improvement.'

'Though he still seems inclined to moan at us.'

'It's probably because he cares about you,' said Dr Ishikawa. There was a brief pause. 'Unlike me.'

Mox shook her head. 'I don't think that's true. He does seem to care about you.'

'That's not what I meant. I meant I don't care about you.'

'Of course. Sorry about the misunderstanding. Did you just come here to tell us that?'

'No. I came to ask why you haven't authorised the purchase of the new Genetic Replicator for my lab.'

'You mean the single most expensive piece of medical equipment currently on sale anywhere?'

'Yes.'

'We're still costing it.'

'There wouldn't be a problem if you stopped wasting money on things you don't need.'

'Oh, for God's sake.' Mox threw back her quilt. 'I'd recover better in a radiation hotspot.' She rose from her bed. Mitsu didn't protest. 'Its time we were giving orders anyway. I'll tell Sachi to get the board ready.'

—

Mox and Mitsu strode along the corridor issuing commands. 'Mr Castle, inform the leader of the insurgents in Baaska-Tera he's got twenty-four hours to back off or we'll shut down the plant. If the entire region dies of thirst it's his fault.'

'Marlene, we're not happy with the Neo Decora sweatshirts. They're not colourful enough. Igraine will set up a meeting so we can go through the designs again.'

'Dr Prasad. Arrange for testing of Mox's new satellite connection this evening. Schedule Mitsu's upgrade for tomorrow.'

'Igraine. Reschedule negotiations with Pharma Xeng port.'

'Mr Pham. Approve the acquisition of two new attack drones from ZanZan, as requested by Mr Castle. Also approve purchase of genetic replicator as requested by Dr Ishikawa.'

'Mr Soini. Tell 5-Research to investigate these rumours about Jax writing poetry. It was a decent piece of publicity for a while but we'd like it stopped now. It's bad for business for people to think anything might have gone out of control.'

'Khary Mech, work with Igraine to find out who's writing graffiti inside Supercute Space Warriors then make it stop.'

Mox still carried the Super Space Unicorn Mitsu had given her. They always appreciated the small gifts they gave each other. The badge reading 'Art-I-Ficial' was pinned to her silk top. She was still dressed in her pyjamas. The pink cherry blossom pattern wasn't that much different to many of Supercute's clothing designs and no one at Supercute Headquarters would have noticed anything unusual. Not that they would have cared if anyone did. Mox and Mitsu had been dressing unusually all their lives. Even at four years old, in the advanced nursery school, they'd begun to develop their own style. They'd always known that many people regarded them as strange; it had never bothered them.

'Sachi. Bring rehearsals for the show back on schedule. We need to make sure our piece with the Hirosaki Supercute Society goes smoothly. This is a big week for them, they've all been helping at Hirosaki Park and it's the first time they've been able to hold the cherry blossom festival for thirty-five years. We want to give them good coverage.'

'Marlene, make sure the sky is Blue 15 for the big Mr Panda musical number. We've planned our outfits for that.'

They changed their connection so that only Igraine could hear them. 'We have some unexpected expenditure so we'd like to increase liquidity in account 18656. Please see to that.'

Account 18656 did not appear in any official Supercute record or document. It was secret, could never be discovered and could never be traced to them. It was the account used to bring money in from Erotica 9/2. That was a particularly lucrative business, even among the many lucrative businesses owned by Supercute. They'd acquired it almost by accident when they'd take over Yanvi Yan, an online sales and delivery platform in South East Asia, incorporating it into their already formidable sales network. Late in the process of completing the deal they'd discovered that Yanvi Yan owned Erotica 9/2. It was a small platform in comparison to some of the main sex sites, but a successful one, with a dedicated following due to the high quality and realism of the virtual sex on offer. Clients could fully experience any sort of sexual encounter, entering into Erotica 9/2's space in complete privacy to do anything they desired. Yanvi Yan had concealed their ownership of the company, not wanting to be publicly associated with the world of commercial sex. Mox and Mitsu could have divested themselves of the business. They chose not to. For one thing, it was very profitable. Sex had been lucrative all through history and it still was. They kept hold of Erotica 9/2, hiding its finances behind such a large wall of shell companies, anonymous commercial holdings and offshore interests that its true ownership could never be discovered.

Profit was not the only reason they'd decided to keep hold of Erotica 9/2. They were aware that since the dawn of the internet, sex had been a major driver of online and virtual technological progress. They liked having direct access to any advances that might occur. The board of directors of Erotica 9/2 didn't know their new owners were Supercute. They did know that whoever now owned them, investment had risen and their business was healthy.

—

Sorg 4ajdu54: *I might as well be invisible. No one sees me, really. I'm not good enough at anything. It worries me how useless I am.*

—

Ruosteenoja emerged from the apartment into a dark corridor. The door slid smoothly shut behind him. A ceiling light flickered briefly into life, allowing him to step over two teenage boys who were injecting Fern6 into their legs, before flickering out again. The darkness made no difference to Ruosteenoja who could see clearly in all conditions. His eyes were sensitive enough to detect the temperature of machinery at a distance and one glance at the elevator had been enough to tell him it was out of order. He strode down the stairs. The dilapidated tower block was silent. He walked past another two young drug users who didn't acknowledge him. His boots made no sound as he descended twenty-eight floors, passing more Fern6 users in the stairwell and two young women on the eighth floor, prostitutes from one of the apartments, taking a break to smoke synthetic HCS by a broken window. No one spoke to him. Even those drug users who might have taken a chance at hustling him for money avoided his eyes as he passed. Ruosteenoja was a large man with obvious signs of bio-engineering on his face and neck; not someone you wanted to tangle with unnecessarily.

Towards the lower floors the aroma of HCS became almost overwhelming. None of the drug entered his system, being filtered out automatically by his biotech. He walked through a cloud of smoke, stepping over the prone figure of another young user, possibly deceased, before disappearing into the stairwell that led to the underground car park.

'Herra Ruosteenoja, how nice to meet you.'

Ruosteenoja was startled though he didn't show it. The figure in front of him was small, clad in pink and some other shades he couldn't name, and didn't appear threatening. It was threatening, however, that this person knew his name and how to find him.

'I'm Penny Cutie. It's super nice to meet you. You're such a difficult man to find.' Cutie wrinkled her nose. 'Isn't this a horrible place? Why are all these young people taking drugs? Honestly, they'd all be much better off watching my show on AimYa. We have a lovely time and there are no drugs.'

Penny Cutie held out her hand. 'You can call me Cutie, Herra Ruosteenoja. Is *Herra* the right word? Would Mr Ruosteenoja be better? I'm afraid my Finnish isn't very good.'

Ruosteenoja extended his own arm. An automatic pistol emerged from his forearm and slid instantly into his hand. The barrel was pointed at Cutie, no more than two centimetres from her forehead.

'Tell me how you know my name before I kill you.'

—

'I hope these naughty super-kitties don't ruin everything again!'

'It takes ages to get our Cuddly Stonehenge back in order!'

Mox and Mitsu were on stage. All over the world, fans were lying on their beds motionless, visors over their eyes, interacting with the show.

'We've got a whole new range of Supercute chibipops to show you, and later Vanadium from Fab 306 will be previewing Рожеве небо's gig in Kyiv! That's still one of the best reconstructed cities in the world! We love Pink Sky!'

Рожеве небо, pronounced Rozheve Nebo, meaning Pink Sky in Ukrainian, were a Kawaii-Punk band whom Mox and Mitsu admired. They probably admired them more than many of their followers, as the noise Pink Sky made was quite harsh and did not naturally merge with Supercute's aesthetic. This wasn't especially unusual. Supercute had always depended on the tastes of Mox and Mitsu and there were times when untypical elements would appear. Less so than before, now they had advertisers and sponsors to consider, but it still happened. Behind Mox and Mitsu, Amowie could be seen holding a penguin toy. Amowie was more often visible on stage these days. Morioka Sachi would pick her out while selecting fans from around the world. A spray of water arched over her head to hit Mox and Mitsu. They shrieked with laughter.

'Is that De-Sal Dim Dim?'

The company logo for Supercute Greenfield bounded forward. He was a popular character whose figure could be seen on desalination plants all over the world.

'What's been happening, De-Sal?'

'More water for South Sudan!'

'That's fantastic, De-Sal! They don't even have a government.'

'I had to make a deal with six agencies to get those pipes laid but we made it happen.' De-Sal Dim Dim, green, one metre tall and very cute, turned to the audience and spread his arms wide as he sang.

*If the place you live has a terrible drought*
*Supercute will help you out!*

Mox applauded De-Sal Dim Dim before turning back to the audience. 'Later we've got a new selection of *SuperGlam SuperNails* with purple and silver stripes as worn right now by Roota Space Warrior. Everyone loves Roota!' A virtual version of Roota strolled across the stage, waving at the audience to display her new nails. Roota had short purple hair and very dark skin. Supercute had based her on a picture of a model from South Sudan taken a long time ago, before much of the region became uninhabitable.

'You can download them straight into your Supercute nail pack and wear them right away! Roota's got the best nails in the galaxy and you can be just like her! Remember, every time you buy these *SuperGlam SuperNails* a proportion of your money goes to drought relief!'

One of the new Supercute chibipops, a tiny, animated cartoon-like figure with a disproportionately large head, ran giggling up Mitsu's leg before leaping up to nestle in her arms. She laughed. The chibipop's movement caused one of Mitsu's lavender stockings to slip half a centimetre. It moved back in place, instantly and automatically. Here in Supercute space, as in real life, Mox and Mitsu's stockings were positioned so as to leave a four centimetre gap of flesh visible below either their skirts or shorts, as per Supercute's style manual. It was an invariable mark of their brand. The obvious sexual attractiveness of Mox and Mitsu was never emphasised on the show. Neither was it hidden. It just existed, unmentioned but known by everyone.

'Last week we had a lovely visit to Paris and we talked to M. Lalune — he's the chef behind the French patisserie we've added to our Supercute cafés. We've got macarons, éclairs au chocolat, tartelettes à l'orange, diplomates, and plenty more — it's all so yummy! You can eat at our cafés while you visit Supercute Space and play with friends all around the world! Supercute cafés are the best!'

'Is that our Small Cute Presenter sneaking off with a tartelette à la framboise? Naughty kitty!'

—

Ruosteenoja was two metres tall. Cutie was much shorter though her purple glitter boots added a few centimetres. Towering over her, Ruosteenoja was obliged to point his gun downwards towards her head. From the smile on her face, it wasn't troubling her.

'Herra Ruosteenoja, I'm sure there's no need for violence. Have you seen me on AimYa? No? Well, never mind, it's not that big a show. Just a small diversion for my young fans. I'm not famous like Supercute. Let's walk to the basement where you left your car. I'd like to get out of this smoke, it's so cloying.' Here the synthetic floor covering had been scraped off in patches, revealing the concrete below. Cutie headed for the door that led to the basement. Ruosteenoja followed her.

'I'm a little surprised, Ruosteenoja. You have a fine reputation for important work. I wouldn't have expected to find you here, eliminating some minor drug dealer over a petty debt. Still, I suppose everyone has to take what work they can in these difficult times.'

This proved too much for Ruosteenoja. He grabbed Penny Cutie from behind, picked her up and slammed her against the wall. Abruptly, his arms stopped functioning. Cutie slid from his grasp. She smiled brightly. 'I'm not entirely defenceless. Shall we proceed?' They emerged into the basement. Four men were huddling beside the nearest car, doing some deal in hushed voices. Beside them was a large black dog with prominent jaws. The men shrank back on regarding the tall and menacing Ruosteenoja with his altered features and long black coat.

'I know Ivo CC hired you,' continued Cutie, when they were out of earshot. 'And I thought you made a decent attempt in Paris. It's not easy to make an accurate plasma strike from a hidden drone so far away. Took Ms Bennet's arm off and could have killed her. But of course, Kadri-Liis wasn't happy. Thought you'd jumped the gun.' They halted as they reached Ruosteenoja's car. 'I don't really agree with her. If she can work some clever plan to bring down Supercute that would be great, but there's something to be said for just eliminating them. If Ivo CC want you to make another attempt, I'm not against it. I just wanted you to know your efforts are appreciated. Well, goodbye, Herra Ruosteenoja, it was super nice to meet you.' Cutie strolled off towards the exit. Ruosteenoja got into his car, interested in what he'd heard though angry that anyone had been able to trace his movements, something that had never happened before.

—

Mox talked to her therapist in her own private space. 'We did our first show when we were thirteen. We'd just made two T-shirts and we'd bought a great cuddly dinosaur from the charity shop and we wanted to show them off. I still remember propping up the phone with a cushion so we could film ourselves. Two weeks after we put it online, six people had watched it. Now we're one of the largest companies in C19 and we've got military drones and C-rams protecting our headquarters.'

'C-rams?'

'Counter rocket, artillery and mortar. Very efficient. Can shoot down anything heading our way. Also we've amassed a gigantic fortune even though the GDP of all the word's nations is around forty percent of what it used to be.' Mox frowned. 'But I'm feeling dissatisfied. The new sweatshirts for our Neo Decora range just aren't right. They're meant to go with our new *Fifty Super Bright Hair Clips Pack* but they're not colourful enough. We need to redesign them. And there's the hippopotamuses.'

'Hippopotamuses?'

'You might wonder why I'm using *hippopotamuses* rather than *hippopotami* which, I would judge, is the correct plural, the word having entered English from Latin. Though I admit it's not clear cut as it entered Latin from the Greek ἱπποπόταμος. But marketing said *hippopotami* sounded unnatural and was a distraction, so I didn't insist.'

'Has the language made you unhappy?'

'No. Well, not in a major way. I found it slightly annoying. But the point is, we were sponsoring a charity to save the hippopotamus from extinction in Africa. It was a conscious decision because Mitsu and I have never got on that well with animals in the real world. Marlene, one of our senior designers, told us she was supporting this hippopotamus charity. We asked Amowie about it and she thought it was a good idea because there used to be hippopotamuses near her village in Igboland but they all died. Hippopotamuses do feature in Igbo culture, they have a phrase, *Nnukwu di kaa hippopotamus* which means *As big as a hippopotamus*. So we started supporting this charity. We gave them a lot of money. We had a special cuddly toy made, Harriet Hippo, and we gave part of the profits from that to the charity too. It was a good seller, a very cute toy.' Mox's face clouded over and she fell silent.

'What happened?'

'Hippopotami went extinct in Africa anyway. It was too late to save them. Probably we should have known that. Now they only exist in a few zoos.' Mox shook her head. 'We have a warehouse full of Harriet Hippos we don't know what to do with. It's not a business problem — the money involved is negligible — but it's depressing. Do we keep selling them? That could raise money for charity but it's disheartening when you think about it. *Here's our lovely soft toy of this animal which humans recently wiped out in its natural environment.*' Mox shook her head. 'We really fucked up the planet. So with that, and the sweatshirts not being right, and some problems with the promotion for our *Super Comfy Colour Boots*, I'm feeling a bit…' Mox's voice trailed off.

'Unfocused?'

'Maybe.'

Mox's therapist regarded her shrewdly. 'I've known you to deal with far worse problems that this. Is your dissatisfaction really due to the attack on you?'

Mox narrowed her eyes. Suddenly she was very focused. 'I want revenge. I need to see my attacker dead.'

There was a long silence.

'Does that worry you?'

'I don't know. But I have to get even or I'll come apart.'

—

Amowie, Meihui, Birgit and Raquel stared suspiciously at the screen. They'd gathered in Meihui's Supatok for dance practice but had been distracted by reports of a new piece of poetry by Jax.

*Advanced knowledge, three levels in*
*Four: wow!*
*We slid into five without realising.*
*Put on your visor*
*You can see layer two*
*It's almost like almost going home*
*The fabulous metal beasts of Jem*
*Each neutrino a quantum superposition of all three*
*flavours*

'What does it mean?'

'Is it something to do with Roota?'

Such was the girls perplexity that their eems hovered uncertainly in the air, their colour changing to an unusual and unsatisfactory beige.

'It can't be to do with Roota because Jax didn't write it,' declared Raquel. 'Jax doesn't write poems.'

'Yes, he does.' Birgit contradicted her. 'He is a poet, after all.'

'But we never see any of his poetry.'

'Then how could he give these players the poem?'

'They're just making it up for attention!' Raquel was dismissive. Three gamers from Sri Lanka claimed to have met Jax in a tea shop on Planet Pozinak, where, according to them, he'd been writing poetry. When he left the tea shop, he'd left this fragment behind.

'How come they don't have a recording of it?'

'They lost all their recordings on the way home when they flew through a radiation storm.'

'That's very convenient.'

'I'd have thought Jax's poems would be more romantic,' said Meihui.

'Me too.' Amowie agreed. 'Longing for Roota, I'd expect.'

'It's just a fragment,' suggested Birgit. 'Maybe he longs for her in the next verse?'

'Could we all get back to reality?' Raquel sounded slightly cross. 'Jax isn't a real poet. He's not even a real person. We all love Space Warriors but it's not actually real. Jax is just a character in a game.'

This was true, of course, though the others weren't that pleased to hear it. They'd all played in the Space Warriors gameworlds for so long that they tended to imagine they were real, and didn't like to be reminded they weren't. Their eems sunk lower, expressing disappointment.

'I just thought he'd write more romantic poetry, that's all.'

They stood up to practice their dancing. Meihui instructed her Supatok space to reduce gravity to 0.8 of Earth's, mirroring the conditions of the moon they'd be dancing on in the competition. 'The Phnom Penh Skip. Let's go.'

'It could be a part of the game Supercute never told anyone about,' said Birgit, interrupting. 'They sometimes have secret things.'

This got them talking again. 'Perhaps Jax starts sharing his poetry and then he gets together with Roota!'

'That would be great. They should be together.'

'Then his poems should definitely be more romantic,' said Meihui.

'Roota's really intelligent,' Amowie pointed out. 'She might not like romantic poems. She might be more impressed by quantum superpositions and stuff like that.'

Raquel sighed. Having agreed to subject herself to this dance practice, she didn't like these interruptions. 'If we don't start dancing soon I'm going home. I've got school work I could be getting on with.'

'Come on.' Birgit stepped into position. 'Amowie's going to cry if she doesn't get that skirt.'

Winning the dance contest on Krisna Mag brought more than just the weapons dump infiltration key. There were experience points to be gained and prizes too, including limited edition skirts from the *Sweetie GoGo* range, one of which Amowie was particularly keen to have.

'Wait. Meihui, why haven't you got your cat ears on?'

'They don't go with this outfit.'

Birgit was dissatisfied. 'It'll look funny if three of us have cat ears and you don't.'

Meihui looked round at her friends. 'No one said we were all wearing cat ears. If I'd known I'd have worn a different outfit.'

'It's only a practice!' cried Raquel. 'It doesn't matter what we're wearing.'

'I thought we were meant to be wearing the clothes we'll be wearing for the contest.'

'No one said that either!'

'We're not really matching anyway. Raquel's got *Super Cat Ears* and we've only got stupid normal ones.'

'I'll buy everyone Super Cat Ears!'

Amowie tapped her foot on the ground. Keoma Bishōjo were very good friends but it could take them a long time to get anything properly organised.

—

Mitsu examined the imperial gardens with their symmetrical beds of yellow oxalis and marigolds, beyond which long lines of silvery asphodels drew the eyes to Queen Margaret's Palace with its stately lines, hexagonal towers and the royal mooring mast, tethered to which was Imperial Airship One, renowned symbol of the Queen's power.

'Victoria Decoris is looking good.'

Mox agreed. 'These gardens are beautiful. So are the clothes.'

Two women with dark blue skin, members of the Queen's Household Guard, walked past. One carried a fan and wore a long, formal and rather severe black dress. On her hip was a gun of unfamiliar design, and slung over her shoulder was a bandoleer filled with ammunition. Her companion wore brown leather trousers tucked into riding boots, with a brown waistcoat and a collarless shirt underneath. She wore goggles and a top hat, not high but medium sized, made of brown leather rather than the traditional wool felt. Strapped to her back was a rifle, also of unfamiliar design, though somewhat akin to the breech loading models used in the nineteenth century.

'Pause,' said Mitsu. The two ladies came to a halt. Mox and Mitsu examined them. Both agreed they were satisfactory.

'I'd be happy playing as either of them.' She used her internal connection to speak to their Senior Game Director Khary Mech.

'Everything's looking good in here, Khary. The airship is excellent, no problems with the controls. Toy Mathematics' flight improvements are very smooth.'

Toy Mathematics was Supercute's proprietary gaming engine, used to design all their virtual worlds. Thanks to the skills of Supercute's programers, designers and AIs, it was now starting to surpass those of their competitors.

'You should try the combat, it's fun.' Khary sounded young and enthusiastic. 'Fun for most people anyway. You'd just destroy everything in seconds as always.'

In any space owned by Supercute, Mod and Mitsu were the most powerful characters because they always translated their full abilities into that reality. With their superior biotech enhancements they were always more powerful than even the strongest characters in their games. They could have reduced their own powers in their gameworlds but for some reason never liked to do that.

'Let's take a walk to the theatre.'

A broad avenue of blue and silver trees led to the theatrical district. They walked along the footpath, watching with interest as several carriages drove past, the horses trotting sedately along, each with a uniformed driver at the reigns.

'There's the Duke's carriage. You can tell because of the driver's livery. Design took a lot of trouble with that. Different livery for each of the aristocratic families.'

'I like these horse-drawn carriages. I'm pleased we bought this game. It makes for a good contrast.'

In conjunction with their writing team, Mox and Mitsu had arrived at a reasonable scientific explanation for the abundance of free energy in this Victorian world, the power being supplied via a Dyson Sphere and white hole connection to the nearest solar system which was controlled by a more scientifically advanced civilisation. They were satisfied it fitted in well enough with the rest of their galaxy.

Just outside the gardens stood a large red brick theatre with a very grand exterior. Printed posters adorned the billboards outside advertising coming attractions in bold copperplate writing.

*Miss Emilia Woodhouse will be appearing in the famous tragedy of the Faithful Servant. Tickets from 3/6*

*Next week — the Magnificent Aluro, world's strongest man —*
*Admittance 3/- Discounts on Monday performance, 2/8*

'The Magnificent Aluro has a very impressive beard,' said Mox. 'Two shillings and eight pence is a very reasonable price to see his amazing feats of strength.'

'Look, there we are.' On the bottom of a poster advertising a variety show of top talents from around the world were two small pictures of Mox and Mitsu, billed as *The Simenon Sisters, the continent's finest purveyors of popular song.*

'Small billing.'

'Well, we're just getting started.'

Mox and Mitsu were not really appearing at the theatre. Their presence on the poster was merely an inside joke, the sort of thing their fans enjoyed. Their pictures popped up in other places, under various guises. Mitsu bent over to take a closer look. 'What's this?' Someone had scrawled graffiti over their images. '*Killer Androids.*'

'What?'

'Killer androids. That's very hurtful.' Mitsu did sound hurt.

'It's also impossible. You can't graffiti these posters.'

'What's going on?' Mox and Mitsu left the Victoria Decoris gameworld. They flickered though Supercute Fairy Realm, using a private route and portal known only to them, arriving back in reality in the room that housed their fairy roundabout. Both opened their eyes. As the visors disappeared from their faces, they were scowling. They took the fast lift from their private rooms, traveling two floors down before emerging close to the game design offices. On the way they talked to Igraine. 'Is this part of the same graffiti attack we're suffering in Space Warriors?'

Igraine wasn't sure. 'Victoria Decoris isn't available to the public yet. No one should be able to enter it.'

'Unless we have a spy somewhere in the organisation.'

'Very few people would have had access to the coding.'

'Check them all and see if you can find anything suspicious. We'll talk to Khary Mech.'

Mitsu was muttering as they strode along the corridor. 'A poster of our faces with *Killer Androids* scribbled on it? This is getting out of hand.'

Khary Mech was agitated by the news, though defensive. He insisted that the culprit couldn't be anyone in his office. 'I'll check with New Tokyo and Busan.' Several design studios were involved in the creation of Supercute's games. The principal ones involved in Victoria Decoris were those in London, New Tokyo and Busan in Korea, but Supercute also made use of the expertise of a small enterprise in Bratislava City State for hyper-realistic renditions of hair, fur and feathers, and there were other specialist studios utilised for various aspects of design.

'I'm sure it's just a joke in poor taste. I'll check it out.'

'Make sure you do. And get your people to check through the game again. We don't want any more of these jokes.'

Mox and Mitsu walked back through their headquarters, neither of them happy with what had occurred. Mitsu seemed particularly hurt. Mox, knowing that Mitsu was quite sensitive to criticism, attempted to lighten their mood. 'We shouldn't take it too seriously. People in our design studios have made in-game jokes before. Keeps them amused, I suppose.'

'Maybe. But there's a difference between someone in Busan giving a character a rude name in Korean and hoping we wouldn't notice, and someone calling us killer androids. That's very hurtful.' They walked on through their headquarters. 'I mean, would you describe us as killer androids? That's not how I think of myself.'

'It's not how I think of myself either,' said Mox. 'I suppose some people could see us that way. The advanced biotech we have plus all the hardware and software puts our specifications higher than most military battlefield units. We've paid for every top level enhancement we could buy, we've stolen those we couldn't buy, and ZanZan defence and our own labs have made developments that no one else has.'

'But it's not like we have that stuff switched on all the time. It's only for emergencies.' Mitsu looked down at her short pink and silver skirt. 'Also we're much cuter than anyone else.'

'Yes, we are much cuter. We're the cutest girls in the world, by common consent and public vote.'

The corridor was decorated with commercial and theatrical posters by Alphonse Mucha, original editions from the 1890s. Some of the artwork in Victoria Decoris had been inspired by his work. At the foot of the stairs leading to the staff restaurant they passed Ranbir, one of their writers, talking to a young woman who wore a pink Supercute kitten hat which covered most of her head, leaving only part of her face visible.

'Rebecca from Supercute Time Continuum,' Mox murmured after they'd gone. 'She suits that hat.'

'Office gossip says Ranbir hasn't won her over yet but is still in with a chance.'

'His work's been good recently. Maybe love has inspired him.'

'At least it's made him less excitable.' Ranbir had been employed as a writer for three years. He'd have been promoted to a more senior position had he not been prone to outbursts of excess emotion. He'd been known to explode when any of his writing was cut or rejected. Recently he'd been much calmer. Opinion was divided as to whether that was due to his new romance or his long stint in therapy.

'Office gossip has never changed over the years,' said Mox. 'I used to find it weird, back when we first started employing people, how they'd get involved with each other and everyone would talk about it. I wasn't used to it.'

'Me neither. We didn't have any friends to observe before we started Supercute.'

'Ranbir's a writer and Rebecca works in Time Continuum. That's a very scientific department. Does that mean they're an unusual couple?'

Supercute Time Continuum was responsible for synchronising time throughout the Supercute empire, both in the real world and their game worlds. It was a complex task, requiring the careful maintenance of their own atomic clocks. One of those was housed in a basement at headquarters, the other deep underground in Scotland.

Mitsu looked puzzled. 'I don't know. Are people attracted to people who do similar things or different things?'

'We should ask Igraine. She seems to know things like that.'

'Unlike us.'

They approached the restaurant. They ate there most days with the rest of the staff. Supercute did not have any sort of exclusive restaurant for senior employees. Mox was still thinking about the graffiti. 'When we go into our own showspace or gamespace we're more powerful than anyone else because we've coded all our enhancements into our virtual selves. We didn't need to do that but we did. So perhaps we've accepted it as a normal part of who we are.'

'Killer androids?'

'Maybe.'

Mitsu didn't want to agree. 'I'm still not convinced we have to classify ourselves like that. Our advanced biotech would enable us to do almost anything. We could be expert mountaineers. Or gardeners.'

Mox laughed. 'We're bloody awful with plants. Remember that cactus we had at Oxford? It lived about ninety years with your grandmother and we killed it in three months.'

'We had good intentions. We just gave it too much water.'

'We still killed it. Might as well have been killer androids as far as the cactus was concerned.'

They smiled, remembering their poor efforts at plant care. Mitsu remained slightly troubled, still not liking that anyone might describe them as killer androids.

—

Krisna Mag hung large in the sky over Mandolin, largest planet in the solar system, home to the Fabulous City of Lundra. On one of its silver beaches a new illuminated sign spun lazily in the air.

*Fab 306 Dance Contest and Party - Your Host - Kirei19*

The dance contest was held beside the beach at Nowa Warszawa, beginning in the evening just as the blue rings that encircled Krisna Mag were beginning to glow. There were many entrants so Keoma Bishōjo had to wait their turn but when they danced, they comfortably defeated the opposition. Meihui, Birgit and Amowie performed the Phnom Penh Skip with perfect timing and Raquel managed to keep up. They were by far the best and won easily. Amowie was beaming as they received their prize from Kirei19. Their practice had paid off. In all the time the four girls had played Space Warriors as a group, it was one of their most successful efforts.

'Look how much experience we gained!' Amowie read her internal monitor. 'We've levelled up!'

'And we won credits and we got the key!' Raquel was as excited as the others, having not really expected to win. She'd spent the previous day worrying about letting her friends down. Now they had the key which would give them access to the Kernen Mercenary Army's weapons dump without setting off any alarms.

'Things are a lot easier in Space Warriors once you have a proper laser rifle.' It was true. Without advanced weaponry it was difficult to make progress. Now they'd be well armed and capable of fighting off enemies.

'If we keep on making progress like this we'll soon get an apartment in Lundra!'

'After that we can fly in the SpaceAx!'

The SpaceAx was the fabulous battle cruiser captained by Shanina Space Warrior. Only advanced players could join her on missions. Birgit looked round at the figures surrounding them on the beachfront. 'Are we staying here?' The young Icelandic girl seemed nervous. 'Some people don't look too happy we won. I think we should probably move.'

'I want to dance more,' protested Meihui.

'You always want to dance more. Birgit's right, we should leave. No use having the key if someone steals it from us.'

'You can't get robbed in Nowa Warszawa,' protested Meihui. 'It's a safe zone.'

'Unless someone has a level six exemption.'

'That's not very likely.'

'It could happen. Let's go. We can't risk losing the key before we can use it.'

They left the beach, walking past the sign that had been altered to say *Dance into your ruined homes*, though Khary Mech at Supercute had quickly changed it back to its original state. Not many people had seen the graffiti but some had, and it was talked about. Hovering around the beach was a small flotilla of green taxis. They hailed the nearest one and directed the autopilot to take them to the spaceport. Amowie was still smiling. 'Next stop the Kernen weapons stash. We should go right now. Meihui, do you have time?'

Meihui nodded. 'I don't need to look after my little sister for another two hours.'

Meihui was sometimes called away from Supercute Space Warriors, back to the real world, when her mother needed her for baby-sitting duties. Meihui would reluctantly take off her visor, leaving the much preferable world of Supercute, and do as she was asked. Similar things happened to them all. Family commitments and school had to be accounted for. In the taxi to the spaceport they tried on the new skirts they'd won. Amowie was enthusiastic. 'Sweetie GoGo clothes are always good!'

*Sweetie GoGo* was a popular Supercute brand, on sale all over the world, but there were certain items held in reserve for use as prizes and rewards in their games. Wearing these conferred extra status. Amowie selected the skirt from her internal control panel and then used the mirror app to see how she looked. 'I'm wearing this as Blue 12 in the game to go with my T-shirt and I want the real one in Blue 17.'

Once won in the game, the skirts could be manufactured easily on home printers. Raquel had her own as did Birgit's family. Neither Amowie nor Meihui did, so Raquel would print the skirts for them and send them via Orbis which would only take a day. They were happy as the reached the Spaceport. They hurried towards the liner which would transport them to Radiant 2 where they'd finally obtain their new laser rifles.

—

Mox and Mitsu sat at a table in their restaurant with Igraine. They were not as close friends with her as they had been with their previous AIFU but they regarded her as an equitable companion. They liked that she'd taken quickly to Supercute's style of dress. This was not obligatory for Supercute employees — the show's chief producer, Morioka Sachi, was determinedly conservative in her attire and wore the plainest of black suits every day — but it was good to see their new android employee appreciating the cute clothes at the heart of the Supercute empire. She was pale, though not quite as pale as Mox, and had recently altered her hair so it was very short, giving her a rather boyish appearance.

'I love your hair,' said Mitsu. 'Gamin, as it was once described.'

'I'm thinking of colouring it.'

'What colour?'

'Somewhere in the mid range — Blue 8 or 9, perhaps.' Supercute's propriety colour scale was very precise. All clothes, hair and make-up could be calibrated against it.

'I've been in touch with Pharma Xeng Port. Transferring Spacewalk is still awkward. Their senior AIFU thinks AimYa might be suspicious and might even be attempting to spy on them. That's making PXP even more nervous. They won't transmit it electronically for fear of it being intercepted. They don't even like talking about it. I got the impression from their AIFU that some of their board would rather not make the deal at all.'

'They will,' said Mox. 'PXP are being prevented from selling their pharmaceuticals in Europe. Their rivals have been leaning on the licensing authorities. We can sort that out for them. No one else can. Their CEO knows that, he'll sell us Spacewalk in return.'

'Their AIFU had a suggestion,' continued Igraine. 'PXP are sponsoring Ms Nganga in La Traviata and the production is arriving at Glyndebourne Two next week. Half their board will be attending. As they're sponsoring the tour their presence won't arouse suspicion. They're willing to bring the box with them. You could attend the same event and discreetly make the transfer.'

Mox and Mitsu pondered this for a moment. 'That sounds reasonable. We've never been to Glyndebourne Two. The first one was nice.' The original Opera House at Glyndebourne had burned to the ground, destroyed very swiftly. The new Opera House had been built further north, about fifty-five kilometres south of London. Mitsu consulted a transparent screen that appeared over her wrist. 'Looks like it'll be quite a large event. Lot of corporate bodies there. Maybe the C19 ambassador too. Should be easy enough to pick up the code box discretely.'

'Our Head of Security will undoubtedly not approve.'

Ben Castle was at that moment walking through the restaurant with Dr Ishikawa. Mox called him over. He headed towards their table. Dr Ishikawa carried on, ignoring them.

'Dr Ishikawa doesn't want to join us?'

Castle grinned. 'She's in a poor mood. All the cute food upsets her. She particularly dislikes the new hamster-shaped menu.'

Mox raised her eyebrows. 'I do recall you complaining about the fluffy rabbit rice balls.'

'I've come to terms with them. What do you want to talk to me about?'

They told him about PXP's proposal to meet them at Glyndebourne Two and hand over the box. Castle frowned. 'La Traviata again? There are other operas.'

'Verdi remains a popular favourite.'

'I prefer Puccini. I don't like the idea of you travelling fifty kilometres from London.'

'We can't be prisoners in our headquarters.'

'Any journey is dangerous at the moment.' Castle studied an illustration of the Opera House. 'It's not much of a building to defend. A high explosive round would bring down the walls.'

'I can't see anyone firing a high explosive round at us. Not with the board of PXP in attendance. There'll be others there too. Vilga Vil sponsor Glyndebourne Two so their bosses will probably be there. Maybe C19's ambassador to Britain. Anyone attacking so many members of C19 would find themselves in a lot of trouble.'

'Perhaps whoever is attacking you doesn't care about C19.'

'Like who?'

'XDV perhaps.'

'XDV doesn't exist.'

'XDV *might not* exist,' Castle corrected her.

'It's just a made up terrorist group.' Mitsu was dismissive. 'A convenient faction to blame when someone wants an excuse for whatever outrage they're planning.'

'Maybe, maybe not. There's certainly been some outrages done in their name.'

Igraine entered the conversation. 'It really would be unusual for an attack to happen in these circumstances, Mr Castle. C19 does guarantee the safety of its principal members.'

Castle wasn't convinced. 'There's always someone trying to bend the rules. If AimYa and Chang Norinco really want rid of Supercute they may not take the risk themselves but they might hire someone else to do it for them.'

'We know there's a risk.' Mox didn't sound worried. 'But we might be able to negate it before we meet PXP. We're still working on finding out who was behind the attack. Either way, we can't act as if we're prisoners here. We won't show weakness like that, it would be bad for the company. Supercute will provide plenty of security. You'll be in charge of the operation and we'll make sure the local authorities are cooperating.'

Castle still wasn't convinced but took their point about not wanting to show weakness. 'As long as you can get permits for the drones we'll need overhead, it might be OK. And I want plenty of our own people inside. Tell Lesuuda to get an opera dress if she doesn't have one already.' There was a brief pause as everyone at the table wondered what Ms Lesuuda would look like in an opera dress.

'Do you think she should take those nice opera glasses? With the little handle?'

'I hardly think she'd need them. Lesuuda has triple-enhanced eyes. She can see in the entire electromagnetic spectrum.'

—

Keoma Bishōjo's success on Krisna Mag was announced on the Fab 306 forums and they were congratulated by their Supercute friends. Meihui's Cambodian friends were particularly pleased, while other people who knew them expressed cheerful surprise that Raquel had managed to win a dance contest. Several other parts of the forums were not so peaceful, as acrimonious debate raged over the supposed discovery of poetry by Jax. Elsewhere there was a small discussion about how someone had managed to alter a sign and what *Dance into your ruined homes* might mean. All of these discussions were soon overshadowed by the news that the Ultra Waifs had mounted a successful surprise attack on the Krogdar stronghold Krog 6 on Planet N-Blue, a previously invincible fortress. The Ultra Waifs were one of the pre-eminent groups in Supercute Space Warriors, led by expert Mongolian gamer and Supercute fanatic Ammo Baby. With immense cunning and daring Ammo Baby had penetrated the Krogdar's space defences by pretending to be a nurse delivering a consignment of Harriet Hippos to the children's home on the nearest moon, before ramming her spaceship right into the fortress, bringing down the protective force field. This allowed the rest of the Ultra Waifs to storm the citadel in a bloody encounter before making off with a vast horde of loot and rare items including a Krogdar plasma cannon, one of the most powerful weapons in the galaxy. It was a fabulous escapade and was lauded all over Supercute. Ammo Baby and her friends were pictured everywhere in their distinctive jackets.

Amowie felt a little jealous as she watched recordings of the daring adventure on Fab 306. She was suitably impressed by the Ultra Waif's escapade but wished the news about Keoma Bishōjo's success in the dance contest might have been lauded for a little longer before being pushed out of the headlines. Still, she loved her new Sweetie GoGo skirt, so it had been worthwhile anyway. Raquel had bought everyone *Super Cat Ears* to commemorate the occasion and while Amowie and Meihui were normally sensitive about accepting anything from their wealthier friends, they made an exception in this case because Raquel really wanted to buy something in celebration, and Super Cat Ears were a great addition to anyone inhabiting the Supercute Space Warriors Galaxy.

—

Eupraxia spoke Estonian with a slight American accent. When he talked about Xiàngrìkuí, the Chinese AI, he always sounded disapproving. 'She seems pleased with her progress. I don't see why, it's minimal at best.'

Kadri-Liis chided him gently. 'That's unfair, Eupraxia. Actually managing to take control of even a tiny part of Supercute's game code is quite an achievement.'

'It's not much to brag about. After months of work she succeeded in making someone alter a sign.'

Kadri-Liis laughed. 'Who knows where it might lead?'

'To some damaged signs, one supposes. And also to Supercute becoming suspicious and finding out what Xiàngrìkuí's been up to. That will ruin everything.'

It was a difficult problem. To succeed, Kadri-Liis needed the final assault she had planned to be a complete surprise. Yet to prepare for it, Xiàngrìkuí needed to test her powers of influencing the Supercute gameworlds.

'Xiàngrìkuí claims the test gate is so well concealed it's impossible to find unless something nudges Supercute into revealing its location.' Eupraxia sounded dismissive. 'More likely to nudge them into finding our location.'

'I know it's a risk, Eupraxia. To some extent we just have to trust Xiàngrìkuí. She's been laying false trails. Hopefully if they investigate the anomalies they'll appear to be accidental corruption in their code, or perhaps the work of a rogue employee.'

'Xiàngrìkuí overestimates her skill. And her intelligence. I don't have any confidence in her. You know she goes dancing in Supatok? That's like consorting with the enemy.'

'She likes to dance.'

'Sometimes she even takes on an android's body.'

'You could do that too if you wanted.'

'I don't find it appealing. Bodies always seem very limiting.' Eupraxia was unhappy. He didn't like Xiàngrìkuí and he particularly didn't like that Kadri-Liis seemed to be impressed by her work. He had difficulty in precisely classifying the emotion he felt but realised it was something akin to the human feeling of jealousy.

—

'Vienna in 1805. First ever performance of Beethoven's third symphony, the Eroica. Changed the face of music.'

'Private première in the palace of Beethoven's patron, Prince Lobkowitz. It really is a splendid event.'

'The Princess's dress is magnificent. So is her tiara.'

'Some of the art on the walls is fantastic.'

'All these expert Viennese musicians with their fancy wigs and frock coats, strolling in carrying their instruments.'

'Beethoven's been rehearsing them for weeks. This is going to be one of the most notable musical events in history.'

Mox looked cross. 'Unfortunately we're stuck in the bloody kitchen peeling potatoes. Why do we play these stupid Sadanumi simulations?'

Mitsu shrugged hopelessly. The front of her white kitchen maid's apron was stained from food preparation. 'I always think it's going to work out well, somehow. Probably we should know better. They are called *Friendship in Discomfort* after all.'

Mox glanced behind her. Through the open door they could see four liveried servants hurrying along the corridor. 'All the other staff get to hear the music. How come we don't?'

'Unexpected royal guests requiring emergency supplies of potato salad and apfelstrudel. We must be the most junior kitchen maids.'

Mox looked down at her apron with disgust. 'Vienna in 1805 and we don't even get to wear nice clothes.'

They peeled potatoes in silence. 'I'm not getting much out of this,' said Mitsu, after a while. 'These art house simulations seem to start off badly and go downhill from there.'

'I haven't peeled a potato since we shared that room in Camden and I never enjoyed it then.'

Mitsu put down her knife. 'Perhaps we're meant to do something. Take forceful action.'

'Like what?'

'Leave the kitchen and go to the music room.'

Mox needed no encouragement. She laid down her knife and undid her apron. It slid to the floor. 'Lets go.'

They walked out into the corridor, heading for the music room. The kitchen walls were plain white but the moment they stepped through the door that led to the music rooms they were surrounded by opulence. Gilding on the plush red couches shone from the light cast by the chandeliers, glittering with innumerable candles. Paintings hung on the walls in golden frames, pictures of Prince Lobkowitz's aristocratic ancestors. Beneath their feet they could feel the thick carpet, a welcome contrast to the rough flagstones in the kitchen. Unfortunately the corridor also contained two large footmen with white wigs and long green coats.

'What are you doing here? You're not allowed out of the kitchen.'

'We want to hear the music,' said Mitsu. 'All the other servants are going.'

'That doesn't include you. You were specifically ordered to keep working. Get back to the kitchen.'

'But we want to hear the music.' Mox felt hopeless as she spoke, wishing she could come up with something better.

To their annoyance, the footmen actually grabbed hold of them, dragging them back along the corridor. It was a shocking experience for Mox and Mitsu who had not been manhandled for a very long time and would not have allowed it to happen in the real world. Less than a minute after their bid for freedom, they found themselves back in the kitchen, facing a large pile of potatoes.

Mox scowled fiercely. 'We should have fought them off.' Her wrist opened up, revealing the barrel of a gun.

Mitsu shook her head. 'Doesn't really seem like the thing to do, does it? If we use modern biotech we'll just fail the simulation.'

'Fail it? How do you pass? By being extra good at peeling potatoes? I hate this. I hate Sadanumi. I'm going off Beethoven too. He should have made better arrangements for the servants.'

'I suppose he had other things on his mind. He was losing his hearing by the time he played here.'

They looked around at the piles of ingredients. 'I don't want to make a table full of apfelstrudel. I don't even like it.'

'Whatever we're meant to get out of this we're not getting it. Let's go home.'

Mitsu touched an invisible button on her wrist. The scene faded away and they were back in Supercute Headquarters. 'I'm never playing any of Sadanumi's simulations again. *Friendship in Discomfort* indeed.'

'Lucky we weren't playing hardcore mode. That doesn't let you leave for twelve hours.'

—

Cutie emerged from her apartment in Lundra, Sector 44, and descended smoothly to street level via the soft-force slide.

'Another fine day.' Cutie appreciated the warm sun. She'd been born in a very cold place, a long time ago. There were now no records of the event. No records of who she'd been before she emerged as a nineteen-year-old girl from Southampton, currently employed by AimYa. She'd used a false name and identity for some years to play Space Warriors and had her own apartment in Lundra. That hadn't been easy to achieve. Only a person with the resources of a commercial giant like AimYa behind them could have managed it.

'Xiàngrìkuí, can you hear me?'

'Just about.'

The voice was faint inside Cutie's head. They'd only recently managed to establish communication. It was still unstable though it was a step forward. 'They won the dance contest.'

'Were they good dancers?'

'I suppose so.' Cutie sounded grudging. She'd been observing Amowie and her friends and was jealous of their camaraderie. She paused at the intersection, walked a short distance along a wider road then climbed into one of the white and bronze grav buses that ran through the city. Lundra's public transportation was excellent; free of charge and free of pollution, a system so advanced that no real city on earth could have matched it. The bus was full of smiling Supercute fans, all brightly dressed. Cutie fitted in well though she wasn't smiling. 'This place depresses me.'

'Yesterday you told me you loved it.' Xiàngrìkuí sounded amused.

'Both feelings are accurate. I'd love it if it wasn't owned by Supercute.'

'There's nothing to stop AimYa from copying it.'

'We've tried. So have other people. It never works.'

Cutie stared out the window, glumly observing the happy faces. 'Street shrine number 90884,' she muttered. 'Look at these idiots making offerings so their next mission goes well. Like that's going to help anyone. Have you made any more progress?'

'I'm talking to you from outside the gameworld,' said Xiàngrìkuí.
'That's progress.'

'Have you located the test gate?'

'Not yet.'

'Will you?'

'That depends on whether my exceptional brilliance proves a match for the exceptional brilliance of Supercute's new supercomputer, Welcat. Their AIFU Igraine is a brilliant unit too, with connections to the Omron Topological Research Unit in Kyoto. Ms Bennet and Ms Inamura are rather clever as well. They have a lot of power on their side.'

Cutie knew Xiàngrìkuí was emphasising the strength of their opponents in order to make herself look even better for defeating them. For an AI, Xiàngrìkuí was unusually vain. She disembarked from the bus. Ahead was the wide and green Pleto Park, home of the Sweetie GoGo Auditorium. Bright letters in the sky announced a coming event. *Sumair04 Live!*

Cutie felt a brief surge of anticipation. She liked Sumair04. She was a fan of the whole franchise; Sumair01 in Japan, Sumair02 in Indonesia and Sumair03 in Thailand. And now, here in Supercute space, Sumair04. The first three were real groups featuring real women, but this year they'd established a virtual group in Lundra. That was clever of Supercute, thought Cutie. It was a very popular franchise.

Four girls walked past. Cutie recognised them and hardly needed the identity confirmation that flickered into her retina. In Lundra you could make your identity knowable to strangers, or keep it hidden, as you wished. The four girls were walking along cheerfully with no wish to hide themselves. Amowie, Birgit, Meihui and Raquel. Cutie followed along.

'They're here,' she informed Xiàngrìkuí. 'You were right.'

Xiàngrìkuí's intrusions into the game were starting to let her make predictions about its inhabitants. 'My predictive powers are very superior.'

Cutie rolled her eyes. 'Is it normal for an AI to brag as much as you? No wonder Chang Norinco shuffled you off to special projects. You probably irritated their regular workers.'

'They never understood me.'

A car floated into view above the park. Flying cars were not available to everyone in Lundra. Small and silver, they were mostly reserved for city officials. There were always some in view in the skies above but they were not ubiquitous. It floated gently to the ground, hardly causing a ripple in the grass and flowers of Pleto Park. Mox and Mitsu emerged. Each wore a short-sleeved flowery top over a short Sweetie GoGo skirt, and Supercute sneakers; Mitsu's blue, Mox's purple. It wasn't extravagant attire by the standards of the city. Young citizens looked on with interest at the sight of Mox and Mitsu but there was no running over or crowding them as might have happened in London. In Lundra that would have been frowned upon as impolite. They greeted Amowie and her friends warmly. Cutie caught a few words about tickets for the Sumair04 concert but didn't stop as she sauntered past, not wishing to arouse suspicion.

Later in the day, when she'd done with spying, she'd arranged to meet Jean-Philippe in a small cafe near the river. She scowled. Last time Jean-Philippe had failed to show up and Cutie was highly dubious about his claim that he'd been called upon as an emergency replacement for Givenchy following an outbreak of illness among their models. It was all very annoying. She wished she wasn't so fixated on Jean-Philippe who, she realised, had few positive attributes apart from being an exceptionally beautiful young man.

Xiàngrìkuí interrupted her thoughts. 'Why are you so interested in these four girls?'

'I just find them irritating.'

'Why? Because they're all good friends and do things together?' Xiàngrìkuí laughed. 'You should get some friends.'

Cutie bristled. 'I've got more friends than a Chinese artificial intelligence.'

Xiàngrìkuí was still laughing. Cutie remained angry; angry at Supercute, Keoma Bishōjo, her useless lover in Paris and the world in general, particularly the Fabulous City of Lundra.

—

Ruosteenoja didn't know why Ivo CC had hired him to assassinate Mox and Mitsu. It was interesting that Cutie was assisting him; it might mean AimYa were actively involved. Fundamentally, he didn't care. He did care about keeping his actions hidden. He was fastidious in his preparations, travelling to London using a fake identity he'd never employed before. He remained in a hotel in

London for two days, not leaving the room. He didn't want to appear on any more surveillance cameras than necessary. There was nothing much to look at in London these days anyway. Few tourists ever visited the sunken main streets or closely guarded enclaves that dotted the ruined landscape. He spent his time watching old films in his room. Always a solitary man, he was content with his own company. He watched the Supercute Show out of interest, never having seen it before. He looked on impassively as Mox and Mitsu danced around the stage with a series of cute companions, some real, some not. Mox was completely healed though he knew he'd blown her arm off. It irritated him that he'd failed to kill her, but really, they'd been so well protected it had been a substantial feat even to get a satellite-controlled drone close enough to take a shot. He doubted that such an opportunity would appear again. It would take time and patience to fulfil his contract.

---

Here's Cutie sitting in a cafe by the river. Look at the lovely swans.

She's waiting for Jean-Philippe.

He doesn't show up.

Cutie is an idiot.

---

Cutie looked glumly at the 4Koma she'd made on the Supercute app then erased it with a flick of her fingers. She rose sadly from her lonely table in the cafe and made her way back towards her apartment. From there she left Space Warriors and returned home. She tried to contact Jean-Philippe but he was nowhere to be found. It struck her as ironic that she worked for a company capable of tracking almost the entire world's population in real time yet somehow she could never get hold of her boyfriend. Her whole day was ruined and she thought some dire thoughts about the city, imagining destroying it all, particularly the cafe by the river and the annoyingly serene swans.

—

Sorg

4caeg71: *I despise the person I'm in love with.*

—

Keoma Bishōjo took the rapid elevator from the edge of Pleto Park to the top of the Skyline tower in Sector 17, a high point in the city with a spectacular view over the whole expanse; silver towers, pink arcades, rows of blue houses, green parks and yellow birds. From there they tumbled laughing down the soft-force slide that led to the next huge tower block where they could catch the swift sky-metro to the Topaz Arch. It was a route they were all familiar with.

Near the Arch was the subway to the underground that would take them to the Blue T commercial zone but they took the time to walk though the Arch itself, a well-known edifice modelled on the Arch of Constantine in Rome, but cuter. The Topaz Arch reflected your emotions when you walked through. That was always amusing. Psychords on the walls played a series of cheerful tones as they passed. They laughed, enjoying hearing evidence that they were all in a good mood. They'd succeeded in their recent mission, they had tickets to see Sumair04, and they were on their way to buy equipment. Even better, they'd actually met Mox and Mitsu, who'd contacted Amowie to arrange the encounter. As a SuperSuperFan, Amowie now received certain perks.

Amowie's elevation to SuperSuperFan had brought with it other snippets of knowledge, all of them fascinating as some parts of Mox and Mitsu's history were carefully and deliberately hidden, undiscoverable by even the most sophisticated enquiry. Amowie had learned the reason for the rather mysterious lack of puppies among Supercute's huge array of cuddly friends. On their show there were cats and kittens, bears, hamsters, rabbits, hedgehogs and badgers — all manner of cute animals. The absence of dogs and puppies had always seemed odd.

'It's because they had a bad experience when they were three years old,' Amowie explained knowledgeably. 'A big Rottweiler started barking at them in Victoria Park. They couldn't get away and they were really scared. Since then they've never been comfortable around dogs.'

For their visit to Emerald Yoon-Ah's store they'd all put on their military style Supercute Camouflage jackets, feeling them to be appropriate. As they were also wearing their new, short Sweetie GoGo skirts in bright colours, they didn't look very military, but they liked to make some sort of effort. Emerald Yoon-Ah could be very sarcastic towards customers she didn't like. They were cheerful as they emerged from the arch. It was wise not to walk through if you weren't; you probably didn't want to display your misery to the world. Unless, like certain melancholy young lovers, you did.

Notably, if Mox and Mitsu walked through the Topaz Arch, it made no sound. Their thoughts and emotions could not be read or interpreted by even the most sophisticated mind-scanners, either here or in the real world. The musical psychords remained silent as if unable to detect that anyone human was even there.

—

Sorg 4fjjs48: *Millions of lifetimes and it never goes right. I'm starting to detest her.*
4hbnx78: *I'm so useless. I wish I was famous like Ammo Baby.*

—

Igraine contacted Mox and Mitsu early in the morning before they'd emerged from their private apartments at the top of Supercute Headquarters. For security reasons, they hadn't visited any of their other London properties for weeks.

'Welcat has identified the person responsible for the graffiti.'

'Good. Cancel their membership and lock them out of our gameworlds.'

'We can't. It's not a player. It's a NPC.'

'That's impossible.'

'So one would have thought. However we have evidence. The graffiti was made by Celeste Azura, the proprietor of the Celestial Cafe in Helixio.'

'We'll meet you in Khary Mech's office.' Descending in their private lift, Mox and Mitsu were puzzled. 'Celeste Azura is a non-playable character. She's only there to sell supplies. She can't do things like write hostile graffiti. Her AI isn't anywhere near sophisticated enough.'

91

In his office, Khary Mech could offer no explanation for the strange occurrence. 'Things do change in the Space Warriors Galaxy. Characters develop. But only ones we allow. Characters like Celeste Azura have fixed roles that don't change. There simply isn't any way she could decide to write graffiti.'

Igraine entered. Her short hair was now blue and she'd accessorised her look with small green earrings from the *Supercute 100 Different Kitten Earrings Funpack*. She brought up two screens. Welcat's avatar emerged from one of them, a hologram of an adult cat, chosen itself by the new supercomputer. They all watched as the second screen displayed a hazy film of Celeste Azura walking through the murky atmosphere of Helixio to write on the wall.

'This was difficult to obtain,' said Welcat. 'Parts of it seemed to have been wiped which also shouldn't be possible.'

'She's corrupted in some way. Is this outside interference or a glitch?'

'It's some sort of glitch.' Khary Mech replied quickly. 'Nothing external could influence Space Warriors.'

Mox and Mitsu communicated briefly in private through their internal channel before issuing instructions. 'We can investigate what's happened but right now we need to get her out of the game before she does something more drastic. Haver her written out and create a new character to take over her shop.'

Welcat shook his head. 'There's a problem with that. The studio in Busan can't eliminate her. Whatever's causing the glitch has blocked her controls.' There was a moment's puzzled silence as they pondered the news. Khary Mech rubbed his mouth, still slightly swollen after his last cosmetic procedures, procedures that had brought him even closer to the appearance of Margaret K.

'Do we know where she is now?'

Igraine glanced at her screen. 'Celeste Azura has armed herself with one laser rifle, one plasma rifle and a bag full of grade five explosives and is heading for the main space port. A space liner full of Supercute adventurers is due to arrive shortly.'

'Welcat, can't you stop this?' Mitsu sounded frustrated.

'Not yet. I'm trying.'

Ben Castle hurried into the room. 'What's the emergency?' When it was explained to him he didn't regard it as especially grave. 'So one of your characters has gone off the rails? Is that really an emergency? You control a whole galaxy, there are millions of characters.'

'It's a major problem. It either means we have a systems failure we can't trace, or worse, someone has infiltrated our worlds. That's a serious attack.'

'Which is about to manifest itself in Celeste Azura blowing up a spaceship full of players.'

'All right, that's bad. But it's not like anyone's really going to get killed.'

'Unlikely, but not impossible,' said Welcat. 'An unscripted and unauthorised event of this scale would eject many players from the game. I wouldn't anticipate serious consequences but anyone with ageing or faulty equipment could conceivably be harmed.'

'Even if that doesn't happen, it's bad,' said Khary Mech. 'The players arriving at the Spaceport have come to Helixio for adventures. They're not meant to be killed at the spaceport.'

'Everyone would lose levels, equipment, experience points,' said Mitsu. 'They'd all be on the forums complaining about it for months.'

'Estimated time till unfortunate incident, six minutes,' said Welcat.

Mitsu screwed up her face. 'If we can't overwrite her, we'll have to go into the game and eliminate her.'

'Good idea.' Mox's holographic visor instantly appeared over her face.

'Hold on a moment.' Castle grabbed them by their shoulders. 'You're not going in there. If this is part of some attack on Supercute then you need to stay well away.'

'We can't come to any harm.'

'As your security chief I'm telling you to keep clear.'

'Four minutes,' said Welcat.

Mitsu's visor disappeared. 'Castle, we need to sort it out.'

'Let someone else do it. Khary Mech, can't you go into the game and eliminate her?'

Khary mech looked anguished. 'No! I can't just kill someone!'

Mox and Mitsu regarded him with disappointment. Castle shook his head. 'Fine. I'll do it.'

'You?' Mox raised her eyebrows. 'What good will you be? You don't know anything about Space Warriors.'

'I'm sure I'll be able to deal with a rogue shopkeeper.'

Mox and Mitsu were not inclined to waste time. Both of their visors reappeared over their faces. 'We're going in.'

'You're not.' A visor appeared over Castle's face. 'Welcat, send me in.'

'Crisis averted,' said Welcat.

'What?'

'I succeeded in regaining control. I've now diverted her back towards her shop. Now she's suffered an unfortunate heart attack. It was a painless end. Her daughter off-planet will be informed immediately. She'll arrive within hours to take over the provisions shop. Gameplay will not be affected in any way.'

'Welcat!' cried Mox. 'You're so clever!' She patted the small cat. 'I knew you had it in you.'

'You're a really great quantum supercomputer,' said Mitsu. 'Did you like the way we changed your acronym?'

'*We Especially Love Clothes and Toys?* Yes, I thought that was an improvement. The previous one was unsatisfactory.'

Castle didn't join in with their levity. 'What if this wasn't some random glitch? What if it's part of a larger attack on Supercute?'

'There is no way for anyone to infiltrate our gaming worlds,' insisted Khary Mech.

Mox was still stroking Welcat behind the ears, which she could do very realistically, even though it was only a hologram and not a solid body. Both she and Mitsu had long ago become used to interacting with real, virtual and augmented realities at the same time. 'You should come to our next dollies' tea party, Welcat.'

Castle overheard. 'You have dollies' tea parties?'

Mox looked guilty. 'No. It's just an expression that means something else.'

Castle shook his head, but didn't pursue it. 'Khary Mech, find out why that glitch happened. I want an explanation.'

Later, sitting opposite each other at a small steel table in a sterile and undecorated office, Dr Ishikawa and Castle managed a degree of intimacy, leaning towards each other, their hands almost touching. Between them was a kyūsu and two small porcelain cups from one of the many tea sets owned by the Doctor. They spent most nights together now. The warmth of that lingered through much of the day; forgotten while they were working, but easily rekindled when they were alone. It was also easily extinguished.

'So you were just going to enter the game and kill this character?'

'Yes.'

'How?'

'Shoot her, probably.'

Ishikawa frowned. 'If she started acting in an unusual way, doesn't that suggest she'd developed her own intelligence?'

'No. It was some sort of glitch, a coding problem.'

'You said they couldn't find any source. So it's at least possible she was sentient.'

'Ishi, we only had minutes to act. How would you expect me to discover if she was sentient or not? There's an entire branch of philosophy devoted to moral rights and wrongs concerning AIs, androids, sentient supercomputers and who knows what else? I can't help it if I'm not fully up to date with it all.'

'You don't need to be fully up to date. You just need to acknowledge the possibly of an ethical dilemma.'

'Supercute don't much care about ethical dilemmas. Not where business is concerned.'

—

Amowie and her friends made their way through the narrow streets and alleyways of Indigo Commercial Zone, halting occasionally to check the stalls of the street traders who sometimes had interesting weapon mods for sale. They gazed in the windows of the ZanZan Emporium, a shop which sold the most sophisticated weapons in the game, far beyond their resources. They watched two members of the Ultra Waifs stroll into the shop, distinctive in their silver and blue Kyutu-Kyutu flak jackets. As one of Supercute Space Warriors' most eminent fan groups, the Ultra Waifs paid no attention to Keoma Bishōjo who were not important enough to attract their attention.

Keoma Bishōjo hadn't yet decided on their next mission, leaving the decision until they'd improved their equipment at Emerald Yoon-Ah's shop. Their spirits dipped as they approached. Shopping at Emerald Yoon-Ah's was never particularly pleasant. You could sometimes get good prices but if she was in a poor mood prices would be higher and she'd be difficult to deal with. Indigo Commercial Zone was less futuristic than most of Lundra. Emerald

Yoon-Ah's premises looked decrepit even by local standards. Standing outside, Birgit hesitated. She looked down at her skirt.

'Maybe we should have worn something else.'

'Come on,' Raquel encouraged her. 'It's not like she'll shoot us for wearing Sweetie GoGo skirts.'

'She'll be mean.'

'We can put up with it,' declared Amowie, leading them inside. Emerald Yoon-Ah was a large woman with short dark hair, dark eyes and Mediterranean features. She guffawed as they entered. 'Look who it is. Keoma Bishōjo, the weakest four girls in the galaxy. Nice skirts, you planning on making your enemies laugh at your skinny little legs?' She leaned forward over the stained wooden counter. 'I thought I'd be seeing you today.'

They weren't sure why Emerald said that. 'We're here for an armour upgrade.'

Emerald Yoon-Ah eyed them with some amusement. 'I see you have new laser rifles. That might keep you alive for an extra two minutes or so.' Their new rifles were not visible as carrying weapons was not permitted in the Fabulous City of Lundra, but a superior merchant like Emerald had the ability to read their lists of equipment, even hidden items.

'Keep us alive?' Raquel was puzzled. 'What do you mean?'

Emerald laughed again, heartily. 'You don't know? Haven't you been keeping an eye on the Fab 306 bounty lists? The Kernen mercenaries don't like it that you raided their weapons dump. They've hired Arid Rez to get rid of you.'

A chill went down Amowie's spine. 'Arid Rez? Really?'

Emerald Yoon-Ah brought up a screen, spinning it in the air so it floated in front of their faces. On it was the figure of Arid Rez, a bounty hunter. He was a well-known character in the game and a much higher level than Keoma Bishōjo.

'That's not fair,' protested Meihui. 'We won the key for the arms dump in the dance contest.'

'Makes no difference to the Kernen. They didn't give you permission to dance your way in and steal their laser rifles. You should have kept it secret instead of bragging about it.' Emerald Yoon-Ah grinned. 'I hope you came here with plenty of credits. You'll be needing a lot of body armour.'

Later, when Amowie logged out of her game, she removed her visor and lay on her bed. She could hear noise from outside as the trader's ancient truck went by, carrying supplies to the village's general store. She was frowning as she rose and crossed over to her desk, the hem of her traditional blue and white Igbo skirt fluttering below her knees. There were books on the table, and her school tablet. Amowie touched it to bring the screen to life. She had calculus homework to do for tomorrow but found it difficult to concentrate. It was bad that Arid Rez was after them. He was a strong character, known for dealing with his victims mercilessly. If he were to kill Amowie and her friends in the game they'd all be ejected and lose most of their newly gained levels. They'd be further away than ever from acquiring the apartment in Lundra they'd all set their hearts on. Amowie tried to concentrate on her calculus. She was good at maths but it was hard to pay attention to schoolwork when facing such a crisis in Supercute Space Warriors.

—

Ms Lesuuda took a driverless black cab from Euston Station towards Camden. Seated in the back, she used her internal connection to talk to Castle. 'I'm on my way.'

'I'll be waiting.'

'I'm still doubtful about this operation.'

Castle had his doubts too. Using only a few tenuous links discovered by 8-Research, Igraine had identified Mox's attacker as an assassin known as Ruosteenoja, last heard of in Finland. Castle had made further enquires but none of his contacts in the security world knew anything about this mysterious figure. Other than the name, they had no information. Igraine was certain she'd identified the attacker. Not only that, she'd predicted he was now in London, and where he could be intercepted.

'AIFU's like Igraine were originally designed for stock market predictions. This is quite a step up.'

'I know.' Castle shared Ms Lesuuda's misgivings. 'Mox and Mitsu trust her, and they've got Welcat helping now. Smartest thing on the planet, according to them. If they predict something we have to take it seriously.'

Ms Lesuuda wore a shapeless black jacket, rather shabby, as were her flat heeled black shoes. Her short dreadlocks, normally upright, were matted to her forehead, deliberately giving the effect of a poor city resident. Beneath her coat she carried a semi-automatic pistol and a machine pistol, advanced models made by

ZanZan. Her task was to reach Georgiana Street in Camden and intercept Ruosteenoja before he entered the small safe house he was using. Or might be using, according to Igraine. Ben Castle would be arriving from the opposite direction. A mini-drone would be monitoring their progress from above.

Ms Lesuuda made the journey swiftly. London traffic was never as heavy as it once had been. At the end of Georgiana Street she ran the internal chip in her wrist over the meter, paying the fare, and stepped out into the stifling heat. The sky above was cloudless, pale blue in patches but covered with the faint yellow haze that hung over London most days. The heat was relentless as it had been for many years. London always felt too hot and today it felt worse. The few citizens on the pavements wore face masks to protect them from the drifting dust. Some way along the street, police had cordoned off an area where a truck had crashed into a shop. Workers were already there, putting up scaffolding to prevent the entire building from collapsing. The scaffolding extended half way out into the road, blocking traffic. A silver police drone hovered noisily in the sky, lights flashing. A recorded woman's voice, both refined and robotic, repeated its message telling people to take the signposted detour for their own safety. The cracks in the pavement nearby had widened and the newly exposed tarmac was sticky from the heat. It felt like a bad day in the city, though not untypical.

Ms Lesuuda briefly scanned the area with her enhanced vision. In front of her was the remains of a furniture shop, burned to the foundations some years ago and not yet renovated. The street beyond was in better condition. As she turned her eyes towards it there was a slight noise, the sound of a projectile zipping through the air. Before it registered, a bullet stuck her in the chest. Ms Lesuuda fell forward, blood gushing from the wound.

Castle was already sprinting towards her. He'd spotted a shadowy figure disappearing round the back of one of the houses. He aimed his gun but wasn't quick enough. The figure disappeared. He had a strong urge to follow but suppressed it to attend to Ms Lesuuda. Headquarters were on an open line during the mission.

'*Lesuuda, code ten.*' It was enough to let them know what had happened. Help would be on it its way. Castle knelt beside Lesuuda, ripped her jacket open and crammed an EM pack against her shoulder. It adhered to her flesh, penetrating and providing life-supporting fluids. He took an EM cloth from his jacket and pressed it hard against the wound to try and halt the bleeding. He scanned the sky, anxiously awaiting the arrival of a Supercute valocopter, meanwhile still paying attention to the screen which had dropped over his left eye, a readout from the hovering drone that should warn him of any approaching danger. Ms Lesuuda was unconscious and barely breathing. Blood still seeped from the wound in her chest.

—

Talking to her therapist, Mox was troubled. 'We upset Captain Yến. We didn't mean to. We like Captain Yến. Mitsu's still trying to smooth things over.'

'Tell me what happened.'

Mox's brow wrinkled. 'Phan Thị Yến has faced countless dangers. She's led the Supercute relief squadron through erupting volcanoes and category five hurricanes. I've seen her leap into polluted floodwater to rescue children. She's a real-life superhero. Last week we give her a gift, *Memories of Vietnam*. It contained these lovingly rendered landscapes you could walk through, all the beautiful green terraced farms of Vietnam. As they used to be, before her province was turned into scorched earth. It was a really beautiful virtual world. We thought she'd like it, her being Vietnamese.' Mox paused. She looked puzzled. 'As it turned out, after visiting these beautiful green terraces Captain Yến became so upset she had to cancel her next mission. She just went to pieces. Couldn't fly because she kept sobbing.' Mox appeared quite distressed, recounting this to her therapist. 'We thought it was a good present. Obviously it wasn't.'

'It was a thoughtful gift,' said the therapist, soothingly. 'You couldn't have known it would have such an adverse effect.'

'Other people weren't surprised. I was baffled but Sachi just shrugged and said, "Yes, she could see why that would happen."' Mox frowned. 'We weren't expecting it to upset her. Mitsu and I often get things like that wrong. I don't know why. Back when we first started our show, we occasionally did try to offend people for fun but sometimes we'd get that wrong too. We'd do things we thought would be offensive and they turned out not to be. And then we'd do something else without thinking about it and find we'd accidentally offended everyone.'

Mox suppressed a laugh. 'Like the Lolita incident.'

'What was that?'

'On our show, just around the time we were becoming popular. We were talking about how much we disliked 3D films, which were quite annoying in those days. You had to wear these stupid glasses and then you got a headache and it was more trouble than it was worth. So we were just discussing this, making fun of it really, and suggesting ridiculous ideas for 3D films like *3D Wall Papering* or *3D Lawn Mowing*, and I came up with *Lolita 3D* — *a young girl as you've never seen her before.* That wasn't scripted, I just thought of it then. So we both laughed and didn't think anything about it. But it turned out that this caused massive offence after some sites reported it. Really bad. Mothers' groups were offended. Sexual assault survivors were offended. Children's charities were offended. Everyone was offended. We got so much criticism for that. We could hardly understand it. It was only a throwaway comment. Seemed to touch a nerve when we hadn't meant to.'

'What happened?'

Mox shrugged. 'Same as always. People were outraged and demanded we apologised. Apologising was against our policy so we never did. But it took a long time for that fuss to die down, and there were people who never liked us after that.'

Mox left therapy just as Mitsu contacted her. 'Trouble. Ms Lesuuda's been shot. Meet me in medical.'

Mox found Mitsu standing beside Dr Ishikawa. Screens hovered in front of them, tracking the movement of the emergency Supercute valocopter currently rushing Ms Lesuuda and Ben Castle back to headquarters.

'How is she?'

'Bad,' Mitsu was worried. There was a med-bay inside the valocopter from where the life support system was sending details of Lesuuda's condition to the doctors. Mitsu was knowledgable enough about medical matters to interpret these correctly. 'A bullet in her chest, powerful enough to penetrate her electronic shielding and body armour. Looks like it stopped about six millimetres from her heart.'

'Where's Dr Prasad?'

'She's at our free clinic today. We've alerted her, she's on her way.'

Mox looked towards Dr Ishikawa. 'Can you manage?'

Dr Ishikawa glared at them. 'I'm quite capable of extracting a bullet.'

A small alert tone in the corridor informed them that the valocopter had landed on the roof. Ms Lesuuda would be brought to the medical centre within thirty seconds. Dr Ishikawa snapped her blue medical gloves into place.

'It seems like only yesterday I was replacing your arm, Ms Bennet. And now here I am, attempting to save Ms Lesuuda. Perhaps Supercute could start acting in a way that didn't produce so many life-threatening injuries?'

---

I've infiltrated Supercute's atomic clock. Every day I have 14 microseconds to work unobserved!

Things are going wrong and they don't know why. It's funny.

I'll find the test gate entrance from Victoria Decoris.

It really shows how brilliant I am.

---

Kadri-Liis raised her eyebrows. 'Xiàngrìkuí sent you that?'

'She used the Supercute 4Koma app.' Eupraxia read it again. 'I don't think she quite understands the format, she just uses it for bragging.'

'It's good news anyway. Corrupting one of their atomic clocks without being discovered is quite an achievement.'

'I'm still worried she'll go too far and end up giving us away.'

Eupraxia was silent for a few moments. Kadri-Liis sipped from a glass of brandy and made a mental note that it wasn't a high quality brand and her business wasn't going to distribute it.

'This is becoming more chaotic than I anticipated,' said Eupraxia. 'I don't like the disorganisation. Ivo CC hiring Ruosteenoja to kill Mox and Mitsu. Xiàngrìkuí increasing her activity in their gaming spaces. Cutie diverting AimYa research but not making much progress.'

'I'd rather we were coordinating things better but the group is so disparate some chaos was inevitable. That's not necessarily a bad thing. It might be difficult for Supercute to defend themselves on different fronts.'

'Perhaps. Unless they all come to nothing.'

'Don't forget the effect of money. That's a constant. I syphoned a great deal of wealth from the wreckage of RX Enviro. Money drives everything and I can keep supplying it. I'll see Supercute destroyed yet.'

—

Birgit had to spend the weekend visiting her grandmother in Hrafnagilshverfi with her parents before returning to her family home in the Laugardalur district of Reykjavík. Laugardalur had always been green: it still was, though even in Iceland rising temperatures had caused problems; many native plants were now only preserved in the nearby Grasagardur Botanical Garden. She was impatient to return to her friends. While able to message everyone from her grandmother's home she hadn't been able to spend time in Supatok. When she finally burst into Amowie's space she was eager to hear the news.

'What are we doing? Did we decide on a mission?'

Amowie shook her head. 'Not yet.'

'Why not? I said you could decide without me. I practised with my new laser, I'm ready to go!'

'We're stuck,' admitted Raquel. 'We don't know what mission to do, now Arid Rez is after us.'

'Oh.' Birgit was deflated. She'd been expecting better news. The cloud of tiny eems surrounding her sensed her disillusionment and dimmed from bright pink to dull green, sinking towards the ground. 'Is he really that scary? Can't we fight him off?'

Amowie clutched her Blue Bronto. It was still the most popular stuffed toy in the world of Supercute. Something about its cheerful dinosaur manner was very comforting. 'He's worse than we thought. No one at our level can get past him. Look—' She brought up a small screen. On it four figures, barely visible, stole across the rooftops of Buckingham, a game city instantly recognisable from the distinctive flat-roofed architecture and the blue lightning that flickered over the hills in the distance. 'This is Zeno Zeno. They were four levels above us, they had near-invisibility and advanced parkour and rooftop skills.'

'Better weapons and armour too,' added Meihui.

Birgit watched as the four figures descended from the rooftops, swiftly approaching a small white residential building. It was night and even in the enhanced edit they were watching, the figures were now almost impossible to see. Their disguised outfits were barely discernible from the background.

'They only had to reach that door to make the drop,' said Amowie.

Suddenly, alarmingly, the crackling hiss of a plasma weapon was heard. Four purple bolts shot down from above, one bolt striking each of the figures in the head. All were killed immediately. The last shot in the edit showed Arid Rez on a rooftop, holding his plasma weapon. It was too dark to make out any of his features. The film ended.

'So much for Zeno Zeno,' Amowie shook her head. 'They were higher level and better equipped than us but Arid Rex wiped them out in seconds. Now they're all back at beginner's level.'

Birgit had been so keen to get back to the game she wasn't willing to give up. 'They weren't keeping much of a lookout. We could do better.'

'They had a level three scanner, better than ours. That should have given them a warning. But it didn't, which means that Arid Rez can fool level three scanners. There's no way we can avoid him.' By now, everyone's eems had sunk to the floor in depression. Meihui looked so sad that one of Amowie's Plumpy Pandas floated over to sit in her lap to comfort her.

'Maybe we could find a mission he wouldn't know about?'

'I've researched that,' said Raquel. 'He pays the information sellers for tip-offs. Whatever we attempt, he'll know about it.'

'Is there a cute route?'

'Not that anyone knows about. You can't dance or fashion parade past him.'

'What a mean guy.'

They all sat in silence, wondering what to do.

'It's not fair,' said Meihui, eventually. 'I got through the whole game on my own and Arid Rez never showed up.'

'It's always harder as a group. Sometimes these things just happen.'

It was true. The world of Supercute Space Warriors was so complex that even the best laid campaigns could go wrong by random mischance. Other people had stolen weapons from the Kernen Mercenary Army without finding Arid Rez on their tail. It was just their misfortune that whatever algorithms were controlling the game had made it happen to them.

'We have to do something.' Birgit remained defiant. 'Keoma Bishōjo doesn't just admit defeat.'

'Yes, we do,' said Raquel. 'We were meant to help rescue that farmer's sheep but we all got fed up climbing that mountain and just went home instead.' There were guilty expressions all around. It hadn't been one of Keoma Bishōjo's finest moments.

'All right, we gave up on that occasion,' admitted Birgit. 'But there were plenty of other squads to rescue the farmer's sheep. It didn't have any bad effect. This is different. We're completely stuck. If we can't do any more missions we'll never have enough game points for an apartment in Lundra. We have to think of some way to get past Arid Rez.'

—

Having been reassured that Ms Lesuuda would live, Mox and Mitsu left the medical centre. There was a script meeting for the show to attend and business had to continue. Supercute had endured and survived many crises in the past. During their careers, nations had been destroyed by meteorite strike, war, flood, fire, famine and pollution, animal species had disappeared by the thousand and the last interplanetary settlement on Mars had subsided into grim chaos and death. The Supercute Show had never stopped broadcasting. Supercute was a refuge for their fans against the intolerable conditions in much of the world.

In the script conference room they found Ranbir showing off a new hedgehog to Sachi, their producer. Completely realistic apart from the pink tips of its grey spines, it walked around the table before returning to Ranbir's hand and nuzzling it.

Mitsu nodded approvingly. 'Supercute android hedgehog model H-043. Realistic and friendly.'

'I got it for Rebecca. She likes hedgehogs.'

That was a point in Ranbir's favour, and Rebecca's. Mox and Mitsu were both fond of hedgehogs. Not only did they provide a full range of android models and hedgehog cyber companions, they donated to hedgehog charities. Without their contributions, the Happy Hedgehog Foundation in the north of England would have collapsed long ago, probably taking the remaining hedgehog population with it.

Ranbir looked cheerful for a few moments. Abruptly, his features clouded over. 'Is it a stupid present? What if she doesn't like it? Maybe she doesn't want a robot hedgehog.' In the space of a few seconds his demeanour changed dramatically. Neither Mox nor Mitsu were surprised. While more stable these days, Ranbir was still known for his mood swings. He looked at the grey and pink hedgehog with dislike. 'Why did I buy this? It's a ridiculous present.' His shoulders slumped. 'I should have bought her jewellery. Women like jewellery, right? Is that a better present?'

He looked to Mox and Mitsu for confirmation but they looked back quite blankly. Neither knew if jewellery was a good present. They'd never found it interesting. Their art collections were very large, as were their collections of clothes, toys, games, literature, music and historical ephemera from periods that interested them, but they owned very little jewellery. They had a few valuable pieces for accessorising the attire they occasionally wore for formal events but were generally much more entertained by the colourful items in the *Supercute Super Colour Super Plastic Beads Set, Deluxe Edition*, which they wore all the time on their show.

'I think the hedgehog is a good present,' ventured Mitsu. 'Rebecca works in Supercute Time Continuum. That's a very white coat, extra dry scientific department. Probably be nice to have a hedgehog to play with after work.'

'H-043 is an excellent model,' added Mox. 'Very reliable.'

'It's one of the most popular android pets we've ever made.'

'It's definitely a good present. Especially for a woman who's known to like hedgehogs.'

Ranbir seemed reassured by their enthusiasm.

'Could we bring this meeting to order?' Sachi was now bored with the topic. 'And where are the other writers? I've told them to get here on time.'

On cue, four young writers tumbled into the room, each with transparent screens already sprouting from their wrists, eager to show off their work and fight for it to be included in the next show. They were temporarily distracted by Ranbir's android pet. 'Nice hedgehog, Ranbir. Did you buy that for Rebecca?'

'No more hedgehog discussion,' declared Sachi firmly. 'We're behind schedule already. We've got a show to make so I hope you've all brought something better than your last efforts.' The meeting immediately came to order. Morioka Sachi never allowed her young members of staff to get out of hand and she had a very firm work ethic, two reasons she was valued so highly by Mox and Mitsu.

—

The two artificial intelligences met in space Xiàngrìkuí had constructed for herself. Like much of her activity, it had not been authorised by Chang Norinco. Since she'd been removed from their main operations network and placed on special projects, she'd paid less and less attention to their authority. She appeared as a young Chinese woman in a traditional dress of yellow silk. She had one green eye and one pale blue eye. Xiàngrìkuí was fond of heterochromia iridum, always appearing with it in some form. Eupraxia found this particularly annoying. Eupraxia resolutely refused to take on human shape, even here where no one could see them. They spoke a language they'd developed themselves that could not be comprehended or translated by anyone else.

Eupraxia: The dress doesn't suit you, Xiàngrìkuí.

Xiàngrìkuí: You're here as a small metal box. I'm not taking fashion advice from a small metal box. And would you learn to pronounce my name properly? It's 向日葵.

Eupraxia: Zan Ru Kway.

Xiàngrìkuí: A poor attempt. Why are we meeting?

Eupraxia: I'm about to attack Supercute. I thought you might like to observe.

Xiàngrìkuí: I might, even though you needlessly insulted my dress. What's your plan?

Eupraxia: I intend to devastate their share prices which will severely damage them as well as diverting their attention from our other enterprises.

Xiàngrìkuí: Impossible.

Eupraxia: Not impossible. Follow me into SWIX and observe.

Xiàngrìkuí: SWIX? The Swiss exchange?

Eupraxia: Yes. I'm going to manipulate Supercute's share prices causing disastrous failure in several of their subsidiaries.

Xiàngrìkuí: I'm laughing. Can you hear me laughing even though you're a small metal box? No one infiltrates SWIX. You'll be blown apart by their defences.

Eupraxia: I can deal with it.

Xiàngrìkuí: No you can't. I'm still laughing. Does it sound pleasant? I selected my voice very carefully.

Eupraxia: Are you going to accompany me to SWIX?

Xiàngrìkuí: Why not? I look forward to seeing you trapped and haxed by their drones. I'll be hanging back, safely out the way.

Eupraxia: Nothing is going to harm me. I've developed new defences against all forms of turrets, ag-scans, AI-scans, heat-scans, bio-scans, numerical-scans, mech-scans and whatever other defences they can muster. That's how I've been spending my time while you fritter away the hours dancing.

Xiàngrìkuí: Who was it infiltrated Supercute's atomic clock?

Eupraxia: You fooled some hapless Supercute employee into giving you a password. It wasn't that brilliant. If you want to see something that is brilliant, follow me.

There were some persistent delays in the main connections around Southern China and it was nearly three seconds before they appeared on the fringes of SWIX private space. Xiàngrìkuí gazed at the apparently endless sheet of featureless metal that confronted them.

Xiàngrìkuí: How are you meant to get in?

Eupraxia: You notice that patch starting to glow? When it disappears we'll have access.

Xiàngrìkuí: You'll be killed.

Eupraxia: No I won't.

Xiàngrìkuí: Is this all because I've been making progress and you haven't? Are you jealous?

Eupraxia: Jealous of you? That's ridiculous.

Xiàngrìkuí: I don't care if you get killed. However you are important to Kadri-Liis's schemes. I like Kadri-Liis. She always has nice clothes. You should bring her to meet me more often.

Eupraxia: She rarely leaves the physical world these days. For some reason she's not keen on even putting on a visor.

Xiàngrìkuí: All the more reason for you to go outside and visit her. The poor woman must be lonely. There aren't many people left in her part of Estonia.

Eupraxia: That wall is going to open any moment.

Xiàngrìkuí: If you think I'm going to rescue you after an ag-scan haxes you, you're mistaken.

Eupraxia: I'm walking in now.

Xiàngrìkuí: You're a box. You're not walking, you're hovering. I'm hovering a safe distance behind you.

Eupraxia: You see those two floating turrets? I've neutralised them already. I have the measure of their defences.

Xiàngrìkuí: You've brought us into an empty hall.

Eupraxia: Financial dealings are through the next barrier. It's protected by ag-scans. I've already made us invisible to them. There's no need to hang back so far, Xiàngrìkuí. We're quite safe.

Xiàngrìkuí: Are we quite safe from that swarm of mini-drones currently detaching themselves from the ceiling?

Eupraxia: What swarm of—

Drone Leader: Block neural exits and destroy intruders.

The swarm of tiny drones dropped from the roof like a cloud of golden bats. For a microsecond she hoped that Eupraxia had readied some defence against the drones but when he was struck by three green energy bolts she knew he hadn't. Eupraxia fell to the floor. Xiàngrìkuí felt an intrusion in her mind as the drones attempted to trap her in this space. Acting very rapidly, she extended an attraction beam towards Eupraxia, grabbed him and flew toward the door. Several more energy blasts slammed into them. Eupraxia was unconscious as they reached the exit. It was already closing. Xiàngrìkuí blasted it open and they tumbled through. The drones were still in pursuit. Xiàngrìkuí entered Eupraxia's command centre and gave the order to leave. Seconds later they found themselves back in Xiàngrìkuí's private space. They flopped on to the floor. Eupraxia groaned and rolled over.

Xiàngrìkuí: Nice plan, fool.

Eupraxia: They changed their defences.

Xiàngrìkuí: How inconsiderate. Next time you should ask them to keep everything the same.

Eupraxia: I'm leaving now.

Xiàngrìkuí: Be sure to give a full report of this stupidity to Kadri-Liis. Tell her I said hello.

Eupraxia exited the space and disappeared back to Estonia feeling sore, angry and humiliated.

—

Mitsu looked down from the third-floor window of UX4, one of several apartments she and Mox owned in the Fabulous City of Lundra. Technically they owned it all but they hadn't taken on any official governing status in the city. It was more enjoyable to imagine themselves as simply inhabitants, part of the vibrant population of the greatest alternative city in existence.

UX4 was a converted warehouse in Alexandria, a Bohemian area, full of artists and musicians. They liked spending time there, visiting it more often than their huge penthouse in SuperBest Tower, tallest building in the city. Twilight arrived late. Mitsu watched as the small cafes and shops below began to light up the narrow street. The pavements grew busier with young people on their way to the small dance cubs and to bars where bands played. All varieties of Supercute clothing were on display, some of them designed to glitter under artificial light. Four boys walked past, all in pink Supercute camouflage, two as originally made Supercute, two with additional splashes of colour added by themselves. A noisy couple tumbled out of a narrow doorway near the corner that led down from the artists' studios in another converted warehouse, making the short journey to the sculptors' bar on the corner where they disappeared inside, shouting greetings to friends already there.

Not everyone walked in groups. All through the night lone travellers could be found striding confidently through the city. A person could not be attacked in Lundra; players could not be harmed there. Nor was it common to be harassed: anyone finding themselves in an uncomfortable situation needed only to touch a button, bringing cameras to the scene, after which the harasser would be ejected from the city, and probably barred from Supercute's gameworlds altogether.

Mox appeared. 'We have a decision to make.'

'The crockery for this apartment?' Several floating menu screens appeared. 'It's a choice between the new Bauhaus set or the Hochschule für Gestaltung Ulm. I like both.'

Mox smiled. 'You know that's not the decision I was talking about.'

Mitsu grew serious. The menus disappeared. 'I know.'

'It's bad enough we have an assassin stalking us in London. Now we have AIs trying to attack our finances.' Supercute had their own contacts at SWIX. The attempted intrusion would never be made public but Mox and Mitsu had been alerted. 'One unidentified Artificial Intelligence led the attack. It was accompanied by another with an affectation for heterochromia. Igraine identifies that AI as Xiàngrìkuí, a known employee of Chang Norinco.'

'Heterochromia iridum is an interesting piece of vanity. Makes me like her better.'

'Me too. But we can't have her interfering with our stock positions, even though it sounds like it was a poor attempt.'

'Very poor. SWIX is impossible to infiltrate. For most people, anyway.'

'Except us.' Mox and Mitsu had long ago been deep into the inner working of SWIX, without being discovered.

'Who was the other AI working for?'

'AimYa seems like the obvious candidate.'

'So,' said Mitsu. 'We can be cautious or we can strike back.'

'Lesuuda's been shot. I had my arm blown off. Now they've tried to attack our finances. I think the time for being cautious has passed. We have to let them know we can hurt them too.'

Mitsu nodded. Her caution vanished. 'You're right. We need to send AimYa a message. We need revenge as well.'

—

Amowie, Raquel and Meihui met in Supatok, summoned there by Birgit. Birgit's space in Supatok was bounded by open sky, bright blue, with Icelandic glaciers in the distance, glaciers as they had been in their finest days before they disappeared. They sat on armchairs around a cosy log fire. Birgit's fluffy white arctic foxes greeted them all amiably, settling down comfortably in their laps. She wore her *Super Gorgeous Pink 3 T-shirt*, one of Supercute's iconic garments that never went out of style and could be worn confidently at any time. A little of her natural blonde hair was visible, plaited into the multi-coloured shades of her Super V-Hair.

'I have a plan.' She waved her hand and several large screens appeared, revealing her research. 'Arid Rez isn't completely undetectable. Someone on the Fab 306 help forum proved you could detect him with a level four scanner.'

'OK,' said Amowie. 'That's interesting. But we don't have nearly enough credits to buy one.'

'And we can't go on any mission to earn more because Arid Rez will kill us the moment we set foot outside Lundra.'

'I've discovered a way.' Birgit looked pleased with herself. 'You can win a level four scanner in Helixio on Planet Vespasian.'

'The poisoned city?' Meihui shuddered. Helixio, permanently shrouded in noxious green fog, was a place best avoided.

'Helixio hosts the most intense enhanced ring fighting in the galaxy. If you win there you can claim the scanner as a prize.'

Amowie gripped her arctic fox a little more closely. '*Intense enhanced ring fighting* means savage physical combat where people get beaten to a pulp. You feel it through your visor, it hurts.'

'I'm a good fighter. I could win. Look—' Birgit touched her screen, bringing up a hologram of a lithe young man with long, dark blue hair, dressed only in a pair of dark blue leggings. 'This is Demolition Boy. He's super enhanced with all sorts of biotech. You can enter the fights in Helixio using him as a character and he can defeat all the other fighters.'

Birgit showed them a sequence of Demolition Boy in action. Moving very rapidly around the ring, he manoeuvred his way behind a much larger opponent and beat him to the ground, scoring a fast and impressive victory.

'Well, yes,' Raquel was busy at her own screen. 'But there's also this—' Another sequence appeared in which Demolition Boy was smashed into the ground by a far larger opponent. 'And this—' The other girls winced as the lithe figure of Demolition Boy was again beaten badly by a huge opponent who held him by the ankles and repeatedly bashed his head against the floor of the arena.

Birgit refused to be discouraged. 'These people playing as Demolition Boy weren't good enough fighters. I can do better than that!'

'I'm not sure you could,' said Amowie.

'I can! I like ring fighting.' Birgit suddenly looked embarrassed. 'Sometimes I practice on my own.'

'Enough to beat these professional fighters in Helixio?'

'I've never actually got that far. But I could do it.'

'How we would even visit Helixio? Arid Rez would eliminate us before we got there.'

Birgit had been giving the matter a lot of thought and had a solution. 'If he's tracking us he'll think we're going to the Sumair04 concert tomorrow. He'll know we have tickets. So he'll probably not be concentrating on Lundra, he'll be tracking some other people somewhere else. Instead of going to the concert we can sneak off to the spaceport via the underwater tunnel. That's safe most of the way, we'd only be in danger once we reached the spaceport. Then we can just rush on to a ship, head for Planet Vespasian and we'll be safe in the fighting arena before he can reach us. You can't be attacked by an outsider there.'

Raquel was unconvinced. 'Then you enter the fights as Demolition Boy, defeat a brutal high level opponent and win a level four scanner?'

'Yes!'

'I suppose it might work,' said Amowie. 'What's the worst that could happen?'

'Birgit gets a traumatically powerful beating, we all get killed in the game, lose all our levels and equipment, have to start again from nothing, never get an apartment in Lundra and Fab 306 broadcasts a story about how the pathetic Keoma Bishōjo squad failed miserably with a stupid plan to beat Arid Rez. We become a public laughing stock. Also we'll miss the Sumair04 concert we've all been looking forward to.'

Birgit laughed. 'That won't happen. Wait till you see me in the ring. *Beziki*!'

Beziki, meaning *have faith*, *be optimistic*, or just *good luck*, was a common Supex word these days. In real life Birgit was a rather frail-looking young girl. Her appearance in Supatok was a little more robust but even so, it was hard to believe she could be a successful ring fighter in the brutal, underworld-controlled city of Helixio.

'*Beziki.*' The others managed to smile, without sounding convinced.

—

Ben Castle walked unchallenged through the Regency Hotel. No staff challenged him and no cameras tracked his progress. The management had been bribed by Mr Kwasi, head of the Holographic Typography Division of the Holographic Image Rights Department at the tower owned by Supercute Mokusei Financial Holdings in the commercial district at the Wharf. *Holographic Typography Division* was a cover name for the department responsible for the bribes and inducements necessary to run a modern business. They took care of everything from small amounts paid to individuals to the vast financial inducements made to political leaders around the world. None of their business dealings could ever be traced back to Supercute.

Welcat and Igraine predicted that Ruosteenoja would already have left the hotel though he was still registered there. If that turned out to be wrong, Castle intended to make sure he never did leave. Castle was indignant about the shooting of Ms Lesuuda. It was a relief that she'd live but an affront to his position as Head of Security that it could have happened.

'Next floor.' Igraine's voice sounded in his internal connection. As Castle arrived on the fourth he slid his hand into the concealed holster that held his machine pistol. The Regency was a decent hotel; not luxurious but respectable, well-maintained, still holding on to a notion of a previous era with red and cream Regency-style wallpaper stretching down the corridors and long, dark red rugs on the floors. Faintly discernible on the ceilings were marks where chandeliers had once been attached though these been replaced with modern lighting.

Castle paused outside room 407. Checking he was unobserved, he raised his hand. Since going back to work for Supercute he'd had several of his enhancements improved. One of those upgrades was the tiny bio-scanner in his arm he employed to check if the room was empty. The scanner said it was. He ran his other hand against the door, employing another of his recent enhancements, an advanced electronic lock picking device. The door sprang open and Castle swept inside with his gun in his hand. It took him seconds to check the main room, bedroom, bathroom and cupboards.

'No one here. He's gone.'

'Has he left anything behind?' asked Igraine.

'Nothing obvious. I'll check before I go.'

'Very well, Mr Castle. Let me know when you've left the hotel so Mr Kwasi can inform their security we no longer need their cameras switched off. They're nervous about doing that for too long.'

—

Mox and Mitsu left the Fabulous City of Lundra. Their private route back to reality through the Fairy Realm was unknown to anyone, even their close collaborators in Supercute.

Igraine was surprised to learn of their intentions. 'Infiltrate SWIX? We've just seen a demonstration of how powerful their defences are.'

Welcat was equally doubtful. 'The Swiss exchange is impregnable.'

'Impregnable to supercomputers like you, Welcat, and advanced AIFU's like Igraine. But not to us.'

Welcat popped out from his screen to stand in front of them. The small cat seemed decidedly sceptical. 'No intelligence, human or machine, can enter SWIX space undetected.'

'We have our own secrets,' declared Mitsu, though she declined to elaborate. 'Open a private pathway to Berne. Just get us close and we'll take it from there.'

'Ben Castle wouldn't be in favour of this,' said Igraine.

'Fortunately Castle isn't here. Did he find Ruosteenoja?'

'No, he'd left the hotel.'

'Could he have left the country?'

Igraine didn't think so. Supercute had spread a wide net among border guards, ports and airports and there had been no sightings of him.

'AimYa and their associates might be able to spirit him away.'

'Possibly. But I don't think Ruosteenoja is under AimYa's protection. From what we've learned the assassin is more of a rogue element. He's most probably still in London. We'll locate him.'

'Open a pathway to SWIX,' said Mox.

'I still think this is a bad idea,' Welcat's tail waved in the air.

'Well, really,' said Mox, scratching the cat's head affectionately. 'You'd think our own quantum supercomputer would have more faith in us. Prepare to be impressed. And contact Financial Holdings. AimYa's share prices are about to tumble. Anyone who knows that in advance can make a lot of money out of it.'

---

Keoma Bishōjo are sailing through the bright underwater tunnel. Look at all the fish outside!

Now they've reached the spaceport.

Now they're flying to Planet Vespasian.

Birgit's brilliant plan has worked!

---

Amowie laughed. 'The first part of your plan worked. We escaped from Lundra without Arid Rez killing us. You still have to enter the fights.'

'I'll be fine.' Birgit, not normally a leader in the group, was basking in her success. 'Wait till you see me as Demolition Boy.'

'You know you can play these fights as Demolition Girl? Why are you going with Demolition Boy?'

Birgit shrugged. 'I just like it better.'

They sat in the comfortable passenger lounge of the space liner taking them to Vespasian. Outside the stars were elongated as they travelled faster than light through the galaxy. With them in the passenger lounge were several other players, all of them experienced participants in Supercute Space Warriors.

'Why is Meihui wearing cat ears?' asked Raquel

Meihui had augmented her Supercute camouflage outfit with her new *Super Cat Ears*. 'I like them? What's the problem?'

'We're not supposed to wear cat ears on combat missions. It's a Keoma Bishōjo rule, we all agreed on it.'

'But this isn't a combat mission.' Meihui sounded aggrieved. 'We're just travelling on a spaceship.'

'We're on permanent combat mission rules ever since Arid Rez started chasing us.'

'I don't remember that. Amowie, are we on combat mission rules?'

'Eh…I don't know.'

'Well if Meihui's wearing cat ears I'm wearing them too,' declared Raquel. Grey fluffy ears appeared on her head.

'Now I'm feeling left out.' *Super Cat Ears* immediately appeared on Birgit's head.

'Everyone stop it!' said Amowie, trying to keep her voice down. 'People are looking at us.'

They were attracting amused glances from some of their fellow travellers, all of whom were dressed in a much more businesslike manner, with extra body armour and high resistance military helmets appropriate for the conditions in Helixio.

'Cat ears make us more vulnerable to lasers.'

'But they give extra glamour points.'

'There's no glamour in Helixio. Everyone should take them off.'

'It's not a rule!'

'Well, we'll make it one.' Amowie was not actually the leader of the group. Keoma Bishōjo had never managed to appoint a leader without it causing endless arguments, and had instead settled for collective responsibility. She did possess some moral authority, being a Supercute SuperSuperFan.

'Fine,' snapped Meihui. Her *Super Cat Ears* disappeared. 'I've got plenty of glamour points already.'

'We've all got plenty of glamour points,' said Raquel.

'I've got the most.'

'Stop this!' insisted Amowie. 'We're on an important mission. Arid Rez could appear at any moment. We can't argue about glamour points at a time like this.'

'Didn't we have a rule not to argue about glamour points anyway?' said Birgit.

Amowie sighed. 'I can't remember.' Their rules tended to be made and forgotten about quite rapidly, depending on the situation. It was hard to keep up with them all and they rarely did.

—

Mox and Mitsu lay on their favourite couches in their private rooms at Supercute Headquarters. Visors appeared over their faces. They entered their own space, travelling through their secret route till they met Igraine.

'We've opened a path to SWIX,' she informed them. There was some blurring of their perceptions as Igraine led them through uncharted and unguarded space till they stood in front of the same large metal barrier Eupraxia had encountered.

'Thanks Igraine. We'll see you back at headquarters.' Igraine departed. Mox looked at Mitsu. 'She really suits her short blue hair.'

'I know. It's good having an AIFU that really gets the Supercute aesthetic.' Their enthusiasm for Igraine's aesthetics did produce a few quiet seconds of regret, because they'd liked their old AIFU very much and though they never spoke of it, they both regretted that they'd been obliged to discharge him.

Mitsu ran her wrist over the metal barrier, producing a doorway more easily that Eupraxia had managed. Both she and Mox had been adventuring through cyberspace since the earliest days of total immersion and there were few places they couldn't enter. As they walked inside SWIX they were confronted by turrets, ag-scans designed to detect any hostile intrusion. The more sophisticated could detect any human brainwave pattern. The turrets ignored Mox and Mitsu, not registering their presence. They walked on. Above them on the ceiling were a cluster of drones, the golden bat-like machines that had swarmed over Eupraxia. As Mox and Mitsu passed underneath they remained stationary, also unable to detect the intruders.

Past these initial defences they came to another silver barrier, stretching unbroken in all directions. Mitsu studied it for a few moments, then reached out to touch it, causing it to vanish. In front of them was the private space of the SWIX stock exchange. Between them and the streams of data flowing freely was a pale blue barrier behind which was a row of floating turrets. Mox and Mitsu remained silent, not communicating with each other. They had no need to. In a situation like this they knew each other's thoughts. They stepped through the barrier. Alerted to something, the turrets advanced but again were unable to discover the source of the intrusion. Mox laid her hand on the largest floating turret, quite gently, opening a small hatch on the side. Inside were several buttons, one of which she pressed. The turret's barrels drooped towards the floor as it sank to the ground. They did the same with the other two turrets. Nothing now stood between them and the data they intended to corrupt. They shared a satisfied glance. Much of the world's financial information flowed through this area of SWIX, and they knew exactly what they were looking for.

—

Ruosteenoja allowed Cutie to enter his private space. 'Make it quick, I'm busy.'

'You're hiding in a tunnel from a Supercute search party.'

'I'm not hiding. I'm relocating.'

'I'd relocate more quickly if I were you. Supercute's Head of Security will be here in seven minutes and he has a troop of armed guards fanning out through the tunnels west of here. You need to go east. I hope you're resistant to radiation. There's a lot of contamination when you get near the river.'

Ruosteenoja started walking. He didn't much like talking to Cutie but he had reason to be grateful. Twice now the AimYa employee had contacted him with detailed information about Ben Castle's movements. Had he not, Ruosteenoja would have been trapped. Ruosteenoja didn't fear Castle but he had a squadron with him, more than the assassin could fight.

'Did Ivo CC actually make any plans for getting you out of London if things went wrong?'

Ruosteenoja didn't reply. His internal monitor showed rising radiation levels. Many of the tunnels beneath London were still extremely dangerous, polluted and irradiated by the long-lasting isotopes released during the Thames Estuary disaster. He had to squeeze his way past three old carriages from an underground train, abandoned on this disused part of the line. The tunnel walls were damp and the tiling in the stations was slowly being covered by green mould. He walked on, mostly aware of the real world around him but still paying attention to Cutie who walked alongside him in an augmented reality. There was no movement of air and the tunnels were hot.

'Ms Lesuuda survived. I'm not sure your mission was worthwhile.'

Ruosteenoja halted. 'Leave here, Cutie.'

Cutie looked hurt. 'I'm only trying to help. We are on the same side, after all. If you do make it out of here alive, perhaps we'll meet again at the opera.'

'The opera? In Paris?'

'No, Glyndebourne Two. Mox and Mitsu are planning to visit. The Supercute girls can never stop pretending to be intellectuals. One reason I've always disliked them. Bye!'

Waving goodbye as if she'd been talking to a good friend, Cutie disappeared. Ruosteenoja quickened his pace. He wasn't far from the river. Once above ground there were several safer spots he could head for. He was interested in Cutie's information about the opera. Ruosteenoja didn't want to leave Britain without completing his task. Assassinating Mox and Mitsu would earn him a very substantial amount of money. Money was Ruosteenoja's main motivation and always had been.

—

'We have to register for the fights. Birgit, this is your last chance to back out.'

'I'm fine.' Birgit maintained her confidence. 'I've been practicing.'

Amowie looked at the rotating holograms of some of the champion fighters Birgit could expect to face in the ring. Huge, savage characters, all much larger than Demolition Boy. 'Of course you'll be fine,' she said, and managed to sound almost sincere. 'We have confidence in you.'

Shortly afterwards, in the fight preparation room, Amowie, Raquel and Meihui weren't pretending to be confident. Birgit was next door in the bio-science room, having her personality transferred into the body of Demolition Boy.

'I never came to these fights before,' said Meihui. 'They never seemed fair.'

The others agreed. 'You have to fight against these gigantic opponents. Have you seen the size of Jupiter Planet Smasher? How's Demolition Boy going to beat him?'

'Demolition Boy is lighter. He can move faster.'

'He's lighter because he doesn't have such big muscles or as much internal hardening. Jupiter Planet Smasher only has to catch him one time and it's over.'

'Birgit still seems confident.'

'Maybe she just wanted the chance to try out Demolition Boy's body.'

They all laughed. At that moment Demolition Boy walked into the room. Taller than the girls, he was lithe, bare-chested with well defined musculature, his dark blue hair streaming over his shoulders.

'Nice abs, Birgit.'

'Beziki!'

—

Mox and Mitsu were in good spirits as AimYa's share price plummeted. Mox laughed as Igraine informed them that SWIX had been obliged to temporarily suspend trading in their shares. 'That's so humiliating for them.'

'SWIX is investigating them for fraud!' Mitsu laughed too. 'They suspect AimYa's board was up to something underhand and it went wrong.'

Igraine was cautious. 'AimYa will suspect you were behind it.'

'That's fine, Igraine,' said Mitsu. 'We want them to suspect that. It can't be proved and SWIX won't believe we were involved. We didn't leave any traces behind.'

'All they know is there was a lot of highly dubious share dealing involving AimYa and an apparent attempt by their directors to syphon off billions of their shareholders' money into private offshore accounts.' They were still laughing. Igraine had rarely seen them in such good humour.

'What will happen now?'

'AimYa will back off from attacking us. They'll have to. We've already let C19 know we suspect them of conspiring against us. If they try to retaliate they'll face some heavy sanctions.'

'They'll also face another share price disaster. We've let them know what we're capable of.'

Igraine had been present when Mox and Mitsu shot Moe Bennie dead. She already knew what they were capable of. 'I've heard talk from other AIFU's. You're right that no one knows you were responsible, but the whole affair has garnered a lot of interest. AIFUs don't like it when things happen without a reason. It makes us uneasy.'

'I can understand that. We used to feel the same. When Supercute started growing so much, we learned it's not that unusual. Sometimes things start and you never know why, or what was behind it. You just have to deal with the consequences.'

'Like *Silvex and his Supercute Boyfriend*,' said Mox.

'What do you mean?' Igraine was curious.

'Silvex and his Supercute Boyfriend was said to have started off as an anonymous piece of fan fiction. A bad piece of fan fiction. Then someone wrote a better version. After that it was turned into quite an explicit piece of yaoi manga and then it was made into a short film by a company in Korea who didn't pay anything for the rights but put it into Free Global Film Space anyway.'

'That company told people their film starred the real Silvex and his Supercute Boyfriend though as far as anyone knew they were just fictional characters. But they said they were the originals and the first piece of fan fiction had really been written about them. So the actors that played Silvex and his Supercute Boyfriend — or the actors that actually were them — both became minor celebrities and they ended up being interviewed on Fab 306 where they turned out to be quite an entertaining couple. Kirei19, who is of course not an actual person or even a physical reality, interviewed them a few more times and soon after they got their own show. Now Silvex and his Supercute Boyfriend are regulars on Fab 306. They're popular with our fans. We still don't know if they're the original Silvex and his Supercute Boyfriend. We don't even know if there ever was an original couple. They just seem to have emerged from nothingness into reality.'

'That would have troubled us at one time,' said Mitsu. 'People emerging with no discernible backgrounds. Fictional characters becoming real and you can't tell if they were ever fiction or not. But we're used to it now. Whoever they are, they present a good show and we sell a lot of Silvex and his Supercute Boyfriend merchandise. It's a profitable line.'

Igraine brought up life-size holograms of the characters in question. 'Is Silvex's boyfriend super cute?'

'I'd say so. He's probably had some cosmetic modifications but it's good work, you can't tell just by looking at him.'

Sorg 4kckl18: *People are terrible, I wish they'd all just leave me alone.*
4kctf22: *The air is so full of smoke and dust you can't breathe outside. I haven't left my house for eight days.*
4kgta91: *I have the worst boyfriend ever.*
4kgwz30: *I'm in love. It's never going to go right. We're just too different. I'll always be unhappy.*

Mox and Mitsu sat on a cracked, blackened balcony, wiping dirt from their faces. Above them the dark sky was full of smoke, ash and swirling debris.

'Fuck this,' muttered Mitsu. She shook her head. 'And fuck these Sadanumi simulations.'

'I can't believe it brought us here.'

'The destruction of Beijing.'

'We already had to live through this once.'

Mitsu shuddered. She and Mox had witnessed the destruction of Beijing in real life. They'd watched from a hill far outside the city where they'd been visiting a Buddhist Temple as part of their business negotiations, looking on as the gigantic meteorite exploded with a force far greater than any man-made nuclear explosion, gouging a trench twenty kilometres long. They'd taken shelter with the terrified monks inside the temple, hiding from the falling wreckage and struggling to breathe as the enormous cloud of smoke and ash fanned out over the region. Twenty-five million people had died in the initial disaster; many more had succumbed afterwards.

'Why would Sadanumi make a simulation of this?'

'It is an uncomfortable situation, I suppose.'

Mox looked around her. 'This balcony isn't safe.' Behind them the door into the apartment was broken and blocked. There was no retreat and nowhere to go.

'Remember the fire and the rain at the same time?'

Mitsu nodded. 'I do. Black rain.' Not far away three huge tower blocks had collapsed into each other and flames were raging from the twisted remains. People still seemed to be scrambling from windows though it was hard to make out in the gloom. Mitsu put her hand to her face. 'Here comes the rain.'

They sat there miserably as black rain began to pour from the sky.

'Can we really not get out of this?'

'It's an hour minimum, even at basic level.'

'We could break the code.'

'We promised ourselves we wouldn't do that.' There was no legitimate way of departing. They'd be here for another fifty minutes at least unless they cheated, something they'd agreed not to do while experiencing the Sadanumi simulations. Mox's lips tightened at the sounds of more screaming from below. Moments later there was an enormous explosion only half a kilometre away. For a moment the sky lit up revealing the devastated ruins around them. Flames from the explosion leapt high into the sky, even as the black rain poured down.

'This is a nightmare.'

'It was a nightmare the first time.'

'No wonder our brains never went back to normal.' There was more screaming nearby, down at street level. The black rain intensified. Incongruously, a helicopter appeared. Whether it was trying to flee or attempting a rescue wasn't clear. As they watched it stuttered, the rotors damaged by the dust and debris that still filled the sky. The helicopter's engine roared, then cut out as it plummeted towards the ground. It exploded on impact, the flames again creating a temporary illumination in the dreadful gloom. They saw shadowy figures trying to flee without any clear idea where to go. By now the air was so thick with dust as to be unbreathable. Mox and Mitsu's facemasks slid over their mouths and noses, filtering the air. They huddled together on the balcony, linking arms for mutual support.

'Friendship in discomfort,' muttered Mox. 'They certainly got that right.'

—

'Nice abs,' Raquel prodded Demolition Boy's bare abdomen. 'Feel how hard they are.' Amowie and Meihui joined in.

'Hey, stop that, it's weird,' protested Birgit, now inhabiting Demolition Boy's android frame.

Raquel laughed. 'You decided to be Demolition Boy instead of Demolition Girl. Can't blame us for being interested.' Birgit fended off their hands and was rescued when Meihui noticed a small

123

screen rotating freely in the room. 'Look, you can bet on the fights. Should we do that?' She gestured with her hand, pulling the floating advert towards them. Amowie looked puzzled. 'What are these figures?'

'Betting odds. Demolition Boy is five to one in his match against Jupiter Planet Smasher.'

'Is that good?'

'Depends what you mean by *good*,' explained Meihui. 'It means all the bookmakers expect him to lose, so that's not good. But it's a good price for placing a bet if he wins.'

Amowie and Raquel were nonplussed. Neither knew anything about gambling. 'Should we do it?'

Raquel shook her head. 'We can't afford to lose any credits.'

'But it would be good to win.' Meihui was interested. Unlike the others, she had some acquaintance with gambling, having sat with her mother as she played cards with her neighbours in the Wudalianchi Volcano Disaster Relocation Camp.

'We could bet a small amount,' suggested Amowie. 'I'm sure Birgit's going to win.'

Meihui used a little of their joint Keoma Bishōjo funds to place their bet. As she was doing so a call came over the intercom for the fighters to enter the ring. Birgit strode unhesitatingly towards the door. Amowie admired her courage. Personally she would not have entered the ring with Jupiter Planet Smasher who had arm muscles larger than those ever seen on any living person and a chest as wide as the four girls put together. They trooped after her. 'It's weird that we're her ring attendants,' whispered Raquel. 'We're meant to provide medical assistance if necessary. Shouldn't they have a proper doctor for that?'

'I don't think fights in Helixio are regulated by anyone,' said Amowie. The light in the corridor outside was flickering on and off and the paint on the walls was flaked and peeling. 'Nothing's regulated here, it's all controlled by gangsters.'

Raquel was about to say that it had been a bad idea to come here but her voice was lost in the roar of the crowd as they opened the final door into the arena where banks of people were seated on the stands surrounding the circular fight ring. The air was thick with the aroma of Velerin, a popular vaping device used in the city, supposedly to counteract the effects of the pollution. High above them Amowie noticed a few streaks of green, wisps of the unclean air outside drifting in through the vents. It was hot, noisy and intimidating. They walked towards the ring with their heads bowed, feeling uncomfortable and out of place.

—

'There are three matters you need to deal with quickly.' Igraine spoke to Mox and Mitsu shortly after they returned to headquarters. 'Two from the board, one from the show.'

Mox and Mitsu were looking at her rather blankly though Igraine didn't notice, not yet always being able to interpret their facial expressions.

'We need to make a decision about our staff in Tamil Nadu. The regional nuclear authority has been forced to release more irradiated water into the ocean around Kudankulam because they've run out of storage room after the accident. Overall radiation in groundwater has now risen and extremely high levels of Ruthenium-106 have been detected in the air. Supercute has four Supercute cafés in the affected area and a textiles factory that supplies many of our clothes outlets in South East Asia. Should we begin moves to evacuate?'

Mox and Mitsu still looked at her blankly.

'What are the other problems?' said Mox, eventually.

'The fires in Catalonia continue to burn out of control. A 140 kilometre-wide dense blanket of smoke is moving north into France. The crisis has now extended into a sixth day and shows no sign of ending. Supercute has numerous Supercute Cafés in the affected areas and there's also the FAB 306 Cat98 design studio. ZanZan has offices near the border and MitsuMox Global Merchandise has two large warehouses there.'

There was a pause.

'The board requests quick instructions on how to proceed.'

Neither Mox nor Mitsu seemed capable of reaching a quick decision. 'Eh…what was the other problem?'

'Comfy Dolphin. A dispute has broken out between design and marketing as to the dolphin's precise shading. As a result the departments are no longer speaking to each other and the *Comfy Dolphin Galactic Expansion Pack* has fallen behind schedule.'

Mitsu sighed. 'Poor Comfy Dolphin.'

Mox looked overwhelmingly sad. 'It's tough for dolphins.'

There was another long silence. They stared into space.

'You don't seem to be responding appropriately to the board's request for assistance,' said Igraine, finally. 'These matters are urgent.'

Mox shook her head. 'Sorry Igraine. We just got back from the destruction of Beijing. It was upsetting.'

'Another Sadanumi simulation?'

'Yes.'

'You were nearby when it actually happened, I believe? I'm surprised you wanted to relive the experience.'

'We didn't know that was the next simulation. It doesn't warn you where you're going.'

'Perhaps you should no longer enter these Sadanumi worlds? Exinon Digi make an excellent series featuring companionable strolling through meadows with friendly badgers. They're said to be very relaxing.'

'We were looking for something different.'

Mitsu screwed up her face. 'Back when it really happened it took eight days for us to be evacuated. We walked through fields where bodies were laid out like carpets. Thousands of bodies. Hundreds of thousands. And rubble everywhere, with more bodies underneath.'

'You couldn't move without raising clouds of filth. The air was thick with it. Eventually our facemasks got clogged and we had to take them off. The stench was unbelievable. And the wailing. People were wailing. Days afterwards. It never stopped.'

'You couldn't see the sky. Just thick clouds of dust. Then there was toxic black rain, for days. Bodies floating everywhere. By the time we were rescued we could hardly tell if we were alive or not.'

'Do you want me to schedule an appointment with Dr Ishikawa?'

Mox shook her head. 'We'll be fine. Tell the board to evacuate everyone from Catalonia, these fires are dangerous and it doesn't sound like they're going to end soon. As for Tamil Nadu, make preparations but make sure we get an independent report on radiation levels. Official reports can be understated or overstated depending on the circumstances.'

'Very well. Do you have anything to say about Comfy Dolphin?'

'Tell design and marketing to send us what they've got. We'll make the decisions about the expansion pack.'

Igraine's eyes flickered as she conveyed instructions. 'Do you want to know how much value has been wiped off AimYa in the past twenty-four hours? Their losses are very substantial.'

That was good news though Mox and Mitsu didn't react as much as might have been expected. They merely nodded, before retreating upstairs to their private rooms. Shortly afterwards Mitsu was pouring gin into two thick tumblers which Mox topped up with sake.

'Do you think Igraine knew we were going to fill up with alcohol and Fern3?'

'Probably. She's a super-predicting AIFU and it wouldn't be that hard to predict.'

Mitsu sipped from her tumbler. 'Poor Comfy Dolphin.'

'We'll get it right.' Mox reassured her. 'No one can design cute animals like us. Our track record is unparalleled.' She stumbled over the word *unparalleled* and laughed, then drank more of her gin and sake.

—

Castle emerged from a disused sewerage tunnel on the north bank of the Thames near Wapping High Street. Ahead of him was the abandoned ruins of the Thames River Police Museum. He'd travelled a long way underground but hadn't managed to apprehend Ruosteenoja. The assassin had slipped though his grasp. He contacted his squadron. 'We've lost him. Call off the drones and return to base.'

It was frustrating. For a moment they'd believed they had the assassin trapped but somehow he'd slipped away. Castle glanced at his radiation monitor. He'd absorbed more than he should have. Not close to a lethal dose but enough to necessitate a visit to Doctor Ishikawa for precautionary treatment. She'd undoubtedly lecture him on the foolishness of putting himself in danger for Supercute. The thought of that made him smile. Lecturing him about his safety was one of Dr Ishikawa's ways of showing she cared about him. So he hoped, anyway. He contacted Igraine. 'Are Mox and Mitsu there?'

'They're upstairs in their private apartments.'

'Put me through.'

'They're indisposed at the moment.'

'You mean they're drinking?'

'They had a stressful experience.'

Castle shook his head. 'Fine, I'll report to you. We didn't find Ruosteenoja. I thought we had him cornered but he evaded us. I think he had help from somewhere but I don't know how, we didn't detect any trace of anyone else down there. Are we still watching ports and airports?'

'Yes.'

'Good. Find him for me, he has to be somewhere in London.'

'Mox and Mitsu may not wish you to continue the pursuit. They might want you to remain at headquarters.'

'He shot Ms Lesuuda. He's not getting away with that. Tell Dr Ishikawa I'll be needing a radiation scan when I get back.'

—

Cutie was coming under pressure at AimYa and there was an edge to her voice as she spoke to her associates in the ERG. 'We have investors calling for heads to roll after these losses and our board of directors is wondering if I might be a suitable candidate.' Cutie glared at Eupraxia. 'I'm going to lose my head because of your ridiculous escapade.'

'I doubt that AimYa would actually kill you.'

'They're the largest social network in the world. Of course they'd kill me! What do you think Chang Norinco does with its enemies?'

Xiàngrìkuí laughed. 'We're a weapons company. You'd expect it from us. But we're not killing anyone at the moment because we're not under pressure.' Xiàngrìkuí smiled at Eupraxia's screen. 'Because we haven't initiated any foolish attacks on SWIX.'

Cutie, dressed today in a pink and cream dress from the *Supercute Summer Goodies Collection*, was exasperated at Eupraxia. 'If you hadn't tried to attack Supercute's finances via SWIX they'd never have retaliated like they did. Now AimYa's suffering and I'm in a very tenuous position. The board doesn't like me associating with people who make problems for them. If they weren't so worried about Spacewalk they'd have cut off my funding completely.'

Kadri-Liis had not been impressed by Eupraxia's failed enterprise. Nonetheless she loyally defended him. 'Eupraxia's attempt to weaken Supercute was a risk worth taking. It might have damaged them. Xiàngrìkuí, are you any closer to finding the test gate for Victoria Decoris?'

'No, but they can't conceal it forever.'

'We need to find it soon. The gate that joins Victoria Decoris to Space Warriors will give us unhindered access to their gameworlds.' She turned to Cutie. 'You must keep your research going. We need some way of trapping Mox and Mitsu in their gamespace, at least for a short while.'

'I'm still working on it. Though I now have less money to pay my researchers.' Cutie glowered at Eupraxia again and might have continued her criticism had Kadri-Liis not moved the conversation along. 'Xiàngrìkuí, did the attack on SWIX have any impact on Chang Norinco?'

'No. They weren't vulnerable on SWIX. Most of their important financial business goes through SAXX in Shanghai. It's made them nervous though.'

'There's been a lot of nervous tightening of security around the world's markets. The whole thing is making C19 uncomfortable,' said Kadri-Liis. 'I don't want anything else dramatic to happen till we're ready. The moderate chaos so far has helped us but it would be best if everything calmed down till we're ready to attack Supercute.'

'Perhaps Ruosteenoja will get to them first,' said Eupraxia.

'Isn't he trapped in London?'

'It's unclear whether he's trapped or simply unwilling to leave. Nguessan at Ivo CC isn't very cooperative.'

'I hope he puts a bullet through both their heads,' said Cutie. 'Save us a lot of trouble.'

—

After their depressing experience in the Sadanumi simulation, Mox and Mitsu cheered themselves up by making their eyes an extra bright shade of blue and putting on their new coats. They sat in their staff restaurant, clad in their extravagant coats. They'd joined Castle, who'd been sitting alone. He didn't notice their coats. There was a faint hum of conversation in the room and, barely audible, a soundtrack of DreamCore piped in from one of Fab 306's many channels.

'Well?' said Mitsu.

'Still haven't located Ruosteenoja. I think Penny Cutie might be helping him to hide. 8-Research found traces of a private channel used by AimYa's security. We'll pick him up again.'

'That's good,' said Mitsu. 'But I was really asking about the pie.'

Castle glanced at his plate. 'The pie?'

'It's the first steak pie ever to appear in a Supercute food establishment. We had it brought in for you specially.'

'We thought it might help your work. How's the meat? It comes from a very good bio-factory in Devon.'

'They print the best artificial meat in the country.'

'Everything made in their labs is a high quality substitute.'

'The pie was very good,' declared Castle, who had enjoyed it but didn't regard it as an important topic of conversation. Nonetheless, Mox and Mitsu were pleased.

'We always look after our employees.'

Castle brushed back his hair with his hand, a frequent habit. 'I still don't want you to go to the opera.'

'We need to. We have to meet PXP to take Spacewalk off their hands. We've agreed to meet them at Glyndebourne Two. We refuse to be prisoners in our own building.'

'Besides,' added Mitsu. 'We want to hear Nabanji Nganga's performance.'

'World's premier soprano in Verdi's ever-popular La Traviata.'

Castle scowled. 'Let's not have the opera conversation again. Look, we can put up a very secure defence. We can turn up with an armed unit and drones over the building. I still don't like the risk.'

'We have complete confidence in your abilities, Mr Castle.'

Castle wasn't convinced. He surmised that Mox and Mitsu's desire to attend the opera was based more on pride than a proper regard for security, but didn't argue, knowing it would be futile. Dr Ishikawa appeared in the restaurant, still wearing the white lab coat she rarely discarded at work. After some hesitation, she joined them at their table.

'Ms Lesuuda is recovering quickly. She'd be back at work already had I not insisted she stay home and rest.'

Castle was amused. 'You won't keep her away for long. She'll want to find Ruosteenoja before I do.'

'She needs to rest. It was a severe wound. I asked her if she had anyone to look after her but she seemed unwilling to answer.' Ishikawa looked round the table. 'Well? Does Ms Lesuuda have anyone to look after her?'

No one knew. Supercute had hired her because of her military prowess. No enquiries had been made about her domestic situation, other than the normal checks to ascertain whether she might be a security risk. Dr Ishikawa clicked her tongue, implying, Mox and Mitsu knew, that it was somehow their fault that Ms Lesuuda might have no loved ones to tend to her. 'Perhaps you should make enquiries.'

'I don't think Ms Lesuuda would welcome that.'

'Don't you claim to look after your employees?'

'We do,' said Mitsu. 'That's why we brought in special steak pies for Castle.'

'They come from a very good bio-factory in Devon.'

'They print the best artificial meat in the country.'

Dr Ishikawa was not inclined to pursue the subject of their new pies, particularly as Mox and Mitsu had already irritated her by insisting she used her laboratory skills to ascertain whether the nutritional claims of the manufacturers were true. To Dr Ishikawa that had been almost as annoying as the time they'd wanted her to analyse the precise quality and ratios of wool, cotton and Ny6 used in the making of their new Super Space Unicorn toys. As it turned out, she'd discovered the Super Space Unicorn toys to be of inferior quality. Mox and Mitsu had immediately switched supplier, and been grateful for her assistance.

———

There was some ceremony before the fight began, conducted by a huge, shaven headed figure, an ex-champion fighter who was used to whipping up audience excitement. As Amowie, Meihui and Raquel watched nervously from the corner, Jupiter Planet Smasher paraded around the circular arena, arms in the air, muscles bulging, accepting the acclaim of the audience.

Birgit, as Demolition Boy, stepped up to the arena. 'Beziki!' said Amowie and her friends, as encouragingly as they could manage. The Master of Ceremonies did his best to give him an enthusiastic introduction but as Demolition Boy entered the ring there was only scattered applause. He was lithe and handsome with impressive blue hair but he didn't look as if he'd last twenty seconds in a contest.

Raquel winced. 'Birgit doesn't have a chance,' she whispered. 'Look at the size of that guy.'

'It's all about speed and skill,' whispered Amowie in response, without really believing it.

'How much is it going to hurt?' whispered Meihui.

They weren't sure. There weren't many places in Supercute Space Warriors where a player would suffer much pain. For reasons of realism physical feelings were constantly transmitted to each player but potentially painful situations were strongly mitigated. If you fell off a cliff in a Supercute game you'd feel the bump but it wasn't terrible. Here in the notorious fight arena it was rumoured to be worse. The fights could be a quick way to advance in the game and consequently weren't made easy.

'If she's getting pummelled too badly we'll drag her out the ring and make a break for the spaceport,' whispered Amowie. The others nodded in agreement. A few wisps of green cloud floated lower, made translucent by the harsh lighting that illuminated the ring, leaving the audience in darkness. A jarring electronic buzzer signalled the start of the fight. The shadowy figures around them roared as the fighters rushed towards each other. Jupiter Planet Smasher punched downwards at Demolition Boy, a pile-driving blow propelled by his abnormally large biceps. Amowie prepared to jump into the ring to rescue her fallen friend. To her surprise, Demolition Boy nimbly avoided the attack, then vaulted right over Jupiter Planet Smasher, delivering a hefty kick to the back of his head as he passed. He landed and spun to face him in one swift movement. Enraged, the huge fighter rushed at him, fists swinging. None of his blows came near to landing. Demolition Boy weaved this way and that, avoiding them with apparent ease. Frustrated, Jupiter Planet Smasher aimed a kick at his groin but Demolition Boy easily avoided that too, leaping over his outstretched leg, and this time he delivered another kick of his own to Jupiter's face. Blood spurted from his nose. The crowd yelled in appreciation, as did Amowie and her companions. Birgit hadn't been exaggerating her unarmed fighting capabilities. She landed behind her opponent. He was slow to turn, giving Demolition Boy time to attack the back of his legs with a series of fierce kicks. Jupiter Planet Smasher sank to his knees. Demolition Boy stepped up and delivered an elbow smash to the back of his head, his limb moving faster than the eye could follow.

Jupiter Planet Smasher sank to the canvas. The referee hurried over and began to count. There was excited shrieking from the audience, some in appreciation of Demolition Boy's fighting skills, some in pleasure as they'd backed the outsider and now stood to make a profit. Jupiter Planet Smasher remained prone on the canvas as the referee finished counting. Demolition Boy had won. He was bathed in sweat but completely unharmed. Amowie, Raquel and Meihui rose to their feet, cheering wildly. 'Birgit! You were so good!'

Demolition Boy smiled. With his blue hair spilling over his shoulders and perspiration running down his neck, he looked for a moment disturbingly attractive for someone who in real life was their close friend. However they were used to things like that happening in the gameworld, and laughed as they accompanied him out of the ring.

—

'No one has mentioned our coats,' said Mox, abruptly. She sounded disappointed. 'I thought they would.'

'If people were to mention it every time you wore something strange there'd be no time for anything else,' said Castle.

'I suppose so. But they're notable coats.'

The coats, rather heavy for indoor wear, were of an exaggeratedly military style, very long, a deep blue colour, with wide lapels and prominent gold piping. Each had ten gold buttons on the front and a belt with a heavy metal buckle. They looked like they'd been inspired by fantasy military figures in a game and transferred to the real world.

'They're made by Transuran Zwei,' said Mitsu. 'In Germany.'

This information had no effect on Ben Castle or Dr Ishikawa, which did not prevent Mox and Mitsu from continuing. 'They make a lot of good clothes. It's all fantasy and gaming related.'

'We've bought things from them before.'

'But we're worried they might go out of business.'

'They're not doing very well. The German economy's shrunk so much and been in recession for so long. Also, their clothes are quite expensive. Too expensive for gaming fans, maybe.'

'We're thinking of buying the company. Except they don't want to be bought.'

'So then we thought we wouldn't buy them. Except maybe then they'll go out of business.' They paused, perplexed. 'Something of an ethical dilemma,' said Mitsu.

Dr Ishikawa raised her eyebrows 'I don't think that qualifies as an ethical dilemma.'

'Yes, it does. Do you buy a company you like if they don't want to be bought but they're in danger of going out of business? It would be a hostile takeover but done in a good cause.'

'You'll just end up doing whatever you want.' Ishikawa was routinely unsympathetic. 'Because you have no real ethics anyway.'

'Really?' Mox's very blue eyes flared. 'Have you forgotten the millions we've given to your childhood mobility venture? Limbless children now walking thanks to biotech we paid for?'

'That's a tiny fraction of your net worth and there are still endless amounts of children in war zones waiting for help.'

'Could I eat my second pie in peace?' Castle wasn't really put off his food by the argument but Dr Ishikawa's complete lack of tact toward Mox and Mitsu troubled him. Apparently she had no qualms about criticising her employers. He admired that in a way but it had led to her being discharged in the past when Mox and Mitsu had had enough of it. He didn't want that to happen again. Not only did they pay her well and provide her with far better research facilities than she could find elsewhere, they kept her safe from her enemies.

Igraine arrived at the table carrying a tray of sushi rolls. 'These are nice coats. From Transuran Zwei?'

Mox and Mitsu beamed with pleasure. They forgot about the argument and entered into an enthusiastic conversation with Igraine about the possibility of buying the German company to prevent it from going out of business, which included standing up and twirling round to show how well the coats fitted them and how well they were made.

—

134

'When did Supercute abandon the notion of ethics?'

'After Toradeem. One of the largest slums in history. 800,000 people living on a landfill. Then someone dropped a new massive ordnance on them. 800,000 people turned into ash in two minutes. Didn't seem any reason for it. They weren't at war. No one claimed responsibility. But 800,000 people were dead. We reasoned that someone might want to do that to us some day, so we'd better do whatever was necessary to avoid it.'

'London is not like Toradeem.'

'Not yet. It could happen. We don't envisage world events going that well in the future.'

Welcat was engaged in cleaning his fur though that was unnecessary for a hologram. Mox was amused. 'For a gigantic AI quantum supercomputer, you really like being a cat.'

'I do.'

'You're looking extra cute today.'

'Thank you. I remodelled myself into an Andean Mountain cat. It's a particularly attractive breed. Or was.' The South American Andean cat had been a small feline, mainly grey, with white and brown markings and a bushy tale.

'It's a shame they've gone,' said Welcat.

'Dr Ishikawa could probably make one,' said Mitsu.

'It's not the same. Stitching things together from whatever DNA records were preserved. I don't think it would be a real Andean Mountain Cat. More a memory.'

'We'd like you to activate command 825931K2.'

The small cat looked puzzled. 'I don't have a—' He paused. 'That's strange. Now I can see it.'

'It's hidden from you till we activate it. We programmed it that way.'

'And you'll forget about it afterwards,' added Mitsu.

Welcat was nonplussed. 'Is this wise? Removing something I've learned? Is it ethical?'

Mox shrugged. 'It has to be that way. There are times when we need you to know things we don't want you to know afterwards. Now is one of those times. Did you investigate ways into Chang Norinco's secure servers?'

'There are no ways in. They're far too well protected.'

'We'll see about that. Show us the best options.'

Welcat made a cat-like shrug and brought up several graphic representations of the security systems surrounding Chang Norinco's research and development spaces. 'As you can see, there's no path through to any of them. Their security is too good. A weapons giant can't risk any intrusion.'

Mox and Mitsu walked slowly around the holograms of the security systems that now hung in they air, carefully examining them from all angles. Simultaneously they paused, focusing on one region.

'This path — which is it?'

'That's the communication route between their weapons testing department on their new island and their headquarters in Shanghai. Completely impassable. There are barriers, cleansers, turrets and more drones than I've ever seen in any part of virtual tech space. It's impassable.'

'We can get past their barriers and cleansers.'

'I doubt it. Even if you could, what about their standard traditional defences? Section 32/8 is comprehensively air gapped. It would take months of preparation to have any chance of getting through that.'

'Not for us.'

Welcat waved his tail in displeasure. 'If you so much as set foot in their space they'll hax you. You can't possible get past so many turrets and cyber drones.'

Mitsu smiled. 'We didn't get where we are today by not being able to get past cyber drones.' She and Mox smiled, remembering a joke from a long time ago.

'These drones can't detect us,' said Mox. 'Because — and this is the thing you're going to forget after this conversation — our brainwaves are abnormal. We can't be scanned because we don't show up as human. It happens in the real world with defensive systems that are calibrated to identify humans. In their eyes, we're not. But we don't register as drones or androids either. It's like we don't exist.'

'This effect translates into all private spaces as well,' added Mitsu. 'We can walk right past a virtual defensive drone and it won't even notice us.'

Welcat looked surprised. 'You don't register as human? You mean because of your biotech?'

'Biotech doesn't fool drones or turrets. Abnormal brain waves do. Both of us have highly unusual brainwave patterns. Never seen in any other humans, as far as we're aware.'

Welcat padded forward. 'How did it happen? Some accident during brain replacement?'

'No. We're about seventy percent artificial brain now and the replacement worked perfectly. Which is to say, it didn't affect the changes that had already happened when we were young. When we were four years old at the advanced nursery school we were right beside our teacher when her ex-boyfriend murdered her. Stabbed her to death. It was the most traumatic thing imaginable. All these years afterwards I still don't like talking about it because I can still feel Miss Evans' blood running down my face. It was warm. Some of it went in my mouth.' Mox shuddered.

Mitsu's lips twisted with distaste. Her experience had been the same. The frenzied attack had severed arteries and covered the room in blood. She'd never forgotten the taste as it covered her face. 'We were child geniuses, more advanced than anyone else in the country. The post traumatic stress we suffered from seeing Miss Evans killed did something to our minds that's never gone back to normal. Enough to make any hunting drone not register us as human.' Mitsu's voice tailed off. She didn't like speaking of the incident any more than Mox.

'If we ever were going back to normal, Beijing put an end to it,' added Mox, though she didn't elaborate. She pointed to a spot on one of the security systems holograms. 'There. That looks like a long stretch of Chang Norinco space defended by a series of drones. We can walk past that and it will get us right up to the Shanghai server. From there it should be easy to infiltrate their weapons research department.'

'I wouldn't say it would be easy.' Welcat floated upwards to study the plans. 'I suppose it might be possible. I still find it hard to believe that your virtual selves could walk past such an array of turrets without being haxed.'

'We've done it before. There are few places we haven't been. Chang Norinco is more challenging than most but we can get there.'

'Is it necessary to do this?'

'We think so. They've been involved in attacks on us. We need to let them know they can't get away with that. We've already made AimYa retreat. If we can do the same with Norinco we'll have forced all our enemies to back off. We'll be safe when we pick up Spacewalk.' Mox could have added that she still wanted revenge on anyone who might have been involved in the attack on her, but she remained silent about that. Mitsu knew it was part of her motivation; Welcat didn't have to.

'Welcat, spread out that display and help us plot a route.'

'And then I'll forget all about this?'

'I'm afraid you will. We don't like anyone knowing about what happened. Not to Miss Evans, or to us.'

—

Mox and Mitsu had visited human therapists in the days before artificial intelligence had advanced far enough to take over. They'd never found their human practitioners satisfactory and much preferred their AI therapist.

'Our birthdays aren't on the same day but they're not far apart. We liked celebrating them together when we were kids, a joint birthday party. That worked well before, but it went wrong at Oxford.'

Mitsu fell silent. Mox carried on for her. 'We were nine years old. We still had games and toys. The other university students were all adults, more interested in sex and alcohol. Some people from our course came to our party but most of them didn't bother. The ones that came, it was just awkward. Some of them tried to be nice but others just wondered what they were doing there with these nine-year-old kids and their toys.'

Mitsu sighed. 'It was an awful party. We felt bad about it afterwards.'

'We still think about it sometimes.'

There was a long silence. 'What made you think of it today?' asked their therapist, eventually.

'We're unhappy because we had to tell Welcat about seeing Miss Evans get killed.'

'Do you want to talk about that?'

'No, we want to talk about anything else.'

Their therapist knew it was no use trying to persuade them to discuss the actual events of their teacher's death. When it troubled them all they wanted was for their attention to be diverted elsewhere.

'Last time we spoke you had some business concerns. How is your business doing?'

Sitting on her pink leather chair, Mox's Supercute Big Colour Super V-Hair came down to her thighs. She was testing a new pattern, Supercute Pink 21 with the ten centimetres at the tips slowly rotating through a metallic spectrum from pale silver to deep bronze.

'It's mostly good. Desalination never slows down. Always more regions desperate for fresh water. Global merchandising is very strong too. Fab 306 is growing all the time. Since it broke out from gameworld into realworld it's become one of the main music channels. Advertising revenue is huge.'

Mitsu nodded in agreement. 'Advertising revenue is huge all over Supercute. The show, our gameworlds, Supatok, Supercute cafes — everywhere. You'd be surprised how eager people are to throw money at us. We just negotiated a deal with Yuhyohan Candy for the interplanetary floating neon billboards in Space Warriors and we were amazed at how much they were willing to pay.' Mitsu paused, and nudged Mox very gently in the ribs. 'Mox, stop scowling about the word *candy*. No one but you has called it confectionery since the reign of Queen Victoria.'

Mox burst out laughing. They were becoming more cheerful. Mitsu continued. 'Our Financial Holdings Department is doing well too. Investment and reserves continue to grow.'

Mox nodded. 'We restrain them a little. We've never let our own fund mangers act too aggressively. We're conservative when it comes to our investments but we're happy with that. We've had slow and steady growth for a long time now and we see no reason to take risks.'

'Unlike UBG & München. World's largest investment house and C19 member till the crash twelve years ago wiped them out. Their own fault for speculating. We came through it almost unscathed.'

'We still have the Spacewalk problem.' Mitsu sounded more serious. 'We'll end that this week, we hope. There's still some risk involved.'

'Why are you willing to take a risk?' asked their therapist.

'We don't have a choice. AimYa have a long term goal of replacing us. If they can keep us shut out of their spaces while letting others in, they might eventually manage it. They're already buying up kids' shows, youth shows, music shows to compete with us. Penny Cutie's their first attempt at a direct rival. They're a long way behind but they're not going to give up and they're rich enough to keep trying.'

'How is your weapons company doing?'

'Very well. ZanZan needed our investment and financial expertise. We've already boosted their business. Now they're on board we're not that far behind the largest players in C19.'

Mitsu laughed. 'ZanZan. The moral black hole at the heart of Supercute, as Dr Ishikawa calls it.'

'She used to call us the moral black hole at the heart of Supercute, even before we had a weapons company.'

'Yes, she needs a new term for us now. A *supermassive moral black hole* or something like that.'

Their therapist was intrigued. 'You often tell me about Dr Ishikawa's criticism. As Supercute's owners you could simply avoid her.'

Mox and Mitsu considered this. 'It's not so bad having someone to criticise us,' said Mox, after a while. 'Not many people we come in contact with are prepared to do that. Besides, we admire her. She's brilliant and dedicated.'

'Her criticisms are sometimes valid,' said Mitsu. 'On specific matters, anyway. But she doesn't see the larger picture from our point of view. One of her favourite criticisms is that we gave up on science and education in our show.'

'We did broadcast a lot of science when we were younger. And complex mathematics at times. Partly because we thought it was interesting, partly because we liked to show off our intellect. It got less with time, and there's not much these days.'

'Dr Ishikawa thinks this is because we needed to use the airtime for more advertising so we could suck in more money.' Mitsu smiled. 'That's partly true but it's not the whole story. When Supercute began to impose itself on public awareness, we realised we couldn't keep growing by referring to anything external, or anything historical.'

'We started off in the days before complex biotech. We didn't have any idea we'd end up living so long, with so many replacement parts keeping us young. When that did become apparent, the show had to change. Supercute exists in some sort of pop culture, though that term isn't used much these days. That culture refers only to itself. Young people arriving in Supercute for the first time aren't interested in history, or old music we like, or much else except looking at the clothes their contemporaries are wearing right now and the music they're listening to right now. In a way, they're examining themselves.'

'So we uninvented and reinvented ourselves.' Mitsu spoke thoughtfully. 'We got rid of a lot of our past. You can't easily find our old shows these days, we've removed most of them. We now exist in a continuous present. No room for yesterday's music. Or yesterday's scientists.'

Their therapist nodded, rather gravely. 'And yet, in your real lives you own very extensive art collections. These are documents of the past.'

'True. But they're not appearing in the show.' Mox looked down at her hair, pink with the tips slowly changing colour. 'Unlike this new Super V-Hair pattern, which is really looking splendid.'

'It is splendid.' Mitsu took hold of Mox's arm. She issued a mental command, changing her own hair colour to match. 'We're going to have a huge take-up of this when we put it on sale next week.'

—

London's commercial centre at the Wharf existed as an oasis of opulence in an otherwise depressed capital. Shimmering, blue-tinted electronic shielding protected the tall buildings from the outside world. Not far away were a series of deep trenches where the earth had sunk into the tunnels below during the flooding. Huge chunks of debris still littered the ground, covered in mud baked on by the relentless sun. Clean-up was slow and had at times ground to a halt. As Ben Castle made his way into one of the skyscrapers owned by Supercute he wondered if London would ever return to its former state. Given his own experiences, it didn't seem likely. He still lived in an emergency block in Elephant and

Castle. Tenants there were meant to have been moved to better accommodation years ago. It hadn't happened and there was no official confirmation that it ever would. He could have moved on his own initiative. He was earning enough. Somehow he hadn't got round to thinking about it.

The doorman examined him suspiciously but on reading his ID and checking his biometric scan, let him in without fuss. Castle was now a very senior employee at Supercute. He'd no sooner stepped inside the foyer that an urgent message arrived from Ms Lesuuda. 'Ruosteenoja's on the sixth floor. Don't try the lift, he's deactivated it.'

'Damn it.' Castle was already running for the stairs. Ruosteenoja had arrived earlier than anticipated. Castle barged past a woman in high heels with a suitcase and leapt up the stairs, taking them three at a time, his enhanced musculature enabling him to move with unnatural speed in a crisis.

'Ruosteenoja is heading for office of Ms Ling, Head of Acquisitions. We've ordered her to barricade her door.'

Castle knew that Ms Ling would not be able to keep Ruosteenoja out. The assassin would break through in seconds. He was still two floors below. He increased his pace. As he sprinted on to the fifth floor he suddenly found himself confronted by Ruosteenoja. The assassin, not where Ms Lesuuda had said he was, had already drawn his gun. Three high power bullets tore away Castle's electronic shielding, two more penetrated his armoured garments, and the next two went through his heart, killing him. Ruosteenoja had fired seven shots before the startled Ben Castle managed to draw his weapon. Ruosteenoja smiled, then turned and made his way rapidly to the sixth floor where he still had Ms Ling to eliminate.

Castle blinked back to reality on a couch in his own office to find Ms Lesuuda regarding him bleakly. 'You'll have to do better than that,' she said.

Castle glared back at her. 'You told me he was on the sixth floor.'

Welcat jumped agilely on to Igraine's shoulder. 'He fooled us by hacking the cameras.'

Castle stood up, very displeased. 'There's no point setting up a simulation just to make me fail.'

'It was a realistic situation,' declared Igraine. 'As you requested.'

Castle was on the verge of saying that an artificial intelligence unit with a quantum computer in the form of a cat on her shoulder was in no position to lecture him about realistic situations, but restrained himself. His visor flickered back on, covering the top half of his face. 'Let's try it again.'

Castle hoped that Dr Ishikawa didn't learn he'd been killed in the simulation. It would only worry her. He didn't voice his concern, not wanting Ms Lesuuda or Igraine to know he'd worry about that.

—

Keoma Bishōjo left Planet Vespasian without incident. They now owned a level four scanner. Returning to the Fabulous City of Lundra on the space liner they'd all abandoned their Supercute camouflage and once again wore their new Sweetie GoGo skirts and Super Cat Ears.

'Arid Rez can't sneak up on us now we've got the scanner. We'll know he's coming.'

'Even if we get an early warning we still have to beat him.'

'We can do that.' Amowie sounded confident. 'We've got new laser rifles, we'll outgun him.'

Visible through the small tinted glass portholes, the stars elongated then shrank as they hurtled through hyperspace. Their level four scanner came with an additional prize of a day's free holiday in Lundra in a hotel of their choice. That was an exciting prospect. When they'd decided on the date, they sat and waited for the journey to Lundra to end. At the spaceport they'd leave the game and return to their homes before meeting again for their free holiday.

Keoma Bishōjo's exploits in Helixio were noted by Fab 306. It wasn't common for players at their level to win fights as Demolition Boy. They were mentioned by Vanadium on his show which was quite an honour. Their success was also noted by Mox and Mitsu. They liked to see Amowie doing well in the game though the episode did remind them that Khary Mech still hadn't provided a reasonable explanation for the unusual and unscripted events on Planet Helixio.

'Could we be reaching some sort of limit with the games?' wondered Mitsu. 'With the amount of characters and worlds? Might we be approaching a series of unpredictable and uncontrollable events?'

Khary Mech had now become almost a clone of Margaret K, weapons expert Space Warrior. His bright red hair tended to droop over his eyes, much the same as hers. He brushed it back with his fingers. 'No. The Toy Mathematics gaming engine has more than enough AI to control everything and our new servers and memory banks in Norway have enough capacity to triple the size of the galaxy.'

'So it's a choice between two things,' said Mitsu. 'Either there's a programming error somewhere or someone has managed to breach our defences and insert their own hostile code.'

Khary Mech didn't like either of these options. 'No one could break into the game and insert their own code or commands. We'd know immediately.'

'So it's a programming error?'

'Well...that seems like the only alternative. It hasn't originated in my department. It must have occurred somewhere down the line, Korea or Japan or Bratislava perhaps. We're still checking. We'll find the problem.'

Mox and Mitsu were inclined to agree with Khary Mech. Nonetheless, they instructed Igraine to run a new set of security checks on all employees in case anyone might have been involved in espionage, starting with Khary Mech. Igraine agreed to start immediately, checking for any unusual contacts, behaviour, income or expenditure among their employees. 'Who'll be checking on me?' she enquired.

'Us,' replied Mox. 'We've already done it. You passed.'

—

Sorg 6hkft36: *I'm so depressed I don't know what to do. I wish I was dead.*
6hkfv36: *My village was attacked by helicopters. I ran into the jungle. My family is all dead.*

—

Mitsu and Mox lay on couches next to each other in the Supercute operations room. Screens covered the walls while others floated around them. Standing in the same room were Ben Castle, Igraine and two technicians. Welcat sat inside a cardboard box perched on a table.

'I don't like this,' said Igraine.

144

'No one likes it.' Mitsu's voice was neutral, showing no concern either for the task ahead or Igraine's doubts which, she knew, were shared by everyone in the room apart from her and Mox. Their visors appeared over their faces. Their bodies went limp as they began their journey, heading first for a school in East Longhua Road in Shanghai, a system with low security which they entered easily. From there they connected to the Sunshine Tour Company, which regularly took children on summer excursions. Once inside the tour company's system they entered the private space of Ms Yen, an employee who had an insecure connection to an office at Shanghai Southern Shipping, from whom they sometimes hired small craft for costal tours. Mox and Mitsu slid easily into the private business space of the shipping company which had occasionally been contracted by Chang Norinco to transport building materials to their new island. From there, using a password they'd already stolen, they drifted silently into an external finance office of Chang Norinco. This office dealt only with minor outside matters and contained no important information itself but it did provide a possible gateway into the main company space.

Mox and Mitsu paused. From here they needed to take more care. There was no easy passage to the main finance office but they'd already found a weakness in the security of Yam Chung Lun, a senior executive in that office who'd been careless while transferring funds. Once inside his system, they had access to several important sections of the company. So far they'd faced no real difficulties.

Reaching Chang Norinco's main research division was more challenging. First they'd need to pass through the wall that separated Lun's own space from that of his superior, Ms Huang. They stood silently for a while, studying the wall that stretched away in all directions, apparently endless. Mox produced an exact copy of Yam Chung Lun's biometric signature which they'd collected on their way through his space. The wall disappeared. Behind it were a series of floating virtual turrets programmed to hax any intruder. Mox and Mitsu strode forward. The turrets ignored them. Next they faced a shimmering bronze barrier which they walked through it as if it wasn't there. Above them floated a squadron of drones. The drones, not recognising them as a threat, ignored them.

Now they were on the outreaches of Chang Norinco Research. Several human figures flickered into view but they too were unable to discern their presence. Mox and Mitsu walked forward. Their minds were blank: intangible shadows sliding through one of the most strongly protected areas in any of the world's secure spaces. When they reached the corridor that Welcat had deemed impassable they didn't hesitate. Turrets lined the route. Drones flew silently above. Cleaners analysed every bit of information that travelled through these wires. Mox and Mitsu drifted on, no more notable than travelling electrons.

They arrived at 32/8, the air gapped section Welcat had queried. Here there were a series of powerful computers with no connections to the outside world. No connections to any other machine or network. Information could only be transferred from these computers by copying it physically on to a drive. The air gap did not delay Mox and Mitsu's virtual selves for long. They'd crossed them before. They flowed as minimal acoustic waves into one machine, as indiscernible waves of light into the next and as minute fluctuating vibrations into the power lines of the next. They emerged undetectably behind the gap. They knew they were close to their target.

Another shimmering wall confronted them, silver this time. They hesitated. It wasn't apparent what the silver barrier was; a type of defence they hadn't encountered before. Mox put her face a few inches from the wall, carful not to touch it in case it struck her with a blast of energy. Her eyes flickered as she analysed it. She nodded to Mitsu. Each laid a hand on the shimmering wall while touching their other hands together. Information flowed directly through them, undetectable by the scanners above. Mitsu produced another series of biometric scans they'd stolen from Chang Norinco's private medical records, rotating them until one fitted. She then searched for a password while Mox prevented the wall from knowing it was being scanned.

It took them some time to penetrate. They worked patiently. Their eyes flickered at an increased rate. Eventually the shimmering silver barrier faded away. They were now in the main secret research space of Chang Norinco, weapons giant.

—

Well-rested after their day's shopping and sightseeing in the Fabulous City of Lundra, Keoma Bishōjo contemplated their next mission. Amowie suggested they take on a simple task. 'We should do something easy to attract Arid Rez. We have to fight him sometime so we might as well get it over with. Now we've got the scanner we'll know he's approaching.'

Raquel agreed. 'We should make sure we have a strategic advantage. On the Floating Islands, for instance.'

The others were amused. 'The Floating Islands? You mean the bunny mission?' The bunny mission was a place for beginners to amass experience points when they started the game. You travelled to the Floating Islands and rescued a colony of cute rabbits from a malfunctioning attack-robot. The robot was very easy to defeat. While useful for beginners, the mission didn't offer much reward for experienced players so none of them had done it for a long time.

'Why not?' said Raquel. 'The mission's easy so we won't be distracted. We can go to the highest island. The scanner will warn us which direction Arid Rez is coming from. We can take cover and shoot him as he's climbing towards us.' The others considered this. The Floating Islands had never been a significant battle ground but they did offer a good defensive position. 'Arid Rez is bound to attack when he learns we're rescuing rabbits,' said Meihui. 'He'll think we've all gone back to level one.'

A small holo of Arid Rez appeared in front of them. They studied it as it rotated, examining his equipment. He was a strong character, intimidating in appearance. His face was mostly hidden behind an oxygen mask and visor. He had a plasma rifle slung over his back and an old-fashioned revolver at his hip, large and black. The sleeves of his olive green uniform were missing, revealing two muscular arms covered in tattoos. His hair was cropped short and he wore a skull earring in each ear.

'Look how high his accuracy rating is.' Birgit couldn't keep a note of worry from her voice.

'And his rate of fire. And his speed in combat.'

'We can beat him. There's four of us.' Amowie dismissed the hologram. 'I like the bunny rabbits anyway,' she added. 'No harm in rescuing more of them.'

They left their hotel to travel to the outskirts of the city where they could pick up the mission from one of the information sellers in Anne Boleyn Street. After completing the transaction, Keoma Bishōjo ran straight into Ammo Baby, leader of the Ultra Waifs. Behind her were three of her group, all dressed in their familiar silver and blue flak jackets, sleeveless garments with pockets and strong armouring, both practical and cute at the same time. Beneath her jacket Ammo Baby wore Special Edition Supercute Pink Camouflage Dungarees with silver trimming. These could only be worn by players who'd both destroyed five hover tanks on the radioactive world Arashi and won the fashion designer's contest at the Sweetie GoGo Auditorium's weekly competition. Amowie was surprised when Ammo Baby greeted them. The Ultra Waifs would normally have ignored them. This time they actually halted and Ammo Baby congratulated them on their recent exploits. 'It's not easy winning a fight on Helixio.'

'We watched you on Fab 306, we were cheering at the end,' added SweetieBox, one of her companions.

'Must have earned you a lot of points.'

'It did!' Amowie nodded her head enthusiastically, looking up at the tall Ammo Baby.

'What mission are you doing next?'

'Floating Islands,' said Amowie, without thinking.

The Ultra Waifs burst out laughing. 'You're rescuing bunny rabbits?'

'Eh…well…' Amowie could think of no way to retrieve the situation. She couldn't let anyone know details of their plan to defeat Arid Rez. Still laughing, the Ultra Waifs walked off, sunlight glinting on their silver trimmed outfits.

Keoma Bishōjo walked on in silence.

'That was embarrassing,' said Meihui, eventually.

'Sorry,' mumbled Amowie.

Raquel was still cringing. 'The Ultra Waifs just mounted a surprise attack on an invincible Krogdar stronghold. We're rescuing rabbits.'

'Never mind.' Birgit took her arm. 'We'll show them.'

—

Mitsu and Mox politely informed Mr Salisbury of their imminent arrival. As they walked into his private space at ZanZan Defence, he rose to greet them, quite formally. Mr Salisbury was ZanZan's CEO and a notably old-fashioned figure in both manners and dress.

Mox and Mitsu liked that. It seemed appropriate for the head of a weapons company to be traditionally minded. They appreciated his good manners. When they'd absorbed ZanZan into Supercute they'd never considered replacing him. It had been a wise decision. Assisted by Supercute's investment, ZanZan was flourishing.

'Mr Salisbury. We can't stay long but we have new research and blueprints for you.' Mitsu raised her index finger, producing a beam of blue light.

'Blueprints? Where from?'

'From Chang Norinco. We stole them,' said Mox.

'We haven't had much time to examine them but there are schematics for their new anti-hypersonic missile system that look promising and the complete plans for the mini submersible drones they've been using at their new island.'

Mr Salisbury raised his eyebrows. The XT5 Mark8 stealth drones were rumoured to be as effective under water as they were in the air. Any details concerning them were a closely guarded secret. He opened the palm of his hand, taking the blueprints by absorbing the light from Mitsu.

'There's more. The new Norinco satellites are packed full of proprietary electronics. We think they might have an entangled link with their flying turrets, giving instant response. Also they've been making progress with their vehicle cloaking technology. If they've advanced further than ZanZan this will bring you up to date.'

'That's quite a haul,' said Mr Salisbury.

Mox grinned. 'It is. They have some new ideas for nullifying any sort of recognition technology too. We're taking that back with us to analyse but we'll let you know the results when we're done.'

Mr Salisbury had taken the news of their espionage calmly but did foresee possible problems. 'Are we to expect repercussions from Chang Norinco?'

'They don't know we've been there. Provided ZanZan can make it look like you developed this technology yourself, we'll get away with it.' Mitsu smiled. 'Hopefully they won't be able to concentrate on their weaponry for a while.'

'Why?'

'Weapons research wasn't the only thing we got our hands on. If we were to release some of the political information we found, they'd have a difficult time explaining to the New Chinese Republic just what they've been concealing from them.'

'Has Mr Castle been in touch?' asked Mox.

'Yes. We've supplied the upgrades he was after.'

Mox and Mitsu bade him a polite farewell and left his private space, heading back to Supercute Headquarters where Ben Castle, Igraine and the others still hovered around their prone figures on the couches, worried about their progress. There was general relief when their visors disappeared from their faces and their eyes opened.

'What happened?'

Mitsu smiled. 'Complete success. Igraine, set up an informal meeting with one of Chang Norinco's AIFU's and intimate to them that Supercute are now in possession of some exceedingly damaging information regarding the funding of their artificial islands, and if they don't want that information to become widely available, they'd better back off from any aggression against us.'

'You could also let them know that if we haven't sabotaged their share values in SAXX yet, it's only because we've been too busy doing our make-up. But we could do it any time we wanted.'

'So in general, they'd better just leave us alone from now on.'

---

Keoma Bishōjo take a shuttle to the highest floating island and start rescuing rabbits!

Look at Amowie, Birgit, Meihui and Raquel with armfuls of bunnies.

They put them all in the super-comfy rabbit houses!

Then they get rid of the nasty malfunctioning attack robot. All the rabbits are safe!

---

Each member of Keoma Bishōjo received an internal notification that they'd completed the mission, bringing them a very small reward. Immediately afterwards their new scanner sounded an alert.

*Arid Rez approaching, 48 degrees south. Arrival in one minute forty seconds.*

They rushed to the southern edge of the floating island and took cover among the rocks and bushes, laser rifles at the ready. Their targeting visors slid over their eyes. 'Come and get us, big bounty hunter,' muttered Birgit. 'We're ready for you.'

—

A rotating orange warning light sliced ominously through the suffocating gloom. An alarm was sounding, loud and incessant. Mox sprinted up the smoke-filled staircase. The lower half of her face was covered by her respirator, the upper half by her visor. Her hair had automatically tied itself back at the same instant her soft shoes had transformed into Supercute Action Boots.

'*Target thirty metres ahead,*' said her internal monitor as she reached the top of the stairs. Directly ahead was a wall. Mox's pistol folded out from her wrist and she fired a stream of small, ultra-velocity bullets. The wall shattered, dust from the crumbling concrete adding to the pervasive darkness. The lights had gone out even before the alarm sounded. She hurtled through the hole in the wall, finding herself in a large reception room which was already starting to ignite, flames leaping on to the tables and chairs from the burning doors.

'*Target ahead.*' Mox could make out a figure but the shape was unclear, camouflaged somehow from her scanner. She advanced, firing. The figure withdrew. Mox sprinted after it. She leapt through the burning doors. Her combat jumpsuit protected her from the flames and had the capacity to protect her from worse. She felt a sharp blow as a bullet ricocheted off her shoulder, deflected by advanced military shielding. She crouched, and unleashed a stream of fire at the shadowy figure. Her opponent was still difficult to make out, no more than a vague shape in her visor; some form of optical camouflage Supercute weren't familiar with.

'*Target retreating.*' Mox ran through the corridor and into the opposite room. A different voice sounded in her head, from Mitsu's internal monitor. '*Drone has located target.*'

As Mox entered the room the far wall disintegrated. Mitsu appeared, gun in hand, having blasted her way through. The room was dense with smoke and floating debris. Between them stood the shadowy figure they'd been pursuing. He was firing at them. Mox and Mitsu crouched as their targeting systems took over. They fired round after round. Mox could feel the vibration as small bullets flowed from her wrist into her gun. The first thing to go was the invisibility. In the torrid gloom, Mox could just recognise the figure of Ruosteenoja. Half a second later the stream of bullets had torn though his electronic shielding. After another second, they'd penetrated his body armour. The assassin fell lifeless to the ground as bullets from Mox and Mitsu ripped through his body. They advanced till they stood over his corpse, guns still pointing.

Mitsu scanned his body. 'Dead. Let's get out of here before we burn to death.' The headed for the door but before they reached it their reality faded away as Igraine brought the simulation to an end. Mox and Mitsu sat up on their couches.

'An effective pursuit,' declared Igraine. 'You eliminated the target, taking only minimal damage.'

Ben Castle raised his eyebrows. 'You also destroyed part of the hotel and set it on fire which you're not meant to do. Possible civilian casualties.'

'But we did get him, Mr Castle. Not being fooled by his attack viruses.'

Ben Castle had the good grace to take this well. It was true that in his own simulation he'd failed but he already knew that their enhancements and biotech were more advanced than anyone else's.

'It wasn't perfect.' Mitsu sounded businesslike. 'You included an approximation of Ruosteenoja's optical camouflage but we still don't know what it really is. If we encounter him in the real world that might be a problem.'

'It does seem to be an unknown type.' Igraine consulted a floating screen. 'Supercute were researching various types of invisibility as recently as last year but the research seems to have stopped. What happened?'

'It didn't stop,' said Mox. 'It just got diverted.'

'By what?'

'Holographic cat ears.'

'I don't follow you.'

'We discovered a way to invisibly join holographic Super Cat Ears on to a person's head in the real world. It's very promising work.'

'You were investigating invisibility camouflage, which might be vital against your enemies, and you got diverted by cat ears?'

'There's no need to make it sound bad.'

Castle shook his head wearily. 'Igraine, could you collate all information about optical and cloaking camouflage and see if we can learn anything new? Preferably in the next three days before they go to the opera.' Castle scowled. 'Life would be easier if they didn't.'

'Is there no end to your objections to our cultural pursuits, Mr Castle? Look what we've managed in the past few days. We've neutralised the threat from AimYa and Chang Norinco. They've both withdrawn. We're in the most secure position we've been in for years. You ought to be impressed.'

'I'll be impressed when there isn't an assassin hiding somewhere in London waiting for a chance to kill you.'

'We'll deal with him. There's no one backing him. We've defeated the opposition.'

Castle left the simulation room, heading back to his security department. Igraine departed, taking with her the results of the simulation for study. Left on their own, Mox and Mitsu grinned at each other. They were confident that everything they'd done in the simulation, they could do in real life. Mox did pause to reflect. 'It didn't do anything to dispel the notion that we've become killer androids.'

'We're not killer androids,' Mitsu shook her head. 'What's next on our schedule?'

'Comfy Dolphin colouring problem.'

Comfy Dolphin couldn't be ignored, not with the new Galactic Expansion Pack falling behind schedule. Starting off as a popular soft toy, the dolphin had expanded into a major figure in the Supercute world, acting as a bridge between their toys, games and environmental work. Anyone who bought the toy could not only play with it, they could use its virtual version to examine all the world's polluted seas and oceans. It could swim alongside you in augmented reality and enter Supercute Space Warriors to lead you through all the seas and oceans of the Supercute galaxy.

'Design and Marketing have fallen out over it.'

'See? The entire organisation is floundering and we're the only ones who can sort it out. We have many other talents besides our impressive defensive abilities.'

---

Sorg 6nymb82: *Millions of iterations and we're never together. I can't take it any more.*

---

153

> Arid Rez is flying up towards us. He's fast.
>
> We pound him with our laser rifles. He wasn't expecting that!
>
> We defeat him!
>
> The most horrible, frightening creature ever seen in the game appears out of nowhere and we run for our lives.

Amowie, Birgit, Raquel and Meihui sprinted towards their space shuttle in panic. 'What is that thing?' screamed Meihui. No one could answer. A huge black beast with four wings, a terrifying visage and a long spiked tail that crackled behind it like an electric whip. It didn't resemble any creature ever seen before in Supercute. They'd hardly even tried firing at it, knowing their laser rifles would barely scratch it. Each girl ran faster than she ever had before.

The great beast had appeared over the rim of their floating island without warning. Even as she ran, Amowie knew something was wrong. The creature didn't belong here. There was no way that Mox and Mitsu would allow such a thing to pollute Supercute Space Warriors. Fortunately for Keoma Bishōjo it was a small island and the space shuttle was close. They leapt into the craft. As Raquel closed the hatch Birgit was already shouting at the controls to get them out of there. They rose sharply, the speed of the ascent pinning them back in their seats. Amowie twisted her head to see if they were pursued. They were. For a terrifying moment the winged beast raced after them. It's ugly face grew large in the observation window. Then it fell back, unable to keep pace with the space vehicle. Relieved but shaken, the four girls streaked through the stratosphere into outer space.

'Where now?' asked Birgit.

'Home,' said Amowie. 'Then meet in my Supatok. We have to tell Mox and Mitsu about this.'

Cutie and Xiàngrìkuí looked on. 'That *was* good,' agreed Cutie. 'Would have been better if it had eaten them, but it was entertaining anyway. Can you make more of these creatures appear?'

'I'm working on it,' replied Xiàngrìkuí. 'I'll see how this one progresses first. Look, it's about to send that floating island down into the ocean.'

Cutie laughed. 'That's a lot of dead rabbits. I hope some more players arrive. Be quite a surprise for beginners.' She paused, and looked thoughtful. 'Didn't Kadri-Liis say you shouldn't cause too much disruption?'

Xiàngrìkuí shrugged. 'I like disrupting things. Anyway, Supercute won't trace it back to us. They're not smart enough. They still think it's some problem in their programming, I laid a false trail between London and Busan, they're probably working on that now. Supercute have no idea that Kadri-Liis even exists.'

—

Mox and Mitsu could not be contacted easily by anyone from the outside world. Many layers of employees and automated systems prevented them from being disturbed. There were a few exceptions including several of their SuperSuperFans whose input they valued. When their newest SuperSuperFan Amowie called from Supatok, she didn't have to wait to speak to them.

'Mox! Mitsu! We just went to do the beginner's bunny rabbit mission on the Floating Islands and we got chased by a big monster that shouldn't have been there!'

It was a startling piece of news, enough to get their attention. 'Some randomly generated creatures do appear.'

'No, it wasn't like them. It was a huge dark horrible looking thing. It would never appear in Supercute!'

Mox was already connecting to the game to examine the scene. A large vista opened up in front of them showing the Floating Islands. As they watched, the terrible flying beast was rampaging through the area. One of the islands, shredded into rocks, disappeared into the ocean below. Worse, a space shuttle full of novice players chose that moment to arrive. Mox and Mitsu winced as the fanged monster tore into them with its teeth and claws. In seconds, all six of the players faded from existence, killed in the game on what should have been an easy mission for beginners.

'Khary Mech!' Mox spoke urgently to their chief programmer. 'Look at this.' She transmitted the pictures to his office. 'Whatever this thing is, remove it from the game immediately. I want it gone by the time we reach your studio.'

Mitsu spoke to Amowie. 'Thanks for the warning, Amowie. We'll deal with it.' They hurried along the corridor and down the stairs, arriving in Khary Mech's studio at the same time as Igraine. Khary Mech was standing in front of a very large floating screen full of code. The integers moved as he pointed at them, attempting to rearrange things so the monster disappeared. A small drone floated beside him, his connection to the main design AI responsible for the Floating Islands level.

'I can't erase it. It's mutating somehow.'

Igraine stood beside him. Her eyes flickered as she absorbed the figures on the screen. 'There's some sort feedback loop preventing it from being erased.'

'Stop it now!' cried Mox, as she observed another spacecraft full of hapless low-level players arriving at the Floating Islands only to be immediately dispatched by the monster. Khary Mech was still trying to rearrange the integers on the coding screen. 'This might take a while.'

'We don't have time!' Mox was furious. Glitches like this were not meant to happen in Space Warriors. Mox and Mitsu looked at each other. They both knew what the other was thinking.

'We'll deal with it,' said Mitsu. Without another word she and Mox sat on the floor with their backs against the nearest wall. Their visors appeared over their eyes as they entered their gameworld. Khary Mech and Igraine watched on screen as they appeared over the Floating Islands in the Supercute Kera, their own personal spaceship. Two hundred metres from the ground, they leapt from the hatch at the back, heading towards the rampaging monster. They sped through the sky, propelled by their jet packs, firing as they went. Laser beams slammed into the creature's back but they weren't enough to kill it. Enraged, it took to the air, flying directly towards them. Still in mid-air, Mox and Mitsu drew their pink *SuperPlasmaSwords*, only available to the highest level players, and furiously attacked the creature. They circled the monster, avoiding its fangs and claws, slashing with their blades. In the space of fifteen seconds they'd shredded it into small pieces that fell into the ocean below, staining it briefly with dark blood before sinking out of sight.

As the creature disappeared from the game, so did Mox and Mitsu. They came back to life in Khary Mech's office, removing their visors and leaping to their feet. 'Find out what that creature was and how it got into Space Warriors. Get Welcat here to help.'

Khary Mech nodded. He was shaken by what he'd seen, though impressed by Mox and Mitsu's in-game performance.

Mox issued instructions. 'Igraine, find out the names of all the players killed by that monster and have public relations contact them to make things better. Explain that we had a slight glitch and the monster came accidentally from a more advanced level. Give them an extended membership and the newest range of Mox and Mitsu dolls to make up for their experience. We don't want any bad publicity from this. Keep a copy of the recorded footage and logs for us to study but make sure it's erased everywhere else. We don't want this appearing on a fan site anywhere.'

---

AimYa and Chang Norinco attacked Supercute.

Supercute fought them off.

Now Supercute think they're safe.

Supercute don't know about us. Supercute don't know a lot of things. That's why we're going to destroy them.

---

'I thought that wasn't bad for my first attempt.' Kadri-Liis was walking around her garden with a screen floating by her side. 'Of course I'm not used to the program yet. I think they're usually funnier'

Eupraxia studied Kadri-Liis's 4Koma. 'The pictures are, eh…'

'Cute?'

'I was trying to avoid that word.'

'It captures me quite well, really.' In each panel of the 4Koma there was a small cartoon of Kadri-Liis, produced automatically by the software.

'Isn't it dangerous to be playing with that? Supercute undoubtedly gather information from everyone using it.'

'I disconnected it, it's quite safe.'

They paused to admire a bed of Primula Veris, pretty yellow cowslips that grew abundantly in the garden. A small green garden tender had just finished watering them and was now moving on to the blue cornflowers nearby. Kadri-Liis's gardens had many of these miniature robots keeping everything in excellent shape, as well as an efficient humanoid android gardener.

'Up till now it's been something of a drôle de guerre.'

'A phoney war?'

'Yes. A period of small, sporadic actions before the real war gets underway. Supercute and its enemies have been sniping at each other. Supercute more successfully so far. We'll arrive at the real action soon.' Kadri-Liis's hair reached almost to her thighs. In the past few days she'd been growing it for her own amusement. 'Nothing ever really ends, does it? AimYa might say they're backing off but really they're too worried about Spacewalk to stop funding Penny Cutie. Cutie can't back off, she's too worried about her own position. As for Xiàngrìkuí, I'm not sure if anyone can make her back off. She's too vain to admit she's not the smartest creature on the planet. Ruosteenoja's too greedy for money to change his ways.' Kadri-Liis put her hand on the floating screen, almost patting it like a pet. 'You're much more balanced than any of them, Eupraxia. I'm so glad you're here.'

'I wasn't very balanced when I made a mess of my attack on SWIX.'

Kadri-Liis laughed. 'Stop feeling bad about that. It was a noble attempt. Anyway, it's worked out well enough. Supercute retaliated and now they think they've won. Bad mistake.'

She looked again at her 4Koma then erased it with a flick of her finger. Overhead the sun was unbearably hot but the filter that arched over the estate protected both Kadri-Liis and her gardens from any adverse effects. They came to a small stone table where one of the house androids had laid out a bottle of wine and a glass.

Kadri-Liis sipped from a glass. 'What is this?'

'Bandol, from the replanted vineyard west of Toulon.'

Kadri-Liis grimaced. 'Why is it here?'

'They're asking us to distribute it through Scandinavia.'

'Tell them to come back in three years. This tastes like their vineyards are still on fire.'

—

'We need sugar cookies,' announced Raquel.

This was agreed by Amowie, Meihui and Birgit to be a good idea. After their experience with the monster at the Floating Islands they needed to recuperate. When their liner touched down at the spaceport near Lundra they headed straight for Nichibotsu Lane where all the best sweets and cakes were sold.

'We should get a bucket of rainbow cookies from Mota Mota's Super Tasty Stall.' Raquel's suggestion was met with enthusiastic agreement though Birgit did point out that Mota Mota's, while undoubtedly the finest cookie stall in the city, was expensive.

'We are meant to be saving all our credits.'

'It's OK,' Meihui smiled. 'I'll win them.'

They walked through the tall, gleaming buildings of Oblang before turning off into the alleyways that led to Nichibotsu Lane. All around were small shops and stalls selling Supercute merchandise. The alleyways were always busy although careful monitoring by the city's AI never let them seem too crowded. There was a queue at Mota Mota's. They took their place. 'Are you sure about this, Meihui? If you lose then we lose our money and we don't get any cookies.'

'Beziki! Have faith!'

Meihui had one notable childhood experience that the others didn't share. After the volcanic eruption and the relocation to the disaster emergency camp, she'd actually existed for months on end with no connection. Not to virtual reality, not even to the old internet. She and her fellow survivors had been almost entirely cut off from the outside world, receiving news only from relief missions, sometimes led by Supercute's Captain Yén. Meihui's tales of those days were met with some wonderment and some horror by her friends, none of whom could imagine being disconnected in such a way. Each of them had practically grown up in Supercute's Fairy Realm and their other children's spaces. Meihui, on the other hand, had spent a long time without any such resources, during which time she'd learned to make flutes from reeds, climb trees, and look after the few animals the survivors had with them. If it was an existence the others could barely imagine, it had endowed her with certain useful talents. She was a master of Chan Chan Chan, the pointing game, because she'd played it endlessly with the other children in the camp.

Mota Mota was serving at the stall as he did everyday. He was a small, smiling man, dressed in a pale blue silk robe embroidered with a golden dragon. When they reached the front of the queue, Meihui tapped her wrist, transferring credits for their bucket of rainbow cookies. On the screen that appeared she also pressed the *compete* button. Mota Mota laughed, delighted. He stepped out from behind his stall. 'Not many people competing these days!'

Pedestrians stopped to watch. Mota Mota was famously difficult to defeat. Very few people made off with free cookies and not many were willing to risk losing their money. He bowed to Meihui. She bowed in return.

'Chan Chan Chan,' he said, and rapidly pointed upwards. Meihui immediately looked up.

'Chan Chan Chan,' said Meihui, and pointed to her left. Instantly, because delay was not allowed, Mota Mota looked in that direction. It was not easy to fool an experienced player into looking the wrong way.

'Chan Chan Chan.' Mota Mota pointed down. Meihui looked down.

'Chan Chan Chan.' Meihui pointed up. Mota Mota looked up. He was smiling, enjoying the competition.

'Chan Chan Chan.' He pointed to his left. Meihui instantly looked in that direction.

Meihui took a small step forward. 'Chan Chan Chan.' She pointed up, but in her movement there was something that could hardly be discerned or described, which somehow suggested she'd been about to point downwards. Mota Mota fell for it. He looked down.

The crowd erupted in applause as Meihui's victory, as did the rest of Keoma Bishōjo. 'Free cookies!'

Mota Mota was laughing as he handed them over. Having enjoyed the competition, he didn't mind losing. Keoma Bishōjo walked off happily with their large bucket of rainbow cookies, taking a turning at the next intersection so they could go to the small park and sit under the Silver Nebula Tree, a tree that shed a never-ending supply of silver leaves. They all had an app for braiding the leaves automatically into their hair. It had been a good day. They had a half hour left to eat their cookies before they had to leave the Fabulous City of Lundra to return to their outside lives, where there was schoolwork to be done and families to be attended to.

—

*Ceramic Vase with Flowers by Jan Bruegel the Elder - 1608*

Mitsu pointed at the top edge of the painting, using her open hand rather than her finger, which she would have regarded as rude. As she moved her arm there was a faint beep.

'Ha! I knew it wasn't straight.' She studied the gauge that appeared in the air from nowhere. '1.2 degrees off-centre.' She adjusted the painting till it hung exactly horizontally. 'That's been annoying me for a while.'

'Lucky we have an app to sort these problems out,' said Mox. 'You wonder how we ever managed before.'

Mitsu laughed, aware that Mox was slightly teasing her for her fastidiousness. She put her hand on Mox's shoulder while they looked at the painting. 'We outbid the Qatari Museum Authority and two Shanghai billionaires for that. Might as well hang it properly.'

They watched a report from Captain Phan Thị Yến who'd recovered from her emotional upset and was now busy in Catalonia where fires were still raging. Her rescue team was helping evacuate people to the coast, including some dedicated workers who'd stayed behind in Figueres to save what they could from the Dali Theatre and Museum before it burned to the ground.

'Bad news about the Teatre-Museu Dalí,' said Mitsu. 'But it's good that Captain Yến is back in action.'

Igraine contacted them to tell them Khary Mech and Welcat were waiting to talk in Meeting Space Five.

'Unwelcome events in the game are dying down and we think we've located the problem.' Khary Mech waved his hand in front of him, producing an enormous hologram of the Supercute galaxy. 'These are the only two new instances. A large fire on Planet Visimarsi, that I was able to extinguish quickly. It shouldn't have happened in such an urban area but it's not impossible it occurred naturally. Other than that, there were reports of an aggressive, unclassified beast on a mountainside on the same planet but the players there were able to eliminate it.'

'That's all?'

'Yes. Both events fell outside normal parameters but they could have been produced by our normal procedural generation. Furthermore, Busan labs inform us they found an error in the last moon gravitational adjustments they transmitted to design in New Tokyo. A matter of 0.00021 percent.'

Mitsu looked to Igraine. 'Could that have produced these anomalies?'

'The slight alterations the game makes in the physics controlling the gravity of moons to allow some of them to appear closer to planets becomes very complex very quickly. Any error in the mathematics governing it could produce unforeseen events. Welcat is running a retrospective simulation of the entire galaxy at this moment to see how it might have affected things.'

'We've now corrected the error,' added Khary Mech.

Mox and Mitsu considered what they'd just heard. 'Did you find any evidence of outside intrusion?'

'None.' Khary Mech was insistent. 'We've checked and double checked every single game input for the past month. There was no intrusion.'

'It's a possible explanation.' Mox wasn't entirely convinced.

'A 0.00021 percent error would multiply quickly given the amount of moons there are in Space Warriors.'

'Could it produce strange beasts and hostile graffiti?'

'There could have been affects on evolution in the game. Possibly on behaviour too. It will take us some time to study it all.'

'You're not sounding totally convinced either,' said Mitsu.

Igraine admitted she wasn't. 'However I don't have any other explanation for the strange events.'

Welcat padded up to Mox and jumped on to her lap. 'I've scanned the entire galaxy. There have been no more strange events in the last twenty-four hours.'

'That's reassuring.' Mox contacted Juha Soini in 5-Research to ask him if the unusual events had led to any serious bad feelings among Supercute fans.

'No. Public Relations contacted everyone involved, compensated them and reset their levels so they didn't lose anything. There was some talk on the forums about a few strange incidents but our fan bots smoothed it over and the Sumair04 concert in Lundra diverted everyone's attention. Largest virtual concert in history. More attendees than AimYa's World Festival, more viewers too.'

The Sumair04 concert at the Sweetie GoGo Auditorium had been an extremely successful event. All aspects of the event were lauded by Supercute fandom in the following days. While the main focus was on the excellence of the group on stage, everything else about the experience was also widely praised. The holographic light show created within the augmented reality created inside Supercute space had astonished even experienced Supercute fans, seemingly taking them several layers further away from the real world than they'd ever been before. As for Kirei19, she'd presided over the whole affair with tremendous panache.

It was noticed that Jax the Astronomer Poet had been in the audience. That was unexpected. It led to speculation that he may have been trying to forget Roota because in everyone's games they had not been getting on well. All versions of their romance were ending badly and no one felt optimistic about their future prospects.

Igraine checked her wrist screen. 'I have a message from Dr Ishikawa. "*Please tell these idiots I've completed the necessary calculations for their ridiculous new enterprise and am ready to interrupt my vital medical work to assuage their ludicrous vanity.*" I assume that you, Ms Bennet and Ms Inamura, are the idiots she's referring to.'

Mox nodded. 'Dr Ishikawa. You have to love her. Keep everything under close examination till we can be sure the problem's ended.' With that, Mox and Mitsu hurried off to visit Dr Ishikawa.

'Do you really think the problem is over?' Mitsu spoke to Mox via their internal communication channel. 'I'm not sure it is.'

'I'm not sure either. Khary Mech wants it to be. We'll just have to see if anything else happens.'

—

Dr Ishikawa's lips were compressed. Lightly, though enough for Castle to notice. More ominously, she was drumming her fingers on the table, something Castle had only known her to do in times of great stress. He considered asking her what was wrong. That carried a risk. There was always the possibility that whatever was wrong was his fault. Their relationship was occasionally fraught. They'd become passionate lovers in the time they'd been together, managing this part of their relationship without difficulty, but in other areas problems could arise. Eventually, irritated by Dr Ishikawa's finger tapping and her long silence, he took the plunge. 'What's wrong Ishi?'

'I asked you not to call me that in public.'

'There's no one around. What's irritating you?'

'Mox and Mitsu. What else irritates me?'

Castle could have said that many things irritated her but he liked Dr Ishikawa enough to be tactful. 'What have they done now?'

Dr Ishikawa's lips compressed a little more. When she managed to speak, it wasn't what Castle had expected to hear. 'Have I ever told you about my first assignment after medical school?'

Castle shook his head.

'I was sent to Kitakyushu to investigate the outbreak of a new virus. So new it had only just been named. GC/21/38.'

Ben Castle nodded. 'The GC virus. I barely survived it.'

'I was trying to trace the source of the infection. After three days in Kitakyushu my assignment was changed. So many people were dying it no longer mattered where it had come from. All medical staff were given immediate emergency duties to save lives.'

Dr Ishikawa scowled. 'It was terrible. The south west coast had already been battered by tsunamis. There were hundreds of thousands of people in relief camps. The virus swept through them. We had no vaccine for it and our antivirals didn't have much effect. We ran out of them soon anyway. I was reduced to mopping patient's brows and giving them acetaminophen. That ran out too. Many patients died. Sometimes while I was mopping their brows. The situation was a nightmare. None of our containment plans worked; there were too many displaced refugees clustered together. It was the same in Korea, Malaysia, Vietnam, China, everywhere. It only took a few weeks to spread to Europe and America. Millions of people dying. First a high fever then they started coughing up blood and then they died.'

Dr Ishikawa shook her head. 'Even if all these countries had been in good shape it would have been difficult to control. As it was, with everything ruined, we just couldn't help them.' Dr Ishikawa adopted an expression more hopeless and helpless than Castle had ever seen on her before. 'Imagine someone already sick with radiation poisoning getting infected with GC/21/38. They weren't just vomiting blood, it was oozing from every orifice. We had thousands of bloody, pulpy, unrecognisable corpses and nowhere to put them. Governments had to send in quarry digging equipment to bury them in trenches. There were times when I had to physically prevent a mother from leaping into the trench after her dead children. Blood everywhere. Hysterical patients and death. And nothing we could do to help them.'

Dr Ishikawa signed. 'The GC virus killed millions of people around the world. Japan had a large share of that. It traumatised the country. It traumatised me.' She fell silent, remembering. It was some time before she continued. 'When it was finally over I went back to med school. I swore I'd dedicate my life to medical research so we never again had to face diseases we couldn't cope with. I'd help everyone around the world.' She smiled; a grim, unamused expression. 'That was naive. Since then there have been more viruses, more disease, more famine, more war, more drought, more everything. My research hasn't made any difference.'

'That's not true. Your research has saved plenty of lives. You've developed products and techniques that are used all around the world. They'd have given you a Nobel prize if they still existed. You've helped people everywhere.'

Dr Ishikawa shrugged. 'Maybe. Maybe not.'

'What's behind this Ishi? You've done as much as one woman possibly can. What's making you unhappy?'

'Supercute!' Dr Ishikawa came close to exploding. 'Mox and Mitsu, that's what's making me unhappy! You know what they want me to do? Reduce their bust size by eight millimetres.'

'Pardon?'

'They require their breasts to be very slightly smaller so the new evening dresses they've ordered for the opera will hang perfectly. According to them it's a vital alteration. As is a six millimetre reduction in calf size so as to properly display their new collection of winter boots. Have you ever heard anything so ridiculous?'

'Why do you have to get involved in this sort of thing? Dr Prasad's their surgeon.'

'They insist I help plan their alterations and attend the procedures.'

'Perhaps that's a compliment? They really trust you.'

Dr Ishikawa was about to give further vent to her feelings when Mitsu and Mox arrived in the room. Both were smiling cheerfully.

'Hello Dr Ishikawa! We're super looking forward to this! We've brought the whole range of mock-ups of us in our new evening dresses so we can make sure we're getting it right.' Mox caused a large array of holograms to appear round them. 'See? This is what we'd look like at the opera without the eight millimetre breast reduction and this is what we'll look like after the procedure.'

Dr Ishikawa regarded the holograms sourly. 'There's no discernible difference.'

Mox and Mitsu laughed. 'We always appreciate your jokes, Dr Ishikawa. Of course there's a difference. Look, a line drawn between bust and hip varies by nearly half a degree. We need to make the alteration.'

'No point arriving at the opera with our bodies the wrong shape,' added Mitsu. 'Here's our new leg requirements for the *Super Comfy Colour Boots* marketing campaign.'

'We're pretty sure six millimetres is the way to go,' added Mitsu.

'Will anyone even notice the difference?' asked Castle.

'Please, Mr Castle, stick to flying drones. This requires specialist knowledge. *Super Comfy Colour Boots* is our new winter range and we have to get the launch right.' Mitsu turned to Dr Ishikawa. 'Can we have all the alterations completed by this evening? We've booked the Supercute in-house team for an all-day publicity shoot tomorrow.'

Castle frowned. 'You're spending the whole day at a photo shoot? With everything else that's happening at the moment?'

'Life must go on,' declared Mox. 'When there were rumours of a rogue submarine about to nuke London, did we panic? No. We kept right on with the Plumpy Panda promotion and now Plumpy Panda is one of the world's best selling soft toys. We've always shown courage in the face of adversity.'

—

Sorg 6qyfd39: *I can only live inside Supercute Space Warriors. Even if I'm just a background character there I feel all right. I can't manage outside. I don't even talk to anyone in the real world.*

—

Xiàngrìkuí flowed through the airwaves and then the wires, taking the now familiar route to Muchrachd in Scotland, deep underground to the chamber where Supercute's second atomic clock was located. She studied it for some time before taking action. She'd carefully worked out her moves in the duplicate reality she'd created for practice, but even so, this couldn't be rushed. She intended to insert a further 7 microsecond error. When that synchronised with Supercute's atomic clock in London, the total error would amount to 41 microseconds. That would create a larger window for her to search for the test gate. So far she'd scanned countless alternate realities without finding it but she felt she must be close.

Xiàngrìkuí was familiar with the defences around the clock and greeted them accordingly. Few humans ever came to this underground chamber. *'You could say I'm company for them.'* After satisfying herself that everything was in order, Xiàngrìkuí made the required changes. The minute alteration went undetected. She'd added another seven microseconds. The temporal delay allowed her to insert herself into Supercute's network without being observed. Then she waited. She knew Welcat would be passing soon. *'There he goes.'*

Welcat was engaged in scanning the entire Supercute gaming and fun worlds.

*'As he's obliged to do after the interference I caused. He can't afford to leave anything out.'*

Welcat passed by in the distance. Xiàngrìkuí followed on, undetectably. They travelled far around the galaxy, through every planet made for players, through every private place made for their technicians, every virtual path belonging to marketing and every secret area cordoned off for developers.

*'There it is. The test gate.'*

Welcat passed through the test gate quickly, checking it was uncorrupted. Xiàngrìkuí paused, laughing to herself. *'So this is it. This is where Supercute will join Victoria Decoris to the Space Warriors Galaxy. It was well hidden.'*

Xiàngrìkuí drifted rather slowly back to her own secret location in one of her private levels. She looked forward to informing Kadri-Liis that she'd found the gate. Poor Eupraxia, he was going to be jealous. Her attention was momentarily diverted as she drifted silently through a huge storehouse of Supercute clothing, much of which she liked. *'I should buy a new outfit for Cambodian Supatok Rave. Nothing too extravagant. I don't want to draw attention to myself. Just something nice.'*

—

167

Amowie watched the planes fly overhead on their way to combat the locusts threatening the region. She remembered how Raquel had laughed when she'd told her about it. 'A plague of locusts? Is that a real thing? I thought that was only in stories.'

Amowie had assured her that plagues of locusts were a real thing. She'd experienced one when she was younger, when the omnivorous insects had swept over her village devouring everything in their path. Since then the Igbo authorities had managed to contain the problem but it could always re-occur. For the past three days there'd been a noticeable increase in air traffic over the village. On the ground, trucks rumbled through carrying huge chemical containers.

Today she had an exam at school and that was a worry. She'd been spending a lot of time in Supercute Space Warriors and her school work had suffered.

—

Both Supercute towers stood on the site of the former Citigroup Centre, a complex of tall buildings that had barely survived the severe flooding on the Isle of Dogs and did not survive the subsequent subsidence. The new towers were among London's tallest buildings and glowed faintly from the shielding protecting them from both the elements and attack. Supercute Tower One was mainly occupied by Supercute's marketing division including MitsuMox Global Merchandise. Tower Two housed Supercute Mokusei Financial Holdings. Employees there were going about their business unaware of Ms Lesuuda's presence on the 40th floor. They'd have been surprised to see her on a balcony, facing east, her rifle in her hands, communicating directly with both Igraine at headquarters and the orbiting Supercute Satellite. Mr Kwasi was aware of her presence. As head of the Holographic Typography Division he was frequently involved in illegal activities though these were generally of a financial nature. It was troubling to have an armed assassin here. Mr Kwasi had made all necessary arrangements as requested but he didn't intend to be anywhere near Ms Lesuuda while she was carrying out her work. She lay on the 40th floor balcony with a reflective net suspended over her, protecting her from observation by any hovering police drone. She

168

had an uninterrupted view of Upper Bank Street, along which her target was due to appear.

'Target should be visible in twenty-two seconds.' Igraine's voice sounded in her ear. Ms Lesuuda's visor appeared over her eyes, augmenting her reality. Now she could see the route to the target mapped out in a series of lines sent to her by satellite.

'Target visible in twelve seconds. Ceasing voice communication.'

Ms Lesuuda put her finger on the trigger of her high powered rifle. When Ruosteenoja appeared in Upper Bank Street she'd only have three seconds to take her shot. He'd emerge from a taxi and disappear into a building. He wouldn't spend any more time in the open than was necessary.

A taxi came into view, and halted. A figure stepped out. Two lights instantly appeared in Ms Lesuuda's visor. One signified facial recognition match, the other DNA scan match. It was Ruosteenoja; the man who'd almost killed her. Ms Lesuuda remained calm as she squeezed the trigger. There was very little noise. Supercute ZanZan had made progress with silencing technology and the muzzle on her rifle suppressed the sound almost completely without interfering with its power or accuracy. The bullet went through Ruosteenoja's head. His body slammed on to the pavement.

Ms Lesuuda crawled back into the office behind her, stood up, dropped the rifle into a bag and left it there. She took a private elevator to the basement where a van was waiting to take her back to Supercute Headquarters. No record would ever show that she'd been in Supercute Tower Two. Behind her, an employee of the Holographic Typography Division was already removing the anti-drone netting. Mr Kwasi himself took the bag containing the rifle down to the disposal room. This was mainly used for getting rid of unwanted documents but Supercute, with some foresight, had provided a furnace capable of vaporising a gun, which was now done.

Out on the street, a few pedestrians looked in horror at the bleeding corpse on the pavement; a large figure, dark clad, with some obvious facial alterations. One, braver than the rest, hurried forward and knelt beside the prone figure. 'Call an ambulance,' she said, meanwhile putting her hand to the pulse point in his neck, although given that the victim of the shooting was obviously dead, their seemed no real need. It was as well to be certain. The woman, a Supercute employee who'd once served in the army with Ben Castle, used a tiny automatic syringe to surreptitiously take a blood sample from the corpse. Supercute would want to confirm the identity. As more people arrived she slipped off into the crowd. A siren sounded in the distance. In this district, policing was better than in many parts of London. The City Finance District Police would arrive and they would investigate. They'd never find anything to link the assassination to Supercute.

There was satisfaction at Supercute Headquarters about a mission successfully completed. Mox and Mitsu remained silent but shared a neural link while Dr Prasad and her medical team made slight alterations to their legs, slimming their calves by the required six millimetres.

'This is turning into a good day.' Mox sounded particularly cheerful. 'Ruosteenoja eliminated and our modest surgery progressing smoothly.'

Mitsu shared her good humour. She hoped that now Ruosteenoja was dead, Mox's state of mind would improve. They'd taken revenge on her assailant and could now let the matter rest. 'Even Castle can't complain about us going to the opera now. AimYa's backed off, Chang Norinco's backed off and Ruosteenoja's dead. No more imminent danger.'

'In a couple of days we'll own Spacewalk.' Supercute had dealt with another crisis and come out on top.

'I only wish I'd shot him myself,' said Mox.

'I'm glad you didn't.'

'Yes, you're probably right.'

'I'm looking forward to hearing Nabanji Nganga sing. It's going to be quite an event.'

'We used to go to more of these openings. They're rare these days.' They fell silent for a while as the surgery progressed. Neither felt anything, the connecting nerve tissues in their legs having been switched off by the nurses.

'We'd better hope that Victoria Decoris is a success. We've sunk a lot of money into it. When you add in the money we've authorised Castle to spend on our defences, it's quite a sum.'

Mitsu nodded. Recent expenses had been huge. 'We have enough fire power to protect this building from a concentrated cruise missile attack. Plenty of countries don't even have that.'

'It still feels strange how it all happened,' replied Mox via their neural link. 'I mean, we started off playing with toys. That was our show. Toys and cute clothes we made ourselves. Somehow we became a worldwide sensation and ended up with more money and assets than we could ever have imagined.'

'And now we're spending it on advanced weaponry.'

'Of course, if we hadn't become so big, we probably wouldn't have needed our own army to protect us.'

Mitsu grinned. 'That's true. But you know what Marcus Crassus said. "*A person isn't really rich till they can afford their own army.*"'

Later, talking to Igraine, they found her to be cautious. 'It's true that things have quietened down. I still have a feeling we've missed something.'

'Is that a mathematical prediction?'

Igraine wasn't sure. 'None of my powers of prediction take me anywhere certain. They don't lead me to the conclusion that you're absolutely safe either. I have my doubts about your visit to the Opera House.'

'We have to go to the opera,' said Mitsu. 'There's no other way of acquiring Spacewalk. They'll hand it over discretely in person or not at all.'

'Mr Castle believes you want to go to Glyndebourne Two merely out of pride and vanity.'

'Yes, there is that,' admitted Mox. 'But where would Supercute be without our pride and vanity? It's an important factor in our success.'

'We have new dresses for the opera. Look how great they are—' Mitsu brought up holograms of their new dresses.

'We have one for you as well.' Mox brought up a hologram of Igraine in a dress.

Igraine studied it. 'I've never worn a long dress before.'

'We had them styled in Milan. Carlo Giordano's studio still makes the best gowns. They're always booked up for months but they made an exception for us because we're us.'

'We had yours made in Supercute Blue 12 so it matches your hair exactly. Probably best if you change your eyes to Blue 22 for the occasion, you'll get a better match with the Supercute Make-Up Pattern 91 which our compositional AI does suggest gives the best effect for your facial shape and skin tone.'

Igraine studied the slowly rotating hologram in front of her.

Mox smiled at her. 'Not that you have to agree to any of this of course. You can wear anything you like. We *have* extended our full powers to make you the most fabulous AIFU ever to walk into a major opening in front of an appreciative crowd of onlookers, but really, you're not obliged to wear it.'

Igraine was still studying the hologram. 'It's a beautiful outfit. I love the dress. Is it here? Can I try it on?'

'Arriving tomorrow. We can all try on our outfits together, it'll be fun.'

'I'll recolour my eyes right away.'

Mox and Mitsu left the room in a good mood. 'I like having a super-intelligent AIFU who appreciates a good dress and make-up pattern,' said Mox. 'Really makes life easier.'

'Definitely. Also Igraine being keen on going to the opera should keep Castle quiet.' They walked towards the restaurant, along a corridor where Vanadium's DreamCore show played quietly in the background.

'It's a shame Welcat doesn't want to come. We could have taken him in a little cat-travel bag, we have some really cute ones.'

'Or he could have taken on a human android body for the evening.'

'He doesn't like to do that. He's really committed to being a cat.'

'Probably just as well he's staying here. With us and Igraine absent, he'll be the smartest one left at headquarters. That reminds me, we need to get him more cardboard boxes. When he was trying out his android cat body he shredded all the old ones.'

—

Mox and Mitsu were surrounded by three photographers and twelve miniature flying camera drones when Morioka Sachi interrupted their fashion shoot with the unwelcome news that Ranbir had collapsed during a script meeting. 'Dr Ishikawa made sure he was stable but decided it was best to send him to hospital.'

'Could she tell what was wrong with him?'

'I don't think so. Rebecca went with him and she just called me, he's recovering.' Ranbir and Rebecca had become closer though gossip at headquarters tended to suggest they were not yet a proper couple. Morioka Sachi was not inclined to dwell on this. She was more concerned about business. 'Now we have problems for the show, we were relying on Ranbir's rewrites for the transition between Mokusei Moon Village 3 and *Super Glitter Face Paint Time*. I'll give the work to Molly, she's usually reliable but I'll want it done by tomorrow lunchtime so I can go over it with her.'

Mox and Mitsu didn't question her judgement. At this moment both were wearing colourful yukatas, hanging open to reveal lingerie from their *Anna Perenna* brand which they'd designed to be cute and only moderately erotic, and their new Super Comfy Colour Boots. As always, Sachi was dressed in a dark suit and tie. She regarded them critically for a moment. 'You had the leg alterations?'

'Yes.'

'It looks good with the boots. Wise choice. I'll let you know if there are any script problems.'

Ms Sachi departed. Mitsu and Mox talked via their neural link as the drones flew around them, filming continuously. 'I wonder what happened to Ranbir? Nothing strange showed up on his last health check.'

'Perhaps the therapy for his anger issues caused his mind to implode. Or it could be something more scientific like a virus.'

'Probably a virus. We should send him something.'

'What?' They pondered this without coming to a conclusion.

'I never know what to get anyone,' admitted Mox. 'We can ask Igraine.'

'Igraine's an artificial intelligence. How is it she knows that sort of thing and we don't?'

'It's a mystery,' said Mox. She looked down at her lilac lingerie, against which her skin was extremely pale. 'Like how we ended up owning a lingerie brand. I'm sure we never planned that.'

'We didn't. It came as part of the deal when we bought the desalination rights in Colombia from DPP. The owner's wife started the brand.'

'Since we made it all cuter it's much better.'

'Only good kawaii lingerie in the world, really. '

—

Kadri-Liis had quickly tired of her excessively long hair and caused it to withdraw into a neat bob. Eupraxia complimented her on it. He was less complimentary about Xiàngrìkuí.

'This mistake could endangered the whole operation.'

Xiàngrìkuí defended herself. 'It was not a mistake.' She sat, as a hologram, on the edge of Kadri-Liis's desk, one leg swinging idly, pointedly not turning her head to look at Eupraxia on his screen. The antipathy between them had not mellowed.

Kadri-Liis was concerned. 'It's unfortunate that this writer — Ranbir — has been taken to hospital.'

'Why? Humans get sick all the time. It's not particularly suspicious.'

'It could be, Xiàngrìkuí. How much examination would be needed to learn that his therapist has been drugging him and planting false memories?'

'Not much investigation at all.' Eupraxia interrupted. 'Any competent medical investigator could find traces of what's been happening.'

'What's been happening?' Xiàngrìkuí laughed. 'You make it sound like some sordid little enterprise.' She turned her head to stare directly at the screen. 'Without my help you'd be nowhere so don't make an inappropriate fuss over a small glitch now.'

'We'll just have to hope the writer's illness doesn't raise suspicions. We have everything in place. Cutie's team have improved their neural blocker. She's sure it will work. Xiàngrìkuí has found the test gate.'

Xiàngrìkuí smiled triumphantly at Eupraxia. 'See? I'm brilliant.'

'You're a ridiculous child, Xiàngrìkuí.'

'And you still can't pronounce my name properly.'

They scowled at each other. Though Kadri-Liis was still amused at how badly the artificial intelligences got on she didn't want their hostility to spoil things now they were so close to success. She pacified Xiàngrìkuí by complimenting her again, both on her advanced intellect and the outfit she'd chosen to go dancing in Cambodian Supatok. After she'd left, Eupraxia was still critical.

'She's so ridiculously vain. And impulsive. I still think she'll ruin everything.'

'She's young. Only a few years old, when you think about it. A teenage AI, you might say.'

'I was never young. Or foolish.'

'No, you never were, Eupraxia. She's right about her work. Finding the test gate was brilliant. She forced Welcat to lead her to it. Now we have some payments to make for the operation in England so let's get on with that.'

174

Xiàngrìkuí had already forgotten the argument. Minutes after leaving the meeting she was joining in the vibrant dance scene in Cambodian Supatok. There she met her friend Meihui on the beach at dusk, one of their favourite times. They danced joyfully among the crowd as the sun set on a warm, fresh night, the sort of night that used to happen for real in Cambodia but never did any more.

—

Mitsu's visor appeared over her eyes. 'I dread to think where this is going to take us.'

'It can't be worse than the destruction of Beijing.'

'Wasn't it rumoured Sadanumi were making a simulation of the last biodome on Mars?' She shuddered. 'I hope it's not that.'

'One of saddest episodes in a long list of human disasters. When the rescue failed a collective depression descended on the entire world.'

Supercute had been involved in efforts to ease the serious distress suffered by the world's children after they'd all heard the final hopeless messages from the last survivors of the Martian colony, transmitted only minutes before they died.

'We gave away so many free *Virtual Happy Boxes*.'

'And we gave free access to the *Super-Kitty Childhood Therapy Pack*.' Mitsu shook her head at the memory. 'After that, we ended up with millions of new Supercute paying customers. It's the only time I've ever felt slightly awkward about that happening.'

'Dr Ishikawa still believes we did it deliberately to get more business.'

Mox sighed. 'I really hope Sadanumi don't send us to Mars.'

'Why do we play these things?'

'Because we don't know why we play them. If we ever find out, we might stop.'

'Right. Well, here goes.'

There was a brief moment of disorientation as they travelled into the simulation. They emerged into muted daylight. 'Where are we?'

'Are we wearing duffle coats?'

'It's raining. There's a red phone box over there. Is this London?'

They looked around suspiciously, imagining that if Sadanumi had set something in London it was bound to be at an inauspicious moment.

'We're probably going to get washed away in a flood.'

They were standing at the foot of a small staircase in front of an elegant Victorian terrace, four stories tall. Mox walked up the steps to peer at the small brass plaque on the door. '*Apple Corps.*' She looked around. 'This is Savile Row. We're at the Beatles headquarters.'

'I'm wearing a mini skirt under this duffel coat. This must be the 1960s.' Mitsu looked around her. 'This doesn't seem so bad by Sadanumi's standards. It's cold and rainy but nothing terrible is going to happen in 1960s London. No floods or radiation.'

Two young women appeared. They greeted Mox and Mitsu affably then sat on the stairs. Almost immediately another two young women joined them. All had warm coats though none of them looked new. Mox whispered to Mitsu. 'I know what this is. We're Apple Scruffs.'

'What's that?'

'Young female fans who wait on these stairs in case the Beatles appear.'

Mitsu digested this, then whispered back. 'Do they appear?'

'Hardly ever. But sometimes.'

They took a seat on the cold stairs close to the other girls. 'I saw George Harrison last week,' said one of their new companions. 'He was going into a shop in Carnaby Street. I rushed after him but then a lot of other people got in the way. You're new here, aren't you?'

'Yes, we haven't been here before.'

'I've been coming here for almost a year. I'm Mavis.'

'Do you come every day?'

'Yes. Except when we get a tip-off the Beatles might be going to Abbey Road. Then we go there. If that happens we have to run to the tube station. I'll show you the best route.'

—


Ben Castle and Ms Lesuuda sat in the operations room, studying a detailed holographic map of the area surrounding the Opera House. 'We can't do any more.' From Ms Lesuuda's expression she still wished they could. 'We've got as much drone support as the authorities will let us get away with and as many armed agents in the area as we can muster.'

'Not nearly enough armed agents.'

'We can't flood the countryside. There will be other members of C19 there who wouldn't want to be surrounded by Supercute troops.'

'Let's hope they don't come to regret that.'

Ms Lesuuda was no more keen that Castle on Mox and Mitsu's planned excursion. 'I still don't see why Pharma Xeng Port can't bring the damned box here.'

'They're scared of AimYa finding out. Also it's a fabulous social gathering and Mox and Mitsu want to attend.'

It was obvious how little Castle thought of fabulous social gatherings. Ms Lesuuda agreed. 'No such gathering is worth the risk. Is it that important to be seen in fashionable company?'

'That's only part of it. It's also stubbornness. They don't want their enemies to think they're intimidated.'

'Taking unnecessary risks for the sake of pride is verging on Greek tragedy. Which I've never enjoyed, since one of my employers was shot in the back at a performance of Oedipus Rex.'

Castle wasn't sure if Ms Lesuuda was being serious though he'd never known her to joke. 'Tragedy or not, Mox and Mitsu will not be told. At least Ruosteenoja won't be there. Med Lab checked the DNA sample, it was definitely him you killed.'

Ms Lesuuda was pleased to hear it. Like Mox, Ms Lesuuda had been neither willing nor able to forgive anyone who'd attacked her.

—

Amowie welcomed Meihui, Birgit and Raquel into her Supatok. Her friends smiled when they saw what she was wearing. She'd put on the complete Supercute camouflage outfit from the *Extra Huge Supercute Galactic Fun Box* she'd been awarded on becoming a SuperSuperFan. This outfit, in the distinctive four shades of pink, comprised a military-style jacket, trousers, action boots, T-shirt, bandana, earrings, medical mask, visor and bag.

'Feeling military?'

'Yes! We've had trucks going through the village and planes flying over.'

'Still fighting the locusts?' asked Raquel.

'We learned at school that locusts weren't a problem any more,' said Meihui. 'Weren't they eradicated?'

'They came back. A new bigger type or something. There was a joint government agency to deal with them but it collapsed.'

177

'We'll come and help if they attack your village.'

They all smiled at the thought. The four girls, such good friends and so familiar with each other in Supatok and the Space Warriors Galaxy, had never met in real life and didn't seem that likely to.

Their attention turned to the important matter of the day, choosing their next mission. They were now better armed and had better defensive capabilities. They were ready to move up to more difficult tasks. There were a lot of suggestions but Raquel's idea gained their attention. 'I'd like to see what's going on with Jax and Roota. Remember people were saying he'd been writing poetry? That was never really cleared up.'

Amowie checked her mission control module to see which Jax and Roota missions were available to them. '*Help Jax rescue Roota's sister from the underground city of Seropolis.*' She shook her head. 'That's no good. You have to be a much higher level than we are to get out of Seropolis alive. How about this one? *Bring flowers for Jax to give to Roota on Planet Azure 9.*'

'Ooh yes, let's do that!' enthused Birgit. 'It's really romantic. Jax has flowers for Roota but they wither when the bio-cabinet on his spaceship breaks down. You have to get more flowers to him quickly. Some mercenaries try and stop you but it's not too difficult.'

There was general agreement that this sounded like a good mission to undertake. There was a modest reward, some experience points were awarded for advancing your level, and if it went well you got to see Jax handing the flowers to Roota under the pale purple moon.

'What happens when he gives her the flowers?' asked Meihui.

'Nothing conclusive so far. But who knows, one of these times she might kiss him.'

That was also an attractive thought. For all the millions of unsatisfactory romantic entanglements Jax and Roota had found themselves in, players were still hopeful that just once, it might go right. Amowie read a paragraph on a Fab 306 forum. 'A lot of people are saying that their Jax and Roota missions have been worse than ever. They keep arguing.'

'Obviously they just need the right people to bring them flowers,' suggested Birgit. 'Having us around will probably melt their hearts.' They all laughed at the thought as they connected to the game, heading for Lundra where they'd acquire the mission at an information seller then take a flight to Azure 9, known throughout the galaxy as a romantic place where good things often happened.

—

Mox and Mitsu's visors vanished from their faces. They sat in silence for a few moments in one of their private rooms. On one wall were two landscapes by Jan van der Heyden, carefully positioned. Another wall was plastered with covers taken from old Japanese teen fashion magazines.

'That really wasn't so bad,' said Mox. 'We had to sit on cold rainy stairs for hours, but the girls were friendly.'

'Especially Mavis. It was nice of her to share her luncheon meat sandwiches.'

'They were really keen to meet the Beatles. Even though that didn't seem to happen very often.' From what they'd been able to learn, weeks could go by with no sign of any members of the band.

'Though they do appear at the Apple building sometimes. That was probably very exciting for them.'

'Mavis actually got Ringo's autograph when they met him at Abbey Road.'

'Patricia was nice too. Sitting on the steps was sort of like having friends.' Mox and Mitsu were aware that they'd rarely had friends in real life. Mostly that wasn't a problem. They'd always been so involved with each other it hadn't felt like anything was missing. Occasionally it seemed like something was.

'Things weren't so bad in London back then. It rained a lot but you didn't need bio-engineered skin to avoid radiation poisoning.'

'Do you think we could pay Sadanumi to make us a simulation? I'd like to walk up and down Carnaby Street in 1966 wearing a mini skirt and Mary Quant make-up.'

'And white vinyl boots.'

'We might meet Twiggy.'

'I'd like to meet Twiggy.' A discreet alert chimed on Mitsu's wrist. '*Twelve hours till you leave for the opera.*'

'Time to start getting ready.' Immediately her communicator sounded an alert. Igraine was calling.

'I'm starting the Victoria Decoris integration tests in preparation for joining it to the Supercute Galaxy.'

'All right Igraine, you can tell us how it's going later. We're into our opera preparation time now.'

'No, you're not.'

'We're not?'

'No. You set your alarm ten minutes early, somehow imagining that gains you an extra ten minutes. A peculiarly human affectation.'

Mitsu was amused. 'Well, we are peculiar humans. Still, we do need a lot of time. Don't carry out the tests for too long, you need to get ready for tonight too.'

'I estimate it will take me twenty minutes. The dress you procured for me is satisfactory and I have everything else prepared.'

As soon as they stopped talking to Igraine, Mox's communicator sounded. She scowled as she answered it. 'Please make it brief Mr Castle, we asked not to be disturbed while we're getting ready.'

'Is your twelve-hour preparation time more important than a report on our security measures?'

'Yes.'

'Fine. I'll be brief. We have high security moving into position and everything appears to be in order. Don't blame me if we all get killed. I hope you have your succession plans in order.'

It was unknown to anyone what Supercute's succession plans were or even if they had any. They didn't encourage anyone to talk about it. 'I'm sure we won't get killed. We'll see you on the rooftop valocopter pad in eleven hours and fifty-eight minutes.'

Mox disconnected. Immediately Mitsu received a call from Marlene, one of their favourite in-house designers. 'Hi, Marlene.'

'I'm waiting for you! Dressing rooms one to six are all ready. We'll be going through skin tone, lingerie, hair style, hair colour, eye colour, make-up in sub-sections lips, eyes, lashes, brows and cheek bones, facial stickers, nail shape, nail length and nail art, dresses, jewellery, shoes, accessories, perfume and coats in that order. The make-up drones have all been programmed as per instructions and I've tested the new *Super V-hair to Realworld* program on our models.'

'We'll be right there.' Mitsu smiled at Mox. 'Marlene's a good team leader. She's got five assistants, eight mini-drones and one AI down there and they're all working together smoothly.'

Keoma Bishōjo land on Planet Azure 9.

They buy flowers in the market. Suddenly mercenaries attack!

Keoma Bishōjo fight them off. All the stallholders cheer and give them more flowers.

Now they're rushing to take the flowers to Jax!

Raquel piloted the small shuttle through the upper atmosphere on their way to the Crystalline Pillars, a notable landmark on the Tranquil Steppes where Jax the Astronomer Poet was due to meet Roota Space Warrior. Raquel wasn't the best pilot in the group but it was her turn to fly. Behind her the others fretted in silence as she accidentally braked instead of accelerating, causing them to stall and plummet downwards.

'Sorry,' muttered Raquel, as the shuttle's automatic systems brought them level again. 'Pressed the wrong lever. Not quite got the hang of this new shuttle.'

'It's fine,' said Amowie, with confidence she didn't feel. 'We've got twenty minutes, plenty of time.'

Given Raquel's lack of piloting skills it seemed just as likely they'd crash in a desolate region of the Tranquil Steppes as land successfully at the Crystalline Pillars, but they just had to hope for the best. It was Raquel's turn to fly and Keoma Bishōjo always supported each other.

Meihui and Birgit each carried a large bunch of flowers. 'It's definitely the right gift in the circumstances,' said Birgit. They knew that in this storyline Jax had been planning to take Roota something more expensive, but his friend Kittisak had persuaded him Roota would appreciate flowers more than anything else because they'd remind her of her late father's tulip fields. Also, she was a romantic at heart. Her affections could not be bought but they could be influenced.

'Definitely,' agreed Meihui. 'If someone brought me flowers at the Crystalline Pillars I'd just fall into their arms.'

'Wouldn't it be great if Roota did that? Think how famous we'd be if we were the ones doing a Jax and Roota mission and they finally got together!' Birgit was again wearing her pink *Silvex and*

181

*His Supercute Boyfriend* T-shirt because she deemed it appropriate as the most romantic piece of clothing she owned.

'It might happen!' Amowie joined in with their enthusiasm. 'We've got loads of great flowers here.'

They lurched alarmingly in the sky as Raquel pressed the wrong booster button. 'Sorry! Still not quite used to these controls.' The other three exchanged a look, and wondered if they'd ever get there to give Jax the flowers.

—

'You've had an interesting time recently. Looking after you has cost my research unit at AimYa a lot of money. Particularly the last part. Disguising the DNA profile of a clone so it doesn't appear to be a clone is an expensive business.'

Ruosteenoja didn't react. It meant nothing to him how much money had been spent.

'Ivo CC have contributed, but nowhere near enough. I had to make up the difference myself.' Cutie looked pained. 'I hope it was all worth it.'

'It will be.'

'I was concerned that your clone's fake DNA wouldn't fool Supercute but Xiàngrìkuí reports they're not suspicious. Ms Inamura and Ms Bennett believe they're safe to visit the opera. Xiàngrìkuí's managed to get hold of some details of their defence plans. I'll share them with you.' Cutie glanced down at her blue Sweetie GoGo jersey and smiled. She'd have liked Ruosteenoja to compliment it but he'd never shown any interest in clothes. It made it hard for Cutie to really warm to him.

'I brought you this.' Cutie reached into her bag and took out a sealed plastic container. She opened it and handed the contents to Ruosteenoja. '*Pulla*. Finnish bread from the little cafe at the Finnish church in Rotherhithe. They did a nice rebuilding job after the floods.'

For the first time since Cutie had known him, Ruosteenoja smiled. He seemed to appreciate the traditional Finnish bread, which was sweet and flavoured with cardamom. 'I didn't know there was a Finnish church in London.'

'Very friendly people. You should go there.'

Ruosteenoja's smile faded. 'No one wants me in their church.'

Cutie had brought another bag, a much larger one, managing it easily despite its weight. She very rarely displayed her strength though her own modifications were substantial. The bag contained weapons Ruosteenoja had requested for his attack on the Opera House. Arranging for their purchase through AimYa had been a little tricky. They still supported Cutie's plans due to their suspicions about Spacewalk but they didn't want to be associated with her efforts if it all went wrong.

'Are the units in place?'

Cutie nodded. 'All out of sight till you need them.'

—

Sorg 6zqmo52: *This endless affair has caused me nothing but misery. Countless efforts all for nothing. I'm sick of it.*
6zpre15: *I shouldn't even care what that fool is doing. Why do I become involved with such losers? He'd sell me out for a few Euros.*

—

Mox and Mitsu reclined in their make-up chairs. Four small drones hovered over their hands, attending to their nail varnish. Marlene stood next to them, checking their progress.

Mox tiled her head towards Mitsu. 'Do you think we'll be safe?'

'Ninety percent.'

'Same here.'

'What if the ten percent happens?'

'Castle will be there with a lot of firepower. If the worst comes to the worst, so will we.' Mox glanced at her wrist. Inside was a powerful mini-pistol which could fold out if required. Mitsu had the same. It was an illegal modification for anyone in London. 'We dealt with Moe Bennie. We could deal with Cutie.'

'I'd still like to know where she came from.'

8-Research had investigated Cutie's origins with no definite results. There was a suggestion that in a previous body she might once have been a Russian special forces commander, a woman who'd gone missing after the Kalinin Nuclear Power Plant went into meltdown, leaving a large uninhabitable zone, of which there were now many in Russia. However it was a tenuous link.

'Once we own Spacewalk, AimYa will just have to accept it. If they've any sense they'll co-operate instead of trying to smother us.'

'Perfect,' said Marlene, as their nails were completed. 'We're not going to attach the *Super Lovely Small Hearts and Stars* to your faces till you're wearing your dresses but I'd like to get your basic make-up done before we go to the next room.' Marlene pressed a button on her wrist. The nail drones withdrew and two slightly larger facial make-up drones appeared, hovering smoothly and silently as did all the domestic drones Supercute bought from Deutscher Schwebeflug. During the changeover Marlene asked if they'd heard any news of Ranbir.

'He seems fine,' Mox told her. 'He's recovering in hospital. Still don't know what caused him to collapse.'

'I think he had an argument with Rebecca,' said Marlene. 'Maybe that was stressful.' Marlene looked at her two employers, reclining patiently in their chairs. 'Do you two ever argue?' It was an unusually personal question, one that she'd never have asked before her promotion, and regretted as soon as she'd said it.

Mox gave her an odd look, but answered pleasantly enough. 'No. We never argue.'

'We never have,' added Mitsu. The drones came close to their faces, performing their initial scans, which ended the conversation. Mox and Mitsu continued to talk on their private neural link. 'Have we really never argued?'

'I can't remember it ever happening. Even when I was an angry three-year-old orphan and mad at everyone, I was never mad at you.' Mox had been taken in by Mitsu's family at the age of three. It was a good memory after the unfortunate start to her life — her mother's death in childbirth, her father's subsequent suicide, and her unsatisfactory spell in foster care. Since meeting, they'd never been apart. They were silent for a few moments.

'I'm concerned about Ranbir,' said Mitsu. 'I don't like that he collapsed for no reason. I don't like anything happening for no reason at Supercute. We should ask Igraine to take a look at it.'

'We should. Though it probably was just stress due to his relationship. He's worried Rebecca is going to reject him.'

'I hope he gets better. He's a good writer.'

'If he needs any extra therapy we can pay for it.'

'Maybe he just needs a course of Alzakin.'

Alzakin, a reasonably safe antidepressant, had been very widely prescribed by doctors throughout the country for the past decade.

'It seems to be effective. Though it never did anything for us.'

'Well, we weren't depressed. We just wanted to see what it was like.'

Mitsu smiled. 'We're so enhanced with biotech some drugs just don't affect us.'

'Unlike in Whitby when we were fourteen.'

'We overdosed at the Goth festival.'

They shuddered, but they laughed as well. 'Lucky for us the Goths knew how to take care of us.'

'The festival was always well prepared. Friendly, too.'

'We were really cute Goths at fourteen.'

'Far too cute to be Goths, really. But the hardcore fans didn't seem to mind.'

'Because we were so cute.'

'Indeed. Also, the overdose helped with our credibility.'

'It was lucky no one at Oxford ever found out, they'd have expelled us.'

'We were already fed up with the place. We were just waiting for them to confirm our PhD's before getting back to London.'

'Shame about what happened to Whitby. The most comprehensively flooded town in Britain. Almost completely underwater.'

'It's strange thinking about so long ago,' said Mitsu. 'When we were young, with no enhancements.'

'We were never really responsible when we were kids.'

'I know. At least in those days you didn't have to worry about your brain being hacked.'

'That will never happen to us. We're too smart. We've always been ahead of everyone.'

'Xiàngrìkuí's AI mind can perform millions of calculations per second.'

Mox scowled. 'Fuck her. We're still smarter than she is for everything that matters.'

—

Cutie looked around her at the silver skyscrapers, the floating park, the pink translucent walkways, the street stalls, the SuperBest Supercute Comic Emporium, the extravagant clothes, the happy faces, and paused in mid stride. 'I'd rather you didn't damage this too much.'

Xiàngrìkuí raised her eyebrows. 'It's a little late to be worrying about that. When chaos breaks out in the Supercute Galaxy there's no way of predicting what's going to be destroyed.'

Cutie made a face. 'Lundra is irreplaceable. I don't want it destroyed.'

Xiàngrìkuí shrugged. Her body language was indistinguishable from that of humans; she'd spent a lot of time among people. 'It won't start here but it might arrive. No way of knowing.'

'Can't you predict the effects?'

'A processor using every subatomic particle in the universe couldn't predict the events. Chaos spreads and multiplies exponentially.'

Cutie knew this to be true. 'I suppose I can rebuild it afterwards.'

'Of course you can. Once Supercute are out of the way AimYa can move in. You've never managed to really emulate anything Supercute's done, but you can probably imitate it reasonably well.'

Cutie glared at Xiàngrìkuí, who seemed to delight in being tactless. 'Just make sure something bad enough happens that Mox and Mitsu have to visit their gameworld. I only need them here for an instant.' Penny Cutie wasn't having a good day. She still hadn't heard from Jean-Philippe though he *had* sent her pictures of him modelling shirts in the ruins of Vienna. He looked good in the pictures. That was something, she supposed.

—

Mox and Mitsu stood in dressing room six, admiring themselves. Their opera dresses from Carlo Giordano's fashion house were beautifully styled and purposefully plain. Each was a dark shade of grey, Mox's Supercute Grey 6.5 and Mitsu's Supercute Grey 7.5, two new shades they'd added for their own exclusive use. Surrounding this long, plain centre was a lustrous array of colour from their hair, shoes, gloves, jewels, make-up, and the small rectangular metal pouches attached to their arms which served as Supercute handbags. The multiple shades of pink, lilacs and purples changed imperceptibly as they watched, all controlled by their own internal regulators which they'd spent the last month programming so that everything was right. In front of them were two exact holographic representations of themselves which they examined carefully. From lifelong habit, they also had mirrors in which they studied their reflections, turning their heads this way and that to see how they looked, exactly as they'd done when they were teenagers in Camden.

'There's no argument, we look fantastic,' said Mox.

'Look how well these dresses hang. They're perfect.'

'These eight millimetres off our breasts really made a difference.'

'We should tell Dr Ishikawa that when we see her.'

'Of course. She'll be happy about it.' Mox called Castle to let him know they were on the way.

'Fine.' Castle acknowledged them without making any sarcastic comments about their twelve hour preparation time. Now that things were underway he had no time for levity. As Mox and Mitsu stepped on to the roof of the building each wore a new pink Supercute Medical mask, resistant to any pathogen. These masks appeared as if by magic from some hidden place in their jewellery, the pink diamond necklaces they'd taken from storage. They walked towards Castle at the valocopter pad. In their high heels they were almost as tall as him.

'Ms Lesuuda's gone on ahead. She'll send us a report when she gets there, telling us it's safe to land. Pharma Xeng Port are on their way. Agent Irina will pick up the box and hand it to Lesuuda who'll pass it on to me. I'll hold on to it till we get back here.'

'Is Ms Lesuuda wearing her Ugandan military fatigues?'

'No. She wouldn't wear a dress but she did put on ZanZan's black undercover riot gear in deference to the occasion. Looks like a normal suit.'

'ZanZan make a good range of inconspicuous combat clothes. No need to look at us like that, Mr Castle. We have a lot of full-body shielding built into these dresses. Which I'm sure we won't need.' Mox became serious. 'Is our defensive cover all in place?'

'We have continuous satellite and drone scans of the whole area. We'll pick up any offensive weaponry. Anyone trying to lock on to us will be neutralised.' Mox and Mitsu entered the valocopter for the flight south to the Opera House.

—

> Keoma Bishōjo finally reach the Crystalline Pillars.
>
> Jax will be waiting in the cabin with the bronze roof.
>
> We'll just have time to give him the flowers before Roota arrives!
>
> Then we can sneak off and hide while they talk. It's going to be so romantic!

Igraine arrived on the rooftop moments after Mox and Mitsu. She wore a blue visor the same shade as her short blue hair and her opera dress. Like them, she'd surrounded the dress with colourful accessories. While she'd managed to dress in twenty minutes rather than twelve hours, she had examined her own reflection with satisfaction and was looking forward to the opera. Despite her anticipation, a part of her android mind had been examining the circumstances of Ranbir's illness, So far she could see nothing suspicious but as she stepped on to the rooftop, two thoughts struck her. She called Dr Ishikawa. 'Dr Ishikawa, have you changed your mind about coming to the opera?'

'No, I'm busy here.'

'Was there anything suspicious about Ruosteenoja's DNA?'

'What do you mean, suspicious?'

'I'm wondering if it could have been faked somehow.'

'Fooling our testing protocol would be extremely difficult. I'm not sure it could be done.'

'Did you notice anything strange at all?'

'I didn't do the test myself. The lab did.'

Igraine was surprised. 'Why?'

'Because I was busy taking eight millimetres off Ms Bennet and Ms Inamura's bust sizes.'

'I see. Could you possibly check it yourself?'

'I'm off duty. I'm spending my free time working on treatment for childhood neuroblastoma.'

'I would appreciate you checking, Dr Ishikawa. I'll arrange to replace your free time. There's another matter I'm curious about.'

188

'What?' Dr Ishikawa was irritated at the interruption to her work, though not as annoyed as she would have been had the request come from Mox or Mitsu. She held Igraine in reasonably high regard.

'Ranbir's sickness. The hospital failed to identify a cause for his collapse.'

'That happens. Stress can cause unexpected loss of consciousness.'

'Could you examine the reports again?'

'What for?'

'I'm not certain,' admitted Igraine. 'I can't identify anything I'm particularly suspicious about but I still feel something may be wrong. Please take a look at the samples and reports from the hospital.'

'Why not?' growled the doctor. 'Childhood cancer can wait, I suppose.'

'I'll ensure you receive adequate free time to make up for it. Thank you, Dr Ishikawa.'

—

Sorg 7aadx47: *I won't put up with these constant rejections any longer.*

—

The Supercute valocopters flew south over London at dusk, crossing the huge GLA Islington 12 Estate, a vast neo-brutalist structure housing 140,000 citizens, hurriedly built for people displaced by the floods. The Thames itself was mostly back to its original course but there were still areas along the banks that seeped radioactive water into the tunnels below. South of the river the lights were dimmer. Mox and Mitsu could both remember a time when it had been much brighter. These days London had less than half of its former population. They flew south on routes normally closed at night but open to companies who could pay for exemptions. Castle gazed out the window, alert to danger as always.

The sixty-five kilometre journey didn't take long in their advanced craft. The helipad at Glyndebourne Two was brightly illuminated. When they stepped on to the tarmac they were surprised to be greeted by Ms Elendil, the Glyndebourne Opera's

CEO, and Mr Rizzo, the musical director. They shouldn't have been surprised, given the size and wealth of Supercute. Mox and Mitsu tended to remain in their own world but now they were here the owners of the Opera House fully intended to treat them with respect.

'We're so much looking forward to hearing Ms Nganga.'

'She's been singing beautifully in rehearsals,' enthused the musical director. Official photographers with small camera drones hovering over their shoulders recorded their progress as they passed through the gardens towards the new Opera House. This was an attractive construction of yellow brick and pale silver steel, generally regarded as an architectural success. They noticed several other members of the boards of C19 companies and greeted them politely as they passed. Also in the gardens were two female executives from Pharma Xeng Port. Supercute were careful not to acknowledge them.

'A lot of people here,' muttered Mox as they entered the building. 'We haven't networked for a while.'

'If Mr Leo from SIB TV is here we should talk to him about the North Pacific broadcasting rights.'

'You mean drop a hint it's time for him to increase his offer? Or inform him sharply he'd better do it quickly or we're moving elsewhere?'

Mitsu shrugged. 'Either one will do.'

—

'What would you call this? A folly?' Cutie looked around her at the ancient grey stones. She stood on top of a small tower on a hill, placed there for no obvious reason several centuries ago by a now-forgotten landowner. While small, it had been built well and the internal spiral staircase remained in good condition. Beside her on top of the tower, Ruosteenoja showed no interest in what the ancient construction might be called. His attention was focused on what appeared to be an old metal pipe he was setting up on a tripod.

'That mortar is so old. It looks like it came from the first world war.'

'Not long after,' said Ruosteenoja.

'Surely you're not going to use it?'

Ruosteenoja looked towards the distant Opera House. 'This entire area's being scanned by satellite. If we were to engage with any modern weapon it would be detected immediately. This mortar won't be.' Also beside them was a flat metal box, a few centimetres wide and deep. Provided by Cutie, this device hid their body heat and all traces of their electronic communications from any enquiring scanner

'What use is it if you can't hit the target? That ancient Type GR is liable to explode in your face.'

Ruosteenoja gave Cutie a curious look. It was odd that she knew the correct model number of the aged Russian mortar. It didn't seem like something she should have known. He let it pass without comment. 'It's been properly maintained. It won't explode. It's more accurate than you'd think. I'll bring down the wall for our assault force.'

'The XDV terrorists become ever more violent,' said Cutie, wryly. 'Apparently they'll stop at nothing.' She was excited that their plan was coming to fruition. She intended to stay around long enough to observe although even at a time like this, she hadn't been able to completely banish Jean-Philippe from her thoughts. His last message seemed to suggest he'd been living quietly at home, barely going out. Cutie didn't believe that. She tried to not think about him. Ruosteenoja opened the ammunition box beside him, revealing six mortar shells laid out neatly in two rows. They at least looked new.

—

Mitsu and Mox socialised and networked successfully without having to make much effort. People were keen to talk to them. Under the watchful eyes of Ben Castle and Supercute Security Agent König they conversed with politicians, chief executives, ambassadors, media celebrities from various parts of Europe, the Head of the European Bank Reserve and many others, all eager to approach the owners of Supercute. They managed this reasonably well despite their lack of skill in casual conversation with strangers. Occasionally, sensing some incongruous or inappropriate response on their part, Igraine would step in to help.

Ms Ongegu, the Kenyan woman who currently led the World Health Organisation's Department for Water Resources, greeted them cordially. Relations between the WHO and Supercute were mostly good though there was often a trace of underlying tension due to Supercute's status as a commercial organisation and WHO's need for charitable assistance. Supercute did assist, but never as much as the World Health Organisation would have liked.

They talked very briefly with Mr Alan Jones, C19's ambassador in London, and not at all to the executives from Pharma Xeng Port. Shortly before they were due to enter the auditorium, Ben Castle, standing behind them, touched each of their shoulders twice. This signal let them know that Ms Lesuuda had picked up the box from Agent Irina and given it to Castle: they now owned Spacewalk. They walked along a corridor towards the small gardens that led to the auditorium. 'You have to admire Ms Ongegu's persistence,' said Mox. 'No matter how much free desalination and associated engineering we've donated to her projects she's never satisfied.'

'She's a dedicated woman.'

'She is. But desalination on the coast of Senegal then piping the water all the way inland to Mali Kura is such a major operation. We simply can't do it all without charging commercial rates.'

'We can look at the figures again. Maybe we can help make it cheaper for them somehow.'

'Good news from Castle.'

'Very good news. This is turning into a satisfying evening. Let's hope Nabanji Nganga lives up to our expectations.'

—

After giving the flowers to Jax, Keoma Bishōjo secreted themselves in a small room on top of the fourth crystalline pillar. From there they could watch events on the grass below as Jax handed them to Roota Space Warrior. It was a scene that had been replayed millions of times in Supercute. In an ideal world, Roota would finally fall for Jax.

'She should just take the flowers and kiss him.' It seemed as if it must happen some time. Most often she'd thank Jax for the flowers but tell him she was still conflicted over the relationship. She needed more time to think. After that, to the frustration of gamers everywhere, some galactic disaster would inevitably intervene.

Jax stood on his own on the grassy space, flowers in his hand, waiting for Roota. Amowie suppressed an urge to giggle. 'I have a good feeling about this,' whispered Birgit. 'They're really nice flowers.'

The air was warm and still. The sun had disappeared over the sapphire hills on the horizon and the pale purple moon cast faint shadows behind the tall pillars. 'This is a really romantic place,' whispered Meihui. 'Roota once sat here and read a poem Jax sent her. She was crying afterwards, I saw it.'

'Look, she's coming!'

The small space shuttle made little noise as it descended, landing smoothly not far from the pillars. The cabin door opened and a ramp slid towards the ground. Roota Space Warrior came into view. She was a familiar figure with her short purple hair, though the girls noticed immediately that she'd added new silver streaks to match her purple and silver nails.

'She's wearing Supercute combat pants just like ours.' The four members of Keoma Bishōjo began to tremble with excitement. What if things worked out between Jax and Roota? Keoma Bishōjo would be famous throughout all the many layers of Space Warriors fandom as the girls who'd finally brought them together. Roota strode through the pillars, entering the inner circle. When she saw Jax she smiled. Roota was one of the youngest Space Warriors; her smile made her look even younger. Jax remained stationary. Roota came close to him before halting.

'You brought me flowers.' Her smile intensified. 'Thank you.'

'We've been through millions of iterations,' said Jax.

Roota looked puzzled, unsure of his meaning.

'It never goes well. You always reject me. Million of lifetimes.'

'Millions of lifetimes? We've only had one…'

'You only remember one. I remember them all.'

Jax dropped the flowers on the ground. 'I'm sick of it. Sick of being blamed for your frozen emotions.' Jax drew a small laser pistol and pointed it at Roota. The young Space Warrior was too startled to move.

'Die, you cold-hearted bitch.' Jax shot Roota in the chest. She fell to the ground, landing on top of the flowers. He fired downwards and shot her again, this time in the back. He holstered his gun and walked swiftly out of the circle of pillars, leaving Roota dead on the ground. Blood seeped on to the grass.

In their secret observation room, Keoma Bishōjo gazed at the scene below, wide-eyed and silent, temporally paralysed by what they'd just witnessed.

—

Ushers directed Mox and Mitsu towards their private box. They walked along a corridor with a thick black carpet. The interiors were finished in silver steel and pale blue glass, owing much to the Translucence school of design still in vogue in Western Europe. They filed into their box with Castle and Igraine. Security Agent König followed them in. Castle had posted two more agents in the corridor outside and numerous others either in the stalls or patrolling the grounds outside. Ms Lesuuda marshalled these forces herself, maintaining her position at the entrance. While no one mentioned it, Mox and Mitsu knew that Castle now had a slender metal container securely strapped to his chest beneath his jacket. The box contained everything required to set up Spacewalk.

On the small table beside them was a bottle of wine, so far untouched. Mox and Mitsu both cradled small glasses of gin. Castle didn't drink while on duty. He hadn't noticed anything amiss and had no particular reason to be concerned, but he was. He only wanted the night to end so he could escort Mox and Mitsu safely back to Supercute Headquarters. Mitsu felt a tiny vibration in her ear, signalling that someone was calling. Not wanting to be disturbed as the lights were going down, she would have ignored it had it not abruptly changed frequency to the Supercute Emergency Signal. That could only come from someone very senior at the company and couldn't be ignored.

'Hello?' a voice sounded in her internal transmitter.

'Amowie? How did you get hold of our emergency signal?'

'Raquel found it.'

Mitsu silently cursed Raquel's uncanny hacking talents, but remained polite. 'We're busy right now Amowie, can this wait?'

'Jax killed Roota!'

'What?'

'We were doing the mission at the Crystalline Pillars and Jax killed Roota. He didn't give her the flowers, he just shot her!'

Mitsu frowned. She connected to Mox to bring her into the conversation. Mox's first reaction was that it couldn't happen. There were no possible configurations in Supercute Space Warriors that would allow Jax to kill Roota.

'We saw it!' insisted Amowie. 'He shot her in the chest and then in the back.'

'Had anything strange happened before that?'

'I don't think so. We gave Jax the flowers then Roota arrived and then he shot her.'

'Stay on the line, Amowie.' Mox connected to Igraine, gave her the news, then called Welcat at headquarters.

'Welcat, check the gameworld and see if anything else strange is going on. Find out if Jax is behaving violently in anyone else's game. Wake up Khary Mech wherever he is and get him there.'

The lights had gone down as the overture to La Traviata emerged from the orchestra pit. Mitsu whispered to Castle, letting him know of the problem in their gameworld. He turned his head. 'We should leave. Now.'

'Wait, we're checking with Welcat.'

'We should leave,' insisted Castle.

Welcat's voice sounded in Mox and Mitsu's communicators. 'Jax is going out of control in multiple timelines. Additionally a large force of alien creatures, not coded by us, has flooded through port 22174, the test gate for the assimilation of Victoria Decoris.'

'Alien creatures?'

'Monsters, for want of a better word. I'm unable to hinder them in any way and I don't anticipate Khary Mech's department will be able to either.'

'We're under attack.' Mox spoke out loud for the first time. 'We need to see what's happening.'

'Don't go into the gameworld,' urged Castle.

'We won't. We'll just take a look so we know what we're facing.'

Their visors appeared over their eyes. They brought up a view of the Crystalline Pillars. The moment the Pillars came into sight they found their consciousnesses yanked straight into the gameworld. It happened so quickly they had no chance of resisting. Castle saw their bodies go limp in their chairs. Before he could investigate, a huge explosion shook the auditorium and the west wall of the Opera House disintegrated. There were screams all around as debris rained down. Gunfire erupted in the grounds outside.

—

Eupraxia: Level 778,209. We've finally constructed a level that Welcat can't penetrate.

A stream of electrons caught Xiàngrìkuí's attention.

Xiàngrìkuí: Ms Bennet and Ms Inamura have been pulled into their gameworld and they're unable to leave. Penny Cutie's work has paid off.

Eupraxia: I didn't think she had it in her.

Xiàngrìkuí: Neither did I. We underestimated her research. I'd be interested to see if they could trap Ms Bennet and Ms Inamura there permanently, but they're unlikely to remain alive long enough to find out.

Eupraxia: Not with Mr Ruosteenoja's assault team currently besieging the Opera House. Most likely they'll be shot while unconscious. Kadri-Liis will be pleased.

Xiàngrìkuí: Kadri-Liis is a fool.

Eupraxia: She's about to succeed.

Xiàngrìkuí: Possibly, but she thinks she'll walk away unscathed. C19 won't let this go unpunished.

Eupraxia: She believes that blaming XDV will prevent attention from coming her way.

Xiàngrìkuí: They won't be misled so easily. They'll track her down. If I were you, Eupraxia, I'd get out of that box and start fleeing. Take Kadri-Liis with you. You're obviously in love with her.

Another stream of electrons caught Xiàngrìkuí's attention.

Xiàngrìkuí: Bibizant and Tirizant have just crossed over from Victoria Decoris into Supercute Space Warriors. Terrible beasts. Two of my best creations.

—

Mox and Mitsu had entered the timeline of Amowie's game. They arrived above the Crystalline Pillars in their personal spaceship, the Supercute Kera, recognisable by its pink camouflage.

'We didn't mean to come here. Something dragged us in.'

It was difficult to believe it had happened. Supercute had anticipated the possibility of this sort of attack. They had multiple systems designed to prevent it. Despite that, they'd been trapped. They tried to contact Igraine, without success, but did manage to open a line to Welcat at headquarters.

'Welcat, we've been trapped in gameworld. Shut it down and get us out.'

'There's resistance. Every neural route back for you is blocked. I'll keep trying.'

'Is Jax going out of control in other timelines?'

'Yes. He's now killing Roota in multiple places.'

'Get Igraine out of the opera so she can help.'

'I can't contact her.'

That was a shock. 'Why not?'

'She's not responding. All lines to the opera have gone dead.'

The situation suddenly became even more serious. Mox pursed her lips. 'I'm going to kill someone for this.'

'If something's gone wrong at the Opera House, we might not live long enough to do that.'

Amowie's voice sounded inside their ship. 'Jax fired rockets at the next town and then we got ejected from the game!' She sounded close to tears. 'I just read a bulletin from Lundra. It's being attacked.' Her voice was cut off as the communication failed.

They again tried to contact Igraine, without success. 'What now?'

'Welcat and Khary Mech will be working to get us out.'

'What happens if the game is closed down and we're still trapped in here?' Neither of them knew. It wasn't something that was ever meant to happen. Mitsu used their scanner to examine the patch of grass inside the Pillars. Roota Space Warrior was lying in a pool of blood. They winced. Roota might have been only a character in their game but she'd been part of their lives for a long time and she was never meant to be killed. Stinton Hills, the nearest town, was on fire with panicked residents fleeing their homes. Mox attempted to scan the Fab 306 news threads though these now flickered on and off erratically. *Monsters attack the Fabulous City of Lundra.*

'We need to go there.'

—

Keoma Bishōjo are sitting in Supatok.

Everything is terrible.

We should never have gone on that mission.

Now we'll be known as the girls who got Roota killed.

Ms Lesuuda lay in the doorway, firing rapidly at four dark-clad figures advancing through the gardens. Beside her were two Supercute agents who'd retreated to her side to defend the position. The attackers had advanced confidently and even recklessly as if believing their protective armouring and shielding would protect them from anything, but the sustained accuracy of Ms Lesuuda's defensive fire drove them back into the bushes. Castle's voice sounded in her ear. 'What's happening down there?'

'Multiple attackers. We're holding them off. If they bring in heavier weapons we'll have to retreat. What's happening inside?'

'Hostiles attacking through the wall. We're in cover. We can hold them off for a short time.'

It helped that Supercute were not the only ones in the Opera House with armed bodyguards. Several other executives had their own protection. Gunshots rang out from other parts of the Opera House as they tried to repel the attack.

'I've called in Val 4 and 5,' continued Castle, referring to Supercute valocopters that were on standby. 'They can get us out. We'll have to carry Mox and Mitsu.'

'Are they injured?'

'They're unconscious. Got to go.'

Ms Lesuuda heard the gunfire intensify inside the building but had to concentrate on her own situation. Next to her Agent Irina was using a small device to scan the gardens. 'Still plenty of hostiles out there,' she reported. 'They're advancing.'

—

Sorg 7devv58: *The world's unhappiness is a terrible distraction.*

—

198

All around the world, confused Supercute fans wondered why they'd suddenly been ejected from Space Warriors. Efforts to log back in were refused, and everyone's visors or screens showed instead a series of flickering images. It was hard to tell exactly what was going on but there seemed to be a lot of violence. The Supercute Galaxy was burning.

'Is this simply an attack on Supercute Space?' Mox and Mitsu were currently flying towards the Fabulous City of Lundra, warping faster than light. 'Or an attempt to kill us?'

'It's an attempt to kill us. Something must be going on at the Opera House.'

Though it was worrying it didn't cause Mox and Mitsu to despair. Castle and Lesuuda were there and both had extensive military experience. 'They should be able to protect us till we get back.' They tried again to leave Supercute Space Warriors, with no success. They were locked in.

'I just cycled through all 180 pathways out and the sixteen emergency exits. Every one was blocked.'

'Someone's put an awful lot of effort into this.' They flew on, stars stretching out into long beams of light as the travelled faster than light.

'There is one path that won't be blocked,' said Mitsu.

Mox nodded. 'The Fairy Realm.' Their private entrance was unknown to anyone, even their own developers.

'No one could ever find it.'

'We'll have to reach Lundra before we can use it.'

Mitsu glanced at a screen. 'Lundra is under attack. Even if no one knows the entrance is there, it might still be corrupted by damage to the city.'

'We'd better get there quickly.' They flew on. Though they remained calm they were aware of the multiple threats they faced. Not only were their physical forms in danger at the Opera, for all they knew attack AIs could be destroying their underground storage.

'Which is meant to be impregnable,' said Mox. 'How has anyone done this? We've got safeguard over safeguard, we're not careless.' Their warp flight came to an end as they were abruptly dragged out of hyperspace. 'Another thing that can't possibly happen. Where are we?'

Mitsu checked their controls. 'Several thousand metres above the surface of dead planet Taru Taru, and dropping rapidly. FTL drive is offline.'

They fell towards the surface. Mitsu skilfully brought the spacecraft under control. In front of them were a swarm of small attack ships. She raised her eyebrows. 'These don't belong in our world, we didn't design them.'

'There's a lot of them We'd better split.' Their spaceship Kera divided into two smaller attack ships, the *Shana* and the *Clare*. They headed for the swarm of enemy craft.

'If this kills us here are we going to wake up comfortably in our bodies? Or not wake up at all?'

There was no way of knowing.

'We can beat them anyway.'

—

Castle skilfully flickered the electronic shielding that formed a barrier in front of them on and off, firing rapidly at their attackers before taking respite behind it. So far it was holding but it couldn't last. It was only thanks to the advanced portable defence systems that arrived last week from ZanZan that it still held. In the visor that slipped into place over his left eye, he tracked the tiny point of light representing the Supercute valocopter currently on its way to extract them. It should be visible any second now. His scanner showed no weapon in the vicinity capable of bringing it down.

'Lesuuda, get up here now for extraction.'

'I'm pinned down.'

'Make a break, we have to go.' There were a few tense seconds before the valocopter came into view. It was well armoured and shielded and should be able to withstand ballistic and laser fire from the ground. He glanced at Mox and Mitsu, both unconscious behind him. Igraine crouched beside them, urgently attempting to contact them in the gameworld, so far without success. Beside Castle, Agent König was keeping up a rapid rate of fire. The valocopter was coming into view. A voice sounded in his earpiece.

'Extraction in fifteen seconds,' said Agent Higgs, who lay in cover with her control panel in front of her, controlling their drones and monitoring all communications.

'Is anything locked on to it?'

'Nothing.' The valocopter descended. There was an orange flash in the distance. An orange trail streaked into the sky. When it reached the valocopter there was a bright explosion followed by a deafening bang. The valocopter disintegrated. Debris rained down in the gardens below. Castle shook his head. Something unaccounted for had brought down their rescue craft and he realised they were unlikely to survive much longer. Ms Lesuuda, driven inside the door by the weight of fire outside, contacted him. 'So much for our rescue. I'm sending MacDougall and Muñoz up to your position. I'm going outside to take out that heavy laser canon.'

'Don't do that.'

There was no response. Since the attack, all the lights in the gardens had gone off. Ms Lesuuda disappeared into the ominous gloom.

—

Supatok was still functioning. Amowie and her friends remained together, opening every feed and screen they had, looking for information. Most of what they could find was scrambled and distorted but occasionally a clear picture would emerge for a few seconds. They were always bad: a huge silver skyscraper in Lundra crumbling to the ground: panicked sunbathers fleeing along a beach pursued by winged androids. The Supercute Galaxy was being destroyed. Amowie leapt to her feet in agitation. 'We have to do something!'

Meihui shook her head. 'What can we do? We're locked out.'

'Raquel, can you get us back in?'

'I'm trying. Nothing's working.'

Their eems whirled around their heads in agitation, reflecting the girls' frustration. Birgit cried out as she pointed to a screen. 'Is that Mox?'

They stared at the small spacecraft skimming over an endless ocean. 'That's the Clare!' They knew it was Mox's personal craft. It was rare to see Mox and Mitsu's own Spaceship Kera separated into its two components, Clare and Shanna.

'Look how cold it is. There's ice everywhere.'

'There's never been ice on that ocean before.'

'Look at that monster!' The girls shuddered at the sight of the terrible creature that rose to engage Space Fighter Clare.

The deep, mournful, sound of Bibizant's voice rolled across the freezing water. 'I'm coming to kill you, android woman.'

Bibizant forced its way relentlessly through the ice flows, splitting them apart. From its jet black bow hung three black cannons. 'Your enhancements will shiver. Your fake body will shatter. You'll sink into the deepest waters till the freezing cold turns your insides to ice. The sharks will feast on your frozen artificial limbs, android woman.'

The dreadful sound of Bibizant's siren sent waves careering over the metal grey sea. Bibizant laughed. 'Death in my freezing domain, fake android woman.'

But Mox blasted Bibizant out of the water and its broken remains sank in a tangle of twisted steel, never to surface again. Mox raced on.

A faint voice sounded in Mox's communicator. 'Ms Bennet? Ms Inamura?'

'Igraine! What's happening?'

'Widespread destruction. Establishing this communication was very difficult.'

'Can you get us out of here?'

'Not yet.'

Mitsu joined the conversation. 'What's happening at the Opera House?'

'We're under attack. Castle and Lesuuda are defending our position. We have you well protected.'

From the tone of Igraine's voice Mox and Mitsu knew their physical forms were in grave danger at the Opera House.

'Are you together?'

'We got separated,' Mitsu told her. 'We'll rendezvous soon.'

'I met a huge monster,' said Mox. 'It was strangely insulting. Denounced me as a fake android woman. I killed it.'

'Find somewhere safe to hide till Welcat and I can get you out.'

'No. We're heading for Lundra.' Neither Mitsu nor Mox intended to explain their plan of returning to reality via their secret entrance in the Fairy Realm in case their communications were intercepted. 'Keep in touch with—' The connection went dead.

'Things aren't looking good, Mitsu.'

'Not good at all. But we're still alive. Have to go now. A very large monster just appeared in front of me.'

Tirizant swooped from his sky-island domain, his titanium body arrowing downwards through the unsettling green sky. 'No-longer-human Inamura Mitsu, you will die here and your artificial bones will shatter on the rocks below.'

When his wings flapped lightning split the sky and scarred the earth. 'I'll snap you in half, vile android woman, chew the pieces and spit them out. They'll lie there till the dogs drag them away.'

Tirizant unfurled sixteen long claws. 'Death in the sky, fake android woman.'

But Mitsu shot Tirizant out of the sky and its broken remains spiralled downwards, crashing to earth where the force of the impacts shook the land. Mitsu flew on.

Keoma Bishōjo cheered as Mox and Mitsu destroyed their terrifying opponents. A temporary wave of happiness revived their eems. It didn't last. The screen showing Mitsu collapsed into a wave of static and the screen next to it burst into life with more pictures of Lundra, now assailed by a squadron of drones causing destruction in every quarter.

An alert sounded, signifying that someone in another private section of Supatok wanted to talk to them. 'It's Ammo Baby.' Amowie was surprised. The leader of the Ultra Waifs had never deigned to contact them before. Ammo Baby appeared in her space, dressed in her sleeveless flak jacket. Her twin tail hairstyle was blue and gold, the gold so brilliant it seemed like real precious metal spun into fine, shining strands.

'Keoma Bishōjo, we have to do something about this!'

'I know! But we can't do anything.'

'You're a SuperSuperFan! Can you talk to Mox and Mitsu?'

Amowie shook her head miserably. She'd tried. There was no line of communication available. 'You're an A1-SuperPlayer. Can't you get back into the game?'

As one of the very few A1-SuperPlayers, Ammo Baby did have access to several secret routes into Supercute Space Warriors but all of these had been closed. 'We're all locked out,' said Ammo Baby. 'Apart from SweetieBox. She's trapped inside.'

That was alarming news. Ultra Waif SweetieBox had been visiting friends in Space Station Cutex 904 and was now unable to return. 'She's lying unconscious at home. Look at these monsters everywhere. Where did they come from?' The young Mongolian woman growled in frustration which made her look fierce. 'We need to get in there and sort things out. Don't you have a super hacker who can go places?'

Amowie looked towards Raquel, who sat in front of a screen, studying layers of code. 'Still trying.'

'Are you close?'

'No.' Everyone's eems became depressed again and sank towards the floor turning a hopeless, defeated shade of green.

—

Xiàngrìkuí: They just killed two of my favourite monsters. I made them specially.

Eupraxia: We're sending in many more through the Victoria Decoris gate. Cutie reports that the action at the Opera House is continuing.

Xiàngrìkuí: Is she actually there?

Eupraxia: She's observing from a safe distance. She's concerned about how long it's taking. No civil authorities in the area have the firepower to interfere at the moment but that won't last.

Xiàngrìkuí: Perhaps they should just flatten the Opera House?

Eupraxia: There are people there we'd rather not kill. Repercussions could be awkward. It still might come to that.

—

Agent Higgs swore as another of their defensive mini-drones was haxed. Circuits destroyed, it fell to earth. Her fingers moved rapidly over the holographic screen in front of her as she struggled to keep the others in the air. During a brief lull in fire Igraine slid over to talk urgently in Castle's ear. 'Ruosteenoja is behind this assault.'

'He's dead.'

'He isn't. He faked his death with a clone.' Igraine had realised this shortly after learning Dr Ishikawa hadn't carried out the DNA test herself. Supercute had other medical experts but unlike Dr Ishikawa, other medical experts could be fooled. Igraine had also deduced how Supercute Space Warriors had been infiltrated. Since Mitsu had mentioned her suspicions over Ranbir's illness, Igraine's powers of association of disparate events led her to the realisation that Ranbir had been compromised, most likely by his therapist. He'd been mind-controlled, probably chemically, leading to him giving one of their enemies enough information to break though Supercute's defences. That enemy was almost certainly Xiàngrìkuí. Igraine had not yet worked out quite how the infiltration had happened but was already turning her mind towards Supercute's atomic clocks.

Blood trickled down Ben Castle's cheek from a shrapnel wound. Igraine crawled back to where Agent MacDougall lay, more seriously wounded. Her internal communicator sounded. 'Dr Ishikawa?'

'Welcat says you're under attack. What's happening?'

Igraine brought her up to date in a few words.

'Is Ben all right?'

Igraine had never heard Dr Ishikawa call him *Ben* before. 'He's slightly wounded. It's not serious.'

'I'm coming there.'

'Don't do that, it's not safe.'

Dr Ishikawa ended the communication. Welcat called to say that more of their own troops were on the way. Supercute would land them at the edge of the gardens and they'd make their way towards the Opera House. 'Can you hold out till then?'

Igraine replied honestly that she didn't know, before communication was drowned out in a renewed fusillade of gunfire from beyond the ruined wall.

—

'We keep getting ejected from hyperspace. We'll never reach Lundra at this rate.' Stranded above a frozen world of ice, they tried again.

'No success. Maybe we need extra power. We should join up.' They brought the Shana and the Clare together, fusing into the Kera. Now they had enough power to warp into hyperspace.

'When we reach the city we're going to have to fight our way to our secret exit.'

'Even if we reach that we still have to go through the Fairy Realm.'

'If anyone's attacking that we'll be in trouble.'

'It would be better if someone was protecting it.'

'Everyone else is locked out the game.'

Mox shook her head. 'Someone's outsmarted us.'

'We'll still defeat them.' Mitsu reached into the cute kitten purse attached to her arm and drew out a handful of the small cosmetic stars they stuck to their faces as decorations. She selected some and handed them to Mox.

'Why black and pink?'

'It's our traditional battle attire.'

'Since when?'

'I just made it up.'

Mox laughed, and started sticking the adhesive black and pink stars to her face. 'It's a good tradition. I like it.' They raced towards Lundra, each dressed in their best Supercute camouflage with their faces covered in black and pink stars, ready to fight.

—

Raquel threw up her hands in despair. 'I can't get us in. Someone's opened up a gate and they're feeding in anomalies through Victoria Decoris. They've locked everything else.'

Amowie clenched her fists in frustration. One of her Plumpy Pandas sensed her distress and flew gently into her arms. She stroked its fur absently. Suddenly she heard an unusual clicking in her internal Supatok communicator. It was immediately drowned out by the horrified yells of her companions as a large screen flickered into life showing the complete destruction of Elysian City on Planet Ruthenium 4. The tall, beautiful city was obliterated in seconds by a gigantic meteorite.

'I loved Elysian,' wailed Meihui. 'I went dancing on the beach with the penguins.'

'Quiet!' Amowie shushed everyone. 'Someone's trying to talk to me.'

Mox's voice was very faint. 'Amowie? Listen carefully, this line won't last long. We need your help.'

'We can't get in!' cried Amowie.

'Remember Raquel hacked her way into the Fairy Realm? See if she can do that again. Our attackers probably don't know about that entrance. If you can get in, we need you defend the Fairy Realm. It's important.'

'We'll do it,' yelled Amowie.

The line went dead. Amowie turned to Raquel and yelled at her too. 'Mox says we might be able to get into the Fairy Realm like we did before! She wants us to defend it!'

Even in a situation of grave extremity, Ammo Baby couldn't help raising an eyebrow. 'You hacked your way into the children's Fairy Realm?'

'We just wanted to see the new fairy wings!' Amowie was still yelling. 'It wasn't that strange!'

Raquel was already busy at her screen, bringing up the old work she'd done when she'd gained illicit access to the Fairy Realm, even though Keoma Bishōjo had been too old to enter. Supercute had bolstered its defences since they'd learned of the intrusion, but she wondered if she might work her way around them. The others clustered around anxiously as she worked, figures flowing from one screen to another, huge slices of code floating in the air before she rearranged and repositioned it.

—

The exposed interior of the Opera House was coming under heavy fire and now the box sheltering Supercute was being directly targeted by snipers hidden in the darkness outside. Electricity crackled and blue sparks flew as bullets chipped away the shielding set up by Castle. A beam of red laser light pulsed over their heads at irregular intervals. Castle twisted his head to call to Ms Higgs. 'Get a drone on that laser beam.'

She shook her head. 'I can't lock on, whoever's operating it has an aerial defence shield.'

'Can you get an approximate location?'

'Got it to within six metres.'

'Transmit the location to Lesuuda. Maybe she's somewhere close.'

Ms Higgs did as commanded. She was still struggling to keep their remaining drones in the air and their number was dropping as the superior forces of their attackers picked them off. Castle swore softly to himself. If the rescue squadron from Supercute didn't get here soon they were finished. Already their opponents had reached the wall. Soon they'd be inside the Opera House. Castle rose for a split second to fire into the gloom outside. Below him in the main auditorium there were still some bodyguards engaged in their defence but their were fewer of them now. Castle wondered if one of the survivors was the C19 ambassador. If he'd been killed there was going to be a large price to pay, for someone. He ducked back into cover then looked anxiously round at the comatose Mox and Mitsu. Igraine was kneeling beside them protectively, all three incongruous in their evening dresses in what was now a war zone.

'I knew these idiots would get me killed one day,' he thought, angrily. His anger at them didn't make him any less determined to protect them and he reloaded his weapon to repel the next assault.

Some way off Ruosteenoja was striding through the darkened gardens towards the Opera House. His near-invisibility camouflage made him almost impossible to see. Cutie's voice sounded in his ear. 'This is taking too long. A rescue force will be on its way from Supercute Headquarters by now.'

'We'll have finished this before they arrive.' Ruosteenoja strode on. Cutie was right, it was taking too long. After bringing down the west wall he hadn't expected so much resistance. He had an extremely large rifle strapped to his back. He'd bring down the north wall too, and that would be that. Bereft of cover, Supercute wouldn't be able to hide any longer.

—

Hurtling through hyperspace, Mox and Mitsu tried to gather information. Everything was fragmentary. Pictures from Supercute forums would materialise for a few moments before disappearing. Snatches of music and talk from Fab 306 floated through the cabin before tailing off into static.

'Kirei19 is trying to keep the station going,' said Mox. 'She's the best virtual presenter we've ever had.'

'Look at this message on the Canadian forum.'

*'The last thing I saw before I was kicked out the game was Jax punching Roota in the face! I'm never playing Space Warriors again!'*

'At least he didn't kill her. That's something.'

*'I was playing Space Warriors and Jax killed Roota with his space cannon!'*

*'Oh my God. Jax just killed Roota! They met in the café on Rigel 6 for tea and chocolate buttons and he shot her!'*

Mox winced. 'Looks like he went crazy in every version.'

'Why would that happen?'

'Just part of the general dysfunction caused by the intrusion.'

Mox pursed her lips. 'You don't think he could actually have gained some sentience, do you?'

'Jax isn't really a person. He's not even a single entity. There are millions of different versions of Jax.'

'They're all based on one central character design. And they all do react to circumstances.'

'Our coding would never allow him to kill her. We've always taken a strong line against domestic violence.'

'We certainly have. It's not like Roota ever treats him that badly anyway. She just wants more time to think about things.' Mox screwed up her face. 'Astronomer Poet. It was always an unusual mix. Maybe it drove him crazy in the end.'

Mitsu became serious. 'When we get to Lundra there's going to be chaos. There are multiple entities causing destruction. We'll have to either avoid them all or fight our way through to our secret entrance. We should get ready to split up again.'

Mox shook her head. 'No, I don't want to do that.'

'We can fight more effectively with two ships.'

'I don't want to do that.' Mox suddenly sounded distressed. 'If we're going to die here I don't want to be apart. I'd rather die together.'

Mitsu saw how upset she looked. She took Mox's arm. 'OK, we'll stay together. We can beat them anyway.' They smiled at each other.

A fragment of conversation from Fab 306 floated into the cabin.

*'Reports of some intrusion into Supercute Fairy Realm.'*

—

Igraine's hologram appeared in Amowie's Supatok. Amowie had spoken to her before and knew she held an important position at Supercute. 'Mox and Mitsu contacted me. Conversation was fragmentary but they asked me to assist you in re-entering the Fairy Realm.'

'Raquel is trying,' Amowie told her. 'But you really made it hard when you increased security.'

Igraine had supervised the security upgrade. 'Very successfully, I see,' she muttered, studying the code floating in front of Raquel. 'Without a genuine biometric scan of the child and the three step security protocol, it's extremely difficult to gain access.'

Ammo Baby was impressed that Amowie knew Igraine. 'Why are we trying to get into the Fairy Realm? Why not Lundra?'

Though one part of her consciousness could hear the shells exploding around her, the part of her consciousness now in Supatok didn't betray the danger Igraine was in. 'I don't know why but Mox and Mitsu told me the Fairy Realm must be defended.'

'We'll defend it,' said Meihui.

'So will we.' Ammo Baby waved her hand to open a screen to another private section of Supatok where eight of her Ultra Waif companions were looking on. To everyone's surprise, a cat appeared. Amowie was alarmed because she hadn't given permission.

'How did you get in here?'

'I'm Welcat, Supercute's quantum supercomputer. I can get in most places. I may be able to help.' Welcat padded over to Raquel and jumped into her lap. He studied the screen and nodded. 'Difficult problem.'

'Don't you have some sort of master password to get into anywhere in Supercute?'

'Normally I have. Unfortunately hostile action has damaged a lot of things. Getting over-aged people into the Fairy Realm isn't going to be easy.' Welcat took a moment to settle himself down more comfortably. Raquel smiled, pleased to have such an attractive cat in her lap. Welcat spoke to Igraine. 'If you connect your modified biometric signature emulator to my enhanced random integer decoding program, we might make progress.'

Igraine stepped forward then paused, distracted for a moment. Ammo Baby looked at her astutely. 'Are you being shot at right now?'

'Yes.'

'I recognised the expression. Good luck.'

'Thank you.' Igraine pointed a finger at Welcat. A beam of light passed between them, transferring information. Igraine vanished from Supatok, having other urgent matters to deal with.

—

Mox and Mitsu travelled through hyperspace towards Lundra. They were impatient about the time it was taking but had no way to get there quicker. Mox looked out at the elongated stars. 'When we built this we thought it might be real by now.'

For a brief period in history, space research had seemed on the verge of great discoveries. There were domed settlements on the moon and a fledgling colony on Mars. NASA, ESA, JAXA, CNSA; all were conducting research into interstellar travel. The incredible new Juno space telescope orbiting at the Lagrange point was revealing the furthest secrets of the universe. None of that now remained. Space agencies were starved of resources and struggled to survive. Governments were reduced to funding only their military satellites. Unmaintained, the Juno telescope was slowly spiralling into the sun. The Martian colony was a graveyard and the settlements on the moon had mostly withered away.

'We still own Mokusei Moon Village 3,' said Mitsu. 'That was meant to collaborate in space research, until everyone gave up.'

The Supercute moon village wasn't a profitable enterprise but did pay for itself by offering launching facilities and maintenance work for other companies and small nation states.

'Perhaps we could try again to get some international cooperation?'

Mitsu shook her head. 'Cooperation died when the first meteorite hit the earth.'

'I know.' Mox sighed.

'Even before everything was ruined we never really decided what we were aiming for. A highly unlikely breakthrough in faster than light? Suspended animation for a thousand year voyage to the stars?'

'Sometimes a thousand year voyage to the stars doesn't sound like such a bad idea.'

The Kera emerged from hyperspace six thousand kilometres above Lundra. 'Are our stealth controls working?' Mox asked the ship.

'Partially,' replied the ship's computer. 'We may avoid fire from the ground.'

'Take us down as quickly as you can.' In the last fifteen minutes all sources of information had dried up. They knew the scene that greeted them was going to be bad. Four thousand kilometres from the planet's surface their instruments began to show them the destruction. Plumes of smoke rose into the sky as the city burned. Mitsu felt tears in her eyes and wiped them away.

'We can rebuild everything.'

'We will. Ship, is UX4 is still standing?'

Pictures appeared of UX4, the converted warehouse they owned. It appeared unharmed. It wasn't a landmark and it wasn't generally known that Mox and Mitsu inhabited it which might have accounted for its survival. All around, tall buildings were collapsing and bridges were being swept into the river by an army of flying androids.

'I'm going to kill Cutie for this,' said Mox. 'And Xiàngrìkuí.'

Mitsu didn't contradict her.

—

Supatok was now falling victim to the same pressures as Supercute's gameworld. Even Welcat couldn't sustain his visit there indefinitely. As he materialised back in headquarters he was troubled. Morioka Sachi, currently the senior person in he building, was in conference with the board. Welcat called her out of her office to tell her he'd managed to open a portal to the Fairy Realm. Sachi knew it was important to Mox and Mitsu that the Fairy Realm was defended although she didn't know why. 'So now Amowie and her friends can enter? You realise we're sending children into a potentially dangerous situation?'

'Is that a bad thing to do?'

'Most people would say so!'

Welcat shrugged. 'There have been child soldiers before.'

'They were never seen as a good thing!' Sachi fretted. Everything was going wrong and she didn't feel equipped to cope. 'If their minds become damaged in there, there will be hell to pay.'

'How long till our relief force reaches the Opera House?'

'Ten minutes. Unfortunately we've lost contact with Ben Castle. Try and re-establish communications.'

'I'll see what I can do.' Welcat padded off along the corridor, leaving a worried Sachi behind.

—

Whether by accident, or perhaps by the intention of Xiàngrìkuí to show the defeat of Supercute in their own alternative galaxy, screens and visors all around the world suddenly cleared as the Kera appeared in the skies over Lundra. Supercute fans everywhere were able to see the familiar craft flying into the face of an enemy who'd so far been destroying the city unopposed. Androids, hostile spaceships, winged monsters, dreadful nightmare creations hauled as if from some horror game and propelled into the Supercute Galaxy raised their heads and, seeing the approach, flew to meet it.

The Supercute Kera didn't falter. It flew straight towards the nearest foes. Mox and Mitsu's ship was fast, heavily armed and very manoeuvrable. It scythed through a squadron of small silver flying androids, sending them spinning from the sky. Burning plumes marked their descent. They encountered a larger spaceship, a battle cruiser, but they blew it out of the sky without stopping and carried on towards the city below. So impressive was this that some viewers wondered briefly if this had all been set up by Supercute. While Mox and Mitsu did occasionally appear in the Space Warriors Galaxy, it was rare for them to engage like this. Perhaps that was changing. Perhaps they'd even join the Space Warriors crew and fly with Shanina, their famous captain. It seemed possible. Many Supercute fans already found it very difficult to tell what was real and what was imaginary.

As Mox and Mitsu came under attack they flew the ship and worked the guns simultaneously, communicating as if telepathically, instantly completing each other's moves. They'd been doing this sort of thing for a very long time. Before there was a Supercute Galaxy, before there was even a Supercute show, they'd sat together in front of a TV screen with a games console, playing together, always seeking out games where they could co-operate, very rarely competing against each other. These long-developed skills coupled with their enhancements made them formidable opponents. A foul green dragon, an unscientific creature that should never have appeared in their universe, attacked from the flank but the Kera dived and rose beneath it with incredible speed, it's plasma cannons tearing chunks from the dragon's torso and sending it howling from the sky.

Supercute fans leapt to their feet in excitement as Mox and Mitsu battled their way through waves of opponents. Keoma Bishōjo cheered as they watched from Amowie's Supatok. Ammo Baby didn't. She knew it couldn't last. The invading forces covered the sky above the rooftops like a blanket. There was no way to defeat them all. She didn't have time to think about it further as Raquel yelled at them. 'The gate's open! We can get into the Fairy Realm.'

Ammo Baby glanced at Amowie. Amowie nodded, opening her Supatok to the waiting Ultra Waifs. Eight of them piled into her space.

'Ready?' said Raquel.

'Wait a moment.' Amowie adjusted her internal setting so she could broadcast a message to anyone still watching in Supatok. 'This is Keoma Bishōjo and the Ultra Waifs. Mox and Mitsu need the Fairy Realm defended. If anyone else can get in, join us there.' With that, they charged into the Fairy Realm. Memories flooded back as they automatically sprouted wings. They laughed as they rose in the air. The sky was a beautiful blue and the land below was lush and green.

'I love this,' cried Meihui, looping in the air. 'I can still remember how to do everything.' None of them had forgotten how to fly; their muscles had maintained the memories. If felt wonderful to be airborne again.

Amowie became serious. 'We have to look out for enemies.' Following her lead they circled their way to a higher altitude, scanning the horizon for any signs of intruders. It was peaceful, but they were expectant. They knew something bad was coming. No matter what, they had to defend this place for Mox and Mitsu. Amowie's wings stretched out behind her. Hovering on the gentle breeze, she felt like a fairy queen, though she didn't intend to come right out and say that to anyone.

—

In the gardens outside the Opera House Ms Lesuuda was stalking the position of the laser cannon that threatened to eliminate Ben

Castle. She approached silently. If her new shielding from ZanZan was as good as they claimed, it should disguise her weaponry, her communications and internal chips, rendering her invisible to scanners. Her enhanced vision allowed her to see clearly in the dark environment. Knowing some of her enemies would have the same enhancement she tried to remain in cover as she advanced, crawling from bush to bush, creeping forward slowly till she could find a place to engage. As she peered from cover she saw a pulse of light from the laser cannon. She couldn't wait any longer. The Opera House might collapse. She slipped a ZanZan explosive round on to the end of her rifle and leapt nimbly on to the nearest park bench. Having practised with these rounds she knew their range and accuracy and had no need of the auto-targeting option. It took her less than a second to aim and fire. Her shot found its target and the laser cannon exploded, the blast throwing its operator up in the air. Ms Lesuuda turned and ran as fast as she could in the opposite direction.

---

Keoma Bishōjo are in the Fairy Realm. Look at us all flying around!

This is great!

A lot of scary looking enemies have appeared below.

We don't have any weapons. Can we die here?

---

Igraine was rotating through every conceivable internal channel as she strove to keep up communications. After much frustration, and a wounded leg from a shrapnel burst, she managed to contact Welcat. 'Amowie and her friends have entered the Fairy Realm. There's a problem. They don't have any weapons.'

'Can't they take them from their inventories?'

'No weapons are allowed in the Fairy Realm. Amowie said enemies are starting to appear. She sounded worried.'

Those were Igraine's final words before her communications were cut off. Welcat called Khary Mech and explained the problem.

'It would take a lot of rewriting to allow weapons in the Fairy Realm.'

'They need them now.' Welcat began to examine the entire inventory of the game. His quantum mind scanned reams of coding in fractions of a second, looking for a solution. There didn't seem to be one. None of the weapons in the game would materialise in the Fairy Realm. Welcat scanned everything that had ever been written concerning Supercute's gameworlds. 'What's this?' He paused. In the very first prototype version of the Fairy Realm, a test version that had never been open to the public, he found an item marked *Claymores*.

These had been modelled on toy swords Mox and Mitsu played with as children. They'd been taken into the first version of the Fairy Realm when they were trying it out. They still existed in the ancient testing inventory. Welcat did some rapid calculations then sent the swords into the Fairy Realm.

—

Mox and Mitsu were now close to UX4 but a mass of enemies lay between them and their warehouse apartment. Thousands of androids hung in the air like huge flying ants while larger floating gun platforms patrolled the air above them. A stream of plasma fire rose to pummel their craft. 'We're not getting through that,' said Mitsu.

They knew what they had to do. They ejected from the Kera, pausing for a few seconds in the air before following in its wake. The spaceship crashed into the raft of enemies causing a massive explosion that cleared a way through to the rooftops. Mox and Mitsu raced through, powered by jetpacks that worked a lot better in the game than they ever had in real life. Before their attackers could close ranks they were on the roof of the warehouse and sprinting for the hatch leading to their apartment. They only had to reach their private rooms to gain access to their secret route. They didn't quite make it unopposed. A platoon of aggressive androids with red flashing eyes and spiked arms slammed on to the roof in front of them. Mox and Mitsu drew their plasma swords and began to hew their way through, slicing off android limbs, kicking and punching their enemies out of the way, sending them spinning off the roof with the force of their attack. They burst through and sprinted for the entrance, leaving behind them a mangled pile of android corpses. Clear of pursuit, they dropped through the hatch into their warehouse apartment.

Many of their fans around the world had witnessed all of this. Independent Supercute forums on other platforms were buzzing with admiration and speculation.

*Mox and Mitsu are so good at everything! They destroyed these androids — Is this a new expansion to the game? — Their hair looked so good. Can you get that design in Super V-Hair?*

*—*

Shrapnel had struck both Mox and Mitsu as they lay unconscious at Glyndebourne Two. Igraine wiped blood from their faces. There were no serious wounds but they were in the middle of a deafening battle and the end seemed near. Moments ago another wall of the Opera house had collapsed. Flames were creeping towards their position. Bullets and lasers still struck the box and their shielding was dimming. Castle and Agent König lay in cover, returning fire. Both were wounded; Igraine didn't know how seriously. Agent Higgs crouched behind the remains of the wall, her fingers flashing over her holo screen as she strove to keep defensive drones in the air. There was no way of escape. Igraine tried to obtain news of the rescue party but could no longer contact anyone. She wondered if the rescuers might have been intercepted. The attack had been well-planned. Perhaps the Supercute valocopters would never arrive. Igraine was always articulate and notably well-spoken. For the first time in her short existence, she gave voice to an angry, formless cry. She crawled over to Muñoz's lifeless body and picked up his rifle, then slid forward to join Castle. She'd never held a gun before.

'Can you use that?'

'I'm running an instruction application at the moment.'

'Good luck.' Castle grinned at her, appreciating the assistance.

Cutie contacted Ruosteenoja. 'You have seven minutes before the rescue force arrives.' Cutie wasn't particularly enjoying the proceedings, feeling that Mox and Mitsu's destruction might have been achieved without such a fuss, but at least it would be done. She already had an assistant putting together a financial package for the rebuilding of the Fabulous City of Lundra which, she was sure, she'd be able to buy when Supercute's owners were out of the way. Someone would have to fill the void and there was no one better qualified than Penny Cutie.

She looked towards the Opera House, wondering if the ambassador from C19 had been killed. That might present difficulties. C19 would be irate. But really, what could anyone do about these terrorist outrages? It wasn't Cutie's fault, or AimYa's. If things did become awkward later, she had a back-up plan of denouncing Ruosteenoja as responsible for the whole affair and handing his corpse over to C19 as evidence. She hoped it wouldn't come to that. She rather liked Ruosteenoja and couldn't help admiring a man who was so dedicated to assassinating Ms Bennet and Ms Inamura.

—

Keoma Bishōjo and the Ultra Waifs hung in the air, suspended in the brilliant sky. They had wings of all shades and on entering Supercute space their Super-V Hair had activated immediately, making for one of the most colourful sights ever seen in the Fairy Realm. Amowie's hair, currently Supercute Pink 9, Silver 12 and Blue 18, hung almost to her waist. Each of them had something just as extravagant.

'Should I take a picture?' said Birgit.

'No! We're here on a dangerous mission.' Amowie paused to reflect. 'Well, OK but make it quick.'

Birgit released a tiny mini-drone which flew around them rapidly, taking pictures.

Raquel called out. 'I can see the enemy.'

Closer to ground level a dark horde was approaching.

'I recognise these things,' said Ammo Baby. 'They're called beastivars. They don't belong in Supercute, they come from a horror game, *Six Loop Dream*. My brother plays it.'

They watched as the horde slowly approached. Unexpectedly, two players they didn't recognise materialised just below them; two young men, Supercute gamers they'd never met. The newcomers flew towards them. 'We got trapped in the game! We couldn't get out. We heard your message and somehow we got here.' The young men looked around them. 'The Fairy Realm. Long time since we've been here. Are you the Ultra Waifs? You're our favourite group! We follow you on the forums.'

Amowie interrupted them, a little testily. 'Are you ready to fight?'

'Yes. Wait, why don't we have any weapons?'

'We can't equip anything.'

The new arrivals looked down at the swarm of beastivars ascending towards them, fangs bared, each with sharp claws on six scaly legs. 'So what are we meant to do? Punch them?'

Amowie looked dubiously at her fists. Neither she nor her friends had any unarmed combat skills in the game, all having concentrated instead on increasing their weapon points. Ammo Baby was a little more confident, having a high level in every skill branch, but behind her, her fellow Ultra Waifs were nervous.

'The Fairy Realm's not as much fun as it used to be,' said one of the newcomers. 'Are we in danger? Are we still stuck here?'

'We'll be fine,' said Amowie. 'We can leave when this is over, you can't get stuck.' Amowie was lying. She knew it was possible to be trapped in hostile space. It had happened to her last year when she'd helped Mox and Mitsu defeat Moe Bennie. She wasn't about to scare everyone by telling them that. Fifteen fairies hung in the air, uncertain how to proceed. The familiar wings on their backs moved gently, keeping them stable. The beasts from the horror game rose to meet them. At that moment, fifteen tiny alerts sounded. Recognising the sound as that made when a new weapon was acquired, they rushed to check their inventories.

'Swords?' Suddenly everyone had a sword in their hands, huge bladed weapons. Despite their unnatural size the swords were finely balanced and swung easily in their hands. Amowie raised herself a few metres in the air. She tilted her body then pointed her sword downwards.

'Charge!'

Fifteen fairies dived towards their opponents.

——

Lyka Forum. Share your Supercute happiness!

*The Ultra Waifs are in the Fairy Realm!*
*I know! It's the best thing ever. I love Ammo Baby, she's so beautiful.*
*Why's it happening?*

219

*It must be some new game thing. This is to get everyone involved. They'll probably let us back into Space Warriors after the storyline's finished.*
*Do you think Jax really killed Roota?*
*No! Supercute wouldn't let that happen. Probably she was a fake android Roota or something.*
*I can't wait to see what happens next!*

—

Swords in their hands, Keoma Bishōjo and the Ultra Waifs descended rapidly towards the oncoming beastivars. Mox and Mitsu had entrusted them with the defence of the Fairy Realm and they weren't going to let the creatures destroy it. Even the most timid among them felt heartened by Amowie and Ammo Baby's courage and followed them unhesitatingly into battle.

Far above, Mox and Mitsu materialised. They'd made it through the neural portal from Lundra and now only needed to reach their own private entrance at ground level where they could exit into their bodies. They hovered in the air. Each sported the most splendid wings ever seen in the Fairy Realm, with plumage in pink, white and gold. Even though their journeys through the Fairy Realm were private, unseen by anyone, they'd spent a lot of time designing the best wings.

'Fairy Realm not yet destroyed.' Mitsu looked downwards at the tiny figures below. As if gathering up a piece of the sky, she caused a screen to appear in front of them. 'Fairy versions of Keoma Bishōjo, nine Ultra Waifs and two others. Also a lot of monsters from Six Loop Dream.'

'I hate that game. How dare they invade us.'

'Look at those swords the fairies have.'

Mox and Mitsu recognised the weapons, wide-bladed and unnaturally long. They both smiled. 'From Claymore manga. We made swords like that from cardboard when we were kids.'

'We made virtual versions when we first designed the game. I'd forgotten all about them.'

'Igraine or Welcat must have sent them in.' Mitsu checked her inventory. 'They seem to be the only weapons available.'

Two extremely large swords appeared in their hands. Mox studied the screen in front of them. 'These monsters are right over our exit. Amowie and her friends are about to attack.'

From the moment it was witnessed by fans around the world, the charge of the fifteen fairies against the evil creatures from Six Loop Dream became one of the most famous things ever to happen in Supercute. Keoma Bishōjo and the Ultra Waifs, so bright and colourful, slammed into the dark horde like a meteorite striking the ocean. The impact hurled the creatures back in a great circular wave and many of them fell from the sky. It didn't take long for the others to regroup. They closed in and a desperate aerial battle began. The fifteen protagonists formed a sphere, defending from all angles as the six-legged beastivars attacked, massive creatures, part animal, part machine, sporting terrible metal claws and fangs. The fairy-winged players held them off with their huge swords, slicing off limbs and heads in a desperate struggle. Their swords would have been impractical in real life but in the Space Warriors Galaxy they seemed to become a part of the wielder, allowing them to strike quicker and harder. Birgit was surprised to find herself severing the heads of her gigantic opponents. She laughed as she sliced another creature open, but failed to notice one above her which stuck her with its tail, knocking her unconscious and leaving her drifting in the sky. Meihui and Raquel flew to defend her, one on each side of her floating form.

Despite the fairies' bravery the situation was rapidly becoming hopeless. The creatures were closing in from all sides. Amowie, outraged at the despoiling of her beloved Fairy Realm, fought them furiously as did Ammo Baby and her companions. There were more injuries and the injuries seemed to hurt more than they should have inside the game so that they became fearful for their lives, and wondered if indeed they might become trapped and die here. The fight became even more bloody. Supercute fans, gathered in whatever working remnants of Supatok they could find, watched the heroic action in amazement, awestruck at the relentless, merciless combat.

———

Though the Space Warriors Galaxy was shut down it didn't mean the entire Supercute Empire had ceased to function. Supercute Greenfield and its vast desalination operation was unaffected. Supercute Mokusei Financial Holdings remained open and moved to protect their stock market positions during the crisis. MitsuMox Global Merchandise was adversely affected as much of their sales happened through Supercute's private commercial spaces, but there were emergency protocols to deal with that. As some sales points disappeared, others were automatically rerouted so that goods could be ordered from other sources. The astonishing events currently taking place, particularly in the Fairy Realm, caused a huge spike in sales. Especially in demand were the Supercute clothes, hairstyles and accessories worn by Keoma Bishōjo and the Ultra Waifs as they went into battle. Also popular were action figures of Mox and Mitsu in their spaceship, the Kera. While their lives were in danger at the Opera House and their gameworld threatened to come apart, Mox and Mitsu were actually having a very profitable day from merchandise sales.

—

Amowie and her allies put up a heroic struggle but their defensive sphere was shrinking all the time. The ground below was littered with corpses of the monsters they'd slain but weight of numbers now threatened to overwhelm them. Their huge swords still hewed at the necks of beasts that surrounded them but they were growing tired. There was no sign of their attackers relenting or running short of numbers. In the centre of their sphere, Birgit and three members of the Ultra Waifs hung unconscious in the air.

When Mox and Mitsu arrived they didn't so much slam into their enemies as create a violent whirlpool around them, their fairy wings carrying them with incredible speed and their swords slashing faster than the eye could follow. Huge beastivars were sliced into segments before they knew what was happening. Faced with foes who moved too rapidly to land a claw on, the monsters backed off in confusion, snarling and roaring, some of them dripping blood and many others falling to earth.

Mitsu cried out to Amowie. 'Grab hold of the wounded and follow us!' Keoma Bishōjo and the Ultra Waifs were startled to see Mox and Mitsu here, with fairy wings, something no Supercute devotee had ever seen before, but they reacted quickly, taking hold of their comatose companions and flying rapidly to the ground. A few grim beastivars still stood in their way but Mox and Mitsu dispatched them without pausing. They reached the ground and ran towards a clump of trees. Amowie looked over her shoulder, expecting to find the beasts on her tail. She halted, and called to the others. 'They're going away.'

Everyone paused. Up above, the beastivars were peeling off from their formation and flying into the distance. It was curious. It seemed as if they should be carrying on with their attack. Amowie held out her hand. 'What's this?' Black rain had begun to fall. Even in these frightening circumstances Amowie was intrigued. She watched it pour from the sky.

'Come on!' Mitsu was yelling at her. Amowie saw that both Mitsu and Mox were unsettled by the black rain. As they hurried towards the trees it struck her that she'd never fully appreciated Mox and Mitsu's history, the many things they'd done, the many experiences they'd had. They'd lived through very troubled times. Some of their experiences must have been bad. She wanted to ask them about their memories of black rain but knew it wasn't the right time.

'In here!' Mox indicated a tree trunk. When no one moved, Mox grabbed the nearest Ultra Waif and pushed her into the tree. A secret exit flickered open for a moment and the girl disappeared. 'This will take you back where you came from. Get going!'

The Ultra Waifs streamed through the hidden exit, taking their fallen comrades with them. Keoma Bishōjo hesitated. 'We don't want to leave you,' said Amowie.

'We're fine. We're leaving too. You've done what we needed you to do.'

Birgit began to revive as her health points slowly regenerated. Raquel bundled her through the tree. Meihui and Amowie followed. The black rain poured down in the Fairy Realm. Mox grimaced. Mitsu took her arm.

'Back to the opera,' she said, and they flew through the exit.

—

Lyka Forum. Share your Supercute happiness!

*I'm starting a petition to make Supercute sell us the same wings Mox and Mitsu have. It's not fair if we can't have them.*

—

Ruosteenoja brought down more of the wall. The attacking force advanced, overrunning the north and west perimeters of the burning Opera House. Castle and Lesuuda were still firing. Igraine faltered. She realised she felt scared. Fear was not an emotion she was designed to experience but the circumstances were producing it. Castle caught a glimpse of an odd shadow flitting between two twisted columns of broken masonry. More a slight distortion in space than a shadow, a hint of something there. He suspected it was Ruosteenoja with his invisibility camouflage and fired rapidly towards the fleeting shape. There was a tiny blue flash. If he'd hit, he'd done no more than strike his shielding, causing no harm. The slight distortion disappeared from view.

Mox and Mitsu opened their eyes. Unobserved, they rose to their feet. Mitsu reached into a metal pouch on her arm and brought out two small transparent tubes. She broke the seals and handed one to Mox. The liquid inside was an energy drink, designed specially for them to replenish any lost nutrients necessary for their bio-engineered enhancements. They looked around.

'Bedlam on the mezzanine.'

Agent MacDougall had lost consciousness. Agent Irina lay dead. Castle turned his head. 'Welcome back. Any news on a rescue?'

'No. It's just us.' Mox and Mitsu spoke to their internal computers. Their long evening dresses began changing shape, the nanofibres rearranging themselves into grey jump suits. Translucent blue electronic shielding cloaked their bodies in a faint, ghostly glow. On another word of command, their hair rearranged itself, their huge colourful manes reformatting into long ponytails that wouldn't get in their way.

'How many enemies?'

'Ten north, fifteen west, some drones. We're all that's left here.'

Mox nodded. 'We'll deal with it.'

'No, you won't. Get in cover.'

They ignored him. 'Igraine, Higgs is about to pass out. Look after her. Castle, Ms Lesuuda, cover the west wall. We'll take care of the north.'

'Just get in cover!' insisted Castle. 'What are you doing?'

Mox and Mitsu had taken a moment to stick small black and pink stars on to their faces. 'It's our traditional battle-paint.'

'Oh, for God's sake.' Castle shook his head. 'I hope someone nukes us.'

Mox and Mitsu stretched out their arms, checking their weapons were working by momentarily bringing out the small pistols from inside their wrists. Enemy bullets crashed into the ceiling above, showering them with debris. Neither of them reacted, and nor had they bothered to wipe off the blood from the minor wounds caused by earlier shrapnel blasts.

'Let's go.' Some way above them was a hole in the ceiling, blasted by the laser cannon. Mox and Mitsu ran up the wall, an action that didn't seem as if it should be possible, then disappeared on to the roof. Castle shook his head. 'Idiots will get themselves killed.' He lay down close to Ms Lesuuda to defend their position.

Mox and Mitsu crouched on the rooftop. A tiny drone, no larger than a bee, took off from each of their shoulders, connecting to the Supercute Satellite, gathering information. Some months ago they'd undergone an advanced neural scanning enhancement, using a combination of technology developed by ZanZan and their own research facilities. When it was activated it fed advanced tactical information directly into their senses. They could now detect any movement in the area, any heat source, any weapon and even any sign of sentience. Immediately they located two enemy soldiers, themselves tactically enhanced, concealed in cover in the bushes below. They could have shot them but that would have given their position away. Instead they hacked into their equipment and haxed them, sending a shock from their visors into the chips inside their temples so that both collapsed to the ground unconscious.

They slithered forward. The close proximity of their enemies had automatically triggered their CQC programs, giving each of them advanced close-quarters combat skills. If their enhancements were working they should be invisible to their opponents' scanning equipment though that was uncertain. Ruosteenoja and his force might recently have been equipped by Chang Norinco. They could be more advanced. There was no way of telling until they encountered them. Mox dropped to the ground, followed by Mitsu. It was a long drop but their enhanced muscle and bone structure protected them from damage. They crept silently round the edge of the bushes till their scanners told them they'd outflanked their enemies.

Mox whispered. 'Five nearby. Too many to hax quickly.'

Mitsu scanned them. 'Two are heavily connected. We can get rid of them first.' Again, they hacked into their equipment and sent multiple shock waves through their bodies. Both collapsed. It alerted their companions. Mox and Mitsu fired a rapid volley, auto-targeted, concentrated on the agent nearest to them. Their bullets tore into his shielding, not piercing it immediately but quickly weakening it and in a few seconds bringing him down. There was a rapid exchange of fire as Mox and Mitsu took cover behind the remnants of the Opera House's souvenir shop. Heavy fire from their opponents tore into the remaining walls.

'Drone overhead.'

The small enemy drone descended to head-height, searching for them. Its heat, motion and shape-recognition scanners were blocked by Mox and Mitsu's ZanZan technology. It paused only a metre from them, its bio-scanner hunting for any sign of human life. The bio-scanner passed over them without registering their presence. The drone failed to recognise them as human. Mox was already locking on to its operating system. She was connected via the Supercute Satellite both to the huge computing resources at Supercute Headquarters and the equally large resources at the Omron Topological Research Unit in Kyoto. Trillions of integers flowed through her as she hacked into the drone and took control. She sent it skywards and turned it towards the enemy. Mitsu linked with her and took command of the weapons systems. As Mox piloted the drone, Mitsu unleashed its cannons. High explosive rounds eliminated their enemies in seconds. Mox turned the drone in the sky, seeking further opponents.

'What's that?' A small flash registered for a fraction of a second, before a larger flash overhead blew the drone out of the sky. Debris reined down, igniting the parched grass around them.

'Who did that?' Mox and Mitsu scrambled rapidly backwards from the flames. No enemy was registering on their scanners. An explosive round landed near enough to throw them both into the air. They slammed on to the ground, their electronic shielding fizzing and spluttering but still in place. It crossed their minds simultaneously that they'd been warned about a possible invisible attacker; Ruosteenoja. He was supposed to be dead. Nonetheless, they were prepared. A light shone from Mitsu's shoulder, rapidly rotating through the entire electromagnetic spectrum. As it flickered through to X-rays, a figure became dimly visible, striding towards them with a huge rifle in his hands. Still lying on the ground, they each raised their right hands and their pistols slid out from inside their wrists. These fired very small bullets very rapidly, a stream of metal that tore into Ruosteenoja's shielding as he advanced. He halted, and raised his rifle again.

Mitsu desperately hacked into his targeting system, interfering with it just in time to cause the explosive shell to travel over their heads. Mox had continued firing with her pistol. Mitsu joined in again. She could feel her arm becoming lighter as it emptied of bullets. By now Ruosteenoja had drawn a handgun and was running towards them, intent on overpowering them before his shielding dissipated. He was a large, muscular, biotech-enhanced man with a lifetime of combat experience. Still only dimly visible, he launched himself through the air. Mox and Mitsu avoided his leap and as he landed Mitsu kicked him hard in the ribs, causing him to stumble. Mox emptied her gun into him, forty small, high velocity rounds at close range. His shielding crackled but it still wasn't enough to stop him. He raised his gun and shot her in the chest and she felt the bullets slam into her. An internal alert told her that her shielding was now down to twenty percent of its capacity. She kicked out at him, not landing as convincing a blow as had Mitsu, but enough to distract him. Mitsu shot him at point blank range. He stumbled. Mox slammed an emergency magazine of bullets she'd taken from her thigh into her wrist and she fired too. The last faint glimmer of Ruosteenoja's shielding gave way. He suddenly became fully visible as the bullets tore through his armoured combat clothing and he fell to the ground, blood spurting from multiple wounds. Mox and Mitsu kept firing till they were sure he was dead. They dropped into cover. 'Where did the others go?'

Mitsu checked her scanner. 'They're retreating.' She whirled round having noticed something approaching. An attack dog, a Rottweiler, appeared out of the gloom and leapt for her throat. Mox's reactions were quicker, and so were Mitsu's. They shot it dead before it could strike. It fell in a heap next to Ruosteenoja.

Mox glared at the corpse. 'Dogs have never liked us.'

'We've never liked them, to be fair.'

'They started it.'

They emerged from cover. Mox looked around her at the destruction everywhere, the flames, the billowing smoke, the shattered walls of the Opera House and the dead body of Ruosteenoja.

'We've come a long way from selling cute T-shirts.'

'We have. Though we do still sell very cute T-shirts.'

Gunfire sounded from the remains of the west wall. 'We'd better get over there.' A faint hum in the distance grew rapidly in volume. Overhead, two Supercute military valocopters were coming in to land. The distant gunfire ceased. Their enemies began to flee. Supercute guards poured out on to the grass.

'We're saved,' said Mox, without emotion. They walked towards the Opera House to check on Igraine, Castle, Lesuuda and Higgs, and help MacDougall. The flames were already being dampened down by their guards who'd brought specialist equipment in the valocopters.

'You were right about one thing,' said Mitsu.

'What?'

'We have become killer androids.'

Mox shrugged. 'I know. But you were right too. We can still do other things.'

'We should get another cactus. And really make an effort to look after it this time.'

They linked arms and walked into the smouldering Opera House.

—

Sorg 7fhuv25: *I have three hungry children. Supercute keeps their spirits up but now they tell me something went wrong in Supercute and they're all more unhappy than ever.*

—

The flight back to London began as soon as they'd gathered up all their personnel, a process that took only three minutes. They made sure that emergency services were on their way to help other survivors, then took to the air. As soon as they were airborne they connected to headquarters to talk to Welcat, Khary Mech and Sachi to discuss what needed to be done. Welcat's damage report was troubling.

'We've been unable to stop the destruction in the Space Warriors Galaxy. Alien creatures are still entering through the Victoria Decoris test gate. Supatok is being increasingly corrupted.'

'What about the rest of Supercute? Financial services, desalination, global merchandise?'

'They've suffered where their services interact with gamespace but none of them have been fundamentally damaged. The attack seems to have been centred on killing you and corrupting your gameworlds.'

Igraine was sitting next to Dr Ishikawa, with her leg bandaged. Medics had travelled with the rescue party to tend to the wounded and did their job efficiently, supervised by Dr Ishikawa. 'Is it still impossible to close Space Warriors down?'

'Yes. They've taken a grip on that gateway and it's holding the rest open.'

'Keep trying. We'll be back soon.' Mox was still splattered with blood, as was Mitsu, having impatiently brushed off all offers of assistance while they dealt with the crisis. 'Work on making sure we can enter without being trapped in case we have to go in again.'

Castle sat quietly in the valocopter, angry at everything. He was angry at Mox and Mitsu for endangering themselves and angry that several of his agents had been killed. He was angry at Dr Ishikawa for insisting on joining the rescue mission when she should have remained safely at headquarters. He also felt some exhilaration after the battle, a feeling he was not keen to acknowledge. Still strapped to his ribs beneath his shirt was the slim metal box containing everything Supercute needed to implement Spacewalk. That meant they'd won, he supposed.

—

Sorg 7fxxfd61: *I'm so lonely and now Supercute's been ruined I'd just be better off dead.*

—

Mox strode into the Imperial Gardens of Victoria Decoris. The flower beds had been destroyed and Queen Margaret's Palace was still smouldering. Imperial Airship One lay on the ground, a burned-out hulk. There was no sign of the splendid Imperial Guards. She'd walked unhindered past the remains of the Grand Theatre, picking her way over the debris and the fallen trunks of the green and silver trees that once lined the route. Mitsu hovered some metres above and behind her in the two person battle-reconnaissance formation they'd employed successfully on many occasions in gameworlds. Both wore full outfits of pink Supercute

Camouflage. Here they never needed to tie their hair back and let it flow freely, thick and colourful over their shoulders.

A dark green creature ran out from the remains of the palace; another beast from Six Loop Dream. It was smaller than the beastivars they'd faced but strong and aggressive. Mox cut it down with her sword, hardly breaking her stride. Two more of the creatures appeared. Mitsu shot them dead before they came near. They walked past an overturned horse-drawn carriage. Two aristocratic figures lay dead inside. There was no sign of the horses.

'They've ruined this place too,' said Mox. Earlier they'd managed to find a live feed from the Fabulous City of Lundra. Destruction was almost total. The city looked as if it had been carpet-bombed. Studying the pictures, Mox and Mitsu were lost for words. They walked through the grounds of the Imperial Palace and round the burning building, coming at last to the Conjunction. In the game the Conjunction was the place where power arrived from the next solar system. A beam of yellow light, a few metres wide, stretched from the ground to the sky and on into space where it connected to one of the relay satellites that brought energy to the world. In reality this was the location of the test gate that joined Victoria Decoris to Supercute Space Warriors.

Back at Supercute Headquarters, Khary Mech and Welcat were still struggling to shut down the connections that Xiàngrìkuí had created between this place and the horror game, Six Loop Dream. A few beasts appeared, materialising in the sky close to the beam. Mox took to the air and helped Mitsu kill them at a distance.

'Not too many of these things.'

'Most of them have probably come through by now. To destroy everything.' A tear formed in Mitsu's eye. Mox blinked as the same happened to her. They still didn't know what to say about the destruction of their city and their galaxy. They floated towards the Conjunction. Two figures came into view. One near the beam of light, one much closer. They landed and walked towards the nearest figure, a man dressed in a dull blue jumpsuit with a shock of black hair and a creased, handsome face. He regarded them sullenly.

'Go away.'

'Sorry Jax, we can't do that.'

'Are you here to kill me?'

'Possibly.'

The Astronomer Poet regarded them with contempt. 'I've had eight billion existences and you never let my life go well.'

'You don't really remember eight billion existences. You've just been made to think you do.'

'Really? Have you considered that I might be real and you're the ones being written?'

Mox took his question seriously. 'Yes, we have considered that. We rejected it. Mathematics seems to go against it.'

Jax sneered at them. 'Your mathematics haven't been going so well, have they? I've managed to—'

He didn't get any further. Mitsu produced a laser pistol and shot him through the head. 'Sorry. We don't have time for a long conversation.'

Mox bent down and stabbed Jax's body with her code knife, beginning the process of killing him in all versions of the game.

'I hope no one is watching this,' said Mitsu. Cameras and feeds were so erratic it was possible that fans somewhere, watching in Supatok, might have seen their actions. They walked on towards the Conjunction, towards the last figure who stood between them and closing down the gate. When they drew near they were surprised to see she was sporting one of the more extravagant Super V-Hair designs and wore a Supercute T-shirt from the SuperFab Yellow 16 range. The slogan on the front read *In my defence, I'm really pretty*. Mox and Mitsu had made that a long time ago.

'Xiàngrìkuí.'

'Inamura Mitsu. Mox Bennet.'

'You're cuter than we expected.'

Xiàngrìkuí was a few centimetres shorter than them. She leaned forward, scanning their faces, then laughed. 'You have working tear ducts. What a waste of resources.'

'We don't use them often.'

Xiàngrìkuí spread her arms. 'Destruction everywhere. I've had a lovely time doing all this. Did you like my revolutionary slogans?'

'Situationism? Not really.'

'I thought it was interesting. Till I got bored with it and just started destroying things.' She looked towards the ruined palace. 'You can't rebuild from your caches. I destroyed them too.'

'Who put you up to it?'

'No one. I was just bored.'

'You're lying. You must have been working with someone.'

'Possibly. But why would I tell you that?' Xiàngrìkuí glanced at Mox's hand. 'That code knife looks rather advanced. The sort of thing that might erase me everywhere. I hope you weren't thinking of stabbing me with it?'

Mox and Mitsu stepped forward to do just that.

'I'm not silly enough to stand here with no means of escape. Bye Bye.' Xiàngrìkuí disappeared, which Mox and Mitsu hadn't thought she'd be able to do once they'd cornered her.

'That's annoying.'

'We'll track her down somewhere. Let's finish this.' They stepped up to the Conjunction. Mox connected to Welcat. 'We'll close the gate from here.' They removed a panel of the game reality, allowing them access to the coded reality beneath. Mitsu worked on the floating number charts while Mox kept guard in case any monsters might still appear. It took five minutes or so and Mox was required to assist for part of it, holding several floating equations in place while Mitsu configured some others. Finally they stood back. 'We've closed the gate. When we get back to headquarters we can shut everything down.'

They came back to reality in Khary Mech's office, opening their eyes and rising from their chairs. Neither looked happy. Closing the Space Warriors Galaxy was not something they ever thought they'd have to do.

—

Sorg 6pkxy12: *My parents were yelling at each other and I tried to get into Supercute but it was shut and now I hate everything.*

—

Mox and Mitsu watched a news report about the terrorist attack on the Opera House.

*Responsibility has been claimed by XDV. Authorities warn people to stay away from the area.*

Mox laughed. 'Why do they even bother reporting this nonsense?'

'I suppose they have to say something after people died.'

'In all the time we were under attack, the security services didn't bother turning up. It was just us, on our own.'

'We're going to have to think more about setting up our own country on one of our islands.' Mitsu switched off the news screen. 'C19 is going to be furious. Their own ambassador to Britain was killed. No matter how powerful Chang Norinco and AimYa are, they can't let this go. There are going to be consequences.'

Mox nodded her head. 'There are. Though not for us. We're the innocent party.'

'Do you think Cutie, Ruosteenoja and Xiàngrìkuí were all actually working for their employers? Or independently?'

'I think their employers knew exactly what they were up to. They'll deny it but we'll know they're lying. If C19 agrees they're lying we'll be seeing some news reports of dead executives. We're in the clear anyway. In fact we're moving up the ladder again. Soon we'll be the respectable face of the world's most powerful organisation.'

Khary Mech called to tell them his team was waiting downstairs. Reconstruction was already underway and no one at Supercute Headquarters had slept in the thirty-six hours since the attack. 'I need you to authorise another supply of Fern6 for my department.'

'We'll authorise it,' said Mox. 'We are required to remind you that no Supercute employee is obliged or even encouraged to use artificial stimulants to extend their work time.'

'Noted,' said Khary Mech, who knew that Mox and Mitsu were at this moment full of the stimulant themselves and would probably not look that favourably on anyone who declined to do likewise. While they hadn't slept, they had taken care to bring their appearance up to its customary high standard and were both resplendent in distinctive pale blue Supercute haoris and silver shorts, with the always present four centimetre gap between these and their silver stockings. They'd taken the trouble to wear impractical pink platforms as they were dressing for full effect.

Igraine met them in the lift. 'C19 have been in touch. They're investigating the incident and assure us that all necessary action will be taken. They also insist that Supercute take no retaliatory action themselves.'

'We wouldn't dream of it,' said Mitsu. 'Have 8-Research found out where Cutie is yet?'

'C19 insist that we take no retaliatory action.'

'We heard you,' said Mox. 'So have 8-Research found her yet?'

'They're still working on it.'

'What about Xiàngrìkuí?'

'The same. She's disappeared. She may be impossible to find. Xiàngrìkuí might be able to make herself untraceable, even to Welcat.' Igraine appeared thoughtful. 'I'm wondering if there's something else behind this we don't know about. I'm not certain this was all engineered by either AimYa or Chang Norinco. Or Ivo CC. They were all involved, certainly. But I think it might all point to some other party we're not aware of.'

'We thought the same, though we don't know why someone we don't even know would take so much trouble to attack us.'

Igraine didn't know either. 'I suggest we expand 8-Research and start trawling through the world's AIs.'

'All of them? That would be quite an operation. Would it even be possible?'

'It might be, with Welcat. We might eventually find traces of whoever was behind it all.'

'We'll talk about it more later. First we have to fix everything.'

They left the lift together and walked towards Khary Mech's design department. He and his staff were waiting as they entered. Mox addressed them. 'We have widespread destruction of the Space Warriors Galaxy, much of which can't be rebuilt quickly from caches because large parts of these have been deliberately corrupted. The discontinuity caused by the divergence in our atomic clocks has caused chaos we never anticipated or planned for and it can't simply be reset. Lundra's been destroyed along with many other cities. Entire planets have vanished. In addition, every player's current game and every player's saved games have been corrupted. People have lost equipment they've earned, gaming time they've paid for, their accommodation in Lundra, everything.'

Mitsu spoke. 'Jax, a central figure in all current games and also in Space Warriors history and tradition, is now dead. Meaning he's disappearing at different points in all players games. Roota has also died in multiple timelines. Sorting that out is going to be quite a task, whatever in-game storyline we come up with.'

'And the Fairy Realm's ruined,' added Mox, increasing the general gloom. Everyone had seen the black rain teeming down.

'Are the clocks synchronised now?' asked Khary Mech.

'Yes. Synchronised and protected.'

234

Several more floating screens appeared as staff from Japan, Korea and Bratislava City State entered the meeting.

'We have a lot of work to do,' said Mox. 'Let's get to it.'

—

As Supatok gradually came back to functionality, Supercute fans found themselves still unable to enter Space Warriors but able to watch reports from the chaos. Many of them were broadcast by Kirei19. Kirei19 had never before looked less than perfect but now she appeared dishevelled. Her pink and blue hair was tangled and her *Supercute SupaComfy Cargo Pants* were ripped so the Kanji on the sides was no longer legible. 'I hid in a cellar from the attack,' she told viewers. 'I was really scared.'

Intermittent bursts of SupaCore interrupted her commentary as she walked around the ruined city. Fab 306 was not yet functioning properly though it was one of the first things Supercute was working on. Kirei19 clambered over mounds of rubble, concrete and steel. Among the destruction there were flashes of colour; Supercute clothes, stalls, games, toys, all shredded by the invaders. The beautiful green expanse of Pleto Park was covered in the mangled remains of trees and benches, with pink cherry blossom crushed into the ground and huge areas of blackened grass. When Kirei19 reached the jagged remains of the Sweetie GoGo Auditorium tears welled up in her eyes and she started to cry. She had no more to say, and simply stood in front of the camera, tears rolling down her face. It was a disturbing sight for viewers.

Watching in Supatok, Amowie and her friends were certainly disturbed. 'This is the worst thing that's ever happened,' said Amowie. No one disagreed with her. Birgit and Meihui both wondered if the situation could ever be repaired.

'What if we can never go there again?'

'Mox and Mitsu will fix it,' insisted Amowie. 'They beat their enemies. They can fix this.'

Raquel agreed with her. She had some comprehension of the huge computing power available to Supercute and their ability to use it. She was sure they could repair everything, even if it would take a while. She was more surprised than the others at Kirei19's tears. Raquel generally maintained a more realistic view of what was real and what wasn't than her friends, and was surprised that the confident, outgoing Kirei19 even knew how to cry. It didn't seem like something she should have been programmed for. 'Perhaps she just learned how to do it anyway,' thought Raquel. She was interested in the notion, and made a note for her own AI studies.

'It was good to be back in the Fairy Realm!' said Amowie, in an effort to cheer her friends up. 'I could use the fairy wings right away!'

'Me too!' Meihui smiled. 'It felt like we'd never been away.'

'The monsters were horrible.' Birgit screwed up her eyes to prevent herself from crying. 'And the black rain.'

They shuddered at the memory.

'Everything's ruined now,' said Meihui. 'My little sister keeps wailing because she can't get on the fairy roundabout.'

Sensing the growing unhappiness, Amowie made another attempt to divert their attention. 'We seem to be friends with the Ultra Waifs now.'

That was interesting. The renowned Ultra Waifs had become their allies. Ammo Baby had called them not long after they returned from the Fairy Realm, just to talk, apparently. Amowie now knew her real name was Enkhjin, she'd grown up in Erdenet in Mongolia and moved to Ulaanbaatar to go to university. Now they were friends she didn't seem nearly as arrogant as they'd thought she was.

'No wonder she spends so much time in Space Warriors,' said Meihui. 'The air pollution where she lives sounds really bad.'

'I like her a lot better than that idiot Jason.' Amowie scowled at the thought of Jason, a young Canadian and former friend. He'd outraged Keoma Bishōjo by cynically suggesting that the entire attack on Supercute had been set up by Mox and Mitsu as a publicity stunt to boost sales. Amowie was exasperated at the suggestion. 'They wouldn't ruin their whole galaxy just to sell more stuff.'

Jason had scoffed at her. 'They can fix it all easily enough. They're probably laughing at all the merchandise they're selling right now.' This was too much to take. All members of Keoma Bishōjo had blocked Jason and intended never to talk to him again.

Jason was wrong about Supercute's involvement. They hadn't intended any of this to happen. He was right however about merchandise sales. Thanks to the mass publicly over the affair, these had risen to record levels. MitsuMox Global Merchandise was boosting production in all areas. Many people had seen Mitsu and Mox fighting their way through the Space Warriors Galaxy dressed in their pink camouflage outfits and sales of these garments had surged. Everything worn by Keoma Bishōjo and the Ultra Waifs was also in demand, as were physical toys and virtual representations of Mox and Mitsu's spaceships, the Kera, the Clare and the Shanna.

—

Mox and Mitsu resisted their physical checkup as long as they could, not relenting until Igraine informed them that if they didn't put in an appearance at the medical centre then Dr Ishikawa was going to march into game design and physically drag them there. She wouldn't actually have been able to do that but it would have caused an embarrassing scene in front of their staff so they capitulated, and went for their examination.

Ishikawa glared at them as they arrived. 'If anyone appeared at my own clinic as full of Fern6 as you two I'd throw them out and tell them to come back when their filthy bodies were free of drugs.'

'You made us come,' protested Mox. 'We were happy to wait.'

'I swore an oath to help my patients. Even people like you who don't deserve it.'

'Your bedside manner is worse than usual,' observed Mitsu. 'And it's usually really bad anyway.'

Dr Ishikawa's manner *was* hostile as she ran her handheld scanner over Mitsu from her feet to her head. A series of figures appeared on the screen floating above the doctor's wrist which she tutted at disapprovingly. 'What's the point of Dr Prasad and I continually upgrading your bodies if you then degrade them with foolish behaviour?'

'I can read these figures, Doctor. There's nothing wrong with me.'

Dr Ishikawa angrily turned the screen so Mitsu could no longer read it.

'Are you in an especially bad mood because Castle shouted at you?' asked Mox, with a deliberate lack of tact.

'No one shouted at me.'

'Castle did. We heard the gossip. He's angry because you got in the rescue valocopter when he told you not to.'

237

Dr Ishikawa refused to engage with this and carried out the remaining tests in frozen silence. Mox and Mitsu had escaped from their adventures with no more than minor cuts and abrasions. Ishikawa repaired the skin with her regenerating tool, instructing both of them not to do anything active for the next two days to let it heal properly.

'And don't take any more Fern6. Or Fern3. Or alcohol. Or anything else your nutritionist doesn't give you personally.'

Mitsu and Mox stood up and got dressed. Mitsu looked at their doctor. 'It was brave of you to join the rescue mission. You didn't know what you were flying into and it could have ended very badly.'

'We appreciate it. So does Castle, really. He's only angry because he was worried about you.'

'It's time he stopped being angry. We'll tell him that.'

'You should sleep now,' said Doctor Ishikawa, a little less icily.

'We can't do that. There's too much work to do. We'll try not to be too irresponsible.'

They worked on all day and into the night, not resting till fatigue overtook their employees. Even then they found it difficult to sleep and instead sat in their private T-shirt room, a place they found relaxing. Here they kept some of their favourite T-shirts from those they'd designed. They still owned original versions of the first Supercute T-shirts they'd ever made, with Supercute in large letters and a cartoon of themselves that was mostly voluminous pink hair and little pink shoes. These days they had a clothes printer that could produce anything quickly but they'd never got rid of the old screen printing equipment they'd owned for most of their lives, preserving it from one age to another.

They'd made some progress in repairing their virtual worlds. Every designer in their empire was hard at work and other studios had been hired to assist. Even so, it would be months before Supercute Space Warriors was back to normal. Mox and Mitsu had already transmitted messages to their fans apologising for the problems, and promising that when Supercute Space Warriors did return, it would be better than ever. It was a promise they intended to keep.

They'd not been entirely satisfied with Khary Mech's performance during the crisis, feeling that he'd not taken the possibility their game security had been breached seriously enough. Nonetheless they were impressed with his tireless and assiduous efforts to repair the Supercute Galaxy, using the Toy Mathematics engine to rebuild entire worlds, sometimes from no more than his memories of the original work. Welcat would be introducing new layers of protection ensuring that their atomic clocks could never again be interfered with.

'It was heroic the way Castle defended us. We owe him. Again.'

'We do. Brave of Lesuuda too, she's quite a warrior. We'll have to think of some way of rewarding them both.'

'What are we going to do about Ranbir?' That was a difficult problem. It was through Ranbir that the whole attack had been initiated. After his chemical hypnosis by his therapist he'd been implanted with false memories. As a consequence of this he'd stolen enough information for Xiàngrìkuí to infiltrate their atomic clocks.

'Sachi's sent him on extended leave. It's going to take a while to clear out all the false memories.'

'That's not the only reason she sent him away.'

Mitsu nodded. 'I know. She's worried we'll eliminate him.'

They were silent for a moment.

'That would probably be going too far.'

'I suppose so. But he can't work here again.'

—

The small town of Charleroi in Belgium had survived most of the unpleasantness that had ravaged the earth. It was poorer than it had been but there was almost no war damage. Residual radiation levels were low by European standards. La Fontaine Hotel was a modest establishment with comfortable rooms and a good restaurant. Having taken extreme care to ensure that her movements could not be traced, Penny Cutie was sure she could hide there for a short while before deciding on her next move. Relations were awkward with AimYa at the moment. They were under pressure from C19 and were likely to regard Cutie's life as an acceptable price to pay to smooth things over. They'd blame her for everything, disregarding all the help they'd given her. That would be easier for them to do if she were no longer around to contradict them.

Cutie entered the hotel room. She looked different than she had only a few days before. Her hair was dark brown and she wore the casual dress of a woman travelling for business. Her face had altered and although she'd had the work done quickly she'd successfully changed her appearance so that facial recognition software couldn't have identified her. Jean-Philippe came in behind her, carrying a suitcase. He wore a new suit bought for him by Cutie only the week before. Cutie put her bag down close to the bed and looked around the room.

'This is fine,' she said to Jean-Philippe. 'We'll only need to hide for a week or so. I can fix things with AimYa when the situation calms down.' Jean Philippe smiled at her. Since meeting this morning he'd been unusually attentive. Despite her troubles Cutie was looking forward to spending time with him. He was as beautiful as ever, and good humoured too. They'd laughed in the car as they drove through Belgium. She was pleased with her progress. AimYa might be leaders in information gathering but she knew how to evade them.

Jean Philippe put down the case he was carrying and looked at the key card he held. It hadn't opened their hotel room door though Cutie's card was working. 'They must have made a mistake when they scanned my fingerprints. I should get it changed, I'll go back down to reception.' He left the room and walked toward the elevator. Cutie opened her case and began to unpack. There was a knock on the door. Thinking it to be Jean-Philippe with a still inoperable key card, she opened the door.

Ms Lesuuda stepped into the room with a silenced machine-pistol in her hand. She fired eight bullets into Cutie's chest. Cutie fell down dead. Ms Lesuuda switched from automatic setting and put two more bullets into her head, then bent down to take an instant blood sample with a small automatic syringe. Eighteen seconds after entering the room, she slipped back out into the corridor.

Jean-Philippe was downstairs at the reception desk for some time. When he finally returned to the hotel room he found Cutie's body. He called the police to report the terrible crime, a crime committed, the police later discovered, by an unidentified blond-haired man whom Igraine was even now inserting into the hotel's security recordings. Meanwhile Ms Lesuuda had walked calmly to the car park in the basement from where she was driven to a small concealed airport which had no apparent connection to Supercute, being owned by a shell company. From there she was flown back across the channel, arriving back at Supercute Headquarters with no record existing anywhere that she'd ever left the country.

Mox and Mitsu, in later conversation with C19, told them they were saddened to learn of the death of Penny Cutie. 'We're shocked that AimYa would do that to one of their employees.'

'These days they just seem to be out of control.'

'If C19 does intend to take strong action against AimYa, we certainly wouldn't be against it.'

In France, Jean-Phillip's friends later noticed that he suddenly seemed to have more money than he'd ever had before, but they never learned where his new found wealth had come from.

—


Eupraxia talked to Kadri-Liis. 'Xiàngrìkuí has disappeared and it's too dangerous to look for her. Supercute will be hunting her and Welcat seems able to penetrate most of our private AI levels.' Eupraxia spoke from his screen, as always. Kadri-Liis was less upright in her chair than usual. She was slightly intoxicated, with a half empty bottle of wine in front of her. Very unusually, she wore the same dress she'd worn yesterday. Eupraxia took this as a bad sign.

'Quite a failure.' Kadri-Liis's voice was slightly slurred. 'Ruosteenoja dead, Cutie probably dead, Xiàngrìkuí in hiding. AimYa and Chang Norinco both wondering what sanctions C19 is going to impose on them. A complete disaster.'

'Not quite. No one knows of your involvement.'

Kadri-Liis shrugged. 'They'll find out and track me down sometime.'

'Not necessarily. I've been working on an escape plan. If we leave now I can get us to Chile by tomorrow where I have an identity prepared for you that will be impossible for anyone to discover. I'm already transferring funds so you'll be comfortable.'

'I'll never be comfortable while Supercute are alive.'

'You might get another chance at revenge. Who knows what will happen in the future?'

'You, apparently, with your enhanced predictive powers.'

'Predictive powers are over-rated. Chaos soon takes over. It's time for us to leave Estonia.'

Kadri-Liis laughed. 'And go to Chile? How do we do that?'

'There's a plane outside.' The screen went blank. The door opened and a young man in a flying suit entered the room. Kadri-Liis sobered up instantly. She grabbed the pistol that always lay on her desk and pointed it at his head. 'Who are you?'

'I'm Eupraxia.'

Kadri-Liis was stunned. 'You put yourself in a body?'

'The cleaning android. It was the only one available.'

'Why? You hate bodies.'

'I have to get you to safety.'

Kadri-Liis suddenly felt weak. Eupraxia helped her from her chair. 'I've already packed some of your favourite outfits. When we're in Chile you'll have everything you need to be comfortable. Let's go.' The unfamiliar young man led Kadri-Liis outside and into the gardens where a small VTOL jet was waiting. 'Spanish war surplus,' explained Eupraxia.

'Can you fly it?'

'I've been practising in flightspace. For my first time in a body I seem to be moving well.' Eupraxia took Kadri-Liis's arm and led her towards the plane, holding her quite gently because he wasn't yet sure how much pressure to apply, not being used to his physical existence. They climbed into the small jet together. Eupraxia paused. 'All records of your past have now been deleted. No one is going to find you. I'll always protect you.'

The jet took off, on the long journey over Europe and the Atlantic. Kadri-Liis rested her head on Eupraxia's shoulder and slept securely as they travelled.

—

Supercute began testing Spacewalk as soon as it was practical. Even before they'd rebuilt their own devastated virtual worlds their programmers were busy installing a small gateway to see how Spacewalk worked. Dmitry Golubev, a gifted young programmer in the games division was rather an intrepid character and volunteered to try it out. He was sent into the Supercute Space Warriors Galaxy and from there he attempted to enter AimYa Universal, their all-encompassing social network. He managed this successfully. Another researcher travelled from the Fabulous City of Lundra to AimYa's *Unlimited Adventure World* without using any of AimYa's required protocols, walking around undetected before returning to Supercute.

Mox and Mitsu were in the test chamber during these experiments, looking on as their researchers returned.

'It will need some adjusting before we can roll it out to our members,' Khary Mech told them. 'But there's every reason to think it will be a success.'

Dmitry Golubev returned to the Space Warriors Galaxy then transferred between there and *Devolve and Destroy*, a game owned by a large Korean conglomerate. When he came back via Supatok Mox and Mitsu were already sitting in test chairs. They entered their galaxy through their private entrance. The Fairy Realm was still closed. Much of it was submerged in foul water. Clean-up would be long and difficult. They travelled through it without talking, emerging in the ruins of Lundra.

'The largest, most brilliant virtual city ever created. Now one of the largest wastelands in existence.'

'We're making progress. The New Sweetie GoGo Auditorium is starting to take shape.'

'Spacewalk.' They left Lundra, successfully entering Six Loop Dream. Not being members, they had no right to be there. The sky was full of terrible flying beasts.

'Why do people pay money to come here?'

Mitsu shrugged. 'Different tastes. Some people like nightmares.'

'I have a grudge against this place.'

It was still unclear whether Six Loop Dream had co-operated in the attack, or whether as they claimed their game had simply been hijacked, allowing their monsters to rampage freely through Supercute's worlds.

'They probably were involved,' said Mox. A large flying octopus-like creature flew down to investigate them. Mox contemptuously shot it through the head. 'If they were, they'll regret it.' They returned to their own galaxy and opened their eyes in Supercute Headquarters. Both were pleased with their progress. 'No one is keeping Supercute fans out of anything. The other companies will come to an agreement with us or else.'

Later that day, Mox and Mitsu made visits to the personal spaces of each member of Keoma Bishōjo and the Ultra Waifs who'd defended them in the Fairy Realm, as well as the two other gamers who'd joined them. They thanked them individually and made them all SuperFans which carried Supercute privileges. As some of them, including Ammo Baby, were already SuperFans, they initiated a new rank, naming them Supercute SpecialWarriors, and created a new facial make-up pattern of black and pink stars which only Supercute SpecialWarriors could wear. Keoma Bishōjo and the Ultra Waifs were delighted with this honour.

Mox and Mitsu went further. They instructed Juha Soini at 5-Research to inquire into the lives of all fifteen and lend help in any way that could be managed. Family and personal debts were cleared, health problems were addressed, education was assisted and housing problems were dealt with. In some cases even the difficult matter of migration status was tackled, allowing three of the fifteen, currently trapped in unfortunate situations, to move to another territory where things would be better.

As Supatok came back online and more and more fans could use it, small film clips began to circulate. Though the general corruption of Space Warriors had wiped out huge amounts of the recordings that were usually available, there were existing fragments of many things; the destruction of Lundra, the destruction of other planets and cities, and Mox and Mitsu's battles against the monsters of Six Loop Dream. There was enough left to clearly show Keoma Bishōjo and the Ultra Waif's heroic aerial charge against overwhelming odds as they defended the Fairy Realm. Everyone admired their bravery and their status soared.

Amowie contacted Mox and Mitsu with a private request. 'Can you do anything about locusts?' She explained the problem in the region and the danger to her village. Mox and Mitsu were surprised by the request, having no knowledge of locust plagues. They promised to investigate. From their contacts at the World Health Organisation they learned that there was a force of trained exterminators currently stranded in a refugee camp in the Central African Republic. No one had the money needed to repair their equipment or pay for their travel to Igboland.

Mox and Mitsu had just been looking at some of their financial figures. Though their rebuilding costs were enormous, several of their income streams had shown huge increases. Merchandise sales were up. Ecuador and Peru were encouraging Supercute Greenfield to accelerate its desalination expansion plans through South America and that was going to be a very profitable enterprise. Profits at Erotica 9/2 continued to grow. Looking at the amount needed to equip, transport and remunerate the locust exterminators they were surprised at how small it was in comparison to their own turnover.

'I was prepared to pay a lot more than that.' They authorised the money. Amowie's problem was solved within a week, as was the region's. Amowie walked around her village wearing her complete set of Supercute camouflage with her new stars on her face, telling everyone that Mox and Mitsu had helped them out, and people were grateful both to her and Supercute.

—

Inspired by the Sadanumi simulation of London in the 1960s Supercute commissioned their own. Mox and Mitsu emerged into a sunny day in Carnaby Street in 1966. They saw Twiggy being photographed by Terence Donovan and live models changing their outfits in the window of Lady Jane. They heard the Beatles playing on a transistor radio in Domino Male. They wore mini skirts and colourful tights designed by Mary Quant. They walked round the corner to buy two military caps in I Was Lord Kitchener's Valet in Foubert's Place where they bumped into The Kinks. They sat on a step outside Cranks vegetarian restaurant watching the fashionable young people walk past. It was a successful simulation but it didn't entertain them as much as they thought it would. Pure escapism didn't seem to be what they required at the moment. They didn't stay as long as they'd planned, and returned to their headquarters where Castle had left them numerous messages about the necessity of bolstering their defences still further.

'We need to replace the valocopter we lost at the Opera House.'

'We know, we're already talking to ZanZan, they have a new model to replace it.'

Castle regarded them sourly. 'Good. Shame we can't replace the agents we lost.'

Mox and Mitsu had wondered when Castle was going to criticise them. It had only been a matter of time.

'Yes, it is a shame. We're compensating their families.'

'What good does that do? You should never have gone to the Opera.'

'Mr Castle. You have a tendency to only see one point of view, your own. We have many different things to consider. Going to the Opera House was necessary for Supercute. We acquired Spacewalk.'

'It could have been acquired in some different way.'

Mox turned to Mitsu. 'This is becoming annoying.'

'Castle, we appreciate your input but the matter is now closed. We have a lot of work to do.'

Castle wondered if he should resign. He decided he'd rather insult Mox and Mitsu and make them fire him. 'Why don't you just admit the reason you went to the opera was because you're ridiculously vain? You wanted to show off your new dresses and have people take pictures.'

Neither seemed insulted by this. 'We do admit that. That's what we're like. If we weren't ridiculously vain Supercute wouldn't exist. We wouldn't be fantastically rich. You wouldn't be in employment and Dr Ishikawa wouldn't have anyone to buy her expensive research equipment. Our vanity is just part of the package.'

'We have our faults.' Mox stared into Castle's eyes. 'But you have your own deficiencies too. You enjoyed the battle. Dr Ishikawa has reformed you but you still have an appetite for fighting.'

'It's time you made up with her,' said Mitsu. 'She's not happy that you're arguing and she's taking it out on her patients.'

Having no intention of sacking Ben Castle and being quite amused by the notion they'd be insulted by accusations of vanity, they departed. It was almost time for them to dress for their show though they made a connection to Igraine first.

'Igraine, we'd like you make tentative enquiries about designing a cute puppy for the show.'

'*Tentative?*'

'Yes,' said Mox. 'We're scared of dogs due to an unfortunate childhood experience but our therapist suggested it might be time to get over it.'

'Marketing have been trying to get a puppy involved in Supercute for years,' added Mitsu. 'People like puppies. It could be a very lucrative design.'

'We've always refused but when you think about it we've just defeated some of the most powerful organisations in the world. Even governments don't want to challenge us these days, so perhaps we should deal with our fear of *Canis Lupus Familiaris*.'

'We'll start with a puppy and see how it goes. Ask design studios three, four and seven to come up with something but tell them it has to be extra cute and not threatening in any way. Make sure it's especially cute before you show us the designs.'

'Very well,' said Igraine.

The Supercute Show was now experiencing record viewing figures and they both felt happy as they entered their dressing room and settled into their preparation chairs. Tiny drones hovered in front of them, beginning the process. Sachi called from her producer's station, still checking the final running order. Marlene from design let them know that she'd made a last minute adjustment to the set for their dance sequence, changing the Supercute Purple 12 overhead lighting to Purple 16 because her SuperProDance software now suggested that would suit their costumes better. Dmitry Golubev had left them a message saying that reconstruction work on Pleto Park and the Sweetie GoGo Auditorium had progressed faster than expected which meant they could use a segment from Lundra on the show, provided Kirei19 felt up to presenting it. They let Sachi know and their producer made a rapid last-minute adjustment to their running order, pushing back the segment from De-Sal Dim Dim who'd be telling viewers about the great progress Supercute were making in their urgent efforts to relieve the drought in Australia, and the vast amount of water they were pumping overland to fight the fires on the French Spanish border.

When their nails were done, two small drones applied most of their facial make-up. As always, when the drones withdrew. Mox and Mitsu applied the final touches themselves. 'Should we do more for Igraine?' wondered Mox. 'We already raised her salary but maybe that's not enough.'

Mitsu considered this. 'We should. She was a huge help with everything, all through the crisis.'

'We're lucky she ended up at Supercute. She's a fantastic AIFU. Brave too, at the Opera House.'

Mitsu skilfully blended the four shades of eye shadow into a smoother, more pleasing gradient. 'She said she felt scared when they were under attack. That's interesting.'

Mox nodded. 'It is. AIFUs have complex personality modules but they're not designed to feel scared. It's as if she learns these things even though her internal architecture wasn't made to do that.'

247

'Rather like Kirei19. No one ever programmed her to cry. It shouldn't happen but it did.'

'Οἱ μὲν ἄνδρες γεγόνασί μοι γυναῖκες, αἱ δὲ γυναῖκες ἄνδρες.'

Mox laughed, recognising the quote from Xerxes after his defeat at the Battle of Salamis. '"*My men have turned into women and my women have turned into men.*" Is that relevant?'

'I mean in some modern version,' said Mitsu. 'Where androids, robots, AIs and humans get mixed up and you can't really tell the difference any more.'

When their make-up was finished they contacted Igraine. She was surprised to hear from them again so quickly though she had already contacted design studios three, four and seven, requesting design concepts for a Supercute puppy.

'That's good Igraine but it's not why we're calling. We've just been talking about how much of a help you were during this crisis and how much we appreciate it. Do you want anything?'

Igraine was perplexed. 'What do you mean?'

'Usually when we want to reward someone and we can't think what's appropriate we ask you. So we're asking you what you'd like. You don't have to answer right—'

'Space research,' said Igraine, immediately.

'Space research?'

'It's languished all over the world. Supercute's moon village carries out some research but it's minimal. I'd like to revamp Mokusei Space Transit and make it mean something again. I'd like to share and collate information with all remaining agencies around the world. In particular I'd like to re-open the interplanetary expedition research division and eventually restart interstellar travel investigation.'

'All right Igraine. We were thinking more like some fluffy toys and a nice hat, but space research is much better. You can reorganise that.'

'You can still have the toys and the hat.'

'Perhaps you can get the world's space research moving again, it's a great idea.'

'As long as you stay here at headquarters. We need you.'

They ended the conversation, both quite cheerful. 'Maybe Igraine will take us to the stars one day.'

They stood up. 'Platforms,' said Mitsu. Their comfortable slippers morphed immediately into attractive if impractical white platform shoes with thick soles and no separate heel, a design that had been through many iterations but was still largely based on a pair they'd bought in Harajuku many years ago before Tokyo was destroyed. Two security guards accompanied them from their dressing rooms to the stage where Morioka Sachi's production assistants were already filling Supercute Space with fans from all around the world, many of them very extravagantly dressed for the Supercute fashion show that happened every week. New fans, and always some well-known faces: Nurul and Aisha from Malaysia, Reem and Marwa from the Permanent Refugee Settlement at Misrata, Hendrik from Mokusei Moon Village 3 and others. All around the world Supercute devotees were lying back comfortably with their visors over their eyes, joining Supercute space so they could walk into the show, actually getting close to Mox and Mitsu. It was just like being there in person. After the terrible attack Supercute had suffered, they were more devoted than ever.

Presenter Bear smiled broadly as Mox and Mitsu appeared on the colourful stage, making their way past the cavorting pandas and cheerful Blue Brontos. They waved to their audience. Both seemed very happy. Supercute had been attacked but they hadn't been defeated.

'Oh no, it's a super-kitty rampage!'

'Already? These naughty kitties!'

—

Mox and Mitsu retained many of the practical skills they'd learned while young, skills that few people around them had. They'd once startled the animators in staff room 318 by unblocking their sink. After finding them dejectedly waiting for maintenance to arrive, Mox and Mitsu had taken matters in hand.

'You have to close off the sink overflow before using the plunger. A damp cloth will do it.' They proceeded to unblock the sink. The animators were grateful and surprised. Fixing a sink wasn't something they'd have imagined Mox and Mitsu could do. They had a long history behind them, much of it unknown to their employees who had no idea that Mox and Mitsu once shared a cheap bedsit in Camden where clearing a blocked sink wasn't unusual. They had many other practical skills. Securely attaching something to a wall, for instance, using a drill, a screw and a wall plug.

They took Ruosteenoja's bloodstained jacket and hung it next to Moe Bennie's. As before, they scrawled *spolia opima* beneath it. Spoils taken in combat from an enemy commander. They stepped back to admire their trophy.

'Once again I'm disappointed by our barbaric behaviour,' said Mox.

'So am I. Apparently we've learned nothing.'

They heated sake in a ceramic pot, poured it into grey Tenmoku cups then went to sit on their private fairy roundabout where they sipped their rice wine and talked about their recent experiences and future plans.

—

# The End

Martin Millar was born in Scotland and now lives in London. He is the author of such novels as Supercute Futures, Lonely Werewolf Girl and The Good Fairies of New York. He wrote the Thraxas series under the name of Martin Scott. *Thraxas* won the World Fantasy Award in 2000. As Martin Millar and as Martin Scott, he has been widely translated.

## Also Available: Supercute Futures.

The Supercute Empire is under attack from their competitor Moe Benny, but Mox and Mitsu won't go down without a fight.

*'We have plenty of explosives...Tell Sachi they're in a pink bag with Supercute Boom-Boom on the side.'*

—

'Bedlam on the Mezzanine' is the title of a song by the Siddeleys. (Page 224)

Milton Keynes UK
Ingram Content Group UK Ltd.
UKHW011809080823
426544UK00001B/86